A HERO
FORGED
in
BLOOD

A HERO FORGED in BLOOD

THE ANCIENT CHRONICLES OF EMPYREA

BOOK ONE

B.H. PRESTON

Canoe Tree
Press

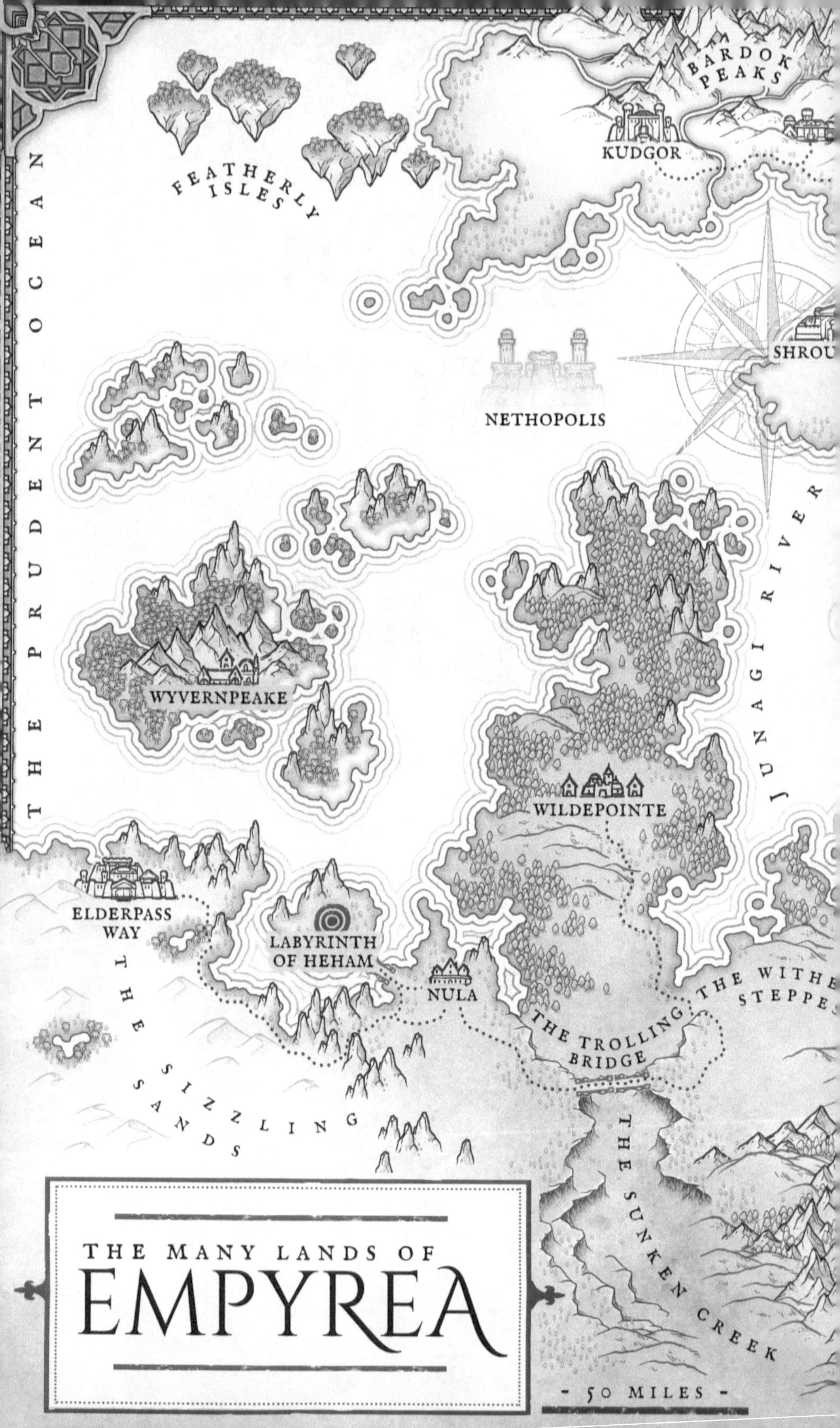
BARDOK PEAKS
KUDGOR
FEATHERLY ISLES
NETHOPOLIS
SHROU
JUNAGI RIVER
THE PRUDENT OCEAN
WYVERNPEAKE
WILDEPOINTE
ELDERPASS WAY
LABYRINTH OF HEHAM
NULA
THE SIZZLING SANDS
THE TROLLING BRIDGE
THE WITHE STEPPE
THE SUNKEN CREEK
THE MANY LANDS OF
EMPYREA
- 50 MILES -

TO THE VAST TUNDRA WILDS
GMAW
HINGTAGA
WHALDALF'S LANDING
THE MYSTICAL CITY OF LUMHAGEN
TYRION
BINICORN'S FARTHING
THE FORGOTTEN FOREST
FAYSPIRE
BRIGHTSHIRE FOREST
WESTRAMORE
THE DESOLATE FIELDS
KARNERGRIEN
ASHLAND
BARREN BADLANDS
DARKVALE VALLEY
TALAIFOTIA
DEEPER INTO THE INFERNAL BARRENS

Canoe Tree
Press

4697 Main Street
Manchester Center, VT 05255

Canoe Tree Press is a division of DartFrog Books

To my son, Calum, to who I dedicate this book. I know you
love reading books, just as I did at your age. I hope you enjoy
this book and always dream!

PRONUNCIATION GUIDE

Adena	*A -DEE-na*	K'Lani	*KAY-laa-nee*
Agwin	*Aug-win*	Kaden	*KAY-den*
Alpheon	*AL-fee-on*	Kel Tyrion	*kel-Teer-ee-un*
Amphisbaena	*AM-fuhs-be-ah-nah*	Kugdor	*Cug-DOOR*
Andaluria	*An-DA-lu-ria*	Lucient	*LU-see-ent*
Ashland	*Ash-land*	Lumhagen	*LOOM-hay-gen*
Asitra	*Ah-SEE-trah*	Luna	*LOO-nah*
Asiz	*Ahh-ZEEZ*	Megalos	*MEH-gah-lows*
Aspis	*AH-spis*	Mercalyptus	*MER-cah-lip-tus*
Bardicus	*BAR-da-cus*	Millicent	*Mil-LAH-cent*
Binicorn	*Bi-na-corn*	Nethopolis	*na-THA-poe-lis*
Blakenshield	*Blay-KIN-sheeld*	Nosegye	*NOWZ-guy*
Brightshire	*Brite-SHAIR-ur*	Omak	*Oh-MAHK*
Bhalla	*BAH-laa*	Orealus	*OR-real-us*
Bonberry	*BON-beh-ree*	Parrotlets	*PAIR-ra-lets*
Briskly	*BRI-sklee*	Trophorus	*TRO-for-us*
Bristlekamp	*BRI-sl-camp*	Pepper	*PEH-per*
Chum	*Ch-UM*	Petey	*PEE-tee*
Cimetes	*SIGH-me-tes*	Rosenhelm	*ROW-sen-helm*
Daneyel	*DAN-yuhl*	Sadunia	*SAH-doo-nee-ah*
Duke	*Dook*	Scruffenfoot	*SKRUH-fin-foot*
Dunntaika	*dunn-tie-ka*	Shroudscar	*SHROWD-scar*
Echethier	*Eh-KAH-theer*	Tha'lassa	*THAW-lah-sa*
Eldrin	*EL-dren*	Truthorium	*TROO-thor-ee-uhm*
Empyrea	*Em-PEER-ri-ah*	Valmyr	*VALL-mear*
Fayspire	*FAY-spai-ur*	Varun	*VAH-run*
Fluteds	*FLU-teds*	Waptoo	*Wop-TOO*
Evias	*EH-vy-ahs*	Woo'apma	*WOO-op-maa*
Gadar	*GAH-darr*	Westramore	*Weh-STRAH-more*
Garth	*Gaarth*	Weylyn	*WAY-lin*
Hintaga	*Hen-TAH-gah*	Whaldalf	*WALL-dalf*
Junagi	*JOO-nah-gi*	Wildepointe	*WILL-da-point*
Karatheas	*KA-rah-thee-is*	Yah'zaval	*Yaah-sha-val*

When the light fell upon the gates of the seven
And the sun once smiled the brightest
Darkness will soon eclipse the moon,
What was once pure is no more,
For the world was not ready for what was in store
Yet there was an arrival of courage and justice amidst two cries
The first did not last through the many lies
But the chosen shall stretch far till the ends of the world
Great Spirit would be his strength, West would be his betrayal
Prepared shall he be, to stop the whims of the deceiver
And thus, the curse over the world shall lift from thee
When the blood flows, and the metals will sing,
Until someone higher into the world that He shall bring

—B.H. Preston

CHAPTER 1

When Kaden woke up to the sweet, aromatic smell of sugary bonberry buns wafting through the air, he knew he had forgotten something special. His mother only baked bonberry buns on consecrated days, days of remembrance, or days of high worship. He lay on his bed, curled up beneath his sleep-warmed blankets, and tried to think of what he ought to be remembering. Was it the anniversary of the Day of Separation? A feast day for Orealus? Or was it one of the unspoken days, days when his mother bowed her head and mixed her tears into the dough she kneaded and shaped, days where a loose word in a sharp ear could bring punishment down on your whole family?

The berries were at their ripest now, and the hot, crisping sugar buns smelled decadent. Kaden's stomach churned like butter, informing the rest of him that he wasn't going to be going back to sleep anytime soon. He wanted to force his stomach into silence somehow—waking up in the morning was always hard for Kaden, and the thought of losing precious minutes of slumber to something as silly as a growling stomach irritated him. He turned his head away from the door and toward his open window, where a delicate breeze that smelled of fresh-cut hay pushed the bonberry scent away. The farmy smell carried his mind outside of these four walls, to his sleepy village of no more than four hundred people at the fringes of the kingdom of Empyrea. Within the village of Ashland, rustic homes sat apart from each other on grassy hills. Beautiful rivers streamed throughout the entrenched valleys into a nearby local creek the locals used to fish. Dirt roads dabbled with cobblestones paved the pathways from home to home, each containing a modest garden of spices, fruits, and vegetables. Kaden could hear the animals in the fenced backyards rousing: a rooster crowing, chickens scratching, as well as goats, sheep, and cows bleating. Mmm, that was better. He sighed, twisting a bit to get comfortable as he settled back into his bed. Just a few minutes more…

"Kaden! Wake up!"

He groaned under his breath, opened one of his eyes, and looked at the sliver of sky through his window. Orange, trending toward pale blue. Ugh, still so early. It was tempting to ignore his mother's call just for the sake of lying here a bit longer.

Suddenly, four large paws pounded the wooden floor up to his door, which burst open so hard that it slammed against the wall. A second later, a tongue wet with sticky saliva and stinking of stale chicken bones and dirty pond water swept along the length of Kaden's face. Sniff—slurp—lick!

"Ugh, Duke." Kaden rolled away from his enormous, overly friendly dog. "Stop it." Duke laid his head on Kaden's shoulder and stuck his cold, wet nose directly into Kaden's ear. "Fine," he muttered. "I'm up. I'm getting up."

He rolled back over and looked at Duke, over two hundred pounds of "pure" hunting dog which stood thirty inches from paw to shoulder. The boy pet his dog's thick, shaggy, soft fur of a reddish-brown brindle. The Empyrean hound had long legs and mighty tails, sharp teeth, and talon-like claws typical of the breed. Droopy triangle ears pushed forward, and Duke's tongue lolled out the side of his short muzzle under his black, twitching nose. Above his master, he danced side to side a little on his front paws, like a puppy. Kaden admired the way the creature's sparkling brown eyes reflected the light from the window and thought back to the day they met. Four years ago, Kaden found the puppy near Ashland Woods and begged his parents to keep the rare-breed dog. Since then, the two had been inseparable.

"Looks like a bear, docile as a hare," was the saying with regards to the breed, and it had undoubtedly bred true in Duke. When he wasn't hunting or protecting his humans, he was as easygoing as any animal could be.

"You're a good boy," Kaden told his dog solemnly, "but your breath is absolutely foul. Have you been rummaging in the burn pit?" He pushed his thick wool blanket back, got to his feet, and scratched Duke behind the ears before reaching for the curtain. "Ma won't like it if you spread the trash around again."

Kaden pulled his curtain open and looked out at the morning sky, brightening above the dark blur of the forest. He and his parents lived at the outer edge of the village, one of the closest families to the woods, where the foraging was good, but the danger was a bit higher. Most of the genuinely fearsome creatures, the ogres and giants of lore, had been gone ever since the great wizard Bhalla saved Empyrea from complete ruin after the old king died in battle. Before his death, King Karatheas's nine united regions prospered until the war. Once their king perished at the hands of the powerful Lucient, the rulers of Nine Pillars fractured the kingdom. Instead of working together, the leaders focused on ruling their respective homelands. Empyrea, a continent named for its kingdom in the world of Sadunia, was a safe place now from what he was told, as long as you weren't caught worshipping in a way you shouldn't or talking about the old days as though you missed them. Not that Kaden knew anything about those days—he'd been a tiny baby when the worst of the war broke out. It was a miracle he and his parents had survived.

Kaden sighed. A part of him wished for something more exciting than another day's worth of chores to do. What was the point of having a hunting dog like Duke if he never got to hunt anything more significant than a rabbit? What was the purpose of all the sword exercises his father made him do if he was never going to wield an actual sword? His father had been a guardsman once before he became a farmer. They went through the drills together, over and over, until Kaden knew them by heart.

He snorted. He could wield a wooden blade with the best of them. It was handy for fending off bad-tempered sows or overly affectionate hounds, but not much else.

"Kaden! I won't be calling you again!"

He'd dawdled too long. "I'm coming, Ma," he yelled back, pulling on a clean set of the simple, sturdy clothes that were a farmer's lot—tunic, leggings, and a stiff wool jerkin over the top of it. He slid his socked feet into his boots and made a quick stop at the outhouse before heading into the kitchen, where a pot of cool, mint-scented water was waiting in the corner for him to wash up with. He did his face, then his hands, and glanced in the mirror hung on the wall above the basin, having to squat to see his hazel brown eyes. When he was a child, the mirror rested at a perfect height on the wall. However, Kaden had long outgrown the frame's position, and the disparity between his height and the mirror's location only became more evident after his last growth spurt. The villagers often commented on the boy's height, at least two heads above even the tallest man they all knew. He had the lean muscles to compliment his thin stature, a natural byproduct of hard farm labor. Combing his fingers through his close-shorn, coarse black curls and rubbing a hand over his light brown face, he finally shook off his sleepiness. He turned to look at his parents.

His mother, Lydia, sat by the wood-fired oven, her dark brown eyes monitoring the bread inside of it while she heated more water for their morning blackroot tea on top of it. Her tight black curls, tickling her shoulders, framed her dark brown face. Her lips were pursed with annoyance—probably from having to yell for him twice—and her free hand smoothed out the worn blue linen of her skirt over and over again. That was a sure sign she was worried and trying not to show it. But why was she nervous? Did it have anything to do with why she was baking bonberry buns?

Kaden's father, Daneyel, had his pocketknife out, and his sharp, dark brown eyes watched as he whittled another peg for the chair he'd been building whenever a lull in the farm's activity let him work on it. His thick, black kinky hair kept its shape even as he moved his head over his work. The knife looked comically small in the man's massive hands, which fit well with his impressive physique built from years of farm work. The tendons of his biceps worked subtly under dark brown skin. One more leg and the chair would be complete. It was a man's chair, broad-seated and high-backed, and Kaden knew his father meant to give it to him at his upcoming birthday when he officially came of age.

A chair. Wonderful. What else could I possibly want?

An instant after he had the thought, he felt guilty for it. Kaden had more than most. When so many other children had lost theirs during the war, he had parents. Kaden had a warm, loving home and had never known great hunger or desperate need. He sat down in his child's chair, chastened, and accepted a mug of tea from his mother. A fresh bonberry bun followed it, and he bit into it gleefully, closing his eyes as the hot, sweet jam inside soothed his rumbling stomach.

"Wha's duh occshun?" he asked around the mouthful of bread and jam.

"Kaden," his mother said with a sigh. "Swallow, then speak. You're not five anymore."

No, he was three times that—but the bonberry buns were such an exceptional food, he felt like a gleeful child every time he got one. He swallowed, washed the bite down with a gulp of tea, then said, "What's the occasion?"

His parents exchanged a look. "There isn't one," his mother said after a moment. "Not really. Bonberry season is peaking, that's all. The Fraynes had some extras from their patch and offered them to me." She looked a little longingly at the empty jar by her foot. "I wish we had a patch of our own, but we're a bit far from the right kind of trees for that." Bonberry briars were parasites, only growing around the thick roots of oak trees. A few of the villagers had an oak on their land, but most didn't.

"I could always go foraging for some," Kaden offered. Suddenly, it seemed like a marvelous idea, lifting a weight off his shoulders that he didn't even realize he'd woken up with. "We spent all day yesterday setting the hay to dry in the fields. Now that that's done, surely today is a good day for a bit of time in the forest. I know where a whole grove of oak trees is, Ma! I could take your basket and bring back more bonberries than you'll know what to do with."

"We've got the sheep to see to today," his father interjected.

"The sheep will still be there tomorrow," Kaden said, trying not to sound like he was begging. "The bonberries might not be." The shortness of their season and the lengths that birds and beasts went to get them off the briars were legends. Kaden wasn't overly fond of sticking his hand into a bush covered with thorns, but he was even less enthusiastic about settling into another twelve hours of farm chores on a beautiful day like this. It felt like it had been ages since he'd been in the forest.

"Daneyel," Lydia said softly. Something passed between his parents, some silent conversation that Kaden couldn't quite understand for all his trying.

"Half a day," Daneyel said a moment later. "If there are any bonberries left out there, they're best gotten in the morning before the birds peck them to pieces. But," he added earnestly, "you take Duke with you. Keep your eyes open for tracks, and if you see any signs of something dangerous, you—"

"Head home right away, I know, Pa," Kaden said, standing up so fast his little chair rocked on its feet. "A half day will be plenty of time. I know just where to go!"

His mother got up from her seat by the oven and walked over to one of the extended wooden shelves above the counter. The shelves were even too high for Duke to get at. She grabbed a weathered basket, laid a clean rag in the bottom of it, and took it over to the oven. She plucked two more bonberry buns out of the heat with her fingertips, then set them in the basket. The sugar sprinkled over the top was dark and glittering, and Kaden's mouth watered. "Provisions," she said with a bit of a smile as she handed it all over to Kaden.

"Thanks, Ma." He leaned in and gave her a kiss on the cheek and was startled when she pulled him into a hug so hard, he felt his ribs protest. His ma didn't give hugs like this very often. What was going on today?

"Be careful," she told him, stepping back and adjusting her shawl around her shoulders.

"I will be," he promised, but really, it was just the forest. He would be hiking for less than a mile, and Duke was bigger than any of the animals in there.

What was there to be afraid of?

CHAPTER 2

The forest was called Ashland Woods, although Kaden wasn't sure why. Did it make sense to name something after ashes when there were none within it? The cursed lands, the areas that had been torn apart by war and burned so fiercely and so deep that nothing would ever grow on them again, *those* places deserved the name Ashland. Then again, Kaden had been eight when he'd named his dog Duke, and there was nothing incredibly regal about the giant hunting dog. People made funny choices sometimes.

As soon as he crossed the boundary between field and wood, the air took on a different timbre. It was as though the sun shined more brightly, even through the trees, and the air smelled a bit sweeter, less like cut hay and more like the fragrant flowers his mother tended in her garden—tiny white snowdrops, giant red lilies, and purple nettles that looked beautiful but stung viciously. There were no flowers here that Kaden could see, but their scent floated on the breeze nonetheless. The sweetness of it reminded Kaden that he was still hungry, and he bit into another bonberry bun as he worked his way deeper into the woods.

Not many people came into Ashland Woods, not even to collect branches for burning or timber to build with. Local groves were maintained and harvested for that, and during the bad winters when the ice was thicker than the snow and the stores of firewood ran low, grown men drew lots to see which of them would venture into the wood for more fuel. Nothing wrong had ever happened to anyone there, as far as Kaden knew, but he was the only person in the village who ever ventured into the forest willingly.

"More bonberries for us," he said to Duke, who gave a gentle *woof* and forged ahead, breaking a trail through the undergrowth a few feet early of Kaden.

It was hot in here, even with the dappled shade from the canopy overhead. Sweat dripped down Kaden's temple, and he wiped his hand across it irritably. "At least it's just sweat this time," he muttered. The last time he'd ventured into Ashland Woods, Duke had charged headfirst into a flock of purple-backed pipers. Their flurry of alarmed birdsong had been enchanting, sounding like a hundred tiny wood flutes all playing in time together. The *mess* they'd left behind as they flew, some of it landing square on top of Kaden's head, had been a lot less delightful.

Insects buzzed through the trees, some of them settling against bushes and branches, others chasing each other through the air as he walked by. Bright, brilliantly colored dragonflies in jewel tones and metallic shades darted this way and that, nipping up tiny gnats and diving down onto the long grasses to perch and fan their wings. As Kaden watched, a lizard the same color as the deep blue sky popped its frill, masking its beautiful markings with a collar of dull, bark-like camouflage as it readied itself to leap at a ruby-colored dragonfly.

Kaden reached out and brushed the dragonfly away. The lizard settled, its frill retracting as it seemed to glare at him. "Sorry, friend," Kaden said with a smile as he passed it, "but it's too peaceful for hunting right now." Perhaps after he'd collected the berries, he'd let Duke go after some of the small game that crept along through the undergrowth—maybe even a boar, if they could find a juvenile. It took more than one hunting dog to safely go after a full-grown boar.

Kaden pressed on absently, his mind distracted even as his body moved with confidence. His stomach growled despite the bun he'd just eaten. Perhaps he should have delayed leaving for some of his mother's morning potage. It was just soup but heartier and more satisfying than the sweet, delicate bonberry buns.

Kaden was so distracted that he didn't even notice Duke had gone stock-still ahead of him until he ran into the big dog's tail. "Duke, what—" he began, then stopped when he saw what the dog was staring at. Inside a small clearing filled with high, wild grass, fifty feet away, was a grazing binicorn. All his indignation at running into Duke melted away, and Kaden crouched down a little lower as he stared. A binicorn! He'd only ever seen one once before, on the outskirts of the village, and that one had been much smaller. This creature, said to be one of Orealus's first creations, resembled a stock horse, with a glossy black coat and two long horns curving back from its head. It had dark eyes that gleamed with attentiveness despite its grazing and a long tail that swished side to side, brushing away the buzzing flies. A fresh *crunch-crunch* sound emanated from its mouth, where it chewed grass with quiet determination.

Kaden knew the binicorn had seen them, and he also knew it didn't consider them a threat. Why should it? Inside the woods, it was king—too large to make easy prey and too fierce for most to even try. He reached out and patted Duke's back and felt the hunting dog quivering. "No, boy," Kaden said softly. "Not this time."

After a second, Duke subsided, and Kaden got both of them back on the path to the bonberry patch. They'd be fortunate with a binicorn in the area if there was a berry untouched at this point.

They got to the stand of oak trees a few minutes later, and to Kaden's surprise, the bushes were primarily untouched. They must have just become ripe—unripened bonberries were so sour that even the birds avoided them unless they had no other choice, but the moment they turned…

Kaden reached out and plucked the nearest round, bluish berry hanging from a stem within easy reach. He popped it into his mouth and closed his eyes as the sweet, bright flavor burst over his tongue. *Perfect.* His ma would be pleased. He set to work picking the berries, wincing whenever a thorn caught the back of his hand. He should have grabbed his leather work gloves out of his room before he came.

Far too often, you don't think before you act. That's a risky habit to get into, son. Kaden could practically hear his father repeating this tired criticism. Hardly a day went by when he didn't hear some version of it from the man, or more rarely, from his mother. Kaden pressed his lips together hard and slowed down a little in his picking. If he came back with scratches all over his hands, his father would look at them and shake his head, and his mother would sigh and fetch her ointments to keep them from infection, and Kaden would feel like a child again instead of nearly the man that he was.

The difficulty was *proving* to his parents that he didn't need that sort of coddling anymore. What were a few scratches, after all? And why should he have to ask their permission to go into Ashland Woods when he was already taller than his father? Regardless of his upcoming birthday, they didn't treat him like a man, and until he did something to show them that he was as solid and capable as they were, they wouldn't.

What would he even do? There was no one to fight now that Empyrea was at peace, there was nothing he could build that his father couldn't build better, and he wouldn't risk setting Duke on any big game for fear of the dog taking an injury. Even now, alone in the forest where most villagers didn't like to tread, Kaden still felt like he was being humored.

"Remember to go no farther than the oak grove," his mother had cautioned just before he set out. "Wilder things can happen beyond that boundary."

She'd given him that warning before but had never explained it. "What sort of wilder things?" he'd asked.

"Mind your mother," his father had snapped from the doorway like he was a little child.

Back home, Kaden had been too eager to set out into the wood to complain, but with time to think about it now, he felt frustrated, even angry, at their treatment of him. "Mind your mother," he muttered under his breath. "What sort of man gets scolded to *mind his mother?*" It was as though they didn't really want him to grow up. Yes, he was an only child, and he knew his parents loved him—too much, perhaps—but, like it or not, they would have to begin treating him like an adult after he turned seventeen. He would get a plot of land, make his own home, tend to his own fields...

Or leave the village altogether, set out along the trade road, and find a bright new future for me! That was Kaden's secret desire, the one he didn't dare speak of to his parents because he knew what their reaction would be—sheer horror. People didn't leave the village—no one had left since the great war. His mother said it was a safe haven in a land of turmoil. Why would anyone want to go?

Distracted by his thoughts, Kaden almost didn't notice when Duke suddenly began to growl. He glanced at his dog, surprised—Duke was a well-trained hunting dog, and he didn't bark when he spotted prey and simply went still. Whatever this was, it was something he didn't like.

Kaden put down the basket of berries and moved over beside his dog. "What is it, boy?" he asked, peering into the trees. He couldn't see anything unusual out there. More thick undergrowth, more insects were buzzing by, more small creatures rustling through the...

Huh. Actually, there *weren't* any tiny creatures moving in the bushes ahead. Not a squirrel, not a rabbit, not even a mouse as far as one could hear, and that was strange. They should be waiting in droves at the edge of the oak grove, desperate to get their greedy little paws on bonberries. Instead, there were… none. None at all.

As soon as he stepped a little farther from the bonberry bushes, a new scent caught Kaden's nose. He closed his eyes and inhaled the savory aroma of a roasted hen. Some*one* was out there, then, someone cooking up a meal in the middle of Ashland Woods. Who could it be? Surely not another farmer, he told himself—Kaden knew his fellow villagers, and nobody would waste a morning making a meal in the forest when they could be eating one faster at home before getting back to work. It had to be a stranger.

Kaden's heart beat faster with excitement. A stranger! He hadn't spoken to anyone outside of the village in over a year, and the last person of any genuine interest had been the traveler who'd rested briefly at his parents' house when Kaden was only twelve. He didn't remember much about the man, just that he kept his cloak pulled tight around his head and shoulders and hadn't bothered to give anyone his name. His parents hadn't demanded it either. They'd just exchanged wary glances while bringing the stranger a bowl of stew and a pint of beer. Kaden knew his father had spoken with the man once he was done eating, but he hadn't been allowed to stay and listen—instead, Ma had sent him to the garden to pick carrots. Carrots! As though carrots were more important than hearing about the outside world!

His stomach growled meaningfully, almost louder than Duke. "Shush," he told the dog. "We should go find this person, speak to them." He rubbed a hand over his middle. "Perhaps offer to share a meal." After all, he had a heaping basket full of bonberries to offer. That ought to buy him at least a *leg* of the chicken.

Duke snarled, and Kaden shushed him harder. "Stop it," he said. "Just because we don't know them, there is no reason not to be friendly." He started forward, careful to avoid the plants with the most burrs—he didn't want to show up at a stranger's campfire looking like a bumpkin with seeds sticking out of his leggings. The smell of meat grew stronger with every step, and after less than five minutes of walking, Kaden found the little campsite. It was empty, and although the bird spitted over the fire was roasted to perfection, no one was there to enjoy it.

"Perhaps they stepped away for a moment," Kaden mused, even as Duke growled harder than ever. "Be quiet!" he added in annoyance. His stomach rumbled harder than ever. "Maybe just a wing," he told himself as he stepped toward the makeshift firepit. He got to within grabbing distance and—

Something snapped beneath his foot. Before Kaden knew what was happening, a net descended from above, trapping both him and Duke beneath its heavy strands. He fell to the ground, spilled bonberries crushed beneath him as he collapsed onto his side.

Breathless and too stunned to struggle, Kaden suddenly heard a deep, malicious laugh begin from somewhere close by.

It didn't sound human.

CHAPTER 3

The laugh began as a rumble and rose to a shrill, malevolent cackle, half a dozen voices creating a cacophony Kaden couldn't escape. He craned his neck as best he could, trying to turn his head toward the noise, but whoever was laughing, they were all behind him. Or they *had* been, before—

A stumpy pair of thick-soled boots that stank of poorly cured leather appeared right in front of his face. "Look what we have here," the owner of the boots said with a low, grunting chuckle. "A long, skinny stick of a human boy. Convenient, that."

"All that time watching the village wasted," another voice complained. "When all along, we could've simply baited the trap with a bit of freshly cooked meat!"

"But is it the right boy?" someone else asked. "It ain't like the Great Lord gave us a picture to know him by. How are we supposed to tell one human's spawn from another? They all look alike to me."

A moment later, a face took the place of the boots, its owner bending down with a grimace on his huge square face. Large, fox-like ears poked out from either side of the malicious green face. Green... *green*? Kaden's mind raced as he tried to make sense of what he saw. Was this... could this be a goblin? From Kaden's disadvantaged position, he counted at least six of the beasts. What were goblins doing outside his tiny, insignificant village?

A heavy hand smacked him across the back of the head. "Pay attention, boy." Nearby, Duke began to growl, fighting at the hold of the nets to get at the creature that was harming his human. "Shut that dog up!" the goblin shouted before turning back to Kaden.

"Look at me," the goblin said. "And mark me well, lad—if you try to lie to me, I'll start by breaking each one of those long, stick-thin fingers of yours. Once I run out of fingers, I'll start in on your toes. And if I get bored and decide to cut them off instead of breaking them, well..." He shrugged. "It's all the same to me, ain't it? Now. What's your name?"

"K-Kaden," he stammered, too shocked to even think of lying. "Kaden Sheppard."

"Eh, just some peasant's name," one of the others said in a disappointed tone of voice. "Reckon we should just cut this one's head off and be done with 'em. We could make a raid into the village, check for—ow! Why'd you hit me?"

"There are six of us and over a hundred villagers, you damn fool," one of the other goblins snapped. "I don't care how useless they are, give a hundred humans pitchforks to hold, and at least one of us will run straight into them—probably *you*, daft as you are." A second later, a thud and Duke's rising snarl suddenly became a whine.

The goblin in charge hit Kaden across the head again. "What did I tell you? Eyes here, lad." Kaden shuddered, unable to control his reaction to the creature in front of him. The goblin's eyes shone like lanterns in the low light of the forest, and his nose was one big scar slicing from just above the brow until the slash bisected a nostril at the bottom.

"Not pretty, am I?" the goblin asked with a grin that displayed a mouth full of black, pitted teeth. "You wouldn't want to look anything like me, would you, eh? A nice young human like you, all that smooth skin, those nice straight bones of yours. Let's keep everything the way it's meant to be, boy.

Now tell me, Kaden." He leaned in close enough for Kaden to smell the dank, rotten smell of his breath. "What do you know of King Karatheas?"

Of all the questions Kaden could have expected, this was at the end of the list? "K-king Karatheas?" he blurted. "I know very little, only that he died years ago—fighting against Lucient, the Great Deceiver—" He stopped as the goblin hit him on the head yet *again*. The pain made him cry out, and that got Duke going again, snarling and writhing so hard that the big dog managed to get his paws under him and press the net up a bit.

"Watch your tongue when you speak of our noble lord, boy. And kill that damnable mutt already!" the head goblin shouted over his shoulder. With the net lifted a bit, Kaden managed to turn his head, and he watched in horror as one of the other goblins, wiry and hard looking, pulled a long, curved blade from a sheath at his back. He stepped toward the net, raising his sword high for a killing blow.

"No!" Kaden begged. "Please, don't!" The goblin just laughed and lifted the sword higher, took one more step and—

—he tripped over the butt of a long spear that suddenly appeared on the ground in front of him. His slash went awry, slicing through a chunk of the net but missing Duke entirely. Duke forced his way out of the rent in the long, solid strands and snapped at the sword wielder, startling him so much he fell to the ground.

Kaden saw Duke's hindquarters bunch as the dog readied to attack, and he knew he had to stop him—they were too outnumbered, Duke would only be killed. No one could take on six goblins at once and win. "Go!" he screamed at his dog. Duke whined and turned his head to look at him. "*Go!*"

Kaden knew the dog didn't want to leave him, but obedience to his master won out, and a moment later, the hunting hound ran into the woods, baying as he went.

"Curse you, Runtling!" the goblin leader snapped. "What were you doing with that spear?"

"I'm sorry!" a little goblin cried out, and for the first time, Kaden saw a member of this savage company that *didn't* scare him. The goblin known as Runtling couldn't be even four feet tall, and his head was so large, his ears even more enormous, that he looked like a child. "I was just trying to push the beast back. I didn't mean to get in Narf's way!"

"Get after the dog and silence it, or I'll spit you on the end of your own spear."

The little goblin made an *eep* sound, then darted into the underbrush, vanishing a second later.

"Told you taking him on was a bad idea, didn't I?" Narf groused as he freed himself from the nets he'd fallen into. "Told you that, but *no*, it was all, 'Oh, Petey's useless, but he's the king's son, taking him on will win us favor.' What kind of favor will we win with Lucient, do you think, when we come back empty-handed because Petey can't—"

"*Shut* it, Narf." The goblin leader turned back to Kaden, no more grin on his face—instead, he looked grim as a pallbearer. "No more delays. We seek a boy in your village, sixteen years old. He would be a foundling, no true child to his parents, someone who doesn't look quite like them even if they've claimed him as their own. Do you know of such a boy?"

Kaden's mind raced. A few other boys in the village were his age, but they had proper parents, just like he did. If he said that, though, would the goblins believe him? More importantly, even if someone did stand out, would he be sentencing one of his neighbors to death if he shared their name? These creatures were... *mercenaries*, his mind supplied, a word he'd learned from his pa one night when word came to the village of a battle fought a few days away from their own small corner of the world. It had been brutal, a battle for dominance between two local landowners, but one of them had had the coin to hire mercenaries to fight for him. It had been a massacre.

Another blow to the head focused his attention. "Are you mute with fear or a simpleton?" the goblin leader wondered aloud.

"He's likely a simpleton," one of the others said with a snort. "What other kind of child would be allowed to wander the woods on a day when he should be working the field? Should have been killed the moment his parents figured it out, but humans are too sentimental to follow through on such things. Do them a favor and kill him now, boss."

Kaden could see the goblin leader was weighing his minion's input, and it finally moved him to speak. "N-no! I'm not. I'm not a simpleton," he said. "There's a family—there *was* a family like the one you're describing, a boy who didn't really look like them. They called him their nephew, not their son, but he could easily have been a foundling. They left, though, two years ago, after—after—"

"After what?" the goblin leader demanded, his burning eyes narrowed in a suspicious squint.

"A man came to visit them," Kaden extemporized, desperate and trying not to show it. "A stranger to the village. He'd come a few times before, but only to see them, and this time—I don't know what he said, but it convinced them to leave. They were gone the next day, their house still full of wares, fields unattended, sheep let out to graze." It wasn't so different from the way that strange old man had visited his own family a while back, Kaden thought. So, it wasn't really a *lie*. It was all based on fact and possibility.

"Hmm." The goblin leader scratched his chin. "What was this family called?"

"The Dar-darveths." Old Man Darveth had died last winter, and he was the last member of his family in the village, but what the goblins didn't know couldn't hurt them. *Too bad.* "I don't know where they went," Kaden went on, his words practically stumbling over themselves to leave his mouth. "They never sent word, never came back."

"Hmmm." The goblin stroked his chin. "Could be the ones, could be. Not much use hanging around here if they're gone. But then, Lucient doesn't steer us wrong. Why send us to this village if our target isn't here?"

"I don't know, I don't, please, I've told you everything I know," Kaden said, feeling a slight fluttering of relief stir in his stomach. "Please let me go! I won't tell anyone about you, I promise."

"Oh, lad." The goblin laughed and shook his head. "Even if you're honest, your time is done! You're as green as an apple to think otherwise. No... we'll track this family, see if you fed us truths or falsehoods. And if you've lied, then rely on this." He leaned in close, his breath a sour wash across Kaden's face, his bright eyes flickering like flames.

"We'll sneak into your village at night and find your home. We'll kill your family and burn your little hut to the ground, slaughter all your animals, and if Petey has failed us and let your dog go free, we'll skin it alive when we find it again. As for you?" He glanced at the ruined chicken smoldering in the remains of the fire. "We lost a decent meal to your hunger, but you'll do nicely to replace it."

Faster than Kaden could blink, a green, grimy, long-fingered hand was clenched around his throat. He scrambled to claw at it, to fight it off, but the goblin leader just pressed his neck harder against the ground. *No... I can't die like this; I haven't done anything yet, I haven't lived! I can't die now!* But breathing was impossible, and the cruel grip on his throat was unbreakable. Stars flickered over Kaden's failing vision, and he hated that the last thing he would ever see was the ugly face of this wicked goblin staring at him.

"*Now*, Duke!"

A familiar bark erupted from somewhere nearby, and a moment later, the goblin leader let go of Kaden, howling in pain as Duke clamped down on his arm. The goblin was rugged, but Duke's bite was powerful, and the scent of blood filled the air.

Kaden, gasping and teary-eyed, barely made out what happened next. One moment the goblins were staring in shock at their leader, who was straining to keep Duke from going for his own neck. Next, they were shouting in terror as a man in a dark cloak, holding a familiar sword, leaped into the middle of them and began to fight with a ferocity that left them stunned for several crucial seconds. Two of the goblins fell before the other two got their wits about them and began to fight back.

Pa! Kaden fought to get his breath back, desperate to escape from the net. He had to help his father… he just wasn't sure *how* to yet.

One of the goblins blocked Daneyel's blade with a small round buckler, then thrust up with a dagger, aiming for the bigger man's armpit. Daneyel danced back smoothly, and the killing blow became a scratch to the forearm. He swung his blade down in a lightning-fast arc, and a moment later, the goblin was left staring at his arm twitching on the ground, totally severed.

The other goblin to survive Daneyel's initial attack was Narf, and he wasn't charging in. He sneaked and sliced and struck with caution, his curved blade as fast as Daneyel's. They blocked and parried, cut and slashed, and fought for dominance. Kaden finally freed his upper body from the net and strained to grab the skewer that had been sitting over the fire—it was a poor weapon but better than nothing. Almost… *almost…*

"Aaagh!" Pain raked like fire across his upper arm, and he jerked away from it as fast as he could, twisting as he did so. It was the goblin leader, bleeding from a dozen bite marks and still tangling with Duke but so focused on Kaden, he seemed unable to feel the pain of his wounds. He held a dagger of his own in his unmarked hand, and a shining line of fresh blood edged the blade.

"It's you," the goblin growled. "You *are* the one. Our Great Lord spoke the truth." He drew his arm back like he was about to throw the dagger right into Kaden. Duke snarled and jerked, but the goblin was determined—even as blood poured from his terrible injuries, he kept his eyes on Kaden. Kaden lifted a hand, helpless to run with his legs still tangled.

Thunk! Daneyel's sword flew across the clearing, straight through the goblin leader's chest and out the other side. The repulsive creature wavered, then fell, the light in his eyes finally going out. Kaden turned to his father, relieved beyond all measure, but then—

"Pa!" he screamed. A second later, Narf ran Daneyel through from behind. "*No!*"

"That'll teach a man to think he can get the best of—*augh!*" Duke was on the goblin in a second, and this time he didn't go for the arm. He caught Narf around the throat and bowled him over onto the ground.

Kaden ignored the awful gurgling sounds and worked himself free of the rest of the net, racing to his father. Daneyel lay on his side, blood pouring from his mouth and around where the blade had penetrated. "Pa," Kaden said weakly, falling to his knees beside him. He didn't... he couldn't... "I'll run home, get Ma, get the healer, we'll—"

"No," his father gasped. "Too... late for that now. You can't... go back, Kaden. You... can't."

"But Ma—"

"No," Daneyel insisted. "Too... dangerous for... both of you." He coughed, and bright red droplets spattered across the leafy ground in front of him. Kaden, helpless and hating himself for it, supported his father's head as he coughed again.

"Go," Daneyel croaked once he could speak. "You must... go. Find... Bhalla." He pressed a unique pendant into Kaden's free hand. "Use this to… help you. Kaden… you—" He shuddered in Kaden's arms. "You are… the son of King Karatheas. The last of that… royal line. I am not your father." He smiled then gently touched a bloodied hand to Kaden's face. "But I have always loved you like a son," he whispered. "Now… find Bhalla. Find him, and live."

"Pa," Kaden said, barely able to choke it out through the tears. "Please, don't go. Stay with me." But it was too late—Daneyel was already gone, his dark, knowing eyes slowly clouding over in death. His chest was still, lungs and heart finally letting go of their burden.

Kaden felt like he was dying himself. "No," he whispered. "No. No, no."

But death would not be denied.

CHAPTER 4

For a long time, it was all Kaden could do to keep breathing. It felt wrong, in every fiber of his body, to go on living while his father—his—the man who raised him lay still on the ground, his great, strong heart no longer pumping. Kaden couldn't help himself—he pressed on Daneyel's chest with his hands, feeling for that heartbeat, listening for a whisper of breath at his lips. With every passing, silent second, the ache in Kaden's own chest grew sharper and sharper until he finally reared back with a cry and turned away from Daneyel's body, buried his fingers in the dirt, and broke apart with sobs.

Crying didn't make him feel better. Nothing could make him feel better now, not even Duke pressing his long snout over Kaden's shoulder and gently licking his face. It didn't help that the fur around the dog's jaw was matted with oily goblin blood. Kaden shuddered and pushed Duke away. "No, boy," he said weakly, but it was something. "Not until you're clean."

Kaden sat back on his haunches and gazed up at the sky. The sunlight was turning golden, the unusual shade of gold that happened as the sun sank well past its zenith, flowing closer to the horizon and spreading its color through the air. It was getting late. His mother would be looking for them both now, waiting for them to come home.

I have always loved you like a son. The words haunted Kaden, made him feel ashamed of his sad, angry thoughts even though he felt entitled to them. Daneyel had loved him. Lydia loved him. He knew she did, but... he couldn't go home. Not with Lucient knowing where he lived, Lucient the Great Deceiver...

Kaden's mind shied away from the very thought of it. *He couldn't be that important.* He was just himself, just a seventeen-year-old boy who, until this afternoon, had never seen actual violence, had never seen someone's death up close. He couldn't think about Lucient looking for him—it would drive him mad with anxiety.

Goblins, though... were somewhat less frightening than the specter of the dark lord and framed his problem in a way he could handle. He couldn't go home, not with *goblins* looking for him. Where *could* he go, then?

Kaden opened his hand for the first time in hours, prying his sore, swollen fingers apart to look at the amulet that lay on his palm. It was about the length of his thumb, a clear crystal with a golden cover in the shape of a tall, five-sided tower. It was strung on a length of simple leather cord that looked long enough to go over his head.

"Find Bhalla," he murmured. But how was this supposed to help him find—

"Whoa!" He almost dropped the amulet as a silvery light suddenly welled up in the center of it, pooling on the left side of the crystal—the side that faced deeper into Ashland Woods. Kaden grabbed the cord and lifted the stone off his palm, and the light faded. He touched it with his skin again, though; it lit up even brighter. No matter how he turned it, the glow always concentrated on the side that led away from the village.

Duke suddenly began to growl just as a small voice off to the side of the clearing said, "It wants to take you to the city of Lumhagen."

Kaden swung around, grabbed the weapon closest to his hand—a curved goblin blade, *ugh*, it made his skin crawl just to touch it—and brought it to bear on the speaker. He couldn't make out whoever spoke to him from the bushes in the lower golden light. "Show yourself!"

"I—oh—no, it's all right!" Leaves rustled, and a moment later, a small, hunched figure crept out from behind a hollyhack bush. "Don't be frightened; it's just me." *Just me* turned out to be a goblin—a familiar one, the one whose spear got in Narf's way when he was about to kill Duke.

But just because he'd done one decent thing where Kaden could see it didn't mean he wasn't an enemy. "Put down your weapons," he demanded.

"I don't have any weapons! See?" The little goblin waved his empty hands pathetically. "I dropped my spear before I left! And I made sure your father and your dog found each other in the woods, and—and—"

"Why?" Kaden asked. He eyed the scrawny, yellow-eyed creature, noticing how short, black hair grew in patches on the goblin's arms, legs, and even neck. Indeed, he must be a spy for Lord Lucient like all the others had been. "Why would you bother helping me? Aren't you supposed to kill me?"

The little goblin wailed and scrubbed his hands over his outsized eyes. "I couldn't do it!" he moaned. "I know goblins are supposed to be tougher and meaner than everyone else, but I've *never* been able to do it! I brought shame to my entire family. This mission was my last chance to prove myself a real goblin before my father removed me from the line of succession." He dropped his hands and looked mournfully at the corpses of his fellows. "Clearly, I failed," he said.

"You can't expect me to feel sorry for you," Kaden snapped. "You—your kind *killed* my fath—my—they killed my father! They were going to kill me too!"

"And eat you, probably," the goblin agreed. "I don't expect you to feel sorry for me, of course not. But... will you at least not mind if I feel sorry for *you*?" He wrung his long-fingered hands. "First you were trapped, then your father was killed, now you have to find the mystical city of Lumhagen, and it's not easy to get there, even with a guide like the one you've got."

"How do you know where I've got to go?" Kaden asked.

"I, um, I heard your father tell you. To find Bhalla, that is. And everyone knows that after the war, the few remaining wizards abandoned Elderkeep and retreated to their hidden city. It's farther from the old capital, Empyrea, and kept secret by the miraculous power of Orealus, that is impenetrable even to Lucient."

He said it all so casually like it really was something everyone knew when Kaden had never heard of any of this before. How much had his parents kept from him? Why was *he* the only one left in ignorance? Another surge of anger welled up inside of him, but he ignored it as best he could.

"But your amulet should show you the way!" the goblin went on a bit more cheerfully. "I mean, you have to survive the forest, and whatever creatures you might encounter along the way, and then there's getting into the city once you arrive, which is a completely different thing than simply finding the place, but… I'm sure you'll figure it out."

Kaden didn't feel so sure. Right now, the only thing he was sure of was that he couldn't go home. What would he even say to his moth—to Lydia—if he saw her? "I'm sorry Daneyel died saving my life from a stupid trap I should have known to avoid"? No, he couldn't face her now, and it wouldn't be safe to go back to town anyway. He scrubbed his free hand over his face and tried to focus.

"I need to bury him," he said, a little croakily, but the goblin pretended not to notice.

"I'll help you," he volunteered solemnly. "There are shovels in some of their packs."

The thought of using goblin gear to lay Daneyel to rest made Kaden feel a bit sick to his stomach, but it wasn't as if he had any alternatives. The only other place to get a shovel was back in town, and he'd already decided that wasn't an option. "All right," he said.

"And, um... I'm Petey," the little goblin said, ducking his head. "Petey Elvenshire. My brother told me that we were forbidden from using our last name, though."

Kaden had to admit, it did feel better to have an actual name to call this oddly helpful creature instead of continually associating him with the bodies strewn across the ground. He didn't say anything, just nodded his head, and after a moment, Petey crossed to the far side of the clearing and pulled packs out of what seemed like thin air, rummaging through the underbrush and piling them in a heap on the ground. *Goblins are really good at hiding things,* Kaden marveled, his grief diminishing for a moment as he watched. *Especially themselves.* He could barely see Petey in the dappled light. It blended so perfectly with the green gray of his skin.

Petey returned a few minutes later with two camp shovels, shorter than what Kaden's family kept around the farm but still decent. They took a moment to haul away the net and drag the goblin bodies further into the woods—Petey with a look of sadness, Kaden resisting the urge to stomp their faces in even though they wouldn't feel it now—then got to work digging a grave for Daneyel.

It was hard going. The ground was crisscrossed with tree roots, one old stump needed to be pried out, and then there was the pain of actually putting the older man into the freshly hollowed grave. Kaden didn't let Petey help with that part, so the goblin busied himself lighting a torch in the twilight. Kaden wound his arms beneath Daneyel's shoulders, and half carried, half dragged him into the cool, wet earth. He lay Daneyel's body down as gently as he could, then used his cloak to cover his face and upper body.

Kaden's knees were cold from where he knelt in the mud, and the sun had gone down hours ago. He shivered, but he wasn't sure how much of that was from the chill of the evening and how much was from the horror of what he was doing now. "I'm sorry," he choked out, laying one hand on his father's covered forehead. "I'm so sorry. I won't... I won't let this be in vain." As much as part of him wanted to lie down in that grave himself, he knew it was the worst thing he could possibly do now. Daneyel had died to save him. Kaden couldn't dishonor his sacrifice. "I love you," he whispered, then forced out, "Father." Then he got up out of the grave, grabbed his shovel off the ground, and began to fill the hole in.

*   *   *

An hour later, the night air was filled with insects, some of them biting, and Kaden and Petey were both covered in soil, but the grave was covered with sturdy rocks from a nearby stream to keep scavengers out, with a simple circle pattern on top of it—the sacred circle of Orealus. Duke sat beside him, and Kaden put one hand on his dog's head as the other traced a circle in the air over the grave. "May Orealus bless and keep your soul, Father," Kaden said emotionally, repeating what he'd heard at funerals in the past. "For you are surely his loyal son, and he shall welcome you into his kingdom with wide arms and an open heart."

For all that Kaden hadn't thought much about death before— no one in the village ever died except old age and, once, a terribly complicated childbirth—he hoped that the prayers were proper. He hoped there was a part of Daneyel out there that would live forever, no longer afraid, no longer in pain. Content.

A long howl interrupted his moment of silence. Duke perked up immediately, a growl emanating from deep in his chest. "Wolves," Petey whispered, his eyes moon-bright in the darkness. He sounded scared. "We need to leave here. They'll be coming for the bodies, but they might not be too picky if they find *us* here too."

"'We?' You mean *you* want to come with *me*?" Kaden asked, surprised despite himself. "To find Bhalla?"

Petey wrung his hands. "I can't return to Shroudscar, not after this! I'd be exiled or worse." He made a sound like a sob. "I know you have no reason to believe me, but please… can we travel together, just for a bit? I don't… I don't want to be alone."

The wolves howled again, closer this time, and Kaden had to admit that he didn't want to be alone either. "Fine," he said after a moment. "But this *doesn't* mean we're friends."

"Oh, I know," said Petey, sadly. "I know that."

"Okay." Kaden cast one last look around, searching until his gaze found his father's sword and sheath lying freshly cleaned on the ground a little way away. He glanced at Petey, who must have been the one to scour the blood off them, but the little goblin wasn't looking his way. Kaden tied the sword belt around his waist, then nodded. "Let's go."

CHAPTER 5

Kaden and Petey didn't exchange more than a dozen words during the rest of that evening's travel through Ashland Woods. They got far enough away from the ambush site to avoid interested scavengers, then decided to settle down for the night and start fresh in the morning.

Stopping made Kaden feel like his bones had dissolved—all the tension and fear and exhaustion he'd done his best to put to the back of his mind came rushing at him so fast, it was all he could do not to fall down in a heap where he stood. He held onto his senses long enough to bathe in the creek—necessary if he wasn't going to smell even more like a grave tomorrow—and then collapsed beside Duke without accepting Petey's tentative offer of preparing food. He would never stay awake long enough to eat it.

He didn't dream. That was the one thing Kaden knew he should be grateful for the next day, when he woke up to early morning sunlight filtering through the trees' delicate leaves, beautiful birdsong echoing through the woods, and the realization that his father was dead and his mother lost to him hitting him like a hammer to the heart, all over again. At least, through all the awfulness of what had happened yesterday, he'd been too exhausted to dream.

In fact, he felt refreshed, rejuvenated, and it seemed so wrong he almost cried again. Daneyel was dead and buried—shouldn't

Kaden feel *more* about that? Feel worse? Why should he get to wake up and feel whole when Daneyel would never wake up again?

"Um..."

Kaden pulled himself out of his panicky, spiraling thoughts to look over at Petey, who stood a few feet away, the toe of one of his oversized black boots digging into the ground as he shyly extended a bowl. "Breakfast?" he asked, then said, "That is to say, I've got breakfast here, and do you want some, not to ask whether you're interested in breakfast at all, because who isn't interested in breakfast?" He scanned Kaden's face with anxious eyes. "Unless you... aren't interested in breakfast? Maybe your people don't eat it. How many meals a day do humans eat, anyhow?"

Kaden coughed to clear his throat. "Breakfast would be welcome," he said. Petey shoved the bowl into his hands so quickly that he almost spilled it. The porridge was savory, not sweet the way his mother—the way *Lydia*—had usually made it, and Kaden was glad for the difference. He didn't want to be even more reminded of her right now. "What's in this?" he asked around a ravenous bite.

"Oh, some oats, some water and salt, a bit of dried meat— but nothing humanoid!" Petey hurried to tack onto the end.

Ugh! Kaden hadn't even been thinking that before, but now, of course, he couldn't help it. "Goblins really eat people?" he demanded. "That's... that's so...."

"*I* don't!" Petey assured him. "I never have; I'd rather go hungry than eat something that I could have an actual conversation with. This is rabbit. Just rabbit." He sniffed the pot again. "Maybe a bit of leftover squirrel too," he added.

Kaden blanched, but his growling stomach demanded more, so he finished the bowl, then handed it back to Petey. Duke had left sometime in the early morning, before Kaden was awake, and came back licking his chops, so Kaden assumed he'd taken care of finding his own meal.

"So," Kaden began, determined to act normal even though his heart still felt broken inside his chest, every beat pulsing with sadness. "What's next?"

Petey looked puzzled. "Doesn't your amulet show the way?"

"Yeah, but..." Kaden pulled it out from underneath his shirt, held it close, and said, "Find Bhalla." The glow lit up again, pointing southeast. "This is a useful spell, but it didn't stop me from almost walking into a bunch of trees last night. And remember when we had to find a shallow spot in the creek to ford because the light led us straight into a rapid?" Kaden looked the amulet over in the bright morning sunshine, twisting it this way and that way and watching the light resettle every time. "I think it's more of a compass than a map, if you know what I mean."

"I think I do." Petey nodded his big head, one long-fingered hand scratching the back of his neck. "Well, there... is a *way*, a path of sorts, I suppose you might call it, that leads in that general direction. It's not a proper road or anything like that, but it's the closest we'll come in leading toward Brightshire Forest."

Kaden frowned. "I thought we were in Ashland Woods."

"Oh no," Petey said earnestly, "those woods are just a tiny part of Brightshire Forest, which some call the Enchanted Woods. This place is huge, home to lots of terribly dangerous things, like wood elves and fairies and binicorns and even a satyr or two."

None of those sounded all that dangerous to Kaden. "The wood elves I knew about," he said because he'd seen a few before on market days in Ashland, the elegant folk stopping by seemingly on a lark. He couldn't imagine that the elves really needed anything Ashland could provide. It was so rural, so far away from everything exciting, *except goblins.*

He steeled his heart and went on. "And the fairies have a city of their own somewhere inside the forest, right? Fayspire?"

Petey nodded shakily. "That's right. Hundreds and hundreds of fairies all in one place, ready to rip the ears off any goblin that gets too close. And don't get me *started* on Binicorn's Farthing. That's a death sentence if ever I heard one."

"So, they… don't like goblins," Kaden surmised.

Petey's eyes welled with tears. "No! No one in here does! And if they *did* like goblins, then they still wouldn't like me because I'm the least goblinish goblin that ever existed!" He tugged on the corners of his long, pointy ears and moaned pitifully. "Hated by one group and loathed by the other," he said with a sniffle. "No one can stand me."

"I can."

Kaden wasn't sure why he said it at first—he barely knew this creature, and Petey *had* been a member of a party sent to kill him, who had actually *succeeded* in killing… well. The point was, Kaden had a lot of good reasons *not* to like Petey and only a few good ones *to* like him, but those few seemed to vastly outweigh all the other considerations.

Petey had risked his life to save Kaden, save Duke, and help rescue Daneyel. He had proven his loyalty, and the least Kaden could do was try to be loyal in return.

"I can," he said again, with more conviction this time. Petey looked desperately hopeful but still didn't speak. "We're in this together now," Kaden said. "So if we run into anyone who thinks you're a normal, everyday bloodthirsty goblin, I'll speak up for you."

"You will?" Petey asked tremulously. "You'll tell them I'm helpful and kind and wouldn't even eat a baby bird out of its nest?"

Yuck. "Yes," Kaden said, trying not to dwell on the image.

Petey's eyes filled with tears again, but this time he was smiling. "Thank you!" he cried, doing a little jig. "Thank you, thank you! You won't regret befriending me, Kaden, I promise."

I hope not. "Now," Kaden continued once Petey stopped dancing, "do you think you can get us to the path? The faster we get to Bhalla, the sooner we're someplace safe."

"I'm sure I can get us there," Petey assured him. "We're very close already. Look up at the tree canopy." Kaden obligingly looked up. "You see how it's getting thicker toward the south? There are actually two paths through the forest—one made of branches trained to grow together to make a road up in the trees and another down on the ground. Only the wood elves use the one in the trees." Petey scratched behind one of his ears and added, "And probably the monkeys, but they're not as scary as the elves."

"So we'll use the one on the ground, then." That was quite a relief—Kaden didn't feel very graceful on his best days, and the thought of trying to walk from branch to branch and keep his balance doing so was daunting. Besides, how would they have gotten Duke up there?

"We can do that, but…" Petey lowered his voice again. "We should be quiet. Really, really quiet. Just in case the elves are around." He laughed nervously. "There's no sense in tempting fate, right?"

Tempting fate… Kaden felt like this whole strange journey was an exercise in tempting fate. If only he'd never gone into Ashland Woods to look for those stupid bonberries. How would things have changed if he'd stayed at home? Would the goblins have attacked the village? Would they still have killed his father, or could they have fought them off together? Would Daneyel still have told Kaden the truth about who he really was?

Would Daneyel *ever* have told Kaden otherwise? He'd kept the amulet from Bhalla for him, but…

Kaden sighed. He was thinking of himself in circles, which wasn't helping him or anyone else. "We'll be careful," he said. "Let's pack up." He nodded his head toward the pile of black leather packs Petey had hauled along last night. "I'll carry one of those." The thought of a goblin pack on his back made his skin crawl, but he wasn't about to ask Petey to carry everything that they needed for the trip.

"Thanks! I was wondering how I was going to manage them all for more than a few miles," Petey said, handing over the least-stained pack with an apologetic smile. "We goblins are much stronger than we look, but… well, anyway, thank you." They cleaned up their campsite and refilled two water-skins at the nearby creek, then struck off toward the thickest parts of the canopy, Duke trailing along at Kaden's heels.

It wasn't easy going among the trees, although Brightshire Forest was undeniably beautiful, especially in the morning when the light made the dewdrops on leaves and spiderwebs glimmer like gems. Now that they were farther away from Ashland Village, Kaden caught occasional glimpses of the long-furred, red-backed monkeys known as mawhaas, whose call sounded like a woman's laugh. Their pelts were both highly prized and incredibly taboo back in town—they were wonderfully warm and beautiful, but killing a monkey was a surefire invitation to bad luck. Sometimes passing traders had them for sale, but even then, no Ashlander would buy one, not if they wanted to keep the respect of their neighbors.

Lost in thought, Kaden tripped over a mossy tree root and almost fell on his face before he caught himself against the massive trunk of a braken oak. Duke nosed at him, Petey looked back worriedly, and Kaden blushed so hard it felt like his face had caught on fire. "I'm fine," he muttered, resettling the pack and Daneyel's sword, which felt awkward and heavy at his hip. "Are we getting close yet?"

"Very close. Look." He pointed a few yards ahead, where Kaden could make out parallel clearings on either side of a long, uneven line of thick-trunked trees. The foliage mainly was cleared there, only dead leaves and long, arcing ferns making their homes beneath the relative darkness that resulted from the woven branches overhead.

Kaden smiled. "That's more like it," he said. "We'll make good time this way. Lumhagen can't be all *that* far away."

"Probably not," Petey said, wringing his hands. His heavy brow was creased with worry lines. "Not very far at all. Maybe not far *enough*. What if... what if they don't... what if the wizards don't let me..."

"Hey." Kaden touched his shoulder. "I said I'd speak up for you, and I will. It will be all right."

Something had to turn out all right after this terrible beginning. This, at least, was something Kaden could try to influence. Something he could do for someone else that might still make a difference in their lives. "It *will* be all right," he promised. "Let's go."

CHAPTER 6

It was hard for Kaden to tell how quickly time passed in the heart of the forest. His whole life he'd lived to the rhythm of the farm, of village life—up as the sun rose, down when the sun set. That part, at least, he could still tell in Brightshire Forest— once he started tripping over tree roots, it was time to make camp. It was the *rest* of the day he had a hard time getting a handle. He didn't know whether it was nine or noon after they'd been walking for a while when the path looked so similar, and the filtered, green-tinged light seemed so constant.

Kaden probably could have asked Petey; he knew. For all that he was a self-professed failure of a goblin, Petey was actually really good at wayfinding. He always seemed to know where they could find freshwater, whether a plant was poisonous or not, and if squatting next to a particular bush to do their business would lead to itching and welts. Kaden had found *that* out the hard way.

The truth was, though, he didn't really *need* to ask Petey anything because Petey seemed to be incapable of staying silent for more than a few minutes at a time. As soon as they were awake in the morning, Petey was chatting about this, that, the flying frog on the bush over there, the tiny two-headed amphisbaena munching on a colony of ants over here. He'd stopped Kaden to point it out.

"They're really rare," Petey said admiringly as they looked at the little golden serpent, no bigger than a dragonfly. "Most types live in the desert. I never thought I'd see one here!"

"They don't have them in your home?" Kaden asked. The little creature startled, suddenly realizing that it was being watched. It coiled the head at the end of its tail over its body, like a two-faced scorpion, and hissed menacingly as it backed away. A second later, it darted under a log, and they straightened up. Kaden had to tell Duke "leave it" twice before the big dog gave up on the idea of following it.

"No," Petey said quietly. "There's nothing beautiful like that in the caves, nothing wild. Everything has either been killed or caged." He sighed and hiked his pack higher on his shoulders. "We should keep moving."

They started out again, but Kaden's curiosity didn't settle. "Why did you grow up so differently from other goblins?" he asked. "Were you raised somewhere else?"

"Um… no, not really?" Petey offered. "I mean, I had a tough childhood. I'm the youngest child of King Remus and Queen Thalia Elvenshire, and by the time I came, everyone thought my mother was well past her bearing years. She called me her little blessing and kept me with her in her private rooms and gardens for the most part." Petey sniffed. "I never even went out into our city, Shroudscar, until my evil brother Garth told me she died. That's when I learned how… different I am from my race."

"Oh… um." Kaden was worried he'd accidentally put his foot in it. He didn't want to bring up the loss of a parent, not when Petey was so kind about avoiding the subject of Daneyel and what had happened back in Ashland Woods. "I'm sorry," Kaden offered, at last, figuring a hint of sympathy was better than ignoring the statement altogether.

"Oh, it's all right," Petey said, even though Kaden could see that it wasn't. "It's been years now, many years. I'm completely over it." He chuckled weakly. "I don't even remember what she looked like anymore. My father had all pictures of her taken down after she died. He—"

Petey stopped so suddenly that Kaden almost ran smack into him. "Why are we—"

"Shh." Petey held up a hand. His ears were twitching wildly, and he turned his head this way and that, searching with his sense of hearing instead of his eyes. "Oh no," he whispered, his long green fingers clenching down on the straps of his pack.

"What is it?"

Petey looked up at Kaden, his bright yellow eyes gone wide as a plate. "Grawlers!"

Kaden shook his head. "I've never heard of those before."

"Wolves! They're a kind of wolf, a, a *big* wolf, twice as big as the normal ones!" Petey was beginning to look downright panicked, turning in circles as though he could somehow see right through the trees.

"Oh." *That* wasn't good. Kaden put one hand on the hilt of his sword. "Do you think we can outrun them?"

"No, they're too close! If I can hear them now, it means they're close enough to smell us. They never give up once they've got a scent. We have to climb!"

"No." His response was reflexive but firm. "We can't. Duke won't be able to go with us."

"He can run! He can—"

"He would never run," Kaden insisted. "He wouldn't leave me. Look, we're both armed; we can fight them off."

"You don't *understand*!" Petey wailed, pulling on the ends of his ears. "These aren't normal wolves! Grawlers are bigger, smarter, and more vicious than any wolf you've ever seen, and they hunt in packs! Some goblins breed them with our domestic dogs to make war pups, and you know how they bait them? With captured *binicorns*! Grawlers love to hunt and fight so much, they'll take on a fully grown binicorn! They're not afraid of anything, least of all us. Please, please." He reached out and tugged on the edge of Kaden's sleeve. "We have to escape, we have to climb, please—"

Kaden gently detached Petey's hand. "You climb," he said as levelly as he could because now *he* could hear them, not barking or howling but letting loose a low, continuous growl. Duke pressed closer to Kaden, responding with a growl of his own. "It's all right. I'm staying here."

Petey sobbed just once, then threw his pack down and pulled his curved sword. It was really too big for him, but he held it in both hands like he had an idea of how to wield it. "I'm staying too," he said in a small voice.

"Thank you," Kaden replied gratefully. "It'll be all right. Keep your back to the trees, and we'll fight them off together." He dropped his own pack, pulled his sword, and positioned himself just in front of a tree as he waited. He felt oddly calm. Maybe he still wasn't recovered enough from Daneyel's death to take other things to heart yet, even terror, but he was grateful that his hands were steady and his eyes were clear.

We can do this. Together. How bad could grawlers really be, after all? He and Daneyel and the other men in Ashland had fought off wolves before, desperate winter wolves that just kept coming until there were enough of their own dead on the ground to sate the hunger of those who still lived. He had handled himself well then. He would manage himself better now.

The growling sound became a rumbling roar, and through the thicket across the little clearing where they stood, the first grawler emerged.

Kaden swallowed hard. His mouth was suddenly gone dry. Maybe they *couldn't* do this.

Petey had said they were big, but this creature was the size of a pony, easily double the width and breadth of an average size wolf—it made *Duke* look small, and he was the most giant dog breed Kaden knew. Its shoulders were hugely muscled, and its front paws seemed more flexible, almost like hands. Its claws were at least three inches long and so sharp they shredded the dead leaves beneath them. Its face was terrifying, the jaw wider and teeth longer than Kaden had seen on *any* animal, and its nostrils were long, deep slits, stretching back along its muzzle almost as far as its dark, glittering eyes. Its fur was black as coal, and when it saw them, it opened its mouth and dropped its long, dark red tongue out, licking its chops greedily.

Two more of them appeared on either side of it. *Oh no.* If the grawlers attacked together, Kaden knew they were through. He might get lucky and take one down with his sword, but there was no way he'd be able to free it before another grawler cut him down from the side. To his left, Duke snarled and trembled with the urge to attack, and to his right, Petey shook just as much, though Kaden knew it was out of fear.

Kaden firmed his stance and lifted his sword. The soft light gleamed along the edge of the blade like liquid gold. "Leave us alone," he said firmly, the way he spoke to both puppies and children when they were naughty. "Or you'll be very sorry." These creatures were supposed to be wise, weren't they? Perhaps his tone, his body language, would sink in. "*Very* sorry," he added, tilting the blade a bit. The lead grawler's eyes followed the tip of his sword for a moment like it was mesmerized before snapping back to him. It shook its head hard, then refocused on Kaden with a fresh growl and a step forward.

"Stay back," Kaden said. The creature took another step forward, carefully avoiding looking at the blade.

They don't like the light. On a hunch, Kaden moved one hand to his amulet. "Find Bhalla!" he shouted, and the sudden glow that surged through the crystal was blindingly, shatteringly bright. He lowered his eyelids to a squint, barely able to see through the crystal's gleam at the grawlers. What were they doing? Would they attack despite the light?

No! Kaden saw them flail, their massive paws churning earth as they scrambled to evade the light's glare. One of them whined, only to wail harder when the lead grawler snapped angrily at its face before darting back into the thicket they'd emerged from. After a few more seconds, the grawlers were gone. Kaden slowly lowered the crystal, and the light faded back to its usual, faint shimmer.

"Wow," he said, stepping forward and lowering his sword. The ground was a mess of paw prints and grawler drool, but the beasts had run away. He laughed. "That was amazing!" It had been so easy, in the end! All he had needed to do to defeat a creature of darkness was a wish for light! "I can—"

Only pure instinct and the sudden change in Duke's breathing got Kaden turning, his sword rising just in time to keep him from being bitten in half by the grawler, which suddenly lunged out from behind a thick tree trunk a dozen feet away. It crossed the distance in almost no time, but it was so intent on attacking him that it didn't protect itself. The force of its leap as it impacted Kaden's shoulders was enough to drive him onto his back—and his sword straight through the thing's belly.

That should have been the end of it, but it wasn't—the grawler refused to admit it was dying and bore down against the blade with all its bulk, snapping at Kaden's face. Duke attacked it from one side, Petey from the other, but it still wasn't enough—the creature seemed bound and determined to get its jaws around Kaden's throat, and he couldn't let go of his sword to grab for the crystal again—if he did, it would only get him sooner.

It snapped its jaws repeatedly, drawing closer with each new effort. Another snap and it would have Kaden—his arms were weakening, and its breath was sickening, and there were two more of them out there, stalking them and *why did I lower the crystal so soon, why didn't I take more precautions, Orealus grant me grace, I'm going to die here.*

Its teeth less than an inch from his throat, the grawler suddenly stopped biting. It made a *hurk*-ing noise, then another, like it was trying to cough or vomit, and then—

Tiny branches covered in buds burst forth from its mouth. A thorny rosebush began to grow right through the grawler, its flowers the darkest color of midnight with pale, starlight-veined hearts. The grawler's glittering eyes rolled back in its head, losing their shine. It slumped on top of Kaden, death overcoming it at last. Kaden struggled to shift it away, but Petey helped him, and a moment later, they had him out from under it. He stared at the blooming, bushy corpse, incredulous.

What had just happened?

"Greetings to you, travelers," a voice said from above his head.

He looked up, wincing at the crick in his neck, and saw a person more magnificent than any he could have imagined. She was small, no bigger than a child, but she hovered in the air with the ease of a dragonfly, iridescent wings beating so quickly Kaden couldn't even really see *them*, just the disturbance they left in the air. Her hair was long, hanging below her waist, and braided with so many flowers, in such a wide variety, that he could barely see its shimmering color—but it was white, pure white of a pale translucent quality. On her head, she wore a beautiful woodland crown made up of wonderful wood twigs that were neatly adorned with more flowers. Her skin was olive toned, glowing like sunlight shining through a dark green leaf, and her big, wide eyes were violet. She wore a simple white shift, but it looked like it was made of fine, shimmering silk. Two other fairies hovered beside her, less adorned but still quite beautiful, each with a slender sword dangling from their belts.

Petey gasped and dropped his sword. He was down on the ground, curled into a ball a moment later, his hands wound around his head like he was trying to keep it from being stomped on as he moaned and whimpered. Duke ignored them all entirely, more interested in how his foe had suddenly turned into a bush that probably smelled like it needed to be marked.

"Gr-greetings," Kaden said once he realized a response was expected. "Um. Did you, ah… do that?" He pointed at the corpse of the grawler, which was now almost entirely consumed by flowers.

"I did indeed." The fairy smiled, and it was lovely enough to make his heart skip a beat. "My strengths lie with earth and air that honor Orealus, and thanks to the enabling of the blessing from his power, I am occasionally able to work minor miracles such as this."

"Um… turning grawlers into bushes using magic?" Kaden guessed awkwardly.

The fairy laughed. "No! Nothing was used of magic. I was born with the abilities that I can use. Orealus chooses those blessed with the gift of yah'zaval[1] which glorifies him through its pure usage. There was also a seed trapped in the fur on the back of its head. I merely encouraged *it* to grow. You see, the seed was planted already, and through Orealus, it grew. Truly, the seed is the hero here. And you"—she glanced at Petey, whose eyes were squeezed tightly shut, then at Duke—"and your brave friends. May I have your names?"

Oh, his ma—*Lydia*—would be ashamed of his manners. Kaden got to his feet and resisted the urge to push the hair out of his face—his hands were filthy with grawler blood. "Of course. I'm Kaden Sheppard, this is my dog Duke, and this is my friend Petey."

"Well met." She inclined her head. "And I am Queen Pepper Shinyfawn, ruler of Fayspire and guardian of the Enchanted Woods."

Oh… Orealus, save me… She was a queen, one of the Nine Pillars' rulers! Kaden made a hasty bow. "I'm very honored to meet you," he said, proud that his voice didn't shake. "Thank you for saving us."

---

[1] Yah'zaval pronounced yaah-sha-val

"You are most welcome. In truth, you have no need to thank me—discovering creatures like this lurking in these woods toward my home is the least of my responsibilities." She glanced at the grawler. "In all my four centuries, I cannot remember beasts like this penetrating so far into Brightshire, so close to my own home, not even during the Great War. They seemed to be targeting you." She looked back at Kaden. "Why do you think that is?"

Kaden paused. "I can't say for sure," he said slowly. "And... please, but I'd rather not—"

"A secret, then?" She smiled gently. "I understand needing to keep a secret. There is something about you, Kaden Sheppard... something almost familiar. Something remarkable. And the company you keep is most interesting."

"Petey is friendly," Kaden assured her hastily. "He wouldn't eat a baby bird out of its nest!" *Ugh, why did I add that in?* But the queen was laughing now.

"I'm sure he wouldn't," she agreed. "Keep your secrets, Kaden, but tell me this at least—where are you headed?"

"To the mystical city of Lumhagen," he said, happy to give her this much. "To meet with Bhalla."

Queen Pepper's eyebrows rose. "Indeed? And you have reason to believe that he *will* meet with you? Lumhagen is no easy labyrinth to penetrate. The spiritual abilities given to them by Orealus are strong enough to keep out even my own people without an invitation."

"We have an invitation," he said. The amulet counted, didn't it?

"Ah. Then I will let you go with my blessing, Kaden Sheppard. You and all your company." She glanced at Petey again, compassion in her gaze. "You are getting quite close. Stick to your path, and before long, you will find an entrance to the city of Lumhagen. I wish you the best of luck entering it."

"Thank you. Um," Kaden said as Queen Pepper and her companions rose a bit higher like they were about to fly off. "I don't mean to pry, but… there were two other grawlers with this one. Are they… what happened to them?"

"Ah," she said. "Of course, you're right to wonder about the safety of the path ahead. I should have mentioned, they will trouble you no further. I have seen to that." Her smile this time was sharper, the look of a person who didn't love a fight but knew she could win them. "One of them has taken root as a young tree, and the other is a patch of ivory broadleaf. Like I said…" Her gaze drifted back to the rosebush, which by now had completely obscured the grawler's corpse. "The seeds are the real heroes."

CHAPTER 7

The rest of their trip through Brightshire Forest passed uneventfully, which Kaden was relieved about and a little unnerved by. He was pretty sure that Queen Pepper, or some of her subjects, were watching over them from a distance, making sure they were safe from further pursuit. That was kind, but... there was also a part of him, a small but noisy part, that resented it. *How will I prove myself to Bhalla if I can't even get to him on my own?*

Then again, Kaden hadn't been on his own for any of this trip. From the beginning, he'd been accompanied by Duke and later helped by Daneyel and Petey. What did it matter if the queen of the fairies made sure he had safe passage to the entrance of Lumhagen? The important thing was that he got there, right?

Plus, Bhalla probably hadn't anticipated goblin mercenaries and vicious grawlers hunting Kaden down when he made this journey. There was no reason to be ashamed of a little extra help when it was the difference between life or death.

That night, when Kaden and Petey made camp and Duke had bounded off into the forest to get his own dinner, Kaden asked, "What do you think the entrance to Lumhagen will be like?"

Petey's ears twitched, a gesture that Kaden had learned by now meant Petey was curious. "I don't know; I've never been there before."

"But are there goblin wizards?" Kaden pressed. "If they seclude themselves the same way, then maybe—"

Petey was already shaking his head. "Oh no," he said emphatically. "Goblins aren't born with the spiritual gift of Orealus. That's for other creatures. Our oldest stories say that every race is born with its own special gifts. Some have great strength, some have ferocity, and some have abilities inside them that they were blessed with from Orealus. Goblins are gifted in endurance." Petey puffed out his chest a little, clearly proud. "We're not the biggest or the toughest out there, but we can outlast almost any opponent given enough time."

"That's a good gift," Kaden said, and Petey grinned. "What's humanity's gift?"

"Flexibility," Petey said immediately. "Not like being-able-to-put-your-foot-behind-your-head flexible"—he demonstrated, and Kaden laughed—"but more like... being versatile! Some humans are great wizards, some are great warriors, and some are gifted with handling animals. When humanity brings all their gifts together, then they become very formidable foes."

He set his foot down and shrugged. "When you can separate them out, though, then they're easy to destroy. Or, um..." He suddenly seemed to get embarrassed, twisting his fingers together until they looked braided. "That's what my arms instructor used to tell me," he muttered. "I would never... *I've* never done that. You saw how bad I was at fighting, I would *never*—"

"I know," Kaden said, quick to reassure his friend. Petey had been even more on edge about his goblin nature since they'd been saved by Queen Pepper. "I understand." He looked down at the amulet resting against his chest, which had been glowing more and more brightly over the past few days without him even having to do anything. "I'm just curious about the doorway. I don't know anything about that type of ability, and if having that type of ability is what it takes to get inside... I don't know what I'll do."

"You'll figure it out," said Petey, sounding uncommonly assured of himself. "Bhalla is the greatest of all the wizards, and he *meant* for you to be able to find him. He must be sure that you can do it. Maybe the amulet itself will get you in, or some sort of force will recognize you when you arrive and open the door that way."

"Yeah, maybe," Kaden agreed, feeling heartened. "You're right. If he wants me to get to him, then he has to make the way in something I can handle, even without possessing my own gift of yah'zaval."

They ate the last of Petey's store of stew that night and let Duke lick the bowls clean before Kaden's manners got the better of him, and he forced himself to actually wash the dishes out in the nearby creek. He lay back on a bed of dry leaves and bright green moss, sweet smelling beneath his lanky body, and stared up into the canopy of the trees.

A monkey swung by overhead, so perfectly camouflaged it was invisible except for the waver of the branches it clung to and the melodic sound of its hoot. Glowing pollen from a lampi plant floated through the air like a slow-moving meteor shower, bright and beautiful, swirling in spirals where a breeze caught it here and there, but there was less of it than Kaden was used to seeing. The fluffy pollen seeds illuminated the backdrop of the forest sky in various locations as they gently danced in the wind. Subtle brightness from the fluorescent colors rendered a calming effect as it chased away some darkness. The air felt a bit damp, and the breeze where it touched his bare skin had just a hint of a bite to it.

They were close to the edge of Brightshire Forest to the north, then, about to enter the land of mountains, wrinkled with peaks and valleys like an enormous replica of Kaden's bunched-up blanket in the mornings. At least, that was the way the land had looked on the map his father had shown him years ago. Tiny lines of blue had run down from the peaks into the valleys, surging to become one thick line as it trailed out over the plains. Small rivers—only in real life, they wouldn't be so tiny, they would be enormous, fed by fresh mountain runoff, and probably shockingly cold.

Would they have to cross a river to get into Lumhagen? Kaden hoped not—he knew how to swim, was taught the way every child in Ashland learned, in the stillness and calm of the lake beside the village, but he wouldn't call himself a *good* swimmer. Could Petey swim? Could Duke?

Duke nudged in closer beside him and let out a *whuff* of foul dog breath that made Kaden gag a little. Ugh, Duke would be fine. If he could survive his own breath, then nothing could kill him. And Petey was resourceful; he'd manage no matter what. And Kaden...

He would do what he had to do.

It wasn't a very comforting thought, but it was firm enough that he was able to calm his mind and drop off to sleep a few minutes later.

*   *   *

It only took an hour's walk the following day to make it to the edge of the forest. As the two approached the break in trees, they heard a colossal crash of water on a rock that could only mean a waterfall lay ahead. It was astonishing to Kaden how quickly the landscape changed—one moment they were surrounded by trees so tall he could barely see the tops of them, his ears filled with the hum and buzz of insect life and the rustle of wind in the leaves, and a moment later the forest ended. It didn't peter out, getting sparser and letting in more light gradually until finally, they emerged from beneath the canopy—the trees just *stopped*, all together, in a neat line. The ground beneath their feet went from soft and loamy to rock hard in the space of a single step. Kaden looked up at the sky and winced—his eyes weren't used to so much brightness at once.

It was worse for Petey, who flinched from the sun and immediately took a filmy rag out of his pocket, tying it in front of his eyes. "Goblins are built for darkness," he said apologetically to Kaden. "Not light. I won't be able to see much out here."

"There's not much to see yet," Kaden said. The line of trees spread east and west, and straight in front of them, fifty feet out, was a rugged wall of stone. It wasn't even a mountain—this was a cliff, steep and treacherous, tufted here and there with greenery but nothing huge enough to wrap a hand around. Pouring down this cliff was a vast waterfall, the sound source that now drowned out the animal noises behind them. The waterfall had the width of more than three men lying head-to-foot. White, frothing water pounded the rock beneath it with vigor before filtering down into a large pond. The water roared and foamed as it hit the stone, splashing and sending sparkling, rainbow-tinted spray into the sky on either side. It was beautiful, but...

"I don't see a door," Kaden said. "Just a waterfall."

The ends of Petey's ears twitched. "It's deafening." Duke seemed to agree, shaking his head from side to side as if to clear it.

"Let's see what the amulet can tell us." Kaden lifted it up in his hand. "Find Bhalla," he said clearly. The light pooled tightly on one side, almost as thin and precise as a string, drawing him forward. Kaden walked, focused on the direction of the light, until—

"Whoa!" Water flowed over the tops of his boots, drenching his feet inside the leather. Kaden flailed backward until his feet were, if not dry, at least not getting any wetter. He looked ahead and frowned. It was just a pool, probably only up to his knees at its deepest, but it led straight into the massive waterfall. The way the water was churning up the bank, Kaden was willing to bet it would hurt like the blazes if he tried to go into it.

"What is it?" Petey called anxiously from behind him.

"It's... the light is pointing me toward the waterfall," Kaden replied, raising his voice above the water's roar.

"Is there a door under it?"

"I can't tell," Kaden confessed. "The water is… there's a *lot* of it."

"This must be the test, then," Petey said, sounding satisfied.

Kaden wasn't so sure of that. "What, to get pounded into the ground by this thing?"

"Maybe to get *around* it somehow," Petey suggested.

Kaden looked again. The cliff stretched as far as he could see in either direction, the only break in the rocky expanse the waterfall in front of him. "Maybe," he said and took a few experimental steps to the right. The light *streamed* out of the amulet, pointing him straight back at the center of the waterfall. "No, this is definitely it. But…"

That was just too much water. There was no way for him to get through it—this much water might knock him unconscious, even if he could stand up beneath it. *Why would it point me here?* he asked himself. *What's the way through?* What was he missing? What did he need to do to find Bhalla?

Faith. The answer came to him a moment later, so simple that, at first, he doubted it just because it was *too* simple. He had to have faith. His journey had been fated to happen—even if the awful incident in Ashland Woods had never occurred. Kaden was still meant to receive the amulet needed to find Bhalla to learn what he needed to know to become… whatever it was he had to evolve into. He wanted to know what he was destined to do—he *needed* to know it; he required purpose. He needed to speak to Bhalla, which meant he needed to get through the waterfall.

All right, fine. If Kaden was *meant* to go through it, if there really was a door under there, then he would find it. He was destined to do this. Fate was on his side. Reassured, he dropped his pack on the ground and motioned for Duke to stay with Petey. "I'll be right back," he said. "I think I know what I have to do."

"Oh—okay," Petey stammered, stepping a little closer to Duke and looking left and right worriedly. "Come back soon?"

"I will." Straightening his back and squaring his shoulders, Kaden stepped deeper into the pool. Water flowed over his boots and crept up his legs, but he pressed on, confident in his decision.

It will let me pass. I'm meant to be in Lumhagen, he told himself. The water grew rougher, colder. The spray in his face made it hard to see. *I can do this.*

Less than a foot from the rush of the water, Kaden's breathing came fast and hard, but he was still confident. *I can do this!* He boldly stepped forward, right into the rushing falls.

The weight of the water assaulted him, knocking him off his feet and down to his knees. This low, his head was beneath the churning surface of the pool, and the waterfall pushed down on him so hard he couldn't even lift his head to make out his surroundings. Kaden flailed, trying to free himself from the press of the falls, but he was dizzy, disoriented. If he went the wrong way, he would go deeper into the water and drown.

If you don't move at all, you'll drown! He tried to crawl forward on his knees below the water's surface, but he slipped again, this time falling to his side. It was getting hard to keep his mouth closed under the water, but all he saw were swirling bubbles whenever he opened his eyes.

No, this wasn't supposed to happen. Kaden was supposed to get through the water! He was supposed to find Bhalla! He was *meant* to locate the door! But he couldn't find his way anywhere but down right now. His lungs ached, but Kaden squeezed his eyes and mouth determinedly shut as he tried to crawl along the bottom of the pool.

Suddenly a solid set of teeth took hold of the top of his shirt. Kaden was towed backward and then up, and he gasped as his head cleared the water at last. Duke had him, Kaden realized, and then a moment later, Petey was there as well, helping to pull him back onto the dry stone. Kaden turned onto all fours and coughed hard, clearing the creeping water from his throat and nose.

"Are you all right?" Petey asked anxiously, tentatively patting Kaden on the back. "Did you see the door?"

"No," Kaden managed around a cough. "I didn't." He turned until he was sitting and stared at the waterfall for a long moment. He looked down at the amulet still on his chest—the light resolutely pointed straight back toward the spot he'd just nearly drowned in. Anger flooded him, chasing away the shivers that wracked his body.

"This is stupid!" he cried. "What's the point of asking me to come all this way to see him if I can't even get into the city?"

"I don't know," Petey said quietly. "This isn't... sometimes *our* trainers would do things like this to us, back in Shroudscar. They would give us a task we couldn't possibly complete and then beat us when we failed, so we remembered our place." He looked down at the ground. "I thought the wizards would be less cruel."

"I thought so too." Petey's sadness seeped through the crackle of Kaden's anger, and he shook his head, more confused now than anything else. "They must be," he muttered, mainly to himself. Bhalla had to be better than a goblin, didn't he? The light pointed him straight toward the waterfall. The door was back there *somewhere*.

But he'd tried to walk right into the water, and it had literally driven him to his knees. He couldn't get through that way; even though he'd had faith in succeeding, he'd *believed* it. Had his belief faltered? Was that the problem?

Well, no, Kaden thought to himself with a snort. *The problem is the big freaking wall of water.* Water which clearly wasn't going to go away just because he wanted it to. So if he wanted to get to the door—which had to be there, it *had* to be, somewhere—he needed to get safely past the waterfall.

He couldn't walk around it, he couldn't swim under it, so he had to go through it. But how?

Kaden ran a hand over his sodden hair. There was something caught in it—a twig. It must have gotten tangled in there when he was driven into the pool. He looked at the twig, then back at the trees, considering. Huh… maybe what he needed was…

He pushed up to his feet and headed back to the trees, staggering just a little bit before he got his feet under him. Petey and Duke followed.

"What are you doing?" Petey asked. "Are you going to ask Queen Pepper for help?"

"No," said Kaden, scanning the edge of the ground for the right thing. Maybe a little farther in… "I don't think she would help me with this, even if she could." Ooh, *there*—but no, that one was too small. He needed something broader. That one? Ugh, too heavy—this was going to be hard enough with just him, no need to make it more challenging with something he could barely lift.

"Then… what are you looking for?"

"For a shield," said Kaden, heaving a log over so he could get at the rotting bark beneath it. Ah, nice. He ripped off a wide swath of it with a grunt, then held it up for a closer look. "Very nice." The piece, curved like a small bridge, was wide enough to cover his head and most of his shoulders, long enough to give him breathing room both in front and behind himself, and the bark itself was thick and sturdy.

"A shield… against the waterfall?"

"Yes." Kaden carried the bark back toward the pool and positioned it over his head. Would he be able to hold onto it? He put it down so that it touched his head, almost like he was balancing a platter there, the way his mother sometimes had, and gripped the edges of it firmly. The water should sheet off around it, and Kaden would be able to see and breathe, hopefully long enough to confirm that he wasn't crazy. "There's a door back there," he said firmly, a promise to both himself and Petey. "And I'm going to find it. But…"

"We'll come after you if we see any sign of trouble," Petey assured him. "Just like before."

"Thanks." Kaden smiled. "You're a good friend." He turned back toward the waterfall, not noticing how Petey's jaw dropped, and stepped into the pool once more. The light in his amulet gleamed brighter than ever, drawing him straight toward the falling water. "I can do this," he murmured, then clenched his fingers around the bark and plunged ahead.

The water hit him like a hammer, making him stumble, but the force of it wasn't quite enough to take him down this time. The bark shield did its job, redirecting the water off the sides and keeping Kaden, if not dry, then at least not thoroughly drenched. His neck hurt from supporting the shield on top of his head already, though. *Get a move on.*

He inched forward, deeper into the falls. There was nothing but darkness ahead of him and more water. He went a foot forward. Another foot. More water, more darkness. It felt like the stone was closing in around him. He faltered, and his grip slipped, almost costing him the shield. *Just a little farther… just another few steps…* He took one, two, three steps, one more even though it hurt, and then—

—the water parted and vanished behind him, becoming a smooth silver sheet. Kaden was in a cave and up to his middle in water. The sound was deafening in here, but he didn't care— for right ahead of him was a set of stone steps leading out of the pool, up to a stone crevice that looked like it had been enlarged by hand. Kaden clambered over to it, shakily climbed the steps, and touched his hand to the stone lintel at the top of the passageway.

His amulet flared with light, and a series of symbols, carved so subtly into the stone that he hadn't even noticed them, suddenly glowed in reply. There were many of them, some beautiful, some frightening, but the one that called to him the most was the sacred circle of Orealus, gleaming like a beneficent golden eye.

"Faith," Kaden said to himself, then laughed. "But not blind faith." He couldn't wait to go through the tunnel and see what waited for him on the other side. *Bhalla and the mystical city of Lumhagen! Finally, I'll find out who I really am.*

But first, he needed to get back to his friends. It would be hard getting all three of them and their packs through the waterfall, especially when one of them was a dog, but Kaden was sure they could do it together.

He thought they might be able to do anything together.

CHAPTER 8

The cave went on for farther than Kaden expected—although why he'd expected anything particular at all, he didn't know. He had never paid very close attention when Daneyel had gone over maps with him, showing him the continent's forests, mountains, rivers, and lakes and how each country fit inside of them. It had all seemed so dull, so pointless—when was Kaden ever going to see any of those other places, after all? He'd be lucky to get as far as the next village on his own, the way his parents hovered.

No hovering now. What Kaden wouldn't give to hear Daneyel rap his knuckles on the kitchen table again, calling Kaden to task for drifting off. What he wouldn't give to feel Lydia squeeze his shoulder in silent sympathy on her way to the stove as she prepared the evening meal.

It doesn't matter. Kaden couldn't go back. All he, Duke, and Petey could do was press forward. And right now, ahead meant a tight squeeze through a narrow rocky hallway, so slender that they had to unpack their gear and carry it through piece by piece before emerging into a more comfortable space.

"This definitely isn't a place they'd use to move troops," Petey commented, tying the last of his pots back onto his pack. "It would take way too long to get people with weapons and armor through here, not to mention how hard it would be to move a lot of supplies."

"I'm sure there are lots of other ways into Lumhagen." Kaden shouldered his pack again and peered into the distance. Was that all just light from the amulet, or was there something more down there? The sound of the waterfall had died away, making their own noises ring louder than he was really comfortable with. Every footstep echoed against the walls, and Duke's panting breaths whooshed through the cave like wind across a field of barley. "I can't imagine a lot of people would have to use this one."

Petey nodded knowingly. "Because most people don't have to prove themselves as you do."

Kaden frowned, but he agreed. He didn't know what would happen to him next, whether Bhalla would be waiting on the other side of the cave or if there were some other trials to get through before Kaden was allowed to see the wizard in person. He hiked his pack up a little higher on his shoulders. "Let's go."

They *were* close to the end of the cave—the light from his amulet gradually became more and more diffuse until eventually they stepped out of the stone walls through a tunnel opening embedded in a hill at the edge of a forest. This forest was different from the airy, ethereal immensity of Brightshire Forest. These trees had rough, reddish-brown bark and bright green-and-yellow leaves that burst upward into the air like fountains; the spiky, glossy foliage was studded with purple and orange fruits here and there. There were all sorts of plants Kaden didn't recognize, from those tall, sharp trees to the heaps of vines strung between them, blossoming with huge white flowers that had speckled faces. Birdsong filled the air, long, tender whistles and brief, raucous squawks, and beyond the trees, the sky looked more blue than usual somehow. Kaden squinted, feeling his instinct draw his attention to this area on the horizon—the very air appeared to shimmer, reminding Kaden of the way he'd seen heat dazzle the distant sky just above the ground of grazing plains. Realization hit him like a brick wall.

"Look, Petey!" he said, pointing. "See the way the air clings to something beyond the trees? There must be some kind of invisible wall."

"Whoa! You don't think—?"

"It *has* to be the city. The wizards must have created some type of force to protect their city. That's where we need to go. Come on."

He led the way down rocky steps carved into the side of the hill, covered in places with smaller versions of the creeping vines that linked the trees. The path was steep, and Kaden almost fell more than once, but he didn't want anyone else to take point. This was his moment—this was what he had been waiting for, the real beginning of his adventure. He would lead the way to Bhalla, and the wizard would welcome them and impart his ancient, powerful wisdom, and then… then…

Well, Kaden didn't know what would happen next, but it had to be incredible, didn't it? Smiling, he stepped down from the final stair onto the gravel path with a resounding *thud*.

He could hear a faint, grinding *whir* over the sound of the birdcalls, and his feet seemed to sink a half inch or so into the ground. "Kaden! Move!" Petey shouted from behind him, but it was too late. Before he could take more than a single step forward, a web of blue light sprung up around him, extending from something beneath his feet and bowing out like loose threads caught in a breeze before twisting back together into a knot about a foot above his head.

Kaden reached a hand out toward the web, then quick as a mongoose pulled it back as soon as he felt the energy humming through the nearest line. He wasn't in direct contact with it right now—the glowing lines seemed to have sprung up from a secret platform beneath him—but he was pretty sure that if he touched any of them, he'd regret it. *It's a trap, a dangerous trap. I should have seen this coming. I should have known that Bhalla wouldn't take any chances.*

"Kaden!" Petey yelped, dropping his pack and running toward the cage on stubby legs. "I'll get you out. Hang on!"

"No, don't touch the—" Kaden's warning came too late. Petey grabbed the nearest glowing bars with both hands and was immediately blasted almost ten feet away from the cage, landing hard on his back at the base of a fanlike tree. He didn't get up.

"Petey!" Kaden's hands twitched with the need to get out of there, to go to his friend. What if he'd been badly hurt? What if the blast had injured him on the inside? Kaden needed to find help, but after what he'd just seen, there was no way he was touching the bars of this thing. He glared down at his amulet, still shining dully in the late afternoon light. *Couldn't you have warned us?* It was painful to just stand there, useless, while Petey suffered.

Actually… "Duke!" Kaden called. Loyal as ever but not quite as prone to rash decisions as Petey—and it was so strange that a *dog* was better at being cautious than a sentient being, Orealus help them—Duke stopped pacing between them and sat down right in front of the cage.

"Good boy," Kaden praised him. "I need you to go get help, all right? Get help. Get—" His voice stuck in his throat for a moment, but he knew the command that Duke would respond to best. "Get Dad," he managed, and Duke's shaggy ears perked up, tongue lolling out in an enormous canine smile. "Get Dad, my boy. Go get Dad and bring him back here."

Duke stood up and shook out his coat, then turned and ran… for about five steps. Then he scrambled back toward Kaden, and a second after that, another glowing, circular trap snapped into existence right where he'd been standing a moment ago.

"Oh, wow," Kaden breathed. From the outside, the cage was… beautiful, actually. Pure energy, bold and bright. It had also been a hand's breadth away from trapping his dog. "Go slow, Duke," he said, slowing his own speech down in hopes it would communicate the need to be careful to the hound. "Slooooow."

Duke seemed to understand. He certainly understood that he'd avoided something terrible, and from the way he was sniffing the air, then the ground, Kaden thought he might be able to scent the locations of the traps and avoid them. It would take more time to bring help this way, true, but there couldn't be all *that* many traps. It was better to take things slow and easy, and—

"Breach! Border breach!" a man yelled in the distance. "Sound the alarm, get some of the city guards down here, now!"

Kaden and Duke both looked up. Where was this person? What was happening now? "We're friends," Kaden shouted into the forest, craning his head in an attempt to make out the person who'd spotted them—or more likely, who'd spotted the ignited cages. "Friends! We come in pe—"

Duke yelped and leaped into the air as a large bolt of bright-red energy sizzled through the air, striking the ground where he'd just been standing. "No!" Kaden screamed, watching helplessly as Duke danced and dodged, trying his best to avoid the attacks. He finally ducked behind Kaden's cage, and the bolts stopped. A group of men in heavy leather armor and wearing short blue-and-white capes ran into the clearing a moment later.

They were all reasonably tall, with brown skin visible in the few places on their legs and arms that the armor didn't cover. They wore metal helmets that reminded Kaden of a bird's head, and Kaden could see now that the white shape on their blue capes was the marble tower, the symbol of the mystical city of Lumhagen. Guards. They had to be the guards.

That was good, he reckoned. Guards were meant to protect the city—indeed, they would see that Kaden and his friends were no threat and release him. "Please," he said, "don't—"

"I've got the beast in my sights," one of the men yelled and let loose with another blast of energy from the dark, metal-ringed staff he held in both hands.

"No!" Kaden watched in horror as Duke barely dodged. "Run, Duke! Go!"

But Duke was beyond listening to him now. His instincts had been triggered; ancient hunting genes activated. His startled barks became a low growl, and after leaping away from another blast, Duke charged the tight knot of men, barreling into them so hard that three of them fell flat onto their backs, staffs knocking together as they hit the ground.

The last man in the group sidestepped Duke's strong lunge and brought his staff to bear on the enormous hunting hound. He didn't fire a bolt of energy, though. He traced a circle in the air with his wooden staff and shouted something that Kaden couldn't make out, and a moment later, Duke froze. He didn't just stop moving—he *froze*, all his husky, trembling muscles perfectly still, his menacing growl silenced, his bristling hair unmoved by the breeze that blew through the clearing.

Kaden felt trembling enough for both of them now, but he wasn't afraid anymore. He was furious instead. How dare they attack them after everything he and Duke and Petey had gone through to get here? How *dare* they do this, after what Daneyel had suffered so that Kaden could find this place?

"How *dare* you!" He hadn't even realized he was shouting until the sound of his own voice filled his ears. The men were getting up now, groaning a little and muttering among themselves, but the last man, the one who had frozen Duke—he didn't look at the other men at all. He stared straight at Kaden, and Kaden stared right back. "We came here in *peace*. There was no need to hurt us!"

"You entered our kingdom through a secret passage, armed with a sword, accompanied by a war dog and a"—he glanced toward Petey and frowned—"a *goblin*. One who appears to have hurt himself before we even got here. What should we think, wild boy?"

"I'm not a boy," Kaden snapped. "My name is Kaden Sheppard. My companions are Petey and Duke." He left off Petey's family name, just in case the men knew about the Elvenshires. "And we were invited here by Bhalla himself." It was stretching the truth *just* a bit, but the heart of it was real enough.

The lead warrior laughed and whirled his staff with one hand, as lightly as if it were made of grass instead of wood and metal. His men looked apprehensive, but he only said, in as dismissive a tone as possible, "Is that so, wildie? Then prove it."

Clearly, this man expected him to fail. Kaden bit back his anger, grasped his amulet tight, and focused all his energy on it. "Find Bhalla," he said firmly, and a second later, the charm blazed so brightly that the bones of his hand were illuminated right through his flesh. He lifted it up and let it dangle, and the brilliant light zoomed toward the city like a shooting star.

The four guards went completely silent, staring at the light for a long moment before looking at each other. The leader opened his mouth at last to speak, but the stillness was broken by Petey instead, who sat upright with a groan.

"Ow," he said, clutching the sides of his head with his long green fingers. His ears twitched uncontrollably, making him look a bit like a massive insect with wavering antennae. "That was dumb," he went on, his eyes still shut. "That was so dumb. Remind me not to try touching the cage again, okay, Kaden?"

"Um..."

"I mean, I've been zapped by things before, I was right next to a tree once when it was struck by lightning, and *whew*, that was a ride, but I've never felt anything like *that*. Ugh."

"Uh, Petey..." Kaden tried to interject, but his friend was going now, and it was almost impossible to interrupt once he'd started talking.

"It must be yah'zaval. Is it yah'zaval? Can your amulet do anything about it? Can you call Bhalla? Try calling Bhalla, see if he'll send a wizard and a doctor out here, because *ow*."

"What kind of goblin speaks like an undisciplined child?" the leader of the guards asked, finally finding his voice. Petey stilled, then cracked one of his eyes open and glanced at Kaden, still in the cage, Duke frozen in place, and the four tall men with staffs.

"I wish I hadn't woken up," he squeaked.

"Petey is my friend," Kaden reiterated. He was tired of standing here, unable to do anything but talk. Talking wasn't going to get him out of trouble... or was it? *You can't catch a mouse without leaving out a bit of cheese,* his mother had always said. Most of the time, you had to give something to get something, and Kaden knew he was in a vulnerable position. He needed to provide the leader of this group a chance to save face.

"I apologize for the strangeness of our arrival," he said, doing his best to sound deferent. "We were just following the light of the amulet. I've only met Bhalla a few times, but he was a friend of my father, and he really is expecting me. If I'd known how, I would have sent word ahead, so we were expected instead of making it look like we were trying to sneak in." He smiled a little and shrugged. "If that had been our goal, we'd have failed miserably at it."

A little self-deprecation seemed to soothe the leader, who nodded once and stepped forward. "True. No spy would be caught by such a simple trap." He jabbed the top of the cage with the point of his staff, and suddenly the glowing web of bars retracted into the ground. Kaden took a tentative step forward and was relieved when nothing else happened.

"I am Evias, captain of the city guard," the leader continued, drawing out the *vee* sound in the middle of his name. We will lead you and your... *group* into the city of Lumhagen to see Grand Wizard Bhalla, but know this. If any of you tries to escape, tries to do a citizen injury, or if the grand wizard isn't really expecting you, cages like these will be the least of your worries." He deactivated the trap that Duke had sprung, then freed Duke with another wave of his staff. The dog collapsed, and Kaden rushed to his side.

"He'll be fine," Evias said dismissively. "Stasis can be painful when you fight it, and an animal like your beast wouldn't know better. He will recover quickly. Get your goblin friend over here."

Kaden looked toward Petey, but Petey was already on his feet and hustling over, wincing under the weight of his pack but not slowing down. "Are you going to be all right?" Kaden asked quietly.

"I'll be fine." Petey offered a lopsided smile. "I've had far worse in Shroudscar."

That really didn't make Kaden feel any better but judging from the impatient look Evias gave them, now wasn't the time to get more details. "Lean on me," he offered after helping Duke to his feet. The big dog was shaky but still growling. "No, boy," Kaden gently chided him. "Stand down. It's okay." *I hope it's okay.*

"You follow directly behind me," Evias said. "Otherwise, you might trigger another of our defenses. Don't wander off for any reason as we head to the Truthoriam2. My men are watching you. Understand?"

Kaden got a steadying grip on Petey's arm, made sure Duke could stand on his own, and then nodded. They headed out, zigzagging along the path at a quick pace. It was hard to keep Petey on his feet, harder still to keep Duke right beside him when the big dog was clearly still uneasy, but Kaden did his best. He didn't even let himself look up from the back of Evias's boots until, suddenly, the light at his feet warped in a way similar to the way his hand could alter sunlight passing through the suds of laundry bubble.

To Kaden's amazement, they were standing on the smoothest cobblestones he had ever seen.

---

2 Truthoriam pronounced *TROO-thor-ee-uhm*

The houses in his village had used heavy flagstones for floors or polished wood, but even the wood wasn't as neatly joined as each of these cobblestones were to the next. And they *walked* on these? What must the buildings be like? Kaden looked up, and…

Kaden gasped. He couldn't help it—they were in the mystical city of Lumhagen! It was the most glorious place he had ever seen, so beautiful he hadn't even been able to imagine a town like this. It was so tall, with rising rings of dark-walled buildings with stucco-beam rooftops all centered on an immense white marble tower that jutted proudly into the sky like Orealus himself had placed it there. The tower's roof, heavily supported by massive pillars, seemed to be solid stone carved in the shape of an enormous book, opened toward the sun.

That had to be where Bhalla lived. He was the greatest wizard of that age—where else would he be found, if not in the city's source of knowledge?

"The library of Lumhagen," Petey murmured, his yellow eyes wide with awe. "There are books and scrolls in there that date back thousands of years, to before the foundings of the kingdoms. There might even be books by goblin scholars in there." His ears twitched, and he looked down. "There was a time when my people were much more scholarly than they are now. No new books have been written in Shroudscar for over a hundred years."

"We'll check when we get there," Kaden promised him, clapping Petey on the shoulder. He felt buoyed up, even more optimistic now than when he had passed through the waterfall and found this city. This place… was seeping miraculous energy. Anyone could feel that! The very air seemed to glow with potential. This was a place where anything was possible, and they had found it! Bhalla was waiting for them!

Before continuing, Kaden looked back and noticed the shimmer in the air of the aura surrounding the city, like the warp of hot air coming off a campfire.

"Move along," said Evias, nudging him with his staff.

Kaden obliged, feeling like they'd stepped into another world. There was color everywhere, more than a whole rainbow's worth of hues. The people of Lumhagen wore variants on silk robes: blockier cuts for the men, more fitted lengths for the women, with winding, elaborate headwraps for everyone. Children ran about in bright silk tunics, laughing and chasing one another through the streets as they dodged the crowds.

It took Kaden a moment to figure out what had caught his eye with the kids; more than the color, it was that each of them seemed to have an identical twin. As he watched, a little boy in red raced over to a girl in blue and touched her shoulder. The girl immediately burst into a shimmering shower of dust that evaporated in seconds while the boy giggled. "What—they—"

Evias glanced back at him with a superior expression. "It's a simple children's game," he said, following Kaden's gaze. "To make playing tag a bit more interesting. You bear the favor of Bhalla—haven't you seen yah'zaval used before?"

"Yes," Kaden snapped, but really he hadn't seen much more than the power that came from the amulet he wore. And Queen Pepper Shinyfawn's gifted abilities, of course, but that was different from this. She had used what was already present in nature to create her fantastic plants, whereas the children were making copies of themselves seemingly out of air. How? What kind of abilities did a wizard wield, and how could people who were so powerful live in such harmony?

Because it *was* harmonious here, that was clear. No one in the crowd seemed angry or jealous; no one spoke badly about someone else or got into a fight, which sometimes happened on market days back home. Every adult appeared to be busy— the women carried baskets of freshly baked bread or hung damp clothing out on ropes stretched between or on top of the buildings. In contrast, others cooked food in clay or metal pots. Yet, others practiced their spiritual abilities in yah'zaval, everything from soaring illusions to simple twinkling lights for distracting a fussy baby. Men sold wares, shouted out to passing customers or friends, or gathered in a circle to have some kind of debate on what sounded like crop yields. Everywhere, people respected the space of those who knelt in prayer stance and made the sacred O in the air while murmuring praise to Orealus.

Evias hustled them along too quickly, giving Kaden none of the time he wanted so desperately to look closer, listen more carefully, take in the sights and even the scents of a bustling place like Lumhagen. He recognized hints of frankincense and myrrh in the air, sandalwood, and something sharp, sweet, and earthy, perhaps spikenard—but smelled a dozen other things that he couldn't name and wished he could investigate closer. They marched up the center of the cobblestone road, and chatter followed them, people wondering who they were, what they were doing here, and—was that a *goblin*? Petey walked even faster, despite his limp, and Kaden stayed right next to him just in case it looked like someone wanted to cause them trouble.

The closer they got to the towering Truthoriam, the less attention people paid to them. They had other things to do— gifts, from the look of it.

One wizard sat behind a table covered with glass vials of boiling liquid heated from beneath by thin blue flames, which roared out of a brazier shaped like a multiheaded dragon. He was watching another wizard working nearby, a tall, bespectacled gentleman who held a book in one hand as he tinkered with some sort of mechanical device with the other. It looked like a kind of telescope, except it was more elaborate than any telescope Kaden had ever seen before, made of copper and gold and covered with buttons and dials. In the middle of the device, splitting it in half, was a glass sphere full of levitating cogs that fit together like the weave of a basket. He would consult his book, push a button, watch a single cog turn, then make a note and do it all over again. Kaden wondered what he was expecting to happen.

He almost ran into Evias's back when the man finally stopped at the entrance of the immense marble tower. "The grand wizard has rooms at the very top of the Truthoriam," he said. "You'd better hope he's really expecting you, wildie."

"He is," Kaden replied, taking comfort from the soft but still insistent glow of the amulet around his neck. Duke and Petey both crowded a little closer to him, and he was very aware of the men standing behind him, their strong staffs at the ready.

Please, let Bhalla be expecting me.

CHAPTER 9

The daunting edifice of the Truthoriam, made entirely of white marble, had a massive staircase leading to an entrance on the second floor. Even from the ground, Kaden could see huge bookshelves inside the floor-to-ceiling windows on the second floor. In the open air, tiny winged feathery birds, eight inches in length, with long beaks and pearlescent bodies, carried books that must have been from the shelves. A trail of glimmering speckles trailed behind as they fluttered throughout the air. The stairs and floor sparkled with internal light, as if thousands of stars decorated the surfaces. Blocky silver and gold mechanisms, not tall enough to touch Kaden's knees, scampered over the slick flooring. They almost looked like toys, except they were far more elaborate than any toy Kaden had ever played with.

Are they alive? And if so, how? Their joints whirred with internal cogs and wheels, and some of the mechanical beings carried or rushed to receive tiny scrolls from wizards, while others dusted, swept, and scrubbed the marble. These miniature men must have been a message-delivery and cleaning system.

Pillars at the top of the staircase lined the edge of an outdoor landing that wrapped around the entire structure. The sculptor of the massive roof had elegantly chiseled the distinct shape of each page that sat atop the book's binding. Windows lined the second story's façade, while the third and top level of the building was made up of two long, curving open-air hallways that encircled the immense statue of the book, which seemed to be treated with a little less reverence than Kaden was expecting. Instead of solemn, serious-faced wizards, he saw more bright and cheerful people sitting out in the shade beneath the book. Many enjoyed the greenery that overflowed from hanging baskets and boxes and having loud discussions with lots of handwaving and pointing, making Kaden wonder if a fight was about to break out.

A young woman in a white robe trimmed with violet met their party at the top of the stairs. "May I help you, Guardian?" she asked. Her voice was polite but with an undertone of *What are you doing here, huh?*

"Wizard Asitra." Evias briefly bowed his head. "We request an audience with Bhalla concerning some potential spies."

Kaden stiffened. Referring to them as potential "spies" instead of mentioning that it was all an accident—or even that it *could* be an accident—would indeed bias this woman, and Bhalla, against them before they even met!

"Hmm," the woman said, tilting her head a bit so she could look past Evias at Kaden, Petey, and Duke. Her dark hair was tightly braided, and it cascaded over her shoulder like a waterfall. "I've never heard of spies that advertised their presence with this type of power before."

Oh, right—*right!* The amulet was still glowing! Kaden had gotten so used to the light that he forgot it was still shining in search of Bhalla. He smiled as politely as he could at the lady— *see how friendly and harmless I am?*

"Nevertheless, we need to see Bhalla at once." Evias sounded curt now. "His rooms will be sufficient for—"

"An audience in Bhalla's star chamber is invitation only, regardless of reason," the woman interrupted firmly. "But fortunately, he is enjoying some quiet and contemplation on the observation platform right now. I will escort these guests—"

"Prisoners—"

"*Guests*," she emphasized, "to Bhalla at once. You know how he feels about disturbing the atmosphere up here with hostile spirits, Evias. You and your men can wait right here, and as soon as I've delivered them to Bhalla and ascertained that all is well, I'll come and release you from your duty toward them."

Evias shook his head. "They are armed and dangerous, and they entered our city through the waterfall passageway. They can't be trusted, especially not the dog." Duke barked once, and Kaden was secretly pleased to see two of Evias's men startle at the big, low sound. "I have to insist that we accompany you."

Asitra smiled. It was the sort of smile a wolf might make as it cornered its prey. "It's touching that you're feeling so protective today but do recall that I am second only to Bhalla himself in the personal defensive ability in yah'zaval. In fact, none of you have been able to bring your weapons to bear since you first stepped foot in the Sanctum."

Wait, what? Kaden didn't quite know what she meant by that—he had no intention of reaching for his sword while surrounded by guards—but her meaning was illuminated when Evias frowned and tried to grab his upright guardsman's staff with both hands. He couldn't do it. It was as though his free hand simply couldn't find the wooden shaft, missing it by the width of a blade of grass each time but still missing it. He grunted, and the hand that already held the staff seemed to strain, endeavoring to change its position. It was no use—the rod stayed vertical, in a resolutely restful posture.

"I protest this interference," Evias said harshly. "You're preventing us from doing our jobs."

"On the contrary. You bringing weapons of war into the peace of the Sanctum challenged my authority first," Asitra replied, folding her arms over her chest. "Or have you forgotten that the security of this place is entrusted to *me*?" She seemed to almost glow with energy, and Kaden was fascinated to see its effect on the guards. The stiffness and fight went out of them, and a moment later, Evias shrugged.

"So be it. I'll hand them over to you, but I'll be waiting for your call to retrieve them once they've said their piece to Bhalla. Outside the Truthoriam, your authority is second to mine."

Asitra lowered her arms and took a more neutral stance. "Quite true. You two." She looked again at Kaden and Petey, then down at Duke. "Pardon me, I meant to say you *three*. Walk with me, if you would be so good. Bring all your things as well, just in case."

They took a moment to secure their packs, then Kaden and his friends stepped around Evias and followed Asitra as she turned and led the way down the left hallway. Kaden only glanced back once, and the glower on Evias's face as he watched them go was enough to make Kaden pick up the pace a bit. He bumped into Asitra, who was almost a foot shorter than him, for all the power she emanated.

"Sorry, sorry!" Ugh, when would he learn to watch where he was walking?

Asitra glanced over her shoulder and smiled. "You're forgiven. Just don't step on my heel with those boots of yours." Kaden glanced down, surprised to find that she was barefoot. "I'm sure you're not what Evias was making you out to be, but you should still be warned. A spiritual ability of compulsion prevents any act of violence from taking place within the Sanctum, either to one another or yourself. If you try to circumvent this pure ability, I will know it and take steps." She stopped then, turned around, and stared Kaden in the eyes. He froze. "You *don't* want me to take steps." It wasn't a question or a threat; it was a simple certainty.

"No, ma'am," Kaden managed, and she smiled again.

"Good! We're nearly at the observation platform, and"—she nodded at his amulet—"I think your power inside your amulet knows it. Prepare what you wish to say to Grand Wizard Bhalla, for your audience begins now."

She pointed toward a platform just a few yards away that jutted out a bit into the air. On the back half of it was a crescent-shaped bench facing outward, and on that bench sat…

Sacred O, *this is it.* Kaden was going to meet Bhalla again at last. He swallowed hard and stepped forward, almost shuffling his feet with sudden nerves. The glimpses he'd gotten of the powerful wizard the few times he'd met with Daneyel had been ruses, of course—disguises to allow Bhalla to travel without being noticed. Now Kaden would be meeting him in all his glory. Would he be stern, authoritative? Would he be kindly and wise? Would he look on Kaden with disappointment or with welcome?

The only person sitting on the bench was humming to himself, hunched over what, from a distance, looked like a star chart. As soon as Kaden stepped foot on the white marble of the observation platform, the person scooted around so they could look at him. Kaden stiffened, unconsciously holding his breath, and saw—

—an old man, clearly once tall but now hunched with age, whose white and beige robe was worn with use. He had wild white hair that bloomed around his head like a snow thistle, and his wrinkled skin was dashed with pale scars here and there. At his side lay a long, pale sandalwood staff, nothing like the menacing weapons the city guard carried. Was it a weapon too, or did Bhalla just use it to help him stand?

Was this *really* Bhalla the Bright?

"Ah. Kaden, son of Karatheas." Now, *this* was more like what Kaden was expecting from the grand wizard, a deep-timbre voice that resonated with authority and confidence. He swallowed hard. "You have come to me at last."

"It's, um… it's just Kaden Sheppard, sir." The *last* thing Kaden felt ready for was to be connected in any way to royalty. Even if it was true, it just didn't seem real. He was Kaden son of Daneyel, not Karatheas.

"But you are indeed the son of the late king, Karatheas, the greatest of his line," Bhalla said, straightening up a bit as he spoke. "You—and I, to my shame—are the only survivors of the fall of Empyrea's capital Karnergrien. You bear great resemblance to your father, Kaden—your height, the shape of your face." He smiled suddenly, and when he spoke again, his voice had lost some of its impressive depth for something more conversational. "Your eyes are your mother's, though. Luna would be pleased by that. You were too young for the color to have settled back then."

Kaden had to sit down. Bhalla politely made a little space for him. "You... you knew my mother?" he said with a shocked look on his face. Inside, Kaden was filled with emotions of happiness and confusion but saddened by their death.

"Of course I did! I knew your family well—how could I not, after working with them so closely, before and during the Great War, to battle the forces of Lucient?" Bhalla sighed and settled into himself a bit, his crooked posture emphasized. "Of course, it didn't work out the way we had hoped... losing your family was a devastating blow to the rest of us. Our Nine Pillars have been fractured ever since, each one keeping to itself in hopes that if the wickedness rises again—and it will, there's no way Lucient will be content with what he has—that it will strike somewhere else." He shook his head. "Short-sighted. Willfully ignorant. Downright cowardly in a few cases, if you ask me, which I know you haven't, but there it is. That's what you'll be up against, Kaden. I hope you're prepared for that."

"I'm not prepared for anything!" He didn't mean to shout the words, they just slipped out that way, but he couldn't take them back. Bhalla was speaking like he expected Kaden to embark on some epic quest. Wasn't his quest *over* now that he was here? "I don't know what you expect me to do, but I know I'm not ready for it. I'm... I'm not *him*, do you see? The prince you rescued, the son of the king—*I'm* not a prince! I'm just Kaden Sheppard, the son of a farmer! I know more about harvesting millet and rounding up chickens than I do about, about evil kings, and great wars and yah'zaval and—listen to this!"

The tale of their trip so far poured out of him like water from a storm cloud. He didn't hold anything back—how could he when Bhalla was looking at him with such gentle intensity? He was the first real bastion of strength that Kaden had found to cling to after Daneyel's death. Kaden spoke of Daneyel, how his idle wandering had led to his foster father's death, how the grawlers had almost killed them, how he nearly hadn't found his way into Lumhagen even with the help of Bhalla's amulet.

"You're expecting me to be someone I'm not," Kaden finished helplessly. Petey pressed close to his back, and Duke pushed up under Kaden's hand. He took a moment to say a grateful prayer for them, then went on. "I've already made so many mistakes. People have died. Think of how much worse the consequences could be if I was treated like a king when I'm really a nobody?"

Bhalla looked at him for a long moment, then held out one gnarled hand. "Give me the amulet."

Oh. Oh, no. This was it. Kaden felt judged and found wanting already. Numbly, he removed the faintly glowing amulet from around his neck and handed it over to Bhalla. The elderly wizard cupped it in his hands, and the glow became almost blinding. "Hm. Hmmm… interesting. Interesting indeed." Without warning, he flung the amulet hard toward the sky.

Kaden gasped and reached for it unthinkingly before realizing that the amulet hadn't been thrown away—it was hovering in the air, a few feet above their heads, in the center of the observation platform. As he watched, the blue sky disappeared, and above the floor, a dark, hollow half sphere formed, like they were looking at a big bowl turned upside down. Misty figures made of light appeared out of the amulet and walked across the darkness above them. It took Kaden a moment to realize that the people depicted were *them*—him and Petey and Duke.

"Wow," Petey murmured from right behind him. Kaden glanced back and saw his friend's yellow eyes had gone lantern bright and broader than he'd ever seen them before. "That's amazing."

It really is.

"I see a young man tested by circumstance," Bhalla said, watching the display calmly like it was something he did every day. Then again, perhaps it was. "I see a young man determined to carry out his father's wishes and fulfill his destiny. Your time was not without trials." The fight scene with the grawlers was suddenly on full display. The amulet showed far more than Kaden had seen at the time—how *close* the beasts had gotten, how intently they'd hunted his party.

"These creatures, like the goblin raiders, were meant to be the end of you, Kaden. It was Lucient's will that you not survive these attacks." Bhalla looked at Petey and nodded his head. "But this young goblin's compassion saved you in the beginning, along with Daneyel and Duke, and the fairies saved you next. Not just any fairy—the queen herself using the gift of yah'zaval!"3

"If it was not for Queen Pepper using the gift of yah'zaval, we would have never made it. Speaking of yah'zaval, can I learn that magic from you?" Kaden asked eagerly.

"Silence!" Bhalla said with a booming voice. "The very word *magic*, otherwise known as dunntaika, is banned in this holy place and is the dark arts practiced by followers of Lucient. Please continue to focus!"

The scene shifted, showing Kaden walking into the waterfall with the heavy bark shield over his head. The image blurred as he entered the water, then gradually stabilized and backed out again. Kaden watched his moment of discovery with the

---

3 Dunntaika pronounced *dunn-tie-ka*

door—had it really been just a few hours ago? It felt like days had passed since then.

Suddenly his figure was surrounded by the sizzling trap. "You had the perseverance to find the way into Lumhagen and the wisdom and patience to negotiate with those who meant you harm." Bhalla clucked his tongue and shook his head. "I'm sorry about that, I meant to be there to meet you, but I got caught up in my research. Damn fool thing to do, with you so close."

"It's… it's all right." As he said it, Kaden realized that it really *was* all right. Looking at this picture of himself, of the things he and his friends had done to make their way here, he suddenly felt—well, somewhat proud. Bhalla was right. It *hadn't* been easy. It had been terribly hard, and the odds had been against them from the very first moment, but together they'd found a way through. *I'm so lucky. I'd never have come this far without Petey and Duke.* And they, he acknowledged, couldn't have made it without him. They were a team.

"You are going to be an essential person, Kaden," Bhalla said after a moment. "Your father knew it from before you were born. I wasn't sure I believed him at the time—I was so certain that Karatheas was the chosen one, the one we were waiting for who would finish off Lucient for good. He had already done so much for the world of Sadunia, for the kingdom of Empyrea, for the regions of the Nine Pillars. How could he not succeed?" Old agonies deepened the lines on Bhalla's face, and he waved a hand toward the amulet.

The picture changed. Now it showed a man in glorious armor, a king on the back of a mighty steed, leading an army into battle. Looking at him, Kaden felt a pang of recognition deep within his heart. *He looks like me.* This was his real father, a man he couldn't ever remember meeting or being held by. "Karatheas did all that we ever asked of him and more," Bhalla said sadly. "It was my visions that led us to war, that brought us face-to-face with the enemy and his allies. If I had not spoken up, if Karatheas had had more time to prepare..."

He sighed deeply and closed his eyes for a moment. "It is a torment that never leaves me for long, the thought that if I had done something different, that could have saved him and so many other poor souls. But I must have faith in Orealus and not let my heartsickness get the better of me." He formed the sacred symbol of O by putting his hands together in that shape in front of his chest. "Do you know what happened next, Kaden?"

Kaden had never been a great student of history, but Daneyel had drilled at least this much into his head. It wasn't hard to get a young boy to sit still for his lesson if he listened to tales of battle, after all. "Um... I think so," he said. "The dark lord Lucient led his generals and all their followers out of the Cursed Lands and attacked Empyrea. King Karatheas launched a mighty defensive charge, but it wasn't enough to turn the tide of the battle, although he came close."

"Indeed," Bhalla said solemnly. "All the gains made, all the light and hope that Karatheas had brought to the world, were shattered when Karatheas died of a poisoned-arrow wound, just a moment away from ending the dark lord permanently. Queen Luna and the older prince and princess died shortly after that. And the youngest"—he gestured to Kaden—"well, that was you. I took you away just before the last stronghold was overrun by the enemy."

"W-w-wait. Why was I the only one to survive?" Kaden stammered quietly. "Why didn't you take my mother, or my siblings, or—were there other children? I thought you saved the land of Empyrea and the kingdom from destruction?"

"By the time I left with you, it was too late to help the others," Bhalla said, his voice full of regret. "I had to leave those I swore to protect: the kingdom, the land, the people, and most of all, your family. Orealus gave your father and me a prophetic vision. The vision has shown your destiny as being the chosen one to defeat Lucient. Your father knew what needed to be done. Your family decided to sacrifice themselves by staying behind to protect you from Lucient.

"And the teleportation ability I used to save you is both dangerous, unpredictable, and undirected. If we hadn't landed in a village where there was someone who could care for you while I recovered from the spell, you would have starved to death beside me as I lay in a healing trance. By the time I returned to Karnergrien, it was completely destroyed from the war.

"It was a *desperate* move, Kaden, but your father's spirit guided me then. I believe it guides us still, even now." He set a firm hand on Kaden's shoulder. "Your father believed that *you* are the chosen one, Kaden. And the more I learn of you, the more I understand his reasoning."

No, no. All the confidence he'd gained in watching his past replay before his very eyes vanished. "I don't think I'm the chosen one. I don't see how I can be. I'm... I'm nobody special! These things you showed me, what we did to get here—anyone could have done that, with help and some luck! That's all I had." He shook his head firmly. "I'm not the chosen one. I can't be. I'm just not..."

He didn't know how to articulate precisely what he felt—fear, uncertainty, and a little bit of hope despite himself, but also... frustration. He wanted *help*. He wanted to learn how to choose his *own* path, not to be chivied into another destiny by one of his two dead fathers! First a farmer, now a chosen one? It wasn't fair!

Kaden knew how ridiculous he'd have sounded if he said any of this out loud, so he didn't, but some of it must have shown in his expression. He also felt a cocktail of emotions. Anger, abandonment, sadness, and bitterness swam through his mind. How could his family just take it upon themselves to sacrifice themselves for him? So much burden laid upon his shoulders.

Bhalla hummed knowingly. "Living in service to ideals greater than yourself is never easy. It is invariably a hard road, often a lonely one. Much can be gained, but it always comes with a tremendous cost. You're right to shun such things, Kaden—any normal person would. But I think there's more to you than what is 'normal.' I believe in you because Orealus guides me to, and because…" He looked back at the crystal amulet, still floating in the air. "Because I am still tormented by visions of the future," he murmured. "And I do not know any more which are true and which are false."

The amulet darkened, its white light turning the rusty color of old blood. More figures appeared, but these ones weren't Kaden and Petey and Duke or the long-gone King Karatheas. These were monsters like he'd never seen before—a terrifying giant, enraged and screaming mindlessly as it charged a group of centaur warriors, smashing them. A dragon came roaring out of a cave, its claws reaching and rending at the group of fairies who awakened it and who tried to flee without success. Ogres and trolls, with strings of skulls dangling from their necks and massive clubs in their armored hands, shrugging off the fiery attacks of wizards as they battled through a group of humans unprepared for such a fearsome foe.

It was death, death in every direction, the death of people that Kaden didn't know but still felt like he was failing, just watching them fall to creatures that he could save them from… but no, how could he? He was so young; he had no abilities, little skill with a sword, and less with a bow. What could he do to stop this? How could he stop it—

"Stop it!" A voice broke through Kaden's reverie, and long-fingered hands reached up to obscure the figures streaming out of the amulet. "That's enough; stop it! What's wrong with you?" It was Petey, and he was glaring at Bhalla. At *Grand Wizard Bhalla*, the most powerful wizard in all of the mystical city, and if Kaden knew anything about this place so far, it was that there were *lots* of wizards. "You're just upsetting him!"

Kaden opened his mouth to object, then realized his throat was so tight that he couldn't even speak. Maybe Petey had a point.

"Ah, my apologies, you're right," Bhalla said. The amulet ceased glowing, and after a moment, it flew straight back to the wizard's hand. The darkness lifted, and suddenly the sky was back, clear and blue, and sunlight warmed the marble floor of the observation platform. "It was terribly rude of me to throw my visions at you like that." He rubbed his thumb over the amulet, shaking his head. "I can't even say that they're definitely true. I've been off before—in little ways, not in big ones, but... between this and the incident with the city guards, I can safely say that this wasn't the welcome I wanted for you, Kaden." He glanced at Petey with a bit of a smile. "Or your friends. Please, let me make up for my poor hospitality now. Asitra!"

The wizard appeared at the edge of the platform just moments later, her hands folded in front of her robes. "Yes, Bhalla?"

"Please see to it that Kaden, Petey, and Duke are given one of the guest apartments on the ground level of the Truthoriam," he said. "One with a door out to the garden, for Duke's comfort. Ensure that they have the means to explore the city without worrying about Evias or any of his lieutenants. We'll talk more tomorrow." The last part was for Kaden, it seemed. "After you've had a chance to rest and think things through. Might I suggest a bit of prayer, as well?" He shrugged one crooked shoulder. "It can't hurt."

Yeah, but can it help? Kaden had never prayed much before, no more than any other farmer with chores to do from sunup to sundown. Maybe he'd try it here, though.

What else could he do?

CHAPTER 10

The guest apartment that Asitra led them to was more enormous than Kaden's whole house back in Ashland. There were separate bedrooms for him and Petey, a sitting room, a kitchen, a patio that led out to a vine-covered garden in full bloom, and a room with a bathtub that *filled itself*. And pulling a cord washed the toilet clean! Kaden had never seen anything like it before.

"This is the result of technology, not our faith in Orealus," Asitra said when she noticed Kaden's dumbstruck look. "Nonetheless, we praise Him for giving us the ability to build such technology," she said while looking at him proudly. "The Truthoriam has pipes set into the walls, connected to a system of aqueducts that transport water from the mountains. It's as simple as good architecture."

"We have something like this back home," Petey added. "In the castle, at least."

Asitra seemed surprised. "Really? I've never heard that about any dwellings in Shroudscar."

"We goblins are very clever builders," Petey bragged. "Our sewer system is *amazing* if I do say so myself."

"Interesting. I've made quite a study of the other races of Empyrea, but this is new information to me." Asitra looked like her hands were itching to hold a quill. "Would you mind describing these things to me in detail?"

Petey beamed. "Sure!"

Kaden couldn't begrudge his friend's happiness—Petey hadn't had a lot of people react positively to anything about his being a goblin, much less asked him questions about it. Still, personally, he felt *done* with wizards for a while. He didn't want to shut himself away in his room, though—it was too early for sleep, and he was far too hungry not to eat something for dinner.

"Perhaps we can sit on the patio while we talk," Asitra was saying to Petey. "I can have a meal brought over from—"

"Actually," Kaden interrupted, a bit surprised at his boldness but knowing he needed to get it out, "I'd prefer to go into town for dinner. If you don't mind."

"Of course not," she said quickly. "I'll get some money for a meal and retrieve my writing implements and be back in a few minutes." She left, and Petey turned to Kaden with a sheepish look on his face.

"I'd... really rather stay behind," he said a bit sheepishly. "It's not that this place isn't beautiful and all, it's just... it's been a long day, and I mean a *really* long day, what with the waterfall and the traps and getting thrown into a tree and everything, and even a goblin can only take so much before they're exhausted, and—"

Kaden chuckled. "It's fine. I understand. It *has* been a long day, but I still feel..." *Like I can't stop thinking about that awful vision, like I'm overwhelmed by everything Bhalla said, about to jump out of my own skin with nerves...* "Like seeing some more of the town, only without the armed escort this time."

"Evias and his guys *did* kind of ruin it," Petey agreed. "Are you sure you want to go out on your own, though? I mean, they say you'll be safe, but we didn't think the city guards would attack us either, so..."

"I'll be all right." Duke shoved his head under Kaden's hand with a soft *whuff*, and Kaden scratched the hound behind the ears. "I'll have Duke with me." The thought was more reassuring than he let on. He definitely wanted to explore, and he wasn't going to make Petey do it with him, but it was nice to have a friend along who'd watch his back.

Asitra returned a moment later, with a red leather folder full of paper and a quill in one hand and a palmful of small copper coins in the other. "Here you are." She handed them over to Kaden. "Half of these should get both you and Duke a good meal. Don't let anyone cheat you."

"I won't," Kaden said, then added, "And would anyone really cheat me? Even here?"

Asitra smiled slightly. "Lumhagen is a haven, enlightened in many ways, but some aspects of human nature are hard to fight against, and one of those is getting the best deal possible."

Kaden nodded, counting the coins before putting them in a small pouch and hanging it around his neck, right next to the amulet. "Thanks."

"Enjoy yourself."

He and Duke left the apartment, making their way through the garden to the main exit. He nodded to the people he passed but made no other communication effort for now. Kaden was tired of talking and even more tired of listening. He wanted to wallow in something new and exciting and mundane for a while, which meant food.

It was noticeably later now than when they'd first arrived, the sky more orange and rose than blue, but the city of Lumhagen hadn't slowed down. The streets were still bustling, people laughing and calling and praying more and more often. The savory scent of spiced, roasted fish filled the air, and in an instant, Kaden's mouth began to water. He glanced at Duke, who was literally drooling. "Yeah, let's get some food," he said with a laugh.

He walked down to the closest corner, where an older woman wearing a headdress the same pastel colors as the sky sat next to a round ceramic pot over a low fire. She looked up and smiled when she caught his eye. "Ah, it's you! We've all been wondering what was happening with you and your friend in there."

"You… noticed us?" Kaden looked around at the crowd, the bustling city streets, and wondered *how* anyone had noticed the three of them in the throng of people out and about. "Why?"

She laughed loudly, slapping her knee. "*Why?* A group of newcomers gets escorted through town by Evias, looking like they came out the worse in a fight, and you wonder that anyone noticed? Lumhagen doesn't get many visitors, lad. And few of those who come here are taken to the Truthoriam by the city guard. If the guard is involved, that usually means a cell is too."

"Oh." That made sense, in a depressing sort of way.

"But now, here you are, out on our streets with your beautiful hound and looking better than you did when you arrived! Is your goblin all right?"

"He's not *my* goblin," Kaden took pains to point out. "He's his own person; we're friends. He decided to stay in the…" It occurred to Kaden that no matter how nice this woman was, he'd only just met her and knew nothing about her. Perhaps sharing the location of where they stayed wasn't the smartest thing to do.

Luckily, his stomach rumbled just then. "Ah, I see you have pressing concerns," the lady said, wagging a finger at his belly. "You've come to the right place. My fish is spiced to perfection, blended with vegetables, and served over fresh rice." She indicated a stack of red and blue bowls beside her. "Two coppers per bowl, or two bowls for three coppers if you sit with Ma Ruana here while you eat and tell stories of the history of Lumhagen."

Kaden had eight coppers with him. The deal was fair, then. "All right," he said, then handed over the coins and sat down on the stoop where she indicated. Ruana pulled a bowl free and piled it with a bed of steaming white grain—rice, something

Kaden had heard of but never tried before—then took the top off her pot and scooped a heaping ladleful of the fish and vegetables over it.

Ruana handed it to Kaden, along with a broad, ornately carved wooden spoon. "For you." She repeated the process, then set the other bowl down in front of Duke. "And *you*! Now." She clapped her hands together as though she was dusting them off, readying them to collect his words. "Tell me what you will about where you've been and what you've seen."

Kaden wasn't sure how much of their story was safe to tell. He certainly couldn't risk being too specific with his own origin, even though he doubted Ruana had ever heard of the tiny village of Ashland or the wood it took its name from. "We traveled through Brightshire Forest to get here."

"Ah, beautiful! I haven't seen it since I was a young woman, but it's a lovely, vast place. Did you see a binicorn?"

Kaden had just taken a bite of his dinner as she asked. Swallowing quickly to respond to her faster was a mistake— the spices were delectable but unfamiliar and scraped down his throat with unexpected heat. He covered his mouth and coughed, then coughed twice more.

"Ah dear, let me get you a drink." She handed over a cup filled with something milky and frothy that cooled the fire almost instantly. "Eating the fish *with* the rice will help too," she advised. After Kaden took a few more bites, she gently encouraged him back to his story.

It was far more relaxing than he'd thought it would be, sitting here with a stranger exchanging tales. He told Ruana little things about the journey, like the sound the red-furred monkeys made as they swung through the trees or the bright color of the little amphisbaena. She reciprocated by mimicking the call of the city's resident songbirds, the bright blue, spike-beaked fluteds.

"They look like they've got a spade on the end of their nose, very funny, but it helps them make the most wonderful sounds.

Stay long enough, and you'll hear a real one," Ruana promised him. At that moment, Kaden wished more than anything that he could stay here, but he already had a sinking feeling in his heart that no matter how badly he wanted it to be, the mystical city of Lumhagen wasn't going to be his home.

*　　*　　*

He eventually finished his meal—Duke had wolfed his down in moments—and thanked Ruana, who patted him on the arm. "It's good to see a meal enjoyed," she said sincerely. "Fine food and good company are truly some of the greatest gifts of Orealus. Come back tomorrow if you're hungry again, lad."

The light, affectionate touch of her hand reminded Kaden suddenly of Lydia. His last memory of his mother was a lot like this moment, an interaction filled with kindness and the warmth and wholeness that came from eating good food. Painful homesickness filled him, almost enough to take his breath away, and he left with just a nod to Ruana.

The sky was darkening, stars appearing by the hundreds as the sun finally let its glory rest for the night. Kaden trudged back up the hill to the Truthoriam, head down, wondering what to do next. It was easier to use the excuse of putting one foot in front of the other than to stop and really have to think, so he kept going, past the Truthoriam and all the houses behind it, until he reached a trail that led into the mountains. It was probably better not to wander up there, considering the last thing that had happened to him in the hills outside of Lumhagen. Kaden heaved a sigh and turned around.

He took a different route back and passed a temple to Orealus on the way down. It was a simple setup, just a white stone building with a marble foundation and the sacred O etched in gold on the front of it. Above the O, Kaden saw what had to be an owl perched at the top of the stone façade. Wasn't it a bit early for owls to be out? He took a step closer, then startled as the "bird" twisted its head toward him with a rusty, scraping sound.

It's a mechanism! Like the little creatures in the Truthoriam! Only this one wasn't dazzling in gold and white. It did have a gold key sitting in the center of its back, but its feathers were black, shimmering here and there with ornate carvings that Kaden couldn't quite make out. Its eyes swiveled in its sockets as it focused on Kaden. It looked so close to an actual animal... were there many of these creations in Lumhagen? These "mechanimals"?

The owl-creature hooted, then spread its wings and took off into the night. Kaden watched it leave, then turned back to the building in front of him. Inside the temple was a space in front next to an altar where whoever could enter and pray. There was an offering dish off to the right side and a box of thin, reed-like candles on the left.

It can't hurt to pray. Prayers to Orealus back in Ashland had often been perfunctory, except during the big ceremonies— something to do once you were done working the fields and before you fell asleep. Maybe it was time for Kaden to take his prayers more seriously.

He got onto the padded leather kneeler and looked up at the O for a moment, then reached into his pocket and pulled out a copper coin. He put it in the offering dish, then grabbed a candle. "Whoa!" It lit without him having to do more than pull it free of the others, glowing with a gentle violet flame. A sign from Orealus, or just more of the combined power of the people of Lumhagen?

A stubby candleholder peeked out from beneath a smattering of wax in front of the marble plaque. Kaden set the candle in it, then looked at Duke. "Sit, boy."

Duke obeyed, and Kaden looked back at the temple and traced the sign of Orealus in the air. "Orealus, bless and keep me, your loyal and faithful son," he murmured. "I..." What could he say that would make the Almighty God pay any attention to him? Despite what Bhalla said, Kaden still felt like a simple village boy, failing to make sense of the wider world.

Perhaps that was enough of a place to start. "I need help," Kaden confessed. "I don't know what to do. Bhalla tells me I've got a future of great responsibilities ahead of me, but I don't see how I can possibly fulfill them all. I'm just *me*! I'm not a prince or trained to lead armies or fight monsters. I need… I need your guidance, Orealus. Please." He swallowed hard. "Please, help me figure out how I can become the person it seems like I need to be. I want to be…" Here came a moment of shame. "I always used to want to be special, but now that I am, I feel sick at the thought of what it really means. Help me to do your will."

The candle suddenly burned out, leaving a scent of lilac and jasmine behind. Kaden blinked, then made the sign of the sacred O again and got to his feet. He felt a little more settled now, even though no sudden flashes of divine inspiration seemed to be hitting him, and walked back to the Truthoriam with a lighter heart.

He and Duke crept into the apartment, which was entirely dark by this point. Judging from the snores coming from Petey's room, he was fast asleep, so Kaden made quick use of the facilities and then got into bed. It was soft, far softer than his bed back home, and the warmth of it lulled him to sleep almost immediately.

"KADEN…"

Kaden opened his eyes, wondering who was calling him so loudly. Except when he looked up, he did not see a ceiling above him—he didn't see anything at all. He was surrounded by light, suffused by it, and it stunned him so much he couldn't even think for a moment.

"KADEN." He couldn't see the speaker, but whoever it was had a deep voice to the point of booming, yet somehow the loudness of it was pleasant instead of painful. "MY SON."

"Or... Orealus?" Kaden asked, forcing himself to speak.

"I AM WITH YOU, KADEN."

"*Oh*." The feeling of love and relief that swept through him almost made him cry. "Thank you, thank you, I... just..."

"I HEARD YOU CALL TO ME, MY SON." The voice softened a bit. "YOU ARE TROUBLED BY YOUR DESTINY."

"I am," he said quietly. "I just don't feel worthy of playing such a big role. King Karatheas was, well... he was a *king*. I'm nothing like him. I've never even seen a castle."

"WHAT YOU HAVE BEEN SHALL PROVE FAR LESS IMPORTANT THAN WHAT YOU WILL BECOME, KADEN. IT IS YOUR DESTINY TO DEFEAT THE EVIL OF LUCIENT THAT IS INFECTING EMPYREA AND STRETCHES THROUGHOUT THE WORLD OF SADUNIA."

"But how?" Kaden begged. "I don't know how!"

Orealus seemed to chuckle. "HOW *COULD* YOU KNOW SUCH A THING, HAVING NEVER DEFEATED THAT EVIL BEFORE? YOUR SOLE DUTY NOW IS TO PREPARE YOURSELF FOR THE WORK AHEAD OF YOU, KADEN, SON OF KARATHEAS. YOU ARE ALSO THE SON OF MY LOYAL SERVANT DANEYEL AND STRONGER FOR IT."

"I don't even know how to *prepare*," Kaden protested. "How can I possibly do all this on my own? This burden... it's just too much for me."

The light around him seemed to contract for a moment. "ALL WILL BE REVEALED TO YOU IN TIME," Orealus said. "I WILL BE WITH YOU ON THIS JOURNEY, KADEN, BUT IT IS OF THE UTMOST IMPORTANCE TO ALL OF EMPYREA THAT YOU FIRST FIND THE TRIBE LEADERS OF EACH OF THE NINE PILLARS AND UNITE THEM IN YOUR DESTINY TO DEFEAT LUCIENT. YOUR FRIENDS AND ALLIES WILL SUPPORT YOU." The light in front of Kaden's eyes became a picture, like the visions that Bhalla had shown them, only so much sharper now. It was as though Kaden was standing within the image itself instead of watching it from outside.

"LOOK," Orealus whispered to him. "SEE YOURSELF AS I SEE YOU. SEE YOURSELF AS WHO I KNOW YOU WILL BECOME IF YOU ALLOW YOURSELF TO REACH THAT HIGH."

Kaden gasped as he saw a man wearing a silvery suit of armor, wielding a long, two-handed sword, and riding into battle. He saw the man cut down the dark forces that attempted to overwhelm him, helped by figures he recognized as Petey and Duke and others he didn't yet know. He saw a shadow he hadn't even realized cloaked the land being lifted, and people of all tribes laughing with joy as their faith was restored. When the man raised his visor, Kaden saw his face and knew himself— older and broader, but still recognizable.

The vision changed, showing him standing side by side with a beautiful woman, smiling at her before he tenderly kissed the smooth forehead of the newborn she held in her arms. "YOU WILL KNOW LOVE," Orealus promised Kaden. "GREAT FRIENDSHIPS AND GREAT JOYS WILL BE YOURS, ALTHOUGH THERE WILL ALSO BE MANY TRIALS AND SORROWS. THIS IS YOUR DESTINY, MY SON. THIS IS YOUR FATE. ACCEPT IT, AND ACCEPT ME INTO YOUR HEART. THE GREATER YOUR FAITH, THE GREATER THE POWER YOU WILL WIELD. YOUR FAITH IN ME WILL BE YOUR SHIELD IN THE YEARS TO COME IF YOU ALLOW IT TO."

"I want to," Kaden said, his heart full of longing. "I want that so much."

Orealus's voice was warm and full of love. "THEN YOU SHALL HAVE IT." The vision faded as the light intensity increased a thousandfold, enveloping Kaden into its power and glory. He felt happier than he had ever been before, like he was experiencing the joys of not just himself but of everyone in the entire world. How could he contain such joy, such love? It should be so magnificent that he was shattered by it, but his soul held—safe in the love of Orealus, his soul held fast.

"IT SHALL ALWAYS HOLD FAST." The voice was softer now, the presence of Orealus not so much diminishing as gradually retracting, like a morningbell flower that closed its petals at night. The flower was still there in all its glory, just curled in, protected until it was time for it to emerge again.

*   *   *

Kaden woke up to the light of a new day, in the same bed he'd fallen asleep in yesterday, but he felt so different now. Everything in him that had been faltering before was bolstered by the visions that he knew, he *knew*, had come from Orealus. Every fear and uncertainty was quieted, and he grinned, then laughed out loud.

"What's so funny?" Petey groaned from the other room. "Really, what is so funny at dawn o'clock in the morning?"

Kaden laughed again. "Come here, and I'll tell you." And once he had told Petey, he would tell Bhalla and see where destiny and Orealus sent him next.

CHAPTER 11

It took Kaden all through breakfast, which had been delivered by a silent man in a white and yellow robe, to explain his vision of Orealus to Petey. It was hard to put into words exactly what he'd seen and experienced because even though Kaden felt Orealus's holy presence still resounding inside of him, he didn't have the language to *describe* that feeling. It resisted his lips, resisted speaking somehow—like it was meant to be his and his alone, intensely private as it had been. He managed as best he could, getting the main ideas across to his friend.

The *other* reason it took so long to explain what had happened was that Petey kept interrupting. He, unlike Kaden, wasn't afflicted with any sort of speechlessness, and he couldn't contain his excitement for longer than it took Kaden to speak a single sentence before he was interjecting somehow, with a "Wow!" or a "Shadows of Shroudscar, really?"

It was a relief to be believed—Kaden had worried a little about that, but if there was one thing he ought to have realized about Petey by now, it was that Petey, in his own way, had the most extraordinary faith of anyone Kaden knew. Not in himself—Petey wasn't exactly brimming with self-confidence— but in his *friends*. In Kaden and Duke. It was humbling to be the recipient of so much faith.

Was this what it felt like to be a king? To be honored by your people, many of whom didn't even know you, and held up as an example for them? Kaden's stomach momentarily veered toward queasiness—it was so much, how could he possibly… Then he remembered Orealus's message to him and their togetherness and straightened his spine. If this was his destiny, he would embrace it. He didn't need to understand it all at once; that would only come with time.

Time, it turned out, was something he didn't have a lot of. Almost the second Kaden and Petey finished their meal of warm meat pies and fresh fruit, a knock sounded on the door. Kaden got up to answer it and was met by a smiling Asitra, who wore a white wizard's robe with a dark purple stole across her shoulders and a purple and blue headwrap holding up her braids.

"Good morning," she said politely, glancing past him to see Petey. "Are the three of you ready for your audience with Bhalla?"

I should have known he'd want to talk first thing. Kaden felt ready for it now, though, prepared in a way he couldn't have imagined feeling yesterday. "Yes," he said firmly, and Asitra blinked once as if surprised. "Should we get our bags, or can we leave everything here for now?"

"Leave it here," she said after a moment, looking at him carefully. "After all, there's still a lot to discuss with Bhalla."

Kaden smiled. "So there is." He patted his leg, and Duke bounded over, ready as ever.

"I'm coming, I'm coming, I'm coming!" Petey yelped before stuffing the last of his breakfast in his mouth. He tried to down some water right afterward, but some of it flowed out of the corners of his mouth, staining his shirt. "Ohngnoo!" he moaned.

"There's more than enough time for you to swallow your water first, Petey," Asitra said in a kind voice.

"Ignaaabuu…" He swallowed, coughed, then drank a bit more water before joining them at the door. "I know, but in Shroudscar, it's considered very rude to make your superiors wait for your arrival," he said a bit breathlessly. "If you were more than five minutes late for weapons practice, you could be beaten or put on sludge-scraping duty."

"What if you were three minutes late?" Kaden asked, curious. "Or four? Or two?"

"Then you had to stay late and keep training after everyone left, only instead of staying for two minutes, you stayed for two hours." Petey sighed heavily as though just the thought of it tired him out. "I stayed late a *lot*, although it never really seemed to improve my fighting skills."

"It's hard to improve when there's no one there to train with you," Asitra noted. "We covered a lot of the architecture and engineering of Shroudscar in our discussion yesterday but didn't have the time to get into social conventions."

"Those are easy." Petey shrugged. "Be mean, and if that doesn't get you what you want, be meaner."

For the first time, Kaden was glad that Petey was with him. Not just because Kaden wouldn't have survived the goblin attack if Petey hadn't been there to help, but because it seemed like Petey had been nothing but miserable back in Shroudscar, except when he talked about his mother.

He put a hand on his friend's shoulder, giving him a bracing squeeze. "Let's go talk to the wizard," he said.

Petey's enthusiasm came roaring back, his eyes going bright and wide and his enormous ears perking up at once as they followed Asitra into the garden. "Yeah! Let's tell him all about your vision of Orealus!"

Asitra glanced at them over her shoulder. "A vision of Orealus?"

"Yeah! He told Kaden all sorts of things, like—"

Asitra held up her hand. "Whatever happened between Kaden and Orealus is a private matter."

"Oh, yeah... good point." The tips of Petey's ears drooped down again.

"I don't mind talking about it," Kaden said. "Or if Petey talks about it."

"Nevertheless, in Lumhagen, we consider such things to be a sacred communication intended for Orealus and the one He speaks to, not to be lightly shared. Especially not by those for whom the vision was not intended." She led the way up the stairs briskly. "Which isn't to say I wouldn't enjoy hearing about it at some point, but for now, I recommend keeping the words of Orealus close to your heart until you feel the time is right for them to be revealed to more than your closest friends."

Kaden opened his mouth, ready to describe what had happened to him, then, after a moment, closed it again. She was right. Petey was one thing but telling every wizard in Lumhagen that Orealus had come to him in a dream before he could wrap his mind around it all himself was a daunting prospect.

Asitra smiled back at him as they reached the top of the stairs. "And so, do you grow in wisdom," she murmured, then turned right, in the opposite direction of the observation platform they'd met Bhalla at yesterday. "He is in his star chamber today and invited the three of you to join him there."

She led them along the path to the other side of the enormous marble statue with its open pages until they reached a building with a round top just behind it. The moment they walked inside…

Kaden shielded his eyes, and Petey actually had to cover both of his. How could it be so *bright* inside a building? Where was all the light coming from? It was sharp, dazzlingly so, brilliant to the point of blinding.

"Grand Wizard," Asitra said calmly, "if you would be so kind as to dim the lights for the moment."

"Oh, are they here already?" There was a sound like a massive wheel turning, and a moment later, the light began to fade. It didn't go out completely—it was as though someone had pulled a curtain over a sun-facing window. Kaden blinked and looked around and saw a complicated system of mirrors and gears and a perforated metal pillar that extended up from the floor at an angle, sliced into a thousand pieces yet still all holding together somehow.

"Oh, *wow*!" Petey exclaimed, his ears perking. "A starscope!"

"Good eye, young one, good eye," Bhalla said with a smile. He looked cheerful this morning, full of energy, his eyes still sparkling from the shower of light that had just filled the room. His robe was pure white, and his feet were shod with white leather sandals. He looked like a part of this room, like he belonged in it. "This is the most complex starscope in the world. It can trace the movements of the solar system, forward and backward, for thousands of years."

"Why would you want to do that?" Kaden asked, taking a step closer. Asitra quietly excused herself, and Duke sat down by the door and began to patiently lick along his haunch.

"Why *wouldn't* you want to do that?" Bhalla replied. "All is Orealus, and Orealus is in all things. That includes every star in the sky, and if knowing more about them can give us greater insight into the will of our creator, then it is a most worthy study."

Kaden thought about that for a moment. "But if Orealus is in all things, equally, then it doesn't matter what you study. Whatever you devote yourself to will be the province of Orealus, and therefore just as worthy of study as anything else, whether it's stars or dirt."

Bhalla's smile grew broader. "Well said, Kaden. Very well said. There's a place for all of us in this world as long as Orealus dwells in our hearts, whether we cast our eyes down to the ground or up to the skies." He tilted his head slightly, white hair bobbing. "Something has... centered you since last we spoke. Brought you great peace."

"I…" Kaden thought about what Asitra said, thought about the fullness of the faith inside him, and how he felt so much yet could tell so little. "Yes, it has," he said at last.

Bhalla didn't press the issue. He just made the circle of Orealus in front of his chest. "Faith in the *O* makes everything possible, even the seemingly *im*possible. May I take that to mean that you accept your fate? Are you ready to begin your sacred duty and unite the nine tribal leaders so that together you can do what must be done to protect this world from the Great Deceiver?"

It still sounded like a lot to Kaden, like more than he should be able to handle. But Orealus was with him. He knew that now, and he knew that there was only one thing he could say. "I'm ready."

Bhalla laughed and clapped him on the shoulder. "Wonderful! Ah, it heals my heart to see you stand so tall and hear you speak with such conviction. Your father—*both* your fathers—would be so proud of you."

Kaden let the sadness that those words elicited wash through him, leaving him still grieving but not desperate with it. "What do I do first?" he asked.

"First! Ah, *first*, I think, it's my turn." Bhalla rubbed his hands together. "You're going out to do a hero's work, after all. You ought to look the part. Give me the amulet for a moment, please." Kaden took it off and handed it over to Bhalla, who cupped it in his palms and looked down at it.

"This amulet only holds a power for what is intended for right now—a useful one, to be sure, but that power of Orealus has served its purpose," he said. He clasped his hands together, then closed his eyes and moved the amulet in a circle, right over the center of his chest. "It must be more," he murmured. "Like you, yourself must be more, so must your tools." White light spilled from the cracks between his fingers, fracturing into all the separate colors of a rainbow after a moment.

When Bhalla opened his hands again, the crystal amulet was no longer pure white. From one angle, it looked blue—rolled slightly to the side, it became green, then red, then pink. "Just as you will play many roles in the weeks and months to come, so shall this amulet work for you," Bhalla said, handing it back to Kaden. "It will still lead to me, but it will also *call* me when you need it to. It will also act as a shield when you have no other means of guarding yourself, and the longer you wear it, the longer the Amulet of Orealus shall help to unlock your own innate, deeply buried secret abilities."

Kaden looked from the amulet to Bhalla in shock. "What sorts of abilities?" he blurted.

"I don't know for certain," Bhalla replied with a shrug. "It's a part of your lineage, though. I have no doubt that *something* will be revealed to you before long. Take heed, though, that you consider the tax on your energy upon each use of the amulet. For, energy may be a renewable source, but this source takes time and rest to renew. We call this source of power Mana."

"Mana?" Kaden clarified.

"Yes, and different feats of yah'zhaval require different amounts of Mana. Now..." He grinned, the expression making him look so much younger that Kaden nearly did a double take. "I think it's time for the really entertaining stuff." He glanced over at the far wall, where a fireplace was set back into the marble, ready for lighting. It was the only gray spot in the entire room. "Grab a stick out of there, Kaden."

Kaden frowned. "A stick?"

"Yes. Any old stick, but make sure it appeals to you."

"O... kay." Kaden walked over to the fireplace and bent over to look at the wood that had been piled in the grate. The highest layer was made up of thick logs, and on the very bottom were bundles of thin wood shavings, obviously kindling. Though there were many long sticks in the middle, delicate enough to burn more readily than the logs but still substantial. Kaden eyed them for a moment, then reached in and pulled one out. He looked it over, wondering what was supposed to make a stick "appealing." Its heft? Whether it would support his weight, like a walking stick? He swished it back and forth for a moment and felt a wobble in the center of it where the wood was cracked. *Not this one.*

He pulled out a second stick, but it was too short. The third was better—long enough to have a good amount of weight but adequately slender so that he could still get his entire hand around it. He turned around to face Bhalla. "This one seems good."

"Excellent, excellent! Bring it here." Kaden came over to him, stopping in his tracks when Bhalla held up a hand. He bowed his head for a moment, eyes closed, then said, "Behold, the power of Orealus," and made the sign of the O in front of his chest.

Kaden blinked and stared at his hand, stunned to find himself holding not a stick but a long, straight sword. It had a substantial cross guard that snugged up nicely against his hand and a round heavy pommel of shining silver, shaped like an O. The grip was dark blue leather, tightly wound and comfortable against his hand, and the blade itself...

It looked like metal at first glance, but a second look told Kaden that it was no metal he had ever seen before. There was the faintest hint of translucence to it when he moved it through the air, as though it couldn't quite decide whether it was a shaft of steel or a beam of light. It didn't reflect light the way metal would either, seeming to absorb it instead.

The blade was well balanced, turning smoothly in his hand as he rotated it, swinging it around his body in a defensive pattern that Daneyel had taught him. It moved so quickly that it almost seemed to Kaden to *want* to move, flickering through the air like a hummingbird. It was long, longer than the stick had been, and heavier, but it felt like a natural extension of his hand. He looked at Bhalla. "It's amazing. I no longer need the old sword that my father gave me. As great as it was, it is not as cool as this new shiny one."

"This is Vrangar," Bhalla said, watching Kaden move with a paternal smile. "The Light-Bringer. It will protect you against more than physical enemies, Kaden. This sword is a shield in and of itself, a light source in the darkness. It will help keep your path clear, both internally and externally."

"Um." Kaden and Bhalla both stopped staring at the sword and turned to Petey, who was meekly holding up a hand. "Is there any chance there's a goblin-sized sword floating around in the ether?" he asked. "Because that one's fantastic, but if I'm going to be watching Kaden's back, then it would be nice to have a powerful weapon to do it with."

Bhalla chuckled. "Of course! I haven't forgotten you or Duke." He nodded toward the fireplace. "Pick out a stick for yourself."

"Great!" Petey ran over and rummaged in the pile, finally pulling out the most giant log in there, almost half as wide as his own body. "This one!" He glanced at Bhalla's stern expression, and his eager grin faltered. "No?"

"Maybe something a little more... you-sized?" Kaden suggested.

"Yeah." Petey sighed. "It was worth a shot. Okay." He put the log back and inspected the sticks instead, finally coming out with one that was maybe half the length of Vrangar.

Bhalla nodded approvingly. "Behold, the power of Orealus," he chanted, making the sign again, and a moment later—

"Wow!" Petey held a wickedly sharp steel dagger in his hand, almost long enough to qualify as a short sword. It tapered to a needlelike point but had one straight edge and one curved edge, so it could be used to slash as well as thrust.

"Loyal Dwingent," Bhalla said. "A weapon that will never fail to strike true when used to save another's life. There is strong energy in that blade, Petey. Treat it well."

Petey's great yellow eyes gleamed with unshed tears as he looked at the dagger, holding it almost reverently. "I will," he promised, and Bhalla nodded once, then turned to Duke.

"And you! I haven't forgotten you, pup," he said, patting his leg. Duke trotted over to him, tongue lolling out, and sat by Bhalla's feet. "A loyal hound, through and through," Bhalla murmured, stroking Duke's head. "Such a mighty companion deserves the recognition of that might." Still petting the dog with one hand, Bhalla closed his eyes and said, one last time, "Behold, the power of Orealus." For a moment, nothing appeared to happen. Then all of a sudden...

It flowed out from Duke's fur: plate armor melding together like liquid gold until every inch of him was covered except for his eyes and mouth. Kaden practically forgot the weapon in his hand as he stared at Duke, awed by the sheer beauty of the armor. Duke got to his feet and shook himself, and the armor didn't make a sound, just moved in perfect sync with him.

"The Thunderlion set," Bhalla said. "Rare and precious armor that will be there whenever Duke is in need. No weapon can penetrate it, and wearing it only makes him stronger and harder, never tires him. And best of all," Bhalla added with a smile, "he can still give himself a good scratch even when he's completely covered by it."

"*Thank* you." Kaden was almost more thankful for this than for Vrangar. Part of him had been nervous about keeping Duke with him on what was likely to be a perilous journey—it was a miracle that the dog hadn't been seriously injured yet, with all the fights they'd gotten into already. Now he could relax a little bit, knowing that he could be near him and stay protected at the same time.

"You're very welcome. It's all due to the ability granted to me by Orealus, of course, but I'm honored to be his conduit for this. Now"—Bhalla turned toward a long wooden table, strewn with papers, along the wall—"let me give you the last thing you'll need to get started."

Kaden nodded, curiosity rising in him. What would it be? A farseeing glass that would let him spy on the enemy from miles away? An elixir that would heal all wounds? Maybe a horn that would allow him to summon allies with just one—

"A map!" Bhalla said, flourishing a small, square piece of paper that was a bit tattered around the edges.

"Oh." *Oh, of course.* Not everything had to be blessed with abilities given to them by Orealus to be helpful, Kaden reminded himself. He took the map from Bhalla, glanced at it, and then looked down again, staring. "What... what are these moving dots?" Petey immediately came over, pulling Kaden's arm down so he could look at the map as well.

"Those are the locations of the tribal leaders of our land," Bhalla explained. "This map tracks each of them, and the closer you get to one, the more the map narrows in on their location. You see how the flower sign of Queen Pepper Shinyfawn is larger than the others right now? That's because you're closest to her. As you get even closer, the map will show more and more details of her surroundings so that you can find her more easily. You must find and unite the tribal leaders as it is part of Orealus's prophecy. They are vital in helping you defeat Lucient and save all of Empyrea." He covered Kaden's hand with his own for a moment. "This is a map that an agent of Lucient the Deceiver would love to have," he said earnestly, his eyes intent. "You must make sure it doesn't fall into the wrong hands."

"I'll take care of it," Kaden promised. "But... what exactly do I say when I find the tribal leaders?"

"You tell them who you are," Bhalla said simply. "You tell them of your quest to reunite the pillar leaders that once followed your father against Lucient. They may not believe you at first, but..." He smiled enigmatically. "I daresay you'll come up with a way to convince them." As fast as he smiled, his face suddenly scrunched, and he sternly cautioned them, "I almost forgot, remember that these gifts will only help you at the beginning of your journey. You must rely on each other and find the armor and sword of Orealus to defeat Lucient and his evil followers."

"Geez, way to ruin the mood," Kaden replied.

"Now," Bhalla said as he clapped both Kaden and Petey on the backs so hard they nearly staggered. "What do you say? Are you young men ready for the next leg of your journey?"

They looked at each other, then at Duke, who just wagged his tail.

"Yes." Kaden felt his faith like a glow emanating from his heart, warming him and giving him confidence. It was time to move on. "We are."

CHAPTER 12

The last time he'd been in Brightshire Forest—could it really be only a few days ago now?—Kaden had been grateful to leave it. While beautiful, it was also a place that had proven downright menacing at times, where he'd been attacked by goblins and grawlers, where Daneyel had *died*. Putting the forest behind him had felt right, like the next step on his journey.

Now, entering it again, Kaden was surprised to find that he felt nothing but excitement and anticipation for whatever happened next. After all, while the adventure had gone poorly in places, he'd also met Queen Pepper here and proven himself in his first real battles. And now they were beginning on an even *more extraordinary* adventure, one that Kaden owned and had to master for the sake of the entire realm. It felt daunting, but with Vrangar at his side and Bhalla's amulet around his neck, he felt capable of facing down evil. It helped to know that his most trustworthy friends, Duke and Petey, were better protected than ever too.

Although, it would be nice if Petey would stop poking things with his dagger every chance he got.

"Yaaah! Eee-yah!" The silvery blade slashed like a firefly through the air, flicker-fast in Petey's hand. "You want a piece of the king?" Petey demanded of no one at all, taking a fighting stance. "You want a *piece* of the *king*? Well then, you're going to have to go through me first, vile varlets! Loyal Dwingent flies faster than the fastest of blades. Ha! Ha-shaaa!" Quicker than

Kaden could see, Petey launched the dagger through the air and into the trunk of one of the enormous braken oaks surrounding them. Up in the branches, a monkey let out a warbling cry.

"Ha, stuck it on the first try! Take *that*, knave!" Petey chortled.

"Um… Petey?"

His friend looked up at him, yellow eyes glowing with contentment. His ears were as pointy as could be, a sure sign that he was happy. Kaden hated to be the one to rain on his campfire, but…

"It's probably for the best if we don't go sticking our weapons into the trees here," he pointed out. "Since we're trying to get Queen Pepper, not to mention King Valymr of the wood elves, on our side."

"Oh, *right*! Right right right, yes, of course." His ears drooping a bit, Petey went to pull Loyal Dwingent out of the tree. He tugged, but the blade held fast. He tugged harder— nothing. Kaden was about to offer help when Petey huffed, grabbed the handle with both hands, and lifted his feet *onto* the tree trunk, heaving himself backward with all his might.

Squick! Out popped the knife, at last, and Petey ended up tumbling head over heels across the soft, loamy earth, finally stopping flat on his back five feet away from the tree.

"Well. That was embarrassing."

Kaden smothered a smile. "There was no one to see you but for Duke and me, and we won't tell," he promised, offering Petey his hand and helping his friend onto his feet. Then Kaden took the map out of his pocket. "According to this, we're actually quite close to Fayspire." Kaden looked around for a clear path through the trees. "I think we could be there before nightfall if we can just find a way around this underbrush."

"We can cut a path through!" Petey offered, then just as quickly added, "Wait, no, that's the same problem, isn't it?"

"Yeah."

"Right. Sorry."

"It's okay. I feel it too." The urge to unsheathe Vrangar and let loose with it, to feel the energy of it as it moved around his body, cutting through imaginary foes, was almost overwhelming. Still, Kaden knew that now wasn't the time to indulge himself. This was the beginning of his actual quest, the quest that Orealus himself had chosen Kaden for, and he couldn't falter. "Let's go…" He glanced at the map, then glanced ahead again. "*This* way."

"Lead on, oh fearless… leader." Petey made a face. "That wasn't very good. Um, lead on, mighty king?"

Kaden laughed as he set off a little to the right, sliding past bushes and pushing branches out of his way. Duke, he was pleased to note, could slide through the clingy brushwood without it sticking to his fur any longer—the Thunderlion armor protected him from more than just blades. That was probably the most incredible relief of all to Kaden, knowing that Duke was so well protected. "I'm not anything close to a king yet," he said, raising a branch out of the way and making sure it didn't *thwip* back and hit Petey in the face.

"Closer than most, but you make a good point," Petey mused. "Hmm… how about just 'Off we go, Kaden'?"

"Sounds good."

It was crisp and dim back under the trees, the occasional shaft of sunlight glinting off the moss or one of the fluttering insects that went skittering by in front of them. In fact, there were more of those insects in this part of the forest than Kaden had seen at any other time in their earlier journey, and they came incredibly close, flitting this way and that, shimmering and sparkling and—

"Oh!" One had stopped right in front of his face, but it *wasn't* one—it was a creature that looked like a tiny version of a fairy, right down to her flowing hair and bright smile, and she waved at him to make sure she had his attention, then curtsied. "Petey, look!"

"Look at wha—oh, hey! Sprites!" Petey said, finally tearing his eyes away from his dagger and noticing them. "They're inhabitants of the fairy realm! Legend says that sprites are the greatest pathfinders in the world—they can find their way through almost anything and lead travelers to safety." He scratched the bottom of his ear. "Of course, if you annoy them, they've also been known to lead people off cliffs."

Kaden looked askance at the sprite, who shrugged her tiny shoulders as if to say, *Hey, no one's perfect.* "Then I guess we'll try very hard to stay on their good sides," he murmured.

She smiled at him, then flew farther back and higher into the air, joining a group of sprites who seemed to dance in the air together, their light glowing brighter and brighter until it coalesced into a globe, with tiny motes floating to the ground like a gentle, starlit rain.

"A sprite trail!" Petey exclaimed, practically jumping up and down. "It's only visible to whoever the sprites decide to lead! To everyone else, it doesn't look like anything at all." The ball of sprites began to move off into the forest, leaving a shower of silver sparkles in their wake. "Come on, let's follow it!"

"I just hope we can keep up." The sprites seemed to be moving awfully fast, and there was still a lot of undergrowth to make their way through... and yet...

It was as though the trees themselves pulled back for them, unraveling branches and shifting roots out of the way so that Kaden and Petey could keep step with their guides. They still nearly had to run to keep the sprites in their sight, but at least Kaden didn't have to worry about tripping and breaking an ankle. Duke, who had already been moving at twice the speed Kaden and Petey had, was running along right below the sprites, snapping playfully at the motes of stardust that glimmered down toward him and sneezing whenever he was lucky enough to catch one.

They kept up the pace for over an hour, heading deeper and deeper into the forest, where the trees became so thick that not a single clear shaft of sunshine illuminated the world around them. The only light was a diffuse, grayish green with occasional reddish tints. There were fewer animals and insects this far in, and the ground was softer and darker.

Great, dewy fronds grew out from around the bases of trees, and mushrooms of all shapes and colors sprang up from rotting logs and mighty trunks in every direction. Some of them dripped, oozing dangerous-looking liquids. Others were long, skinny stalks that climbed around their tree trunk homes like ladders, and yet others glowed in the dimness, in soft blues and purples and one brilliant, intense orange that Kaden could barely look away from.

There was a tug at his elbow. Kaden looked back at Petey, whose bright yellow eyes were narrowed with suspicion. "Did you see that?" he hissed to Kaden.

"See... what?" Kaden panted. Despite the coolness of the air, he'd been moving quickly enough for long enough that he had to work to keep his breaths even.

"The plant!"

Kaden gestured all around them. "Which... one?"

"The one that's following us!"

He glanced back. There was no movement, not even the stir of a brief breeze. Everything was perfectly still. "There's nothing there."

Petey seemed nonplussed. "I could have *sworn* that something was following me."

"You must be imagining it." Kaden glanced ahead—Duke was almost out of sight, and the stardust trail began to fade. "Come on, we've got to get a move on if we're going to catch up."

They ran for another few minutes, almost getting as close to the sprites as they'd been before, when Petey shouted, "Oi! I know you're there, you annoying twit! Show yourself!"

"Petey!" Kaden turned around to see his friend standing ten feet back on the path, shaking Loyal Dwingent at the trees. He sighed and went back, putting a hand on Petey's shoulder.

"Petey, I know it's kind of creepy in here, but really, we have to go."

"It's not the creepiness!" Petey insisted, not moving from his defensive stance. "I grew up in a place with way more creepiness than this. It's the *spying*! If it would just come out into the open, that would be one thing, but nooo, it has to sneak around, it has to be all—"

"If we don't go now, we're going to lose the sprites," Kaden insisted.

"Just another moment! Let me listen!" He tilted his head slightly, ears twitching like he was straining as hard as he could with them, searching for any sound of his follower. A full thirty seconds later, he finally relaxed, his shoulders slumping dejectedly. "I know it's there," he said, scuffing one thick-toed boot against the ground. "I just can't see it or hear it right now."

"Even if it is there, if it hasn't actually bothered you yet, it's probably best to leave it alone," Kaden advised as he began to turn around. "Now come on, we've got to catch up to—" His voice vanished when he looked ahead and saw only the vast, crowded darkness of the trees. There was no glowing trail to be seen, no constellation of stardust to lead their way and light the path. There was only brushwood, back again to give them trouble, and gray air, and quiet. "Duke?" Kaden called out.

Nothing.

He began to push ahead, forcing his way past a set of thorny branches that bit into his clothes and left a scratch mark along his left cheek. "Duke?" he called again, louder.

Still nothing.

The temptation to draw his sword and start hacking the path clear was strong, *so* strong, but Kaden held back—just barely. Breaking his way into Fayspire would be a poor beginning to his quest. He needed Duke back, though. He couldn't do this without him. Where had the sprites led him?

Kaden cupped his hands around his mouth and shouted as loudly as he could into the darkness: "*Duke!*"

A resounding "Woof!" sounded from somewhere in front of him. A minute later, Duke appeared, practically glowing in his armor, his tongue lolling in a doggy smile like he didn't have a care in the world.

"There you are." Kaden fell to his knees and wrapped his arms around his hound. A surge of relief rolled through him. He never liked being separated from Duke, and even though the dog was better prepared to handle himself alone than ever, Kaden still worried for him.

He drew back just enough to look the tall, shaggy animal in the eyes. "Don't run off like that again." Duke licked his face in reply. Kaden grinned and wiped his cheek with his sleeve. "Ugh, you gross thing."

They might have lost the sprites, but perhaps Duke would be able to pick up their scent again. Or maybe they wouldn't even need them to find Fayspire—Kaden still had the map, after all. He drew it out and looked at it again. Yes, they were almost directly on top of the sigil-marked Queen Pepper. She had to be close… but where was she, then? Where was her city? Why couldn't he find it?

You must have faith. Orealus wouldn't abandon him, and neither would Kaden abandon his quest. He shut his eyes and murmured a quick prayer, making the sacred symbol of Orealus right over his heart. He would simply have to—

"Kaden! Kaden, look up!"

Kaden opened his eyes to Petey's wild exhortation and found his own breath taken away before he could even reply. It was as though the forest had suddenly unfolded all around them, bracken and boughs which had been indistinguishable from the background suddenly in stark relief, some of them resembling buildings, others part of support structures that extended all the way up the thick trunks of the ancient oaks. The glowing, ladderlike fungi encircling the trees had unfolded into *actual ladders*, or something halfway between a ladder and a stair, with both handholds and footholds. Kaden could make out voices over the hum of insects now, murmuring fairies wondering who he was and what he and his friends were doing here. And when he looked up even higher…

"*Wow!*" There was an entire city up there, with houses and walkways, perches and staircases, and perhaps a hundred feet further south was a bright, shining enclave so unique and resplendent that it had to belong to royalty. "It's amazing!"

"I've never seen anything like it before," Petey agreed breathlessly. "And I've seen *lots* of mushrooms over the years, let me tell you. I assume the fairies can tolerate them all together like this because they have some sort of innate immunity to their spores, and—hey!" He jumped nearly a foot in the air, spinning around and glaring at the thing perched just behind his feet. "I knew it!" he shrieked, reaching for Loyal Dwingent. "I *am* being followed!"

"Petey." Kaden laid a quelling hand on his arm. "Look at where we are. Look at all the people." They were being watched, undoubtedly by a lot more fairies than were visible right now. The last thing they needed was to kill someone's pet… um… "What is it?" Kaden asked. It looked like something between a puffy-capped mushroom and a rabbit. Even as he watched, it hopped up and down in place, letting out an excited puff of phosphorescent spores.

Kaden grinned. "Whatever it is, I think it likes you."

"Well, I don't like it," Petey snapped, not drawing his blade but not relaxing his hand either. "I don't like things that sneak up on me and then pretend not to be there when I spot them and then sneak up on me again and then spit venom on me and try to dissolve my face, and—"

"Wait." Kaden held up a hand. "What venom?"

"No, *this* thing hasn't done that, but back in Shroudscar, there are these speed snails that can crawl along the ceilings and hit you in the face with their spit at ten paces, and… let's just say I ran into one on my first trip out of the palace." Petey grimaced and rubbed at his right ear, which, now that Kaden looked at it, *was* a little rougher along the inner edge. "It didn't go well."

"Well, I don't think this one is going to spit venom at you." They watched it hop again. Duke sniffed it, then sneezed so hard his armor appeared for a moment. "So, we should…"

"See Her Majesty, Queen Pepper Shinyfawn," a voice behind them announced. They all turned together to see a male fairy, dressed in armor and carrying a spear, hovering a few feet behind them. Despite being shorter than Kaden, he looked pretty fierce. His skin was green, not too dissimilar from Petey's, but it glowed where the goblin's absorbed the light, and the long hair that flowed beneath his helm was golden. "She's expecting you," the fairy continued, gesturing at the nearest ladder with his spear point. "Climb to the top, then turn and walk to the right. I will meet you there." He flew up and was lost to the crowd as he reached the canopy level.

"Uh, I guess we…" Kaden looked at the nearest ladder. The steps were about half as wide as his foot, and the handholds were waist high for him. It wasn't going to be an easy climb. "Go up." He glanced at Duke, then turned to Petey. "You go first. I want to be behind Duke to help him if he needs it." There was no way he would leave his dog down here, all by himself, and he was confident that Queen Pepper knew that.

"Oh, good idea." Petey looked down at the mushroom creature. "Whereas *you* can sit right here until the end of days, mister!" Then he turned and stalked off to the ladder.

Kaden glanced down at the mushroom, which sure enough began to *hop hop hop* after Petey. He stifled a smile and gave

Duke a gentle nudge. "Go on, boy," he said, and Duke began to climb, with Kaden following right after.

It wasn't easy. Duke must not have seen the colors the same way Kaden and Petey did because he had to sniff out each step before feeling confident enough to put his foot on it. By the time they reached the top, all three of them were tuckered out—neither Duke nor Kaden could make noise without Petey whirling around and anxiously asking to help.

It was a relief to see their guard again, a familiar face among the sudden *crowd* of fairies, all of them different, beautiful, and sometimes fluttering a *little* too close for comfort. The countless fairies' wings made a sound as elegant as dragonflies fluttering.

"Who are they?"

"Where did they come from?"

"Look at the weapons! The sprites said they had weapons. Should they really be here?"

"The sprites wouldn't lead anyone here who meant us harm…"

"Look at the doggie! I wanna ride it!" That was a young fairy with thick curly hair the color of moonlight, pointing excitedly as her mother tried to shush her.

Kaden was caught between laughing and shying away. He took a moment to absorb his glorious surroundings. Simple suspension bridges made of rope and wood connected the structures. The sturdy treehouses made up the shops, homes, and meeting places for the fairies. With only a few oil lanterns scattered here and there, the primary lighting was moonlight, starlight, and thousands of fireflies that enjoyed the company of the fairies. A hint of honeysuckle and other fresh flowers wafted among the treetops. Pine dominated the aroma both inside and outside. The air, uncontaminated by the traditional city smells, carried a sweet scent that seemed to reveal the happiness of the trees. The guard led them to cross a bridge, which squeaked under their weight, into the bright oval room at the end of the walkway. Fortunately, the crowd's noise ceased, cut off like there was more than a simple threshold separating them. It had to be from the power of Orealus

This room wasn't immense like the Truthoriam, but looking around, Kaden sensed he was in the presence of great power. There were plants of all kinds here, spilling over the floor and climbing the walls and falling in waves from the ceiling. Some of them moved like they were wafting in a breeze, even though the air was still. Others snapped and sparked, and still others dripped nectar that smelled as sweet as honey. In the center of it all was Queen Pepper Shinyfawn, much like Kaden had last seen her, only this time her eyes glimmered pink, not purple.

"My friends," she said, stepping—not flying, which was odd for Kaden after seeing so much of it—down from her throne, a chair that looked like a living part of the tree itself, and over to them. "I'm grateful to see you well, yet also surprised by your appearance here. Did you not find entry into the mystical city of Lumhagen?"

"We did," Kaden said. "We met with Bhalla, just like we intended." Well, not *quite* like Kaden had intended, but close enough.

"And?" Queen Pepper prompted after a moment.

"And he gave us a quest."

"And ways to defend ourselves!" Petey crowed. "Behold, Loyal Dwingent!" He pulled the dagger and held it aloft, where it was immediately claimed by a tendril of an enormous bell-shaped plant with red and brown streaks coloring its broad, firm leaves. "Hey! Give that back!"

Queen Pepper hid a smile behind her hand. "I should have mentioned, wielding a weapon in my throne room is not permitted. Some of these plants act as my bodyguards."

"I wasn't going to hurt you!" Petey said earnestly. "I would *never* do that."

"I know," Queen Pepper soothed, "but my plants don't. I'll see it returned to you as soon as possible." She turned back to Kaden, her face not quite as serene as it had been. There was a line of worry in the center of her brow. "Tell me more of your quest."

"We have to unite the tribal leaders of Empyrea," Kaden said, quiet with the weight of it. He saw it hit her the same way, with a magnitude that spoke of the epic, perhaps impossible nature of it. "Lucient is gathering his minions again, preparing for another assault. If we don't combine our own forces and stand against him together, no one in the world will be safe from him."

"No," Queen Pepper said, her worry lines growing deeper. "I fear that you are right. I've sensed a shift in the balance of the forest over the last few years, a balance that hadn't changed since the last great battle. No grawler should have dared to come so deep into my realm and into the realm of my neighbors, the wood elves. They should not have *dared*, and yet they did so, without hesitation." She shook her head.

"After my husband, Faedner, died during the last great cataclysm protecting King Karatheas"—Kaden flinched and hoped she didn't notice—"my sole wish was to avoid such pain again in my lifetime. That false hope made me weak, turned my eyes away from trouble so that I only focused on the beauty I wanted to see instead of the ugliness that I *needed* to see. Brightshire Forest has suffered for my lassitude. I cannot allow it to continue."

She flew up now, coming face to face with Kaden. "You three came here to ask me to accompany you on this quest," she said, her voice full of certainty.

"Um, yes…" Kaden coughed to clear his throat. "Yes, we did," he said, much more firmly.

"Then I am honored to accept. My personal guard and I will join you in convincing the rest of the tribal leaders of the kingdom of Empyrea to make an accord with us and prepare for battle." A single tear rolled down her cheek. "All my dreams for a peaceful future have been nothing but lies I told myself, lies to bandage over my wounded heart. I must trust that enough time has passed that my heart will no longer break at the onset of war."

"Squeak!"

The solemn moment was broken by a bit of noise from near the ground. "Oh no, not you again!" Petey moaned. They all looked down to see the little mushroom, hopping and squeaking as it cavorted around Petey's feet. "I'm sorry," he said miserably to Queen Pepper. "It's been following me. I tried to get it to stop, but—"

"Oh no, don't try to stop it!" she exclaimed, lowering herself to look at the little thing. "By the Sacred O, I've not seen one of these in years," she marveled. "A frolicking toadstool! They can live in stasis for decades and catching sight of one is a sign of good fortune ahead. To have one so excited by you that it follows you about?" She beamed at Petey. "It's considered a tremendous honor!"

"Great. I'm... so honored." They all watched the toadstool spray another puff of spores into the air. "How do I, um, get it to *stop* following me?"

"Oh, it stops when it wishes to. You can't *force* a frolicking toadstool into anything. The more you try, the more stubborn they get. But what a great sign for our quest! You might as well give it a name."

Petey looked in despair at Kaden, who just shrugged. There was no helping it. If Queen Pepper thought the toadstool was a good sign, then they'd have to tolerate it. They needed all the good fortune they could get, after all.

Even if it came in the form of a tiny hopping mushroom.

CHAPTER 13

A single night was plenty of time for Kaden to feel done with Fayspire. It wasn't that the place wasn't beautiful, because it was—it was stunning. It wasn't that he was afraid of its height, necessarily, although he didn't like the peril it put Duke in. Because so few barriers blocked the edges of platforms, he had to ensure the dog took care with their every step. It certainly wasn't that he didn't like the people. It was just... there was *no* privacy, None.

Once Queen Pepper announced her intent to travel with them, she hosted a banquet in their honor. The food was all vegetarian—no meat here, not even for Duke, but he didn't seem to mind the blend of chopped nuts and mushrooms he was given. That was fine, but the hush that had overcome the banquet hall every time one of them spoke had been... odd. Kaden didn't think him telling Queen Pepper that he liked the peargerine juice was all that momentous. And that watchful silence had followed them back to the quarters they were given, with fairies flitting by their glassless windows every few seconds, peeking in and moving on, looking in and moving on. They were just sitting there!

Petey didn't even notice. He was so wrapped up in his new pet. Not in a good way either. "Stop spraying that stuff at me!" he cried after the air around his head filled with purple spores for the third time in five minutes. "Why are you doing this?"

Kaden smiled, momentarily forgetting their audience. "Maybe it's how the little guy lets you know he loves you. Like when Duke gave me a lick." At which point Duke obliged with a lick right up the side of Kaden's face, which—*yuck*. But he scratched behind Duke's ears anyway.

"I don't need to be loved by a toadstool!" Petey glared balefully at the hopping, squeaking, mysterious mushroom. "I'm going to call you *Bug* because you keep on bugging me."

"You have to be careful about letting on, though," Kaden said, nodding meaningfully at the windows, where several faces disappeared as soon as they saw Kaden looking at them. "Being picked by one is considered a tremendous honor, remember."

"I wish it had picked you," Petey said morosely. "Or Duke. I'm not cut out for tremendous honors."

"Funny, you seem to like having Loyal Dwingent well enough."

Petey clutched the dagger to his chest. Queen Pepper had been able to get it back from her guard plant after the banquet, and he hadn't let go of it since. "This is different! This is a *weapon*; it's objectively useful! What use is a toadstool?"

Kaden had to think about it. "It's a... well, it's a friend," he said at last.

"I have friends. I have you and Duke, and Bhalla and Asitra. See? I've got so many friends, I almost can't add you all up on the one hand. I don't *need* another one."

Kaden lay back on his slender cot and sighed. At least the bed was long enough, one that the fairies gave to visiting wood elves, but it was awfully narrow. He had almost gotten used to the way the wooden buildings swayed pleasantly with the wind, a feeling Kaden imagined as similar to riding a boat at sea. "I think we're going to need all the friends we can get before long," he said. "Tell me about Kel Tyrion."

"I really don't know that much about it," Petey said apologetically. "Wood elves are notoriously standoffish. Their town is on the far side of a lake, and there's no way to get there except by boat. They have their own language, their own customs, their own army… no goblin has ever been there before, as far as I know."

That sounded a bit ominous. Kaden tried to be encouraging. "Then you'll be the first."

"Yeah, maybe. If they don't shoot me through the head at five hundred paces just for showing up and polluting their air. Like *this* thing does," he said between coughs as yet another spray of spores wafted around his face.

"Let's get some sleep," Kaden decided. They would try to reach Kel Tyrion by tomorrow evening, although he had no idea if they'd move that fast with Queen Pepper and her attendants along. He laid a cloth over his eyes—there was nothing else he could do to dim the glow all around them—and fell asleep to the sound of Duke's gradual snores and Petey's mutterings at his new pet.

*   *   *

They left early the next day to a mournful fanfare from the fairies, who all seemed quite nervous over their queen leaving them. She had dressed down, losing her regalia and shiny clothes in favor of something more woods friendly, and her personal guard—two of them, whom she introduced as Millicent and Redfern—were wearing hardy, practical clothes and carrying much plainer spears than they'd wielded before. Subtlety—or perhaps even subterfuge—was apparently a big part of the plan going forward.

As they left, her people singing softly behind them, Kaden turned to Queen Pepper and asked, "Why are they so sad?"

"Oh," she said, trying to smile but not quite managing it, "they're just a bit worried for me, that's all. The last time a ruler left Brightshire Forest, he never returned. I've barely left Fayspire since that terrible war, and my people have come to… rely on my presence, I suppose."

"She's like everyone's mother," Millicent, a tough-looking female fairy with long, pale-blue hair, said. She was tall, for a fairy, yet nimble. She wore the battle scars on her face like makeup, and her dark brown eyes only grew darker as she spoke. "Any child is distressed when their mother leaves them for the first time."

"It's good for them," the other fairy guard, Redfern, added. With flowing red hair and light brown eyes, this female fairy had a stature similar to most fairies. She appeared feisty even in her features, a round face, pointy nose, and narrow lips. "They need to learn that they can survive without constant guidance. Our queen spoils them with her attention." "Oh, you two," Queen Pepper said fondly. "I notice you were both the first to volunteer to come with me. Was that solely for the sake of my safety, or did you not want to leave me either?" Redfern coughed nervously into her hand and flitted ahead. "We'll be all day getting to Kel Tyrion at this rate," she snapped. "Let's move!

*   *   *

It actually only took four hours to make it out of the woods and to the edge of the lake that sheltered the beautiful city of the wood elves, thanks to Queen Pepper and her guard knowing the quickest routes in the forest. Trees practically stepped aside to let them through, and as they emerged onto the pebbly beach at the edge of the lake, she looked back at the forest and said, "Thank you, my friends." Kaden probably imagined it, but he thought he could almost hear the trees whisper words of love back to her.

"Well," Petey said, stumping down to the water's edge and looking dubiously out across the lake, backed by tall, jagged mountains. A waterfall cascading down from between two peaks fed the waters, making them ripple slightly even this far out. "Here we are, I guess. But how are we supposed to get all the way over there? There are no boats." He kicked a pebble into the water, breaking the glasslike stillness of the surface with ripples. Bug hopped after him, dogged in its pursuit.

"Hmm. That's a fair question," Queen Pepper admitted. "If it were just myself and my guards, we would fly over, but the three of you don't have that option." She tilted her head thoughtfully. "I suppose we could go over and ask them to send boats back for you."

"No, thank you," Kaden said firmly. He needed to stand on his own authority now, not use Queen Pepper's influence to get people to pay attention to him. "If we can't go over together, then we'll stay here until one of them comes to us."

"What makes you think we haven't been tracking you since you came within a mile of the edge of the forest?" a new voice asked.

The whole party swung toward the woods, and Kaden was shocked to see four wood elves emerge from the trees—scouts? Or perhaps nothing more than a hunting party, given the deer that one of them had slung over his shoulder. Either way, they were armed with bows, and each had an arrow pulled back to full draw. "Why do you outsiders seek to enter Kel Tyrion?" the foremost of them asked.

"Prince Eldrin," Queen Pepper said chidingly, pulling her hood back and revealing her long white hair. "That's hardly a polite way to greet your neighbors."

The one who had spoken—Eldrin, Kaden assumed— immediately lowered his bow. His companions followed suit. Kaden took the measure of him as he stepped forward. He had long ears that corkscrewed outward to points at their tips. He was tall, maybe even a little taller than Kaden himself, and had long, almost translucent blond hair and a face free of blemishes. His almond-shaped eyes appeared to contain a ferocious storm in their bluish-gray color. He was nearly as slender as the massive bow he carried, but he wielded the weapon like the draw was nothing. "Your Majesty!" Eldrin said. "What are you doing here? I mean, Father is always pleased to see you, but we didn't miss a message, did we?"

"Not at all," Queen Pepper assured him. "I'm not here for myself, Eldrin. This quest has far more serious consequences."

Eldrin's stormy eyes narrowed. "You. On a quest."

Queen Pepper sighed. "I know. It's hard to believe."

"Try impossible. I didn't think you ever went farther from home than my father's halls."

"Watch your tone when addressing our queen, elfling," Millicent snapped in her lady's defense.

"Or what?" he challenged.

"Or I'll shove my spear so far up your backside you'll get splinters in your teeth!"

"Please." Kaden had to interject, had to stop them before someone said something they'd regret. "Please, that's enough. We didn't come here to fight." He inclined his head to the wood-elf prince. "My name is Kaden Sheppard, and Queen Pepper is here because of my quest."

Eldrin looked him over, then laughed. "A ragged young human, a shaggy hound, and a—Orealus above, is that a *goblin* with you? Are the three of you on a quest? What sort of quest could be so important that it would convince this noble lady to leave her home?" He might be speaking dismissively of Kaden, but he'd gone back to using a respectful tone for Queen Pepper.

"A worthy one," Kaden said. "I'm rallying all the tribes of Empyrea against the Great Deceiver, Lucient. Queen Pepper has come along to represent her people and to help me persuade others to join our cause."

The wood elves looked disturbed, muttering to each other under their breath. Eldrin paused, then asked, "Who are you, to be the leader of such a quest? You're not a wizard, despite that amulet around your neck."

"No, I'm not," Kaden agreed. "Grand Wizard Bhalla gave this to me before I left Lumhagen."

"Who *are* you?" Eldrin snapped again.

"I told you. I'm Kaden Sheppard. I'm *also* the only surviving child of King Karatheas."

Now the elves looked stunned. Eldrin found his voice first. "That's not possible. My father said that no one could have survived that war."

"Bhalla was able to get me to safety. No one else, though." Not the parents he would never know or any of his siblings. "I was raised by a former armsman of Karatheas's in a town called Ashland."

"That tiny hamlet?" The prince recovered a bit of his hauteur. "And you think growing up *there* has in any way prepared you for a quest like this? You must be mad."

"Eldrin," Queen Pepper said with a sigh. "Bhalla himself has vouched for him."

"The word of that dotty old wizard doesn't carry any weight with me."

"Then we will see what it means to your father, instead." Queen Pepper shook out her hair, hovering in the air like a vision, powerful and mysterious and beautiful all at once. "Or do you mean to turn us away here, on your very shores, like we are a group of marauders? Know that I've come on this quest because I believe in it with all my heart, Prince Eldrin. You're right to think that I wouldn't leave Fayspire otherwise. If you have any respect for my opinions, you will take us to King Valymr so that we may be heard."

Eldrin stared at her for a long moment, then back at Kaden. Finally, he said, "My men and I will bring the boats around." Then he turned and left without another word, vanishing into the trees.

Kaden stepped up beside Queen Pepper. "I didn't mean for you to have to take the lead here," he said, quiet and apologetic. "I should be able to do this on my own."

"Kaden." She smiled brightly at him, one hand reaching out to touch his cheek in a motherly fashion. "What good am I as an ally on this quest if I don't use my influence to help you? You will have plenty of opportunities to lead the way in swaying others to your cause, but for now, when I am still so close to my element, why shouldn't I help? Valymr has known me for many years, and he will give more credence to what you say if he sees that you have my full support. That's all."

"It's just good diplomacy," Petey added. "You have to use all the resources at your disposal to get the outcome you want. My mother has negotiated truces between warring goblin clans in all sorts of ways—even with a drinking contest once!"

"Exactly," Queen Pepper said with a chuckle. "As your reputation grows, Kaden, you'll have less need of assistance, but this is only the beginning of your long journey. There is still time for you to grow into your power."

Part of Kaden wanted to protest—he shouldn't *need* time. He'd been given this task by Orealus himself. He was blessed; he should be *ready* for it. But he wasn't foolish enough to turn down help—especially when it was clear that, to Prince Eldrin at least, he was nothing more than a fable or a fool.

Speaking of the prince… he and his companions returned from the woods carrying two long, slender boats over their heads. They set them down on the edge of the water, and Eldrin indicated the close one. "You here, Karatheas's son. Your people can go in the other one." He heaved the deer into the rear of it so that its hooves would poke Kaden in the back. "Or does the water scare you?"

Kaden might not be accustomed to dealing with royalty, but he'd had more than enough experience dealing with casual bullies back home. Daneyel had always said that you were responsible for teaching people how to treat you, that you couldn't rely on the kindness of others—you had to be prepared to stick up for yourself from the start.

Kaden thought of his foster father, of how hard Daneyel had fought for him and how much he'd learned from the man, and stepped forward. "I'll be fine," he replied. "Maybe you'd like me to teach you how to properly load a boat like this, though? You seem a little confused about what to do with that deer."

Petey snickered, and Queen Pepper's guards looked like they were smothering smiles. Eldrin frowned. "Just get in," he snapped. Kaden did—but not before moving the deer, so the hooves were pointing the other way.

Eldrin and two of his people got into the boat, unhooking slender, reedlike paddles from the side. Quick as the wind, they set out across the lake, with the fairies flying beside them. Kaden made sure Petey and Duke followed in the other boat before he relaxed.

"What, you don't trust me?" Eldrin asked.

"I don't know you," Kaden replied with as much diplomacy as he could manage. "But I'm sure that will change."

"We'll see."

Since there was no role for him to play in moving the boat, Kaden focused on his surroundings instead. He'd never been on a body of water so big before—there had been a few ponds near Ashland, but nothing as immense as this lake. The air was cool and full of moisture from the giant waterfall flowing down the mountains behind Kel Tyrion. It was constant background noise, like a heartbeat for the entire city. The graceful buildings, emerging from the waterfall's mist, looked like cathedrals made as giant log cabins of vertically stacked wood. Moss and ivy grew freely up and through the windowless structures. The elves' buildings appeared one with nature, a perfect symbol for their symbiotic relationship with the land and its creatures.

Ducks drifted slowly across the water, quacking occasionally, and other birds flitted overhead, singing their songs as they inspected the surface of the water for long-legged glider spiders and clusters of gnats. Here and there, a fish jumped up, making its own play for the insects that called the lake home, and everywhere the air smelled fresh and sweet. As they got closer to Kel Tyrion, Kaden saw why—every building was wreathed in thick growths of honeysuckle, the flowers ranging from the palest yellow to the deepest goldenrod. The air was thick with the aroma of these flowers, as well as with berries and honey. *It's so beautiful. Even if the wood elves turn us away, at least I'll have the memory of this place in my heart.*

They crossed the lake almost too quickly. Kaden wouldn't have minded spending hours out on the water, but he knew that this next meeting would be a pivotal one for his quest. He'd met Queen Pepper before he even knew what his purpose was, and she had helped him without question. But here… well, if Eldrin were any example, then Kaden wouldn't be surprised if he had to fight to be taken seriously by King Valymr, even with the fairies' help.

The elves paddled the boats right up onto the shore, into wood-reinforced grooves that had been designed to hold incoming ships. They scraped gently, then settled, and Eldrin and his companion leaped out onto the ground. Kaden followed a bit more clumsily, ending up soaking both his feet in the wet sand.

Petey and Duke weren't faring any better, although Duke seemed to be enjoying the wetness immensely. He romped along the water's edge, chasing a minnow or a frog, perhaps. Eldrin laughed. "How does an animal like this qualify as any sort of mighty companion for a quest? He's a puppy, not a predator!"

"Hey!" Petey snapped. "You don't know a thing about him!"

"I know that he's—what's that?"

"What?"

"*That.*" Eldrin pointed at Petey's shoulder, where Bug had just hopped up and was settling in.

"Oh." Petey's ears drooped for a moment, then straightened. "That's my toadstool, and if you have a problem with him, you can just keep it to yourself, got it? He might not be big and powerful like Duke, but he's..." Petey shrugged, and Bug released a spray of pink spores into the air. "Not totally useless, I guess?"

Eldrin didn't seem inclined to laugh. "You got a frolicking toadstool to join your quest? *How?* Where did you even find it?"

Kaden and Petey exchanged a glance. "It found us," Kaden said. "Or Petey, really."

"It's a fair sign, don't you agree?" Queen Pepper asked sweetly.

Eldrin, finally looking unsettled, just said, "Follow me to my father's throne room. But know that if you draw a weapon there, his guards will have you skewered before you can move two paces." He stalked off toward the city, clearly expecting them all to catch up or be left behind.

Kaden and Petey scrambled to get moving, and Duke caught up after one last attempt to catch the creature in the lake.

"Skewered, ha," one of the fairy guards muttered. "Big words from an oversized pain in the—"

"Redfern, shhh," Queen Pepper gently chided her companion as she flew along. "Give him a chance to save face. That's all this is. Valymr will listen to us. He will have to."

"Because he'll understand how important it is?" Kaden asked, lengthening his stride a bit.

"That," Queen Pepper agreed. "And because... well, he has his own memories of the Great War, his own losses to deal with, just like I did. I feel that the ghosts who have haunted him since then will not be able to lie silent now that you're here, Kaden."

Kaden frowned. "What do you mean?"

"It isn't my place to say," Queen Pepper murmured, her face solemn. "Just... believe me when I tell you that the reception we receive from the father will likely be very different than the one we received from the son. Eldrin is a fine young elf, but he takes many things for granted. I think that some of those blind beliefs may come to an end today."

She didn't say anything else, and after a moment, Kaden turned his attention back to his surroundings. The city of Kel Tyrion was reminiscent of Fayspire, in a way, because it was built out of a forest. However, while the fairies constructed buildings on top of trees, the wood elves assembled right inside them. These structures were not log cabins but rather housing fashioned of living trees still growing from the ground. The trees here seemed to be of a different type, too, or perhaps just older, with massive, smooth trunks that fit so closely side by side it was hard to tell in places whether it was one tree or two. Maybe they had grown together. Perhaps they'd been molded that way for a hundred, a *thousand* years. Kaden didn't know. He wished he felt bold enough to ask.

Eldrin led them to an elaborately carved doorway taller than the tallest house back in Ashland. Inside, the air was even chillier than out, where they were misted by the waterfall, and the lack of windows gave the whole place a vague, secretive feeling. The lights were either emitting from the gift of yah'zaval or the most carefully tended fires Kaden had ever seen, captured in glass globes and set at ten-foot intervals down the hallway. The floor was wood, but it seemed as hard as a stone and highly polished. Duke's claws *click-click-click*ed on it, and he almost slipped as they went around a corner.

One of the elves snickered, and Kaden had to rein in his temper. He couldn't afford to get into an argument right now. He needed to save his breath for convincing King Valymr of the necessity of his quest.

They were led into a long, tall hall. This one had a window, one single window at the very top of it, that let in just enough light to give the air a bit of a golden haze. On the far side of the floor was a tall, straight-backed chair covered with silver leaf— or perhaps it was solid silver, Kaden didn't know. In that chair sat an elf with hair even more of a golden blond than Eldrin's and elegant clothes the color of a forest in autumn—red, gold, and brown. He wore a surprisingly delicate silver crown on his head, with a bright red jewel centered just above his eyes, and his long, curving, pointed ears were twined with silver and red as well.

He was the very picture of a king, powerful and forbidding, and Kaden felt his breath catch in his throat. What could he say to make this elf see things from his perspective? How would he possibly convince Valymr that his quest was real?

Eldrin said something to the elf king in a language that was alien to Kaden's ears... yet he somehow understood it. He glanced down at his amulet, which was glowing faintly against his chest. Was this some of Bhalla's abilities that Orealus blessed him with?

"—don't know why they truly want an audience with you, Father," Eldrin continued.

"I'm afraid I do, my son," King Valymr said heavily. "And we will not speak Tah-thynian now. It would be rude to our guests."

Eldrin appeared stung. "The fairies understand it just fine."

"I'm not talking about the fairies." King Valymr met Kaden's gaze, and in a moment, Kaden felt like the elf had learned far more about him than most people would in a week. "You truly are Karatheas's son," he said wonderingly. "I had heard rumors of your escape, of course, but I never paid them much heed."

"I am," Kaden said, a bit haltingly, but knowing his friends were there backing him up gave him strength. "I was raised in Ashland until recently. My foster father was killed by goblins seeking me out. Eventually, Petey, Duke, and I"—he indicated his closest friends—"made it to Lumhagen, where we met with Bhalla. He told me—"

"That Lucient the Deceiver is on the move again." King Valymr smiled mirthlessly. "Of course he is. After all this time…" He looked at Queen Pepper. "And you believe what he's saying?"

"I do," she said gravely. "I defended him from a pack of grawlers in Brightshire Forest. *Grawlers*, so close to the heart of my kingdom? It can only mean that Lucient has detected the threat that Kaden here poses and is moving to stop him before he gains the allies he will need to move against the Dark One's forces."

"I suppose it does." Valymr bowed his head. "I still held out hope that it wouldn't come to this, though."

"I know you did." Queen Pepper flew up to hover beside him. "We both did, for our own reasons," she said kindly. King Valymr looked at her with a bitter, hopeless expression, and she laid a hand on his shoulder. "I would have locked myself away in the safety of Fayspire for the rest of my life—and you likewise would have grappled with the guilt of your retreat at Karatheas and Lucient's final battle in the Great War for just as long—if it meant there was no more darkness to contend with. But there is, and it has come calling. We, who remember the Great War, must answer it."

King Valymr sighed deeply. "So, we must, indeed. But I have not the heart for this quest, Pepper. To go forth as you do would break me, I fear."

She gave him a smile. "I know of one in your family who yet has a heart for adventure."

Kaden looked between the two of them, wondering just what was going on. Eldrin seemed to wonder, but unlike Kaden, he was bold enough to speak up. "Father? I don't understand. What are you talking about? What do *you* possibly have to feel guilty for?"

"Many things," the king replied. "Things that I've kept from you your whole life. Things that I tried to lock away within myself, but the truth always comes calling in the end." He looked at Kaden. "The kingdom of Kel Tyrion will answer your call,

Kaden, son of Karatheas. But I cannot be the one to accompany you on your quest." His lips twisted into a cruel parody of a smile. "I fear I would be of little use at this stage in my life." He gestured to Eldrin. "Fortunately, I have a son of great strength who is ready for an opportunity to come into his own. Prince Eldrin will accompany you henceforth."

There was a moment of dumbfounded silence, and then...

"What?"

CHAPTER 14

"You can't be serious, Father!" Eldrin went on before Kaden even had a chance to speak up. "We know nothing of this human other than what he claims to be. He might be lying about being the son of Karatheas!"

"I'm not!" Kaden exclaimed because there might be wisdom in silence, but he wasn't going to let *anyone* get away with calling him a liar.

"He isn't," King Valymr confirmed. "I would know him anywhere. He looks exactly like his father did at that age."

Kaden's heart leaped a bit at the thought of learning something new about his father. "You knew him as a young man?"

Valymr tilted his head a bit, his eyes going distant. "I knew him from the time he was a baby. Wood elves are a long-lived people, if not quite as long as our friends the fairies." He nodded toward Queen Pepper. "All of us knew there would come a time when we would have to face Lucient again. The times of ease and goodness had lasted too long—and while that lying serpent still lives, no time of plenty can ever be assured." His gaze drifted away from all of them, perhaps into a hazy vision of the past. "We knew another confrontation would come and that Karatheas would likely be the king to lead us into battle. It made sense to get to know him from a young age."

"So, wait." It was Petey who spoke now, sounding a little incredulous, his ears turned down in a sure sign of fear… or perhaps anger. "You knew King Karatheas ever since he was a baby, and you *still* ran away during his final battle? How could you *do* that to a friend?"

"Don't you dare speak to my father in such a manner!" Eldrin shouted, nocking an arrow on his bow and aiming it straight at Petey's heart.

Queen Pepper surged forward just as Kaden moved to cover his friend. Still, it was King Valymr who brought the proceedings to a complete halt by standing up and shouting, "That is *enough*!" in a voice so loud it echoed through the great chamber and down the halls, absorbing every other sound into its fury. Eldrin immediately lowered his bow, looking both stunned and chastened. Petey looked like he was about a second away from bolting out the door.

King Valymr left his throne, walking straight toward his son. It took Kaden a moment to realize that the elf was limping badly. Eldrin moved to help him, but Valymr held up a hand. "No," he said, his voice gentle again. "You must know this, and I deserve to face the truth." He looked at Petey. "The battle with Lucient was a time of incredible chaos," he said, his face serene but his voice flat with pain. "Not an hour into the fight, I was taken down by the ogre lord Omak. He and his honor guard cut a path of blood and suffering through my contingent of fighters. I was nearly blind with agony, and when I heard Karatheas's horn sound, I thought at first that it was a call to retreat.

"By the time I realized my mistake, my guards had borne me beyond the rage of battle, and I… I could not force myself to return to it. I had already lost half my people, and the rest were barely any better off than I was. I made a choice." As pained as he sounded, his eyes were unflinching. "I chose to take my people and flee. I've regretted not staying myself to help King

Karatheas since then, but I haven't regretted preserving my own people. The cost was already so high, and our kind is so few…"

He looked at Queen Pepper, who bowed her head. "An elf or a fairy might go hundreds of years before producing their first child," Valymr said quietly. "And they rarely have more than two or three over their long lives. Our populations are in a delicate balance in the best of times, but during the war? Too many losses could end us permanently."

Now he looked back at Kaden. "Judge me however you will, my prince, but I ask that you not think harshly of my people or of my son."

Kaden's heart hurt just being asked for this kind of forgiveness. "I don't think it's my place to judge your actions, given that I've never been in a battle like that before," he said, going slow so he could think through everything before he spoke it aloud. "I can't know what it was like, but I do know how terrible it is to lose people you love. I wish for his sake—for my father's sake—that you'd stayed, but I won't condemn you for the past. I'm grateful to you for listening to me now and giving me your support."

"Graciously put." King Valymr inclined his head. "I'm honored."

Eldrin looked between the two of them like he thought they were both crazy. "This isn't right," he said, his growing sense of confusion evident. "This can't be right. Father, I don't… I don't understand!"

Valymr nodded. "I'll explain things to you tonight. Tomorrow, you will leave with Karatheas's heir and his companions. War is coming, and our people will have a part in it, whether I wish it or not." He held his hand out to his son, who let himself be led away, but not without a searing backward glance at Kaden.

"Oh, *he's* going to be a jolly traveling companion," Petey said sourly. "An absolute delight, I'm sure."

"Eldrin is an excellent warrior," Queen Pepper said as the majordomo of the palace stepped forward to take care of their group. "And once his temper calms, he's reasonable enough. He'll be all right."

"But will *we?*"

Kaden thought Petey's concerns were a little overblown. After all, Eldrin was the prince, not the king of the wood elves. Indeed, he would listen to his father's directions… wouldn't he?

Just like you always listened to Daneyel and Lydia?

Maybe things would be rougher than Kaden hoped. But he wouldn't borrow trouble. He had the feeling it would find him regardless.

The night passed quickly enough, Queen Pepper telling them stories about fairies and wood elves and anything else they thought to ask about before they all turned in. The following day, though, proved to be even less auspicious than Petey had predicted.

*   *   *

Eldrin appeared next to his father that morning in the throne room dressed all in black, a stern, stubborn look on his face. King Valymr seemed to be tired like he'd been up arguing half the night—and perhaps he had.

"Where do you make for next?" he asked after ensuring that they were well supplied for the road ahead. The fairies had done their best, but the elves at least ate meat, something that Queen Pepper's people abhorred.

"Kugdor, I think," Kaden replied. He'd talked it out with Petey and Queen Pepper and decided that the sooner he could get the hardy dwarves on his side, the better. Not to mention, now was one of the only times the dwarven kingdom would be reachable by the outside world before winter storms closed off the land route to Bardok Peaks for months. They could try to find a ship to take them, but dwarves didn't have reputations as great sailors, and they were unfriendly enough to outsiders that few human vessels were willing to tempt fate to trade there.

Kaden had thought about asking Bhalla for a portal there. The wizard had offered his help, after all, and it was incredibly tempting to simply skip the days and weeks of travel for the speed of a teleportation ability, but... the deeper into this quest he got, the more Kaden was convinced that he *needed* that time. If he was going to build an alliance, he couldn't just do it under the banner of his dead father, a man he couldn't even remember. He needed to be known for himself, which meant getting to know everyone he asked to join him against Lucient. Not to mention, Kaden wasn't certain just how much faith-fueled Mana his crew would need in order to succeed at yah'zhaval as complicated as teleportation.

So, if that meant traveling for the next week or two with a surly elven prince by his side until Kaden figured out a way to get through to him, then he'd do it.

King Valymr nodded. "To meet with King Bardicus Blakenshield. You've picked a good time for it." He gestured to Eldrin. "My son has led two diplomatic missions to Kugdor in the past five years. He knows the quickest paths to get there and how to avoid any scouting patrols that might venture out of Shroudscar." Petey shivered, and Kaden stepped a bit closer to him. "He'll gladly help you get there."

"Yeah, he looks real glad about it," Petey muttered. Kaden had to resist the urge to hush him because elven ears were almost as big as goblin ears, and he had a sneaking suspicion that Eldrin could hear the slightest whisper from this range.

"That's very kind," Queen Pepper put in, always ready to play the peacemaker. "We're all grateful for your belief in this quest and your support. No one more so than me, Valymr."

He graced her with a smile. "I appreciate the opportunity to pay my debt, even though it comes at the price of my pride. But

I would ask that you look over my son for me, Pepper. The pride I can afford to lose, but blood I cannot."

"Father." It would have been a whine if Eldrin hadn't been so stone-faced. "I'll be fine. I haven't been a child for over a decade now."

"You will always be my child," Valymr said, tucking a strand of his son's hair behind his ear before pulling him into an embrace.

For a moment, just a moment, Kaden was desperately jealous of Eldrin. The elf was dressed for a funeral, or perhaps for an evening of reciting questionable poetry outside someone's window, but he had his father *right there*, a father who loved him and cared about his future. Kaden had two of those in his life and lost them both before he was even grown to adulthood— before he was even old enough to preserve the memory of his first father.

Eldrin pulled back after another few moments, then turned briskly away from King Valymr and strode past the rest of them out of the throne room. "Boats are waiting for us," he called out as he left them to catch up.

Kaden bowed quickly to the king before hurrying after his son. His final glance back at the monarch saw him sagging onto his throne, one hand over his face. Kaden swallowed hard and looked away. Some things were too private to witness.

The ride back across the lake was fast, the journey along the edge of the woods swifter with Eldrin scouting ahead. They had an elven escort for the first day, with four of them kept solely to their prince and ignored everyone else but Queen Pepper. After they left, Kaden expected Eldrin to start joining the rest of them, at least for meals if he insisted on scouting alone, but he refused.

The first day, Kaden let it slide. Eldrin was probably missing his father, missing his friends. Kaden knew how that felt, and sometimes you needed quiet around you to work through how you felt about things. The second day, he made more effort to invite Eldrin into their group and even got Queen Pepper to help him, but Eldrin spurned their invitations.

"Why would you welcome the son of someone you regard as a betrayer into your midst?" he'd said with a challenging sneer. "I'd rather spend my evening staring at a stump than dealing with your distaste."

"There's no distaste," Kaden had assured him.

"We would be delighted with your company," Queen Pepper had added. Eldrin just turned his nose in the air and stalked off to settle down by himself fifty feet away.

Queen Pepper rubbed her hands together fretfully, her wings beating so fast Kaden could barely see them. "I don't know how to soothe him," she confessed.

Redfern scoffed. "He doesn't need coddling; he needs a swift kick in the behind."

"Ooh, I volunteer!" Millicent said. The pair laughed, but to Kaden, it was no laughing matter. This was another test of his leadership, a trial to see if he could bring someone who had no reason to like him and plenty of reasons to loathe him into the fold, and he *needed* to pass it. He needed to make Eldrin a genuine part of his group, one who was content to be with them and believed in their cause instead of suffering their company as part of his father's penance.

"I don't know what to do," he said quietly to Petey late that night when everyone else but Redfern, who was standing guard, had gone to sleep.

"You need to find a way to make him feel useful," Petey replied around a yawn. "That's how we goblins do it, anyway. Everyone has a role to play, and each role is dependent on the others to make us into an effective unit. It works... mostly."

"What was your role?" Kaden asked, too tired to notice how Petey's ears were already curling in on themselves.

"Uh... I was the butt of every joke. The one who fetched things for everyone else. The one who... you know, it doesn't really matter, just—believe me, it wasn't a perfect system, but at least it keeps the rebellions down."

"Sorry," Kaden said softly.

"It's okay." Petey fell asleep shortly after that, but Kaden was up long into the night, thinking about what he could do to bring Eldrin more fully into the fold. He made the symbol of Orealus over his heart as he finally closed his eyes, hoping for divine guidance while he slept.

*   *   *

Kaden didn't wake up any more inspired than when he fell asleep, but he *did* wake up groggy, grumpy, and not in the mood to be shouted at. That, of course, was the first thing Eldrin did when he noticed Kaden was finally stirring.

"Our great leader graces us with his presence at last," the wood elf said with a sneer. "Are you always the last one to wake up in the mornings, or did you only now decide to let your underlings do your share of the work while you indulge your new station?"

"What are you talking about?" Kaden groused as he sat up, wiping his eyes.

Eldrin waved a hand. "Look around you."

Kaden looked, and… *wow*. The camp was already mostly broken down, a pot of hot tea was brewing over the fire, and there was a serving of traveler's hash sitting on a plate a few feet from him. Duke was staring at it and drooling, but he didn't go so far as to eat it, which was nice.

Petey scowled at Eldrin from where he was tending to the fire. "You looked tired. I thought it would be nice to let you sleep in a bit," he said to Kaden defensively.

"Just the sort of thing I'd expect a sycophantic goblin to say," Eldrin retorted.

"Hey," Kaden said. "There's no need to be rude to him." He glanced around. "Where are Queen Pepper and her guards?"

"She found a patch of bindweed that she wants to collect for her medicine chest. I told her I'd mind camp while the little prince slept in."

Kaden sighed and reached for his food. "Give it a rest."

"Oh, I'm so sorry." Eldrin inclined his head, but there was nothing gracious about it. "Would you prefer I be just like everyone else and worship the ground you tread on? I'm afraid that's not going to happen. To me, you're just a random human who got dropped into a lineage he doesn't deserve and who has command over people who are his betters in every way."

Ouch. But Kaden could see why Eldrin thought that. After all, he'd come to Kel Tyrion and basically shamed Eldrin's father into not only approving his quest and handing over his son to join them but into revealing his private shame. Eldrin had to *hate* Kaden for that, and yet he was still here because he was dutiful to his father.

Suddenly, Kaden knew how he might get through to Eldrin. Ugh, it wasn't going to be fun, though.

He ate his breakfast and took a moment to relieve himself in the nearby woods, then returned to his bedroll and began to pack it up. He moved Vrangar aside and watched Eldrin's eyes follow the weapon. "Do you know any swordsmanship?" Kaden asked.

Eldrin scoffed. "Probably better than you."

"Maybe," Kaden replied. "Let's find out. Do you want to spar?"

Eldrin gaped for a moment, then looked as though a fish had leaped right out of the water and into the bottom of his boat. "You want to test yourself against me? Truly?" he asked with a smug grin on his face.

Kaden shrugged. "I need the practice, and you're here."

"I can spar with you!" Petey interjected, looking between them anxiously.

"No, I'd rather Eldrin do it." Kaden picked up Vrangar and whirled it a few times—still sheathed, of course. He wasn't about to spar with the blade bare. He looped the tie that could be used to hold the sword to his belt around the hilt, then tightened it so it wouldn't fall off. *There. As close to a practice blade as I can get.*

"Very well." Eldrin wound his own blade up in a unique, elegant fashion. It was smaller than Vrangar and would move much more quickly, no doubt. Kaden raised his sword into a guard position and steeled himself for the first attack.

It came faster than he'd imagined. One moment Eldrin was ten feet away. The next, he was right in front of Kaden, cutting up in a motion that would leave him gutted if the blade touched him unsheathed. Kaden jumped back, parrying down and bringing his sword around in an arc for a return strike to Eldrin's head, as Daneyel had taught him. Eldrin blocked with ridiculous ease, then cracked the flat of his blade against Kaden's shoulder. *Snap!*

"You're very slow," Eldrin said with a smirk. Kaden didn't reply, just cut again, this time swinging for Eldrin's midsection. Eldrin danced back, then brought his sword down for another low cut. Kaden parried, Eldrin arced up again, and this time Kaden parried the strike coming in at his shoulder.

Hey, I'm getting the hang of—

Snap! This time the flat of Eldrin's blade cracked against Kaden's thigh. His muscle burned, and he knew he would have a bruise there. "Still too slow," Eldrin mocked. "What was Bhalla thinking, letting you lead this party? You don't have the *skills* to lead us." He struck again, and Kaden parried. He felt the sword hilt warm a bit in his hands, and his next parry was more effortless than the first. Was the power of the blade waking up, even though he'd left it sheathed?

Not yet, he murmured in his head. "I didn't ask to lead this group," he panted, still managing to block Eldrin's strikes but unable to launch any of his own. The elf was just too quick.

"Then why *are* you leading it?" Eldrin snapped before he jumped and turned in a massive downward blow that would split Kaden's skull, sheathed blade or not, if he let it. He blocked the heavy strike, then raised his foot and kicked Eldrin square in the stomach. The prince stumbled back, looking shocked.

"Because Orealus gave me this task," Kaden panted. "And I will do everything in my power to achieve it, whether I'm the best choice for it or not."

Eldrin scowled with great anger and attacked again, a flurry of blows that struck like lightning. Two of them slipped past Kaden's guard, one to his ribs, the other to the same spot on his shoulder as the first strike. He grunted with pain and nearly dropped his sword.

"*Why* did he give it to *you?*" Eldrin angrily shouted. "You were raised as a peasant! You can't fight properly, you've never traveled, you don't even remember your own parents! Why *you?* Why not let *me* avenge my father's disgrace? Why force him to share it with the world?"

There is the heart of it. Kaden had no time to revel in the discovery, though—Eldrin was already landing more attacks. He wore an angry scowl on his face while hitting so hard that Kaden nearly backed out of the clearing and into the trees. He looked at getting a serious injury if he stumbled, and Eldrin continued to attack.

As soon as he thought it, of course, it came true. He caught his left heel on a root, tried to arrest his fall, but it was too late. Kaden went down hard on his back, and Eldrin leaped into the air, his blade slicing down like a scythe. Kaden raised Vrangar with one hand to block, already knowing it wouldn't be enough to completely stop the blow. His other hand brushed against his amulet as he struggled to bring it up to Vrangar's hilt, and then—

A wave of light traveled across Kaden's body and down to his blade. The moment Eldrin's sword touched it, the light transformed into a concussive force, sending Eldrin flying backward. He hit the ground nearly ten feet away, his blade spinning out from his hand. He didn't move.

Kaden stared at the amulet, which was glowing faintly, almost smugly. What... was... *that*? Bhalla had said that the charm would bring out his natural skills—was this a part of that? Or were the amulet and his sword working in concert to shield him? There were so many things he didn't know the answer to yet.

Kaden glanced at Petey, who was holding on to Duke, like he'd had to restrain the dog from intervening, and looked utterly dumbfounded. Kaden nodded his thanks, then pressed to his feet with a groan. Lifting himself proved more challenging than he expected, and he remembered what Bhalla had said about expending power. *How much Mana did that maneuver cost me?* he wondered. He staggered over to Eldrin's side to make sure the elven prince was all right.

Eldrin's grayish-blue eyes were wide open, staring blankly at the sky. His chest moved, but it looked like the breath had been driven out of him because he was barely gasping. "Here," Kaden said tiredly and reached an arm under Eldrin's shoulders to help him sit up.

As Eldrin coughed weakly, Kaden began to speak. "I have so much to learn," he said, as honest in his words as he could be. "I know that. I'm far less prepared for a quest like this than someone born to lead, like you or Queen Pepper. Even Petey has more experience as a fighter than I do. I'm no diplomat, and I'm not well traveled. All I am is the son of a legendary man that, you're right, I can't even recall. And I'm supposed to be able to carry this burden on my own?"

Kaden laughed, but he wasn't feeling amused. "It seems like a joke. When I first found out, I thought it had to be a mistake. There was no way I could unite all the tribes—I'm nobody! Why would they listen to me?" He sighed and glanced up at the sky. Clouds were beginning to roll in, turning the blue to gray.

"But Orealus called me to this task. Whether I think I'm ready for it or not, I must do this. My saving grace comes from the fact that I don't have to do it alone. I have Duke to protect me and remind me of where I come from, Petey to keep my spirits up, Queen Pepper to show me how a leader can act with compassion and still be strong. Even Redfern and Millicent can teach me about preparedness and honor. And you?" Kaden took a deep breath. "I hope that you'll teach me to be a better fighter and keep me humble. I hope you'll help us get to a place we've never been and meet with tribes you're familiar with. I also hope you know that I *want* you to be here, not because I am interested in hurting or humiliating your father. King Valymr is one of the strongest people I've ever met."

Eldrin finally did move on his own, wiping his hand across his eyes. "He is," he said hoarsely. "And he deserves better from his son. I could have hurt you badly during this bout. I… I *wanted* to hurt you for a moment. I'm sorry."

"I'm the one who made you hit the ground so hard you almost broke a rib," Kaden pointed out. Eldrin chuckled.

"It takes more than that to break me… how did you do that, by the way?"

"I'm not entirely sure," Kaden confessed. "It's one of the things I'm trying to figure out now. There's too much I don't know about what I'm capable of with the sword and amulet and how to work them in fighting."

"That's where we start, then," Eldrin said, and it sounded like a promise. Kaden grinned and held out his hand. After a moment, Eldrin grasped Kaden's wrist and shook it firmly. Kaden returned the gesture.

"What in Orealus's name *happened* here?"

They looked over to the edge of the clearing to see Queen Pepper, her hands on her hips, staring at them. Her guards, their arms full of greenery, looked stunned.

"Just making friends!" Petey said, his voice high pitched. "Just having battles and making friends and using weird magic, it's all perfectly normal!"

Orealus would save him if this was Kaden's new standard. Except, come to think of it, it probably was. He began to laugh. Eldrin joined him after a moment.

Well, that's one way to build a bridge, I suppose. Kaden hoped that convincing King Bardicus Blakenshield to join him would result in fewer bruises, but he didn't regret any of it.

He had found a way forward. Right now, that was all that mattered.

CHAPTER 15

Traveling through a snow-covered land was nothing like traveling anywhere else, Kaden quickly found. At first, he found amusement in the light flurry of snowflakes that dusted the ground. As they approached the mountain range and the snow piled higher and higher, the whimsy wore off.

The route to Bardok Peaks, where King Blakenshield and his dwarven kingdom of Kugdor could be found, was a lengthy one. First, they crossed a stretch of water vaster than any Kaden had ever seen before, then they climbed up into snow-capped mountains that went higher and higher until they disappeared into the clouds. Seeing them from a distance had been an awe-inspiring sight. Actually walking into them…

That was a cold, considerably less awe-inspiring experience that threatened frostbite. Their very bones felt frozen as their teeth chattered and their muscles ached with shivers. Along the mountainside, gray stone and black granite peeked out from a blanket of snow. The wind howled between the peaks like a living creature.

"Have you never seen snow before?" Eldrin asked, not nastily—he wasn't nasty anymore, which Kaden was genuinely grateful for—but more like he simply couldn't believe it. "Your town wasn't that far south."

"We got dustings during the winter, sometimes, and the stream threatened to freeze every now and then, but nothing like"—Kaden flapped a hand at the winter landscape all around him—"*this*. I didn't even know it could pile up so high!"

"And this is nothing," Petey said from where he was fashioning a little woolen hat for Bug. Petey had come around on his insistent little pet and was trying to spoil the hopping toadstool as much as it was possible. If it had been a dog, he would have made it fat with treats by now—a cat, he would have filled it to the brim with cream. Since it was a mushroom, he made do by making it little costumes and ensuring that it was protected against the weather when it rode on his shoulder. "During the winter, it gets *intense*. This is nothing but a late summer storm."

"So the snow will melt soon?" Kaden asked hopefully, rubbing his arms with his bare hands and trying not to let on how cold he was. Did the amulet have a way of keeping him warm?

"No, probably not for weeks!" Petey replied.

"Here." Eldrin thrust a leather-wrapped bundle toward Kaden. "Take these. Orealus only knows what my father would say if I let our new leader in the fight against Lucient die of frostbite."

The bundle turned out to be a heavy wool-lined jacket, a wonderfully soft knitted cap, and a pair of large, cumbersome leather gloves that Kaden nonetheless put on with glee. He felt better almost instantly, but... "Won't you get cold?"

Eldrin shook his head. "Not at this time of the year. Elves don't feel the weather the way humans do. Otherwise, we'd never be able to live on our lake—during the winter, the wind blows the water so hard that it freezes along the edges and crawls up our shores, sometimes almost as far as the door to the castle itself."

Wait, what? "You're joking," Kaden insisted. "Snow doesn't crawl. It isn't alive like that."

"It can be when the wind gets behind it."

"Only on bodies of water like yours," Queen Pepper said, turning in a graceful arc to face them. "Don't tease him so, Prince Eldrin."

Eldrin grinned. "Sorry, Your Majesty, but it's too hard to resist sometimes. He makes such an easy target."

"Try harder," Millicent said dryly. Queen Pepper looked at her with big, disappointed eyes, and she tacked on a "Your Highness."

"Why aren't the three of you cold?" Kaden asked. He wasn't surprised Duke was having nothing but fun, running around and marking every snowdrift he could sniff, but the fairies were wearing clothes suitable for a temperate forest, not a snow-covered mountain.

"While we're not built as hardily as the elves, we have natural innate abilities from birth that more than compensate for a change in climes," Queen Pepper explained. "Fairies only exist due to the grace of Orealus and the abilities in yah'zaval, after all." She smiled sweetly. "Have you never wondered how our wings, so delicate and slight, can support our frames? If we were truly light enough for them to lift us on their own, we would be at the mercy of every strong wind that blows through Fayspire!"

Now that he was looking at them... "Your ability helps you fly?"

"It helps us do many things."

"Like fight," Eldrin murmured.

Redfern glared at him. "I can fight well enough to beat the bottoms of a dozen elves with or without my abilities."

"Care to test it?"

"I'm a goblin!"

Everyone suddenly looked at Petey, who clapped his hands over his mouth after realizing just how *loudly* he'd yelled. "Um... I meant to say," he continued, a lot more quietly now that everyone was staring at him, "that goblins are, um, we're well adapted to cold environments down in the, y'know, the caves and everything, and we... uh... we don't get chilly either. Um."

Kaden knew that Petey had just spoken up to diffuse the conflict that had been brewing between their companions, and he came to his friend's rescue. "Then I guess I'm the soft spot in our group for this leg of the journey. I'm relying on all of you to help keep me on pace and on *you*"—he gestured at Eldrin—"to get us to King Bardicus as quickly as possible."

Eldrin looked up toward the windy peaks, his expression uncharacteristically serious. "If the weather was perfect right now, it might take three days to get to his kingdom's entrance. With this snow, it will more likely be a week, and that's if we keep a steady pace and don't get into trouble with rockfalls or avalanches."

Kaden frowned. "What's an avalanche?"

Eldrin rolled his eyes but wrapped an arm companionably around Kaden's shoulders. "Ah, my prince. You have so much to learn."

Kaden did have a lot to learn about travel in this part of the world—not just learning how to manage the cold, but how to cover his tracks, what kinds of animals could still be found foraging through the woods or searching over the rocks for uncovered plants or pieces of lichen. The constant white of the snow was broken up here and there by towering trees with blue, green, or dark-purple needles. Queen Pepper showed him how to make a tea from the tips of those needle clusters—it tasted foul, but she swore it would keep him hale and healthy. There were also gray and black rocky outcroppings, and once, in the hollow of a rotten, half-frozen stump, a cluster of brittle bluebells, so shining and fragile they looked as though they were made of glass.

Eldrin handled most of the hunting and showed Kaden how to identify different animal tracks in the snow. "They show up differently when they have to break ground," he said, pointing at the long, dragging prints that really didn't look like they'd been made by a hare. When Eldrin came back an hour later with a white-furred rabbit next to a mountain pheasant hanging from his hand, Kaden had to admit that the elf knew what he was doing.

It was sort of a relief being with Petey and Duke, to be honest. They were as lost as he was—not that Petey didn't have some experience traveling in the snow, but it had never been at less than a forced march, and he'd always been responsible for the grunt work—clearing snow, finding firewood, digging out a latrine. He didn't know the first thing about tracking or foraging here, and Duke…

Duke was clearly more interested in enjoying himself than hunting. The snow continued to be novel to him, even on the sixth day, when Eldrin assured them all that they were nearly within sight of the massive stone arch marking the entrance to the dwarven kingdom. "It's built into the side of the mountain, so it isn't as obvious a thing as it sounds, especially not right now." He stared up the hill pensively from their campsite for the night. It was still light out, but there was a light snowfall that would make continuing more complicated than it was worth. "I'd like to scout it out. To make sure I'm leading you in the right direction."

"I thought the prince of Kel Tyrion *never* got lost," Redfern said in a too-polite tone.

Eldrin scowled. "And I thought the queen's guard was supposed to be diplomats as well as fighters, yet look at you two."

"Perhaps both of you could scout ahead," Queen Pepper suggested in a way that made it very clear she was *not* recommending it. She required it. "That way, we can all rest easy tonight. Can you be back before sundown?"

"Easily," Eldrin promised, then looked at Kaden. It was becoming a habit—everyone was looking to him before making their final move, and it was both inspiring and intimidating to him.

"I think it would be beneficial," Kaden agreed. "I'd like to know how close we are."

"Close enough that we should start being careful," Eldrin said. "We're getting into rough territory. The lowlands are pretty wild, but some creatures live up here in the heights who aren't afraid of elves, men, or dwarves, and you never know where they might be lurking."

Kaden swallowed, wanting to ask but not wanting to keep looking like a total neophyte. Petey saved him the trouble. "What kind of creatures?"

Eldrin grinned and winked. "That would be telling! I don't want to spoil the surprise, after all." Then he set off up the hill, the snow almost seeming to part for him. Redfern, of course, flew above it and seemed to take a bit of pleasure at being just a tiny bit ahead of the prince.

"It's as though he's just a hundred again," Queen Pepper said, shaking her head as she looked after her bodyguard. "Honestly." She turned to Kaden. "I thought I would take Millicent and go looking for some lacy lattice to go in our stew tonight. It's a kind of vine that grows tight to the trunks of certain pines, and it's a bit tough but quite delicious."

Kaden knew better than to immediately trust the fairy queen's assertion of what was delicious and what wasn't, but he was certainly willing to try it. Anything to give them a break from the monotony of eating the exact same meal three times a day. "That sounds great."

"Will you be all right on your own?"

The question bothered him. He wasn't a *child* anymore, and he knew it was just how Queen Pepper was and that she didn't mean anything by it, but he still felt a curl of irritation in his gut. "I'll be fine. I've got Duke and Petey and Bug, after all."

Queen Pepper smiled. "So you do." A moment later, she and Millicent were whizzing away through the trees.

Kaden looked at Petey. "Just the three of us. It feels like old times."

"Four of us," Petey said with a grin, which quickly turned into a frown. "No, wait, just three of us." He gestured to Bug, who was sitting on his shoulder in his latest jaunty cap, letting out occasional puffs of pink spores. "Where's Duke?"

Kaden looked around so sharply a tendon in his neck burned from it. "Duke?" he called out. There was no answer. That was… bad. The big dog knew to *always* answer his call. "*Duke?*" Still nothing, and calling out any louder might draw unwanted attention.

Kaden got to his feet and started looking for tracks. Duke had been in camp with them. He *had*, Kaden recalled it clearly, so it was just a matter of finding him. There should be tracks, where were they—ah, there! He followed them to the edge of the little clearing in which they'd set up camp, and that was when he ran into trouble. The tracks became indistinct, already filled by the falling snow in places and obscured by the fading sunlight. Nevertheless, Kaden trudged out into the woods for fifty feet before admitting that he had no idea where to go next.

Petey had followed behind him, worry evident in his face and in the heavy droop of his ears. "What now?" he asked.

"I need to find Duke." It was all Kaden could do to keep the panic welling in his stomach at bay. "I need to find—" It struck him like a shaft of sunshine through the clouds. "The amulet!" He reached up and clasped it in his hand. "Its powers must be able to lead us to him!"

"But how will you—oh wow!" Both of them were shocked as a light burst from the amulet, already reading Kaden's intention and responding to his need. Orealus answered his desire through the power of the charm without having to ask. "That's, um…

really bright," Petey said after a moment. "Maybe you could tone it down a little?"

"Right, yeah." Kaden took a few deep breaths, mastering his fear, and the light from the amulet thinned enough that the reflection of it against the snow didn't wholly dazzle their eyes. He looked left, where the light was pointing. "This way."

Petey followed him on a winding path through the trees, one that led uncomfortably far from their camp. The light was getting dim, and Kaden could sense that his friend was about to suggest they turn back and wait for help from the others when—

"There!" He heard it now, Duke's barking. It reverberated oddly like it was bouncing off the rocks somehow. "He's close!" He broke into a run, following the trail of light as it led him closer and closer to his faithful dog. He was going to hug the stuffing out of that dog when he found him. He was going to yell himself hoarse at that dog when he finally reached—

"*Whoa!*" One second, Kaden was on solid ground. The next an entire sheet of snow fell out from under him, sending him tumbling down a steep, rocky wall into a pit. He hit the bottom flat on his back and groaned as his sword Vrangar dug sharply into his ribs.

"Kaden! *Kaden!* Are you all right?"

"F-f... fine," he managed after a second, forcing his eyes open. "Stay up there." The last thing he wanted was for Petey to fall down a hidden hill too. A second later, he laughed, weak but joyful, as Duke bounded over and began licking at his face. "Ugh, *dog*." Kaden ruffled Duke's fur beneath the armor. "Why do you have to get into so much trouble, huh?" Kaden sat up with a wince. "Where are we, anyway?"

"Um... I think you're in a... in a..."

It wasn't like Petey to be so timid when they were alone. "In a what?" Kaden called up.

"Ogre hole!"

Pain forgotten, Kaden jumped to his feet, pulling Vrangar free a second later. That booming, malicious voice was definitely not Petey's. "Who's there?" he shouted into the swirling snow.

The voice, more profound than thunder, laughed an evil laugh. "Who do you think?" it ground out as though it was forcing the words around a mouthful of boulders. "What makes an ogre hole, human? Who makes a *dinner hole*? Dinner for *me*." A shape began to materialize out of the snow ahead of Kaden—dark and looming, nearly twice as tall as a man and three times as broad. "Dinner for *us*!"

Us? Surely there can't be— But there were two more of the shapes appearing beside the first one, not quite as tall but just as menacing. Kaden had never seen an ogre before, but he knew he would never have mistaken the creatures for anything else. These were brutes from legend, scarred and muscular, with heads that seemed small on top of their massive shoulders and hands that were probably big enough to envelop Kaden's entire head. Their skin was ruddy with thickly applied paint—at least, Kaden hoped it was painted because he didn't want to think about how many creatures must have died for all three of the beasts to cover themselves with that much blood.

In their hands they held clubs made of massive branches studded with sharpened bones and antlers. The one in front grinned, showing off teeth like plowshares. "Little human and little dog," he grunted. "A good meal for a cold night."

"Not an easy meal," Kaden promised, keeping his voice level despite it wanting to break. Beside him, Duke growled, baring his own fangs. "Come any closer to my blade, and I'll cut you down with it."

"Don't want an easy meal," the ogre boasted. "Want a fight. Fight to warm the blood, fight to make us strong. *Fight!*" He pounded on his chest with his own club. The needle-sharp points bounced right off his rocky skin. "Fight us, little human! Fight me, then *feed* me!"

"Fight," the other ogres began to murmur, warming to the battle cry. "Fight, fight, fight, *fight*—"

Orealus, save me. I'm going to have to battle three ogres at once. Kaden didn't even know where to start with the brutes. How quickly did they move? How fast were those terribly strong arms of theirs? If he dodged one blow, would he move into another? And how would he protect Duke?

At least Petey had escaped. If he was getting help, Kaden only had to hold the ogres off until backup arrived. He tightened his jaw and raised his blade, prepared for the fight of his life. The lead ogre stepped forward, lifted his club high into the air, and then—

Bang-bangbangbang-bang! The sound of two huge rocks beating a rhythm against each other filled the twilight sky. A spray of what appeared to be sparks, bright and white, floated away on the breeze above Kaden's head. Well, they *looked* like sparks, but they didn't really *move* like sparks...

The ogres froze for a long moment before one of the shorter ones growled, "Dwarves."

Bang-bangbangbang-bang!

"Dwarf war drum, dwarf battle flare," the other grunted. "Dwarves are close. Better to fight them, better to feed on."

"No!" the ogre in the front yelled. "Fight and food right here in front of us! We fight now; feed now!"

"Dwarves are stronger than humans!" the first one snapped, pointing his club upward out of the hole. "Dwarves heat blood. Dwarves fill belly! Dwarves are better food!"

Bang-bangbangbang-bang! The rocky rhythm was getting louder and more insistent now.

"Are close," the second ogre said, actually looking a little bit nervous. "Ready for a fight. The drums are close."

"Drums are useless! Food is *right here*!" The ogre in front brandished his club again, clearly done with arguing. "We eat now!" He turned back to their human prey and brought his club down in a great, whistling smack, hammering it into the spot where Kaden had been standing just a moment ago.

Of course, he wasn't there any longer.

Kaden had been shocked to see something that looked like a long, dark rope slide down the slope and land beside him. He glanced up and saw Petey—ears spread wide, eyes glowing bright yellow—gesture for him to climb just as the last of the sparks wafted away overhead.

Kaden didn't hesitate. He sheathed Vrangar, grabbed Duke around the middle, hauled the big dog close, then snatched the rope—no, it was a *vine*—with his free hand. He climbed as best he could with his legs, but it was hard enough to keep his hold on the rope and Duke simultaneously. Petey somehow managed to haul the two of them up over the edge of the pit before the ogres even noticed they'd left.

Kaden pushed Duke up ahead of him, making sure the dog was all right, before getting up to his knees. Petey threw the vine aside, panting from the work of pulling. Bug was on his shoulder, glowing strangely bright, as though a star had taken up residence inside of him. "How did you—"

"Ssshhh!" Petey whispered sharply before picking up a nearby rock. He smashed it in a now-familiar rhythm against a stone on the very edge of the artificial cliff. The ogres began to argue. "They're dumb, but they have good ears." Petey set the rock down carefully. "Come on, we need to leave now!"

"But won't they follow us back to camp?"

"We can't fight them by ourselves! We have to—" Both of them stopped talking as they heard a heavy *crunch-crunch* that heralded one of the ogres moving toward the cliff. It began to climb. Kaden, Petey, and Duke backed away, Kaden drawing his sword again.

"It's too late," he said grimly. "We'll have to fight them here. Hopefully, they can only come at us one at a time, and at least we'll get the first strike as they crest the edge."

"Their heads are the hardest parts of their whole body!" Petey protested. "I don't know if even Vrangar will be able to make a dent in them."

"Well, we have to try!"

One of the ogre's massive hands appeared first, followed by the top of its bald, snowy head. Two glittering eyes seemed next, and it grinned as it bellowed, "No dwarves, but goblins! More meat for dinner! More fight for—"

Thwack! An arrow came speeding by behind them and struck the ogre right in the eye. Kaden couldn't tell how deep the shaft penetrated, but the ogre roared in pain and fury and clapped its hand over the wound. In doing so, it lost its hold on the cliff's edge and toppled straight backward. Kaden heard the other ogres shout as their comrade landed.

"Do you think the brute fell on his friends?" Eldrin asked as he came up beside him, another arrow nocked and a fierce grin on his handsome face.

Kaden's whole body flooded with relief that he and Petey— and Duke and Bug, of course—were no longer by themselves. Redfern came up beside Eldrin, spear at the ready. Kaden asked, "How did you two find us?"

"We followed the lights," Redfern said. "A hopping toadstool only expels that kind of powerful energy in times of great peril. We knew it had to be serious."

"It still is," Petey said worriedly. "Not even an arrow to the eye is enough to take an ogre out for long."

The four of them peered over the edge. Sure enough, fifteen feet below, the ogres were regrouping, clattering their clubs and pumping each other up to do violence. "That's... a lot of ogres," Eldrin remarked. "Maybe we should..."

"Allow me to assist," Queen Pepper said, flying over to them through the trees with Millicent in her wake. "We saw the lights," she explained to Kaden and the others before glancing down.

"My *goodness*, an ogre sinkhole! I wouldn't have expected one of those so close to Bardicus's very doorstep."

"My queen, perhaps we should—" Redfern began, but Queen Pepper simply held up her hand.

"These sinkholes are quite effective traps but so unstable," she said serenely. She lifted her arms and closed her eyes, exhaling softly, and a moment later, the heavy snow around them began to glow with light. It became brighter, brighter—the glow reminded Kaden of the sparks that Bug had released into the sky.

A moment later, the snow melted to water, all of it gushing down over the cliff's edge like a great wave. It carried gravel, then the rocks at the top of the treacherous sinkhole trap down with it, flowing over the ogres in an enormous gush and burying them completely.

The light faded, and Queen Pepper opened her eyes. "There," she said with satisfaction. A moment later, she fell to the ground.

Kaden moved toward her, but her guards were already there, lifting her up. "I'm fine," she protested weakly. "My faith is strong, but my yah'zhaval will be out of commission for some time. Just need to rest to rejuvenate my Mana."

"You overtaxed yourself," Redfern snapped. "And even an avalanche of rocks won't be enough to keep them down all night."

"Luckily, we won't have to camp out tonight," Eldrin said, his tone boastful even as his eyes were worried. "It turns out we're closer to King Bardicus Blakenshield's realm than I thought we were. Another hour of walking and we'll be there.

"We'll be at the kingdom of Kugdor."

CHAPTER 16

Kaden wasn't sure what he'd expected as they passed through the enormous pillars that signified the entrance into the dwarven kingdom of Kugdor. It wasn't that he'd thought it would be *abandoned*. He'd just expected there to be more of an air of… hauteur, perhaps? Dignity?

After all, this was the home of Bardicus Blakenshield, the Skull Smasher, the king who'd led his people with a fierce tenacity in the last war against Lucient. Kaden's foster father, Daneyel, hadn't said much about the leaders of other tribes that Kaden remembered, not even during his history studies. Still, he'd talked enough about Bardicus for Kaden to remember some things. *A mighty warrior… small in stature, but larger than life in ferocity… definitely someone you didn't want to face across a battlefield.* With all of that buildup, and with what Eldrin had let drop here and there, at the very least, Kaden was expecting a more formal introduction to the king.

What he got was a pair of enormous axes casually barring the way into the mountain before they'd gone more than two paces. "Who goes there?" one of the weapons' wielders demanded. The dwarf was almost two feet shorter than Kaden but probably twice as wide and wore thick metal plate mail that covered practically everything except for his heavy, bushy beard and the tip of his bulbous nose. The mail was engraved with the symbol of a war hammer, one side blunt, the other side ending in a pointed spike. Kaden had never seen anything like it before.

Eldrin pushed his hood back before Kaden could speak up. "Well met, Guardians."

"Oh." The two dwarves exchanged a look, then put their weapons away. To Kaden's astonishment, they turned and walked over to a small table he hadn't even noticed in an alcove a few yards distant, where a lantern burned just enough to provide light for what looked like an interrupted card game. "What're you doing back so soon, then?" the one who'd spoken a moment ago asked before picking up a tankard and taking a long, deep pull from it. "It hasn't even been a year, elfling."

Eldrin sighed impatiently. "Rest assured, it's not because I missed *you*, Hammertoe. This is business for the king's ears only."

"That right?" The dwarf looked over the rest of the party, his expression staying resolutely bored. "Business so important you needed a coupla fairies, a human, a wolf-dog, and a—what's that lad there?"

"Goblin, sir!" Petey squeaked miserably.

"A goblin, really?" The second dwarf doffed his helmet and peered more closely at Petey. "Well, so you are. At that, a titchy little one and growing mushrooms out of his head. A pretty motley group, Your Highness."

"So we are," Eldrin agreed, his smile strained. "So you can imagine the importance of a mission that would bring such a motley group together. We need to see Bardicus."

Hammertoe shrugged. "Go on, then. You know where he spends his days."

Eldrin frowned. "The last time I came here, I was given an escort to the king."

"Eh." The dwarf shrugged. "Can't spare one this time around. We're on the lookout and won't be relieved for another twelve hours. If we left the door unguarded to take you to the king, he'd have our hides for unprofessional conduct."

"Why can't he get someone to relieve you?" Queen Pepper asked before Eldrin could. "Or provide different guardians to act as our escort?" Her voice was gentle but thready with fatigue. Kaden saw Redfern and Millicent draw in more closely around her, ready to reach out if they were needed.

Hammertoe also doffed his helmet, then inclined his head politely. "Begging your pardon, Majesty, but every other dwarf is taking part in the festivities tonight."

"The festivities? *Again?*" Eldrin exclaimed. "Those were happening when I was here almost a year ago! I thought they only occurred every five years!"

"Eh." Both dwarves shrugged. "King Blakenshield decided he wanted them more often than that."

"By Orealus's Oath," Eldrin swore, then turned to Kaden. "When I was last here, the king and his entire royal retinue were all drunk as monkeys after a ripe fruitfall. The festivities are a national holiday for the dwarves, one they traditionally partake in once every five years. Apparently, the king has made it an annual affair. Two weeks of unending revelry—"

"A month," one of the dwarves said. Eldrin looked at him, astonished.

"Wait, *how* long?"

"It's for a month, now."

After a second, Eldrin began to laugh. "A month! A month of festivities every year! Do the ogres know about this? Because if I was your enemy, this would certainly be the moment I'd wait to barge my way into your kingdom."

"Of course, the ogres know it," Hammertoe said, affronted. "Why d'you think *we're* here?"

"We can handle an ogre," the second one snapped. "And we've got the alarm up and ready to raise if more come our way.

A little group like you doesn't warrant that kind of attention, though."

"Perhaps not," Kaden put in. The dwarves glanced uninterestedly at him. "But we just tangled with *three* ogres less than an hour down the slope. Three ogres are long odds for anyone, even a pair of stout warriors like yourselves."

"Three? Naw," Hammertoe said, but there was fresh worry in the furrow of his brow. "That can't be right. They don't work together like that, not unless they're *made* to. You must've counted wrong, boy."

"I left an arrow in one of their eyes," Eldrin countered. "And Queen Pepper Shinyfawn buried them herself in their own pit trap, but they'll dig out before long, mark my words. They'll be hungry and angry too. You might want to think about commandeering some help at the gates tonight, just in case."

The dwarves looked at each other for a long, silent moment. Then Hammertoe broke into a wide smile. "A whole group of ogres! *That* would make for a *real* festivity, wouldn't it!"

"Aye, it would," the second one said gleefully, already reaching for his ax. "I'm tired of beating you over and over again. There's no sport left in it."

"Wait a moment." Kaden stared at them, uncomprehending. "Are you *happy* about the ogres?"

They stared right back before the second one said, "Are you joking? Of *course* we are! It's been terrible boring around here lately."

"Too true." Hammertoe put his helmet back on. "Right, looks like you get an escort after all. I'll take you to the king and organize a hunting party. We're going to have some *fun* tonight!"

Inside the tunnel, lit only by their escort's torch, the layers upon layers of rock muffled the wind. The sound of the visitors' shoes on stone, along with every other sound, echoed off the cave walls. The boisterous sounds of deep voices and hearty laughter came from the occupied portions of the caverns. They heard the occasional drip of water from stalactite to stalagmite. Bats' rubbery wings flapped, and rats squeaked and scurried about. The mines smelled of mildew, bat droppings, and stirred-up rock dust. However, the aroma of kerosene and burning wood wafted from the caverns occupied as residences and meeting places, marked by the addition of metal doors to certain archways. The damp air seeped into the visitors' mouths, tasting of sediment. Yet, once into the heart of the kingdom, Kaden barely had time to admire the beauty of the immense caverns they were led through on the way to the king—ceilings so high he could barely make out the titanic stone figures holding them up, the buildings on either side of the broad walkway set back into the stone itself, each one faced with precise mason work and carved with intricate, crystalline figures. Jewels crusted the gilded pillars that supported the magnificent, vaulted ceilings above polished granite floors. The stonework was a curious sort of beautiful, so novel to him that the sheer alienness of it made him gape in wonder. The group passed various types of mining equipment and scaffolding. Minecart tracks ran along many of the tunnels to facilitate the transport of minerals. Various precious gems, including diamonds, sapphires, and rubies, glinted in the torchlight. Sometimes, dwarves traveled on wooden trollies propelled by mechanical levers. Still, they were clearly taking advantage of the carts for pleasure and not work. Their boisterous joking and laughing echoed in the tunnels, and they each held at least one wooden cup, spilling their drinks as they went around turns.

"Is this anything like Shroudscar?" he whispered to Petey.

Petey shook his head, making Bug bounce. "No. Nothing like it." That was all he seemed willing to say. Before Kaden could decide whether to press him on it or not, they arrived at another immense door, this one glowing with light and echoing with raucous laughter.

"Welcome to the King's great hall," their escort said, walking up to a thin sheet of bronze set vertically in front of one of the doors. He picked up the padded hammer sitting at the base of it, then walloped it so hard that the sharp, metallic sound made Kaden's entire skull ring. "Hey! Got visitors!" the dwarf roared into the sudden silence.

"Well, get them up here so we can get back to the party then," an even louder voice roared back, and the room exploded with new chatter.

The rich, hoppy smell of beer—no, wait, the dwarves called it *grog*, didn't they—was heavy in the air as the guardian led the way into the vast hall. Massive, crackling fireplaces lined the walls, and each pillar held a torch. Kaden blinked in the warm light, his eyes adjusting after the dim tunnels. The whole place was positively seething with dwarves, all in various stages of armed, many of them very clearly drunk off their feet. Huge platters laden with roasted meat were laid across the long tables, as well as dark, heavy loaves of bread and the occasional dish of salad or cooked vegetables. Their guardian escort shouted to various dwarves he recognized as they walked by.

"Gemson, get your face out of that mug and back under your helmet where the rest of us don't have to look at it! Scaventin, where's Scavent—*hey!* Yeah, I'm talkin' to you, you worthless pile of hair! Where's your ax? Go and fetch it already!" Kaden had no idea how the dwarf didn't run out of breath with all the shouting he was doing.

There was a throne at the far end of the room—it was hard to miss. The thing was clearly designed after the mountain it resided in and was almost as big—but that wasn't where they were headed. Instead, Hammertoe led them deeper into the press of dwarves, bumping against their party and their peers like pebbles knocking into each other during a rockslide, until they reached a thick circle of dwarves three people deep, all of them roaring and cheering at whatever the spectacle in the middle of it was.

Kaden was tall enough to see over the crowd, but it took him a moment to realize what he was looking at. At first, it just seemed like a brawl, half a dozen armor-clad bodies charging into each other over and over again. Kaden gradually made out that, in fact, most of the bodies were set against *one* of the dwarves, the one in the center of it all. He was slightly taller than the rest and had a more oversized helm with broad, winglike shapes sticking out its sides. He was also *throwing* every attacker that came within range, either to the side of him, over his shoulder, or in one case so high up in the air that the crash the dwarf made when he came down was loud enough to overwhelm the roar of the crowd for a moment. None of them got up again. They just lay there rocking back and forth and groaning.

"Ha*ha*!" the dwarf in the middle of the fray shouted. "Got to try harder to get the better of *me*, my lads! Who's next? *Who's next?*" He stared out into the crowd and made eye contact with Kaden.

Oh, no. Kaden didn't look away fast enough, and a second later, the dwarf let out a sound of pure berserker energy. This wasn't the sound of a rational being or even a warrior in the middle of a battle. This was the sound of someone lost in bloodlust, lost in their own power, and Kaden knew he couldn't run fast enough to escape that.

The mighty dwarf charged, barreling through his people like a boulder, and before Kaden could do more than raise his hands, he'd been grabbed around the waist, squeezed in a pair of arms stronger than a blacksmith's irons, and thrown into the air with a triumphant shout.

The world seemed to slow down. Even as he was in motion, Kaden found himself able to focus on everything happening around him. His companions were in a state of chaos, mouths opening as they began to shout. Redfern had already started to fly up toward him, but there was no way the fairy would reach him in time to do more than slow the hard landing he had ahead of him, and Queen Pepper's ability was exhausted. If he came down the wrong way on that hard granite floor…

Then don't. You're in control of your body, your mind, your weapon. Save yourself.

As soon as he thought it, the way out seemed clear to Kaden. He arched his back, taking himself from a gangling sideways sprawl into a smooth twist, and pulled Vrangar free at the same time. Not just the blade—the entire sword, including its scabbard.

As he turned toward the ground, Kaden raised the sword high above his head, and just before he landed, he brought the flat of the blade down on the very top of the dwarf's helmet with a resounding *CLANG*. His feet hit the ground at the same time the giant dwarf's bottom did, the force of the blow knocking the warrior down.

The sudden silence in the hall was so startling that Kaden almost dropped Vrangar. He stared apprehensively into the crowd, where only second ago dwarves who had been cheering and carousing were now staring blankly, mugs of grog forgotten, mouths agape.

Eldrin was the one to break the silence, and he did it with a wry grin and a flourish toward Kaden. "That's one way to introduce yourself to Bardicus Blakenshield, my prince!"

Bardicus… wait, this dwarf was the *king*? Kaden backed up a step and lowered his weapon, looking apprehensively at the dwarf he'd knocked down, who was already getting back on his feet. The entire hall seemed to hold its breath as the king took his helmet off and examined the dent on the top of it with a frown. He turned his dark, glittering eyes on Kaden, and for a second, Kaden was more afraid of him than he had been of the three ogres.

"Well, damn," the dwarf king said at last. "I suppose that's what I get for letting my blood get the better of me. Hammertoe!"

Their dwarf escort stepped up smartly. "Aye, sire?"

"Who the hells have you brought into my kingdom without so much as a formal announcement?"

"Why be formal?" Hammertoe asked. "We all know the elf prince, don't we? Besides, they came with good news!" He smiled a broad, toothy grin. Several of his teeth, Kaden noticed, were either capped by or entirely replaced with gemstones. "Ogres, just down the valley. These lowlanders have already tangled with them."

Bardicus perked up instantly. "Ogres? More than one?"

"*Three!*" Their escort rubbed his mailed palms together gleefully. "Ripe for a hunt, they are!"

"That many, altogether?" The king looked over their party, lingering on Kaden, then Eldrin. "Lucky lowlanders to have lived through it."

"Luck be *damned*—" Eldrin began but stopped when Queen Pepper shook her head ever so slightly.

"Take ten dwarves," King Bardicus said after a moment, wiping his forehead with a hand before jamming his helmet back on his head. He accepted a tankard of grog from another dwarf, and that seemed to mark the end of the tension as voices began to rise in conversation around them once again.

Hammertoe frowned as his king drained the tankard in one long swallow. "That's too many of us to make it much sport."

Bardicus smacked his lips together as he lowered the tankard. "Sport of any kind is hard to come by lately, lad. We don't open a vein of gold just to hoard it for ourselves. Get on with you, then."

"Yes, sire," Hammertoe muttered, then turned and began to walk away, shouting out more names without a single backward glance. The king, meanwhile, waved away the inhabitants of a nearby table and sat down, then gestured for them to do the same.

"No ceremony here, not during the festivities," he said expansively, motioning for another dwarf to bring over a whole tray of mugs.

One was plunked down in front of each of them, and the dwarf carrying it paused to whisper in Kaden's ear, "Well done, settin' him back on his heels like that!"

The king pointed a thick finger at his server. "Out of here with your rot, Malacheen, or I'll let the lad do the same to you!"

"As if I'd leave *my* head open like that," Malacheen said with a mock sneer before dancing out of range of the king's thrown tankard. Grog splattered all of them, and Queen Pepper sighed the sigh of the very put-upon. Bardicus started in on another mug, and Kaden took a moment to more carefully examine the king sitting across from him.

He was tall for a dwarf. Kaden knew that better than most now—tall and immensely strong. His beard was reddish brown, the color of an old wine cask, and was kept neater than any other dwarves Kaden had seen so far. He had a head that looked almost too large for his bulky body and hands that seemed like they could crush rock. Kaden was surprised that he wasn't bruised just from being grabbed in hands like that.

"I confess, the last thing I expected tonight was an influx of visitors. Eldrin, what sort of bee got up your father's bum to have him sending you out here again so soon?"

Eldrin's glare was so hot it should have scorched the king's clothes. "It wasn't *his* idea, and I'll thank you for being more respectful of my father in my presence."

"Eh." The king waved the criticism off. "Whose idea was it, then? Pepper's?" He looked at her now. "You haven't changed a bit, Your Majesty," he said, but he didn't sound pleased to see her. "Still as smooth-faced as the sheerest cliff I've ever scaled."

Kaden frowned. Was that a compliment or an insult? He couldn't quite tell. Neither could Redfern or Millicent, from the way they were exchanging glances. Queen Pepper, for her part, gracefully inclined her head. "And you also look just the same, King Bardicus, even if you do smell a bit worse for wear."

To Kaden's surprise, the dwarf began to laugh, slapping his knee with his free hand as the rest of his grog splashed to the floor. There was practically a pool of it around him by now. "Ha! Given that you last saw me drenched in blood and sweat, that's saying something, that is." He glanced at Kaden. "So, Pepper. You finally dragged yourself out of your forest, and you came all this way with a too-tall human boy, a goblin, and some pets." His eyes narrowed. "Too tall and too familiar. I know what you're here for now, and the answer is no."

Eldrin bristled. "You don't know why we're here."

"I might not be the sharpest ax in the land, but I know a recruiting party when I see one," Bardicus retorted. "Especially one with a boy who looks too much like King Karatheas for comfort. Some bastard get of his, I suppose?"

"No," Kaden said, a bit hurt but determined to hide it. "I'm my father's true son. Bhalla saved me before the final battle."

"Eh, so you say." Bardicus grabbed another tankard and took a long swig. "Not that it matters to me. Blood is blood, but either way, I won't be dragged into a fight that's not mine."

"Bardicus, helping us fight against Lucient is the righteous choice," Queen Pepper said.

The dwarf king just shrugged. "What do I care for righteousness? Where has Orealus been all these years, eh? Letting Lucient kill his chosen one, letting his armies devour our people, rip our homes apart—I haven't forgotten the last war, not at all. We dwarves are better off well out of another one."

"It's a chance to regain your honor," Eldrin pressed.

Bardicus Blakenshield laughed. "What honor do I need beyond taking care of my own people? I won't be part of another hopeless cause, not ever again. I won't let my hopes be raised like that just to have them dashed to pieces, like a piece of cheap glass masquerading as a diamond. No. If Karatheas could have held us together, he would have, I've no doubt of that." The king looked directly at Kaden. "Your father was a canny one, a great leader—for a human. He did his best, but it wasn't enough. Against Lucient, nothing will be enough."

"So you'll just hide here forever?" Petey said, his voice squeaky with fear but still firm. "Even if you're not being used, like us, hiding away makes *you* partially responsible for the damage Lucient will wreak upon the world."

King Bardicus growled—literally growled. "I won't be chided on the subject of *responsibility* by a *goblin*. You want to fight about what I should be doing, we can fight right now! I'll—"

"But you're so bored," Kaden interjected.

Bardicus Blakenshield stopped his slow rise from the bench. He looked at Kaden for a long moment, then sat back down. "Aye, I am," he said, softer now. "We all are. My people are born fighters, and they've been spoiling for a good one for over a decade. But just because they want it doesn't mean I'll go throwing them at every little war that comes their way, and that includes yours, lad. You want to prove you can handle the responsibilities of a king? Then prove to me that you're more than just a figurehead, that any army you lead will have a real chance to defeat the Great Deceiver. Show me that, and I will reconsider my stance on joining your fight. Until then?" He shook his head. "Not a chance, lad, not a chance."

Kaden nodded, disappointed but not crushed. If Bardicus Blakenshield was a prime example of how dwarves fought, perhaps best they did not join until there was actual *fighting* to do. Otherwise, everybody in their party might end up thrown through the air at some point. "That's fair, I suppose."

"You can take 'no' well enough, at least," King Bardicus said. "So, I'll not send you away from my kingdom *completely* empty-handed. There's a man you ought to be looking for, a man eager to prove himself in the service of anyone who'll get him close to a fight with Lucient. He finds work as a mercenary and can sometimes be found in the company of a disreputable old satyr. He's a canny one—knows the land, knows the people in it, and always knows where a fight can be found."

"What's his name?" Kaden asked, his interest piqued.

Bardicus drained his grog, belched appreciatively, and slammed the tankard down on the table. "Weylyn, lad. He goes by Weylyn, the Son of the Wolf."

CHAPTER 17

The sun seemed almost cruelly bright as the party descended Bardok Peak the next day, at least if Petey's grumblings were any gauge of it. The air was too cold, then too warm, the ground was terribly rough, and Bug felt heavier than ever.

Kaden was inclined to agree, shielding his eyes from the light that reflected brightly off the snow. He wasn't as miserable as Petey seemed to be, but it was a near thing.

"I did warn you two about the grog," Eldrin said with absolutely no sympathy in his tone whatsoever.

"I only had a single cup," Kaden muttered, rubbing his temple as they finally left the last of the snow behind them and reached a scree field above a scenic, vividly blue lake. He'd have appreciated the view more if his head wasn't pounding like a farmer setting fenceposts. "It was a *toast*. I couldn't refuse."

Eldrin shook his head. "You need to learn to fake drinking and fast, or you'll never last around the dwarves. They toast absolutely everything, large or small, and believe no meal is complete without a pint or two of grog. Morning *and* night."

"How do they even manage to rise from their beds in the morning?" Petey moaned, stumbling a little ways down the scree field. Tiny rocks shifted beneath his feet, dark and jagged, and he almost fell before Redfern caught the back of his cloak and hoisted him straight.

"Dwarves sleep on beds carved from boulders," Eldrin said with a laugh. "Wouldn't you want to get up too?"

"Keep drinking the water I gave you both," Queen Pepper instructed from her place at the front of the party. "The herbs in it will clear your heads and soothe your stomachs." An evening's rest had done wonders for her, and she seemed renewed after her light-filled exertions yesterday. Kaden wasn't going to make a habit of asking her to help like that, though—seeing her laid so low had been frightening, almost more frightening than dealing with the ogres themselves. The thought of losing one of these people, people who were following him not just as a leader, but that he counted as friends… he couldn't imagine it.

Speaking of things he couldn't quite imagine, his memory of what the dwarf king had told them last night was rather blurry. They needed to go find a man named Weylyn, which means they had to travel to… "Where are we going again?" Kaden asked after taking a long pull from his waterskin. The herbs made the drink bitter, but he *did* feel a little better with every sip he took.

"Whaldalf's Landing," Eldrin replied, peering out into the distance. "It's a fishing village just north of the peaks here and a good spot to catch a bigger ship heading for other parts of the coast. If this Weylyn person is in Westramore, then we're definitely going to want to sail there. It'll take another week's march to get to the village, though, and the terrain is… challenging."

"More mountains?" Petey asked, curling his hands over his enormous ears and tugging fretfully at them. "Because even *I'm* getting tired of mountains, and I've spent most of my life in them."

"It's not… the mountains, exactly." Eldrin shared a look with Queen Pepper. After a moment, she inclined her head and sighed.

"There are more than a band of ogres out there who could cause trouble for us," she said, her lips terse. "If we're fortunate, we won't run into any of those beings on our trip."

"But when have we been fortunate thus far?" Redfern muttered.

"We're all alive," Kaden pointed out. He felt a little foolish stating the obvious, yet it seemed like it needed to be said. "Even though we've been attacked more than once. I'd call that pretty fortunate."

"Well, now we'll *certainly* be attacked," Eldrin said with his odd blend of merriness and contempt. "Since you've just tantalized the forces of darkness with that little speech." He began to stride ahead, picking out a safe path for those without wings to follow. "Come on. We've got to keep a good pace if we're going to get to Whaldalf's Landing in good time."

Queen Pepper explained a bit more about their surroundings and their potential dangers when they made camp that night. "These mountains used to be quite the stronghold for Lucient's forces," she said as she stirred that evening's pot of stew. Somehow, she managed to keep changing the flavor of it enough to make it palatable—Kaden didn't want to think about having to choke down the same exact thing day and night.

"Of course, the dwarves have always lived here and defended their territory fiercely," she went on, "but those ogres we met back in the forest are far from the worst this region can offer. There are also some very fierce trolls."

"And fallen spirits," Redfern said.

"Don't forget the goblins," Petey added with a sigh.

Eldrin grunted. "Dark elves," he almost spat.

"Dragons," Millicent put in as she added some herbs to the pot. "Bandits, human and otherwise."

"And those poor giants," Queen Pepper finished sadly. "I felt so sorry for them in the last war. They've been enslaved by the Great Deceiver for a very long time."

"You'll feel less sorry for them after one of them smashes your father's leg so badly the bones couldn't be put together again," Eldrin snapped and stood up from the fire. "I'm going to check the perimeter." He stalked off into the darkness. Queen Pepper looked meaningfully at Redfern, who rolled his eyes but grabbed his spear and flew off after Eldrin.

"He was quite young when his father was wounded," Queen Pepper said softly. "I think having King Valymr return home permanently damaged has scarred Eldrin as well, in some ways."

"At least he *had* a father to come home to him." Kaden winced as soon as the words left his mouth—he didn't mean to sound so petulant, so *angry*. Yet he couldn't deny that there was a part of him, a part that seemed to grow day by day, which resented the fact that he would never know his real father.

He'd had Daneyel, his Pa, who had done right by him and been a loving paternal figure in his life, but there had always been a... a *distance* there. Kaden hadn't understood it for the longest time, but now he thought he did. Daneyel had loved him. He was sure of it. But perhaps he had never quite been able to accept Kaden as his son, not when he'd first met him as the son of his king.

"Loss is always hard to bear," Queen Pepper said, laying a small, cool hand on top of Kaden's. He looked down, surprised to see that he'd clenched his fist so tight that his nails were cutting into his palm. "Whether it is the loss of a parent, or a spouse, or an ideal."

Oh. Of course, Queen Peeper lost her husband too. The fairy she had been married to for centuries, if what Kaden knew of her long lifespan was true. He opened his mouth to apologize, but Pepper just shook her head.

"The greatest balm for a loss like that is love and faith," she said with a smile and inscribed the holy symbol over her heart. "I have faith in Orealus and in my friends. I have a love for my people and all of you here. I'm not alone, despite the many losses I've faced over my life, and I have the chance to make the world a better place now. How could I lose myself to sadness and anger when I also possess such joy?"

Was it possible for a person to be *too* good? Kaden felt both heartened and a little dismayed by the queen of the fairies. How could he ever become the kind of leader she was, someone who had a love of her people yet still commanded respect thanks to her abilities? The way she worked her abilities was impressive, but she didn't need it to inspire the best in Redfern and Millicent. Even Eldrin treated her with deference, and Petey just about fell over himself to do whatever she asked.

When Kaden looked up from his ruminations, he found her still watching him. "Whatever you're wondering about, it will come in time," she said.

"Can you read my mind?" he asked quietly.

"No, my dear, just your young face." She patted his cheek, then passed him a bowl. "I think this is just about ready!"

It was good that Pepper was there to keep them well fed because the trek was even more arduous than Eldrin had said it would be. The mountains were jagged, broken up at the bottoms by boulders left behind by ancient glaciers, and it seemed like every turn brought a new sort of peril, whether from nature in the form of rockslides or enemies of one kind or another.

Twice they had to detour around old battlefields to avoid vengeful fallen spirits, whose wails set every hair on Kaden's body on end and made Duke bark nonstop. Once, they were almost found by a goblin patrol, and it was only Petey's sharp ears and an unexpected spray of truly foul black spores from Bug that kept the other goblins from venturing further into their hiding place.

"We should have just fought them," Eldrin said between gags once the goblins were gone. "Anything would be better than this filthy stench."

"It's not—so—" Kaden couldn't quite finish the sentence before turning around and vomiting in the far corner of the cave.

"Oh, for the love of Orealus." Millicent pulled a jar out of her pocket, uncapped it, and wiped the corner of a handkerchief in the contents. She quickly smeared a line of it beneath Kaden's nose, then Eldrin's, and Duke's, too, for good measure. "Mercalyptus oil blocks the smell. And it will dissipate completely in another few minutes, you absolute children."

"Next time, offer the oil *faster*," Eldrin said, but he had stopped gagging, at least. He helped Kaden straighten up. "You all right?"

It was a strange way to bond, but if it worked for Eldrin... "Yes, I think so."

"Then let's get going, and keep a distance from this little *menace* and his vile pet!"

"Hey!" Petey protested, patting Bug on his toadstool head. "I'm not a menace!"

Eldrin grinned. "But you don't deny you could be considered a vile pet."

"*Hey—*"

"Dear friends," Queen Pepper said, more than a hint of sharpness in her tone. "I would greatly love to make camp a little closer to the coast tonight, so we'd best get moving, don't you think?"

There was only one thing any of them could say to that. "Yes, milady."

After a week of battling their way past crevasses and cliffs, around unexpected snow, and through thorn-encrusted trees, they were finally within a day's march of Whaldalf's Landing. Even better, the beach was clear of the boulders that had obstructed it for most of their trip, so their final leg could be made by walking along the flat, pale sandbank, the only obstructions the occasional grass-topped dune or outcropping of twisted, gnarly pine trees that had been bent into fantastic shapes by the constant wind. It was a welcome reprieve.

"What is Whaldalf's Landing like?" Kaden asked Eldrin as they marched along at a brisk pace. Petey was right beside them, while Queen Pepper and Millicent flew a few paces back, and Redfern took the lead.

"Oh, it's a typical human fishing village—smelly and sooty and very gray." Not the grand ole ship depot of a village that was once renowned for its trade, medicine, marketplace, and exotic fish in the old times. He plowed ahead before Kaden could do more than make an offending noise. "The color isn't their fault, at least—the buildings are made from mountain slate, which is wonderful for keeping the damp off but comes in gray, light gray, or dark gray. And the smell is mostly from fish, not human waste. They're pretty decent about that. It's a fairly dismal place, but there are spots of brightness in it. The grand market, for one. They're the biggest village around for leagues, and once every two weeks, the smaller merchants pile into the Landing and—"

Kaden didn't even know what he was seeing before his body was in motion, shoving the elf flat down onto the sand as he grasped his amulet and poured his will into it. *A shield, a shield!* Not five feet away from them, a barrage of thin black arrows, their tips crusted with green, were suddenly caught in the golden light of Kaden's amulet. The closest one was less than a foot from his own face.

"Dark elves," Eldrin gasped, leaping to his feet and pulling out his own bow. "It's an ambush!"

"From where?" Kaden demanded.

The next round of arrows answered that question, arcing high from a distant copse of trees and coming down at an angle that would deliver them over his shield. He tilted the light barrier from the amulet to knock them aside, but he was beginning to feel the effort of using it in such a new way. His chest tightened, and his vision began to blur with fatigue.

"Release it!" Queen Pepper shouted, her hands raised in a position of power. Kaden dropped the shield, and a powerful spray of seawater jetted past them a moment later, knocking aside the arrows Kaden had caught as well as the others that were still incoming. A moment after that, Redfern, Millicent, and Eldrin darted inland for the grove of pine trees the attack had been launched from, Eldrin already firing into the low branches. Kaden heard someone scream.

Another arrow flew his way. He didn't bother to use the amulet's power this time, simply cut it out of the air with Vrangar. "Come on!" he said to Petey, then charged after the others, Duke running hard at his heels.

The fight was raging by the time Kaden got to the trees. Four dark elves held their own against Eldrin and the fairy guard, pressing them hard. Kaden ran into the mix and swung at one of the two attackers who had cornered Eldrin. The dark elf parried with two single-edged blades and turned to face him fully.

He was both quite like Eldrin in appearance and nowhere close at all. They were of a similar height, and their ears and facial features had the same shape, but the dark elf's hair—all of their hair—was either stark black or pure white, nothing in between. This one had white hair and dull, grayish skin that seemed to absorb, not reflect the sunlight. His irises were lantern-yellow, similar to Petey's, but his pupils were blood red.

"Ready to die, then?" he hissed, and quicker than Kaden could blink, the dark elf attacked with both blades, blocking Vrangar with one knife while slashing the other toward his belly. It was such a fast attack that Kaden wasn't able to deflect it.

Fortunately, he didn't need to. Duke had already grabbed the dark elf by the leg, clamping his massive jaws around the creature's calf and jerking him off balance. The dark elf screamed with pain and fell, but even in his agony, he managed to thrust his knife back at Duke. Duke's armor manifested just as the blade struck, and it scraped harmlessly off the dog's side. The dark elf's eyes widened.

"What magic is this?"

"Nothing you'll ever see again," Kaden snarled as he raised his sword high, ready to strike down straight through the dark elf's heart. Then... he hesitated.

He knew he shouldn't stop—every nerve in his body was clamoring for him to finish the blow. But he had never killed another person before, not even one of the goblins who'd murdered Daneyel. At that moment, it felt impossible that he should *ever* be able to kill someone like the being before him, someone with thoughts and feelings, someone with a face and a name. How could he do it? What gave him the right to end someone else's life?

"—den! Kaden, look out!"

Shaken out of his daze, he glanced toward the warning—but too late. An arrow took him in the meat of his upper left arm, knocking Kaden down onto his side. He bit back a scream. The wound burned like *acid*, sharp and terrible, like no pain he had ever felt before. The dark elf he had loomed over a second ago got to his feet and, with a bloodthirsty smirk at Kaden, ran off toward a nearby boulder field. Kaden watched him go, shaking like a leaf as reality set in.

Failed. You failed. Failed, failed, failed... When the next wave of excruciating pain came, Kaden couldn't keep the yell inside.

"Oh, no." Millicent was beside him in an instant, ripping the arrow out—Kaden screamed again—and tying a bandage to his arm, not *on* the wound, but just *above* it. "Oh no, oh no..." She looked away toward someone else for a moment. "Get the queen!" she shouted, then looked down again, her violet eyes wide and scared.

Petey dropped in beside him a moment later, his ears quivering with fear. "What happened?" he whimpered.

"Poison arrow," Millicent replied, almost briskly enough to mask the tremor in her voice. "I've cut off the blood flow to the limb as best I can, but I'm sure some of it's slipped into his body by now. If too much of it makes it to his heart…"

"He'll die." That was Eldrin, nothing teasing in his voice now. He sounded cold, stark. "He'll die, and this will all have been for nothing."

"He will not die."

Queen Pepper touched his neck, and a wave of warm, soothing energy flowed from her hand down his shoulder and into his arm. The acid burn eased, and Kaden felt his muscles begin to unknot a little. "He will not die," Pepper repeated firmly. "Not if we get him to Whaldalf's Landing in time. Those people have lived alongside the dark elves for generations. If anyone knows the secret of combatting their poisons, it's them."

Eldrin snapped his fingers suddenly, animation rushing back to his face. "The Davenrich family! They traffic in herbs and medicines, and their stall always seems to have a line on market day. We need to get to them."

"How will we get him there?" Petey asked.

In answer, Eldrin bent down, grabbed Kaden's good arm, and used it as a lever to sling him over his back. "I'll get him there," he said grimly. "The rest of you just need to keep up." He set off at a brutally fast pace, jostling Kaden with every step. The pain came back, the wound's burn encompassing his entire arm now, even with Queen Pepper using her ability to combat it. Kaden just clamped his jaw, shut his eyes, and held on to his sanity for dear life.

With all his energy focused so tightly on enduring the pain, Kaden didn't have a good sense of how much time was passing. It felt like it could have been days since Eldrin had picked him up, and yet when the elf suddenly laid him down, he was genuinely shocked that the sun was still in the sky. Kaden stared muzzily at the faces hovering over him—Petey and Queen Pepper, Eldrin looking tired and angry and worried all at once, and… wait, who was this girl? What was she saying?

Kaden's hearing faded in and out with every breath, but there was no mistaking the authority in the strange girl's voice as she said, "We must get him to my mother. Pick him up again and follow me. Now!"

CHAPTER 18

Drifting up out of the soft, soothing darkness that cradled Kaden felt like floating in the ocean. He had never sailed on the ocean before, but he remembered Daneyel telling him stories of it, the terrible depths and many creatures, and the simultaneous danger and beauty of it all. "Merfolk are rumored to live there," he'd said one night, pointing at a spot on the map, "in a great secret underwater city. There are also beasts in the depths who would dwarf even a giant."

Kaden sighed to himself, remembering how his father had looked as he spoke of such things—a bit distant, a bit longing. Had he ever been to the ocean himself? Was it like this there, cool and dark and comfortable? Was it…

"Mother, I think he's waking up."

Wait, who was that? It was the voice of a woman, but not Queen Pepper or Millicent. Perhaps not a woman, but a girl… she sounded young, but her intonation was soft and sincere.

Warm fingertips pressed firmly to his wrist. "His heart rate is increasing a bit," an older woman said. "He's starting to come out of the healing sleep. Good."

"But you said it would take another week!" the young voice exclaimed.

"I said it *might* take another week." The warm hand released him, and Kaden fought to blink his eyes, to show some other sign of consciousness. "I also said he might wake up faster, and so he is." He heard a low chuckle. "Not too surprising, if he really is who his companions say."

"Do you believe them, Mother?" the girl asked. "Really? Could he actually be King Karatheas's son?"

The older woman sighed. "I don't really know what to think of the tales they're telling. I want to believe them, Ada, but... ah. Look." He heard the smile in her voice. "He really *is* waking up."

How could she tell? It was only then that Kaden realized he was finally getting somewhere with his efforts to blink. The darkness behind his eyelids split in the center, revealing the fuzzy image of a ceiling illuminated by muted candlelight. A face bent over him, and the fuzziness slowly resolved into the most beautiful girl that Kaden had ever seen before. She had light brown skin that practically glowed in the candlelight and long, curling black hair held back from her face by a band of blue cloth.

Her eyes were the most astonishing thing about her, though— they glittered like drops of dew on a fresh spring leaf, like, like... what were the gemstones called, Kaden had never seen one before but... *emeralds*, that was it. If they were indeed as precious as people said, then they had to be at least as beautiful as her eyes.

The girl rolled her eyes and leaned back. "He's awake, but he's obviously not thinking clearly."

Wait, what? Had Kaden actually said some of that... out loud?

"All of it," the girl said. "I've never been compared to a wet leaf before. Am I meant to be complimented or insulted?"

"He's just waking up after four days of sleep," the older woman said from somewhere to the left. Laboriously, Kaden turned to face her. With a similar hair style and skin tone, she looked like an old version of her daughter, at whom she was shaking her head. "The last thing he needs right now is the piercing side of your tongue. Go and tell his friends he's conscious again, but don't let them in until I say."

"Yes, Mother." The girl got up and left without a second glance.

The older woman laid a hand against Kaden's forehead, and he noticed she had light brown eyes. "Don't mind, Adena," she said absently. "She's never met a person yet she couldn't find something to argue about with. I *would* recommend keeping any more compliments to yourself until you're a bit more cogent, though." She removed her hand. "Your fever is completely gone, so we can't blame anything you say on delirium now."

"Where'm... I?" Kaden managed after clearing his throat. Ugh, his mouth was so *dry...*

The woman seemed to read his mind, propping his head up as she brought a cup of water to his lips. A little of it spilled down his cheeks, but Kaden got a few blessed swallows down in the process. "You're in Whaldalf's Landing," she said, taking the glass away and wiping his face. Kaden felt a bit embarrassed to need such basic help, but he was so exhausted he could barely keep his eyes open even though he'd just woken up. "I am K'Lani Davenrich, an herbalist and fisherwoman. Your friends brought you to me after you'd been poisoned by a dark elf."

Memories of the fight suddenly flooded back into Kaden's mind. He stiffened. "Are they all right?" he asked hoarsely. There had been so many arrows, and they'd been outnumbered...

"They're all fine. You were the only casualty." She smiled briefly, and the expression made her look years younger—much more like her daughter, except for the fact that Kaden hadn't seen Adena smile yet. "Your friends have been quite concerned for you, but for all their battle prowess and spiritual abilities, they couldn't fix this.

"I drew the poison out of your blood with special teas and poultices over the first three days," she continued, "but it wasn't until last night that I could tell you were truly on the road to recovery. And now you're awake! That's speedy progress."

Kaden wondered a little bit at that. He'd always been healthy but not immune to the sicknesses that had cycled through his village. Had the amulet helped him survive? He fumbled a hand for his neck… yes, there was the crystal. It lit up at his touch, lightening the room and making the shock on K'Lani's face very easy to see.

"Oh, my." She shakily made the symbol of Orealus over her chest. "You—but that's a wizard's tool, for it to work like that. Are you a wizard?"

Kaden shook his head. "No." He knew he didn't have that kind of power, but… Bhalla *had* said that the amulet would enhance the hidden abilities within him over time. Did that include a slight resistance to poison? Was that why he'd recovered so quickly?

"Then you really are the…" K'Lani stood up abruptly, pressing a hand over her mouth. Kaden was surprised to see her eyes had filled with tears. "Oh, I didn't believe it," she whispered. "I didn't want to believe it. It's been so many years, and we lost so much. We all lost so much… I couldn't let myself believe someone in the king's family might have survived the final battle."

This was more than the reaction of a simple village woman. "What do you know of the final battle against Lucient?" Kaden asked.

"More than I want to. More than… no." She shook her head. "I won't relive this now, not right now. I need to think, I need to—your friends, they want to see you. I will get them." She exited the room quickly but left the door open. More light pooled in, and Kaden released the amulet, which faded to a gentle, almost unseeable glow. The quaint room had hardwood floors and grey stone walls and was furnished only with the chicken-feather bed, a sturdy wardrobe, a nightstand cluttered with an oil lamp and dark bottles of liquid, and a small writing desk and chair.

What had just happened? How had he upset her? What did she know about the fight against Lucient?

All of these questions would have to wait, though, for a moment later, Duke bounded into the room, closely followed by Petey. Kaden chuckled weakly as his dog immediately began to lick his face. "Ugh, gross," he murmured.

"Kaden!" Petey's eyes were wide and so bright they could have been reflecting the moon. He sat on the edge of Kaden's bed, making the chicken-feather bed dip. "You really are awake! Oh, thank Orealus, we were all so worried about you. Even Eldrin was, and you know that expressing concern of any kind is as painful as setting a broken bone for him—"

"Hey," Eldrin protested, crossing his arms as he entered the room. "I express myself just fine. If I'd needed to worry about Kaden after a little wound as he got, then he wouldn't be worthy of leading me."

"Says the elf who carried him for three hours on his back," Queen Pepper said, flying neatly around Eldrin's shoulder and coming to the other side of the bed. She landed softly on the floor and patted Kaden's shoulder. Her touch was just as refreshing as K'Lani's but far more comforting. "I'm so relieved that you're awake again," she said. "K'Lani told us you were doing well, but she didn't want to expose to you any additional ailments by allowing us in and out of the sickroom."

"She said I wasn't clean enough!" Petey scoffed. "Me! I'm the cleanest goblin ever... next to my mother, of course. And I even washed Duke!"

"Thank you," Kaden said. Surrounded by his fellow travelers, his friends, basking in their company... it was enough to bind his throat with grateful tears. He knew he'd come close to death, too close, but at the same time, Kaden was relieved that he was the only person to be harmed during the fight. Except... "Where are Millicent and Redfern?"

"Helping Ada ready her family's goods for the market," Pepper said. "It's not for another two days, but apparently much work goes into brewing herbal remedies and preparing poultices and medicines for sale. Many of the treatments K'Lani specializes in are also known to us and, assisting in their preparation is the least we can do for all the help she and her daughter have given you."

"It's a good thing you aren't staying much longer," K'Lani said from the door. She sounded much brisker now, and from the way she stood, hands on hips, she'd clearly regained control of her emotions. "Your people are too efficient. I'll forget how to brew my own potions at the rate they're going. Now." She clapped her hands. "You've seen he's recovering well, but he's also tired. It's time for you all to leave."

"Can't Duke stay?" Kaden asked at once. He hadn't realized how much he missed his dog until Duke was with him again. Now he couldn't bear the thought of being separated from him again so soon. During the fight, Duke had saved his life; the dog was his first companion, and his oldest friend. "At least until I fall asleep?"

K'Lani smiled slightly. "I suppose so."

For a moment, with his dog beside him and a woman who reminded him so much of his mother looking at him with a caring expression, Kaden almost felt like he was back home. Almost, but... what would his mother—would *Lydia*—say if she could see him now?

Would she be proud of him? Disappointed? Sad? How would she manage the coming harvest without Daneyel and Kaden to help her?

Kaden felt his throat begin to close again, and his eyes start to well. He took refuge in burying his face in the scruff of Duke's neck, and the rest of his companions quickly and quietly left the room, with soft farewells trailing them out. K'Lani was the last to go, and when she shut the door, it was calm and dark again in the room—relaxed, but not quiet anymore, not with Duke's steady, panting breaths and the scratch of his nails against the slate floor as he pawed his way closer for easier petting access. Kaden just hugged his dog and breathed, and soon his most worrying thoughts deserted him, and he slept again.

The next day, Kaden felt well enough to get out of bed. K'Lani agreed to let him sit in the main room and watch Ada bustle about, readying more wares for the market. At the same time, K'Lani herself ran their local store and put the rest of his friends to work hauling in fishnets—or in Queen Pepper's case, tending to the vast herb garden surrounding their modest cottage.

"What can you possibly have left to do?" Kaden asked, staring at the tall stacks of bundled herbs and glass bottles stacked by the front door. He itched to do more, to go out and walk in the open air, but given that he'd been a little winded by the walk here from the bedroom, it was probably best he stay still for now.

"Mark them all with our crest, of course," Ada said, not even looking at him as she stirred the freshly melted beeswax in the cauldron in front of her. She added a few drops of a dark, gluey liquid, and the pale wax gradually turned vivid blue.

"What's that stuff?"

"Toxin from the glands of the glox fish. It's not toxic anymore, of course," she added, snickering at what Kaden assumed was a horrified expression on his face. "Heating it nullifies its destructive properties, and this has been reduced by a lot. Probably a hundred fish glands went into making this one little bottle."

She checked the color in the cauldron against a sample seal on the stone table to her left, added one more drop, then nodded to herself. "This was our family's signature color before the war," she said. "Mama told me it took her years to find a way to replicate it after we came here. She used to make it from a special kind of sea plant, but that doesn't grow this far north."

"Your family had a signature color?" Kaden was confused. "Why?"

Ada rolled her eyes. "Don't you know anything about court life? Aren't you supposed to be the son of King Karatheas?"

"I was a baby when the war happened," Kaden replied, stung. "And *you* weren't even born, I bet."

"I've still been educated on the *basics*, of course."

"I'm sure that was nice since you didn't have to hide your existence under pain of getting hunted down and murdered by Lucient's spies." How was *that* for basics?

They glared at each other for a moment before Ada's shoulders finally relaxed. "Aristocratic families who frequented the royal court usually had crests of some kind, to show off their family's history," she said at last. "Most had a color, or a combination of colors, worked into the crest as well. My family, the Davenriches, our crest was a white and blue circle, with the blue representing ocean waves.

"This color," she continued as she stirred the wax a bit more, then lifted the spoon so he could get a better look, "is the color of southern coastal waters on a sunny day. *Our* color." She sighed and put the spoon down. "Or so my mother tells me." She grabbed a wooden stamp from the table, then set a bundle of dried herbs down in front of her and dribbled a little of the wax on the strip of cloth holding it together. She waited a moment, then pressed the stamp into the wax. A tiny blue circle, creased with waves, was left behind. "There. Now people will remember who they bought their wares from." She sighed and stared at the pile of goods by the door. "This is the dreariest part of preparing for market day, honestly."

"Let me help," Kaden offered. It wasn't the walk in the sunshine he was craving, but then again... it was cloudy out today and something he could do.

Ada looked dubious. "Are you sure? My mother will be upset with me if I let you overwork."

"I can do it while sitting down," Kaden pointed out. "How could I overwork?"

"I'm sure you could figure it out."

Kaden opened his mouth to say—what? To snap at her, to cajole her maybe—then Petey suddenly skidded in through the front door, nearly falling over one of the piles of herbs. "Ada, we need you at the docks!" he said, completely ignoring Kaden for the moment.

"Why?" she asked, her eyes narrowing. "What happened?"

"We, um… maybe got the nets a little bit tangled?" he said, scratching the back of his neck with one hand as his ears drooped sheepishly. "And then Redfern flew in to untangle it, but a wave drenched his wings, and now he's tangled too, and—he's all right, he's floating fine, but we can't get him out, and the nets are getting worse, and the wind is starting to pick up and—"

Ada dropped the stamp and pulled her waist-length, waterproof slicker over her shoulders. "Let's go," she said, stalking out without a single look back. Petey grimaced and mouthed *Sorry* at Kaden before scampering to follow her.

Kaden took advantage of Ada's absence to move over to her chair. He made sure the heat of the fire was just enough to keep the wax liquid, stirred it a few more times to work out some lumps, then reached for another bundle of herbs. *Drip, drip…* blue dots struck brown twine, like flowers blooming out of well-tended soil. Kaden pressed the abandoned stamp down into the wax, then grimaced as he pulled it away. He'd waited too long— the wax hadn't taken the crest well.

He scraped it off with his fingernail, then tried again. *Drip, drip, drip…* this time, he pressed the stamp down almost as soon as the final drop hit, but it still didn't look right—now the picture seemed too loose, too splashy. Like the wave was but a ripple in a pond, vanishing into nothing, instead of the force of nature it was meant to represent.

"Let me help you," a voice said from behind him. Kaden almost jumped out of his chair before he realized it was K'Lani. She lifted up the other chair and brought it over to the table next to him. "Here," she said, taking the spoon from his hand. "Watch. Count." She let three drops of wax hit the bundle of herbs. "One... two... now." Then she pressed the little stamp down and lifted it up a full second later, leaving a perfect imprint of a wave behind.

She handed back the stamp. "Now you try." Kaden grabbed a new bunch of herbs and gave it a try, counting under his breath and pressing firmly. "Not so hard you bruise the herbs," K'Lani chided, and he eased up a bit, then lifted it away entirely. "Better. Try again." Kaden did, feeling self-conscious as she sat there and watched. Each new attempt was better than the last, though, and a pile of marked bundles gradually grew on the table beside them.

Finally, K'Lani spoke. "Your friends have insisted that you're the child of King Karatheas and Queen Luna. I knew both monarchs in my youth. You do have the look of the king about you, but that could be mere chance. How can I believe that you are who they say you are?"

"You don't have to believe it," Kaden said. This was something he'd thought about a lot. Confronting the rulers he was trying to sway to his side was one thing, but announcing himself to the common folk of Empyrea was something else entirely, something he knew he wasn't ready for yet. He didn't cut a commanding figure right now; he wasn't a shining light and an inspiration to the masses. Not yet. Maybe not ever. "It won't affect you, either way, I promise."

K'Lani shook her head. "That's where you're wrong, I fear. If you were nothing but a charlatan with some tricksters on his side, trying to convince everyone you were royalty in exchange for gifts and services, then yes, you would be nothing to me. But if you are who they say, if you really are the son of the last great king of Empyrea… that's something that could affect me significantly.

"What do you think of my daughter?"

The change in subject matter was so sudden Kaden almost choked on his quick inhalation. "She, um… she seems very… um…" *What do I say? What's the courtly thing to say?* "Competent," he settled on, then cursed in his mind. *What mother likes to hear her daughter praised as "competent"? You should have said lovely, you should have said passionate, you should have said she is more beautiful than a dream—well no, maybe don't go that far—*

K'Lani just smiled with satisfaction. "She is quite competent, isn't she? I've taught her everything I could these past seventeen years, and she's consumed it all with fierce interest. Adena, or Ada as we call her, is my youngest child. I didn't even know I was carrying her when everything fell apart." She didn't look at Kaden but had her eyes trained on the window.

"I lost my husband, my brothers… so many people to the war. When I came to Whaldalf's Landing, I swore I would never look back. My children and I would live out our lives in peace, in ignorance of the wider world." Her hands tightened in her lap. "Of course, it's never that simple. Darkness finds you wherever you are, but I did my best. My older three adapted to life here in the village. My son owns a fleet of fishing vessels, and my other daughters are happily married. But Ada…

"She's like her father." K'Lani laughed softly. "She never even met him, but she's so like him. Brave and adventurous, always wanting more out of life. She's a fighter, through and through."

"I can tell," Kaden said, because boy, could he.

"She's not always an easy personality," K'Lani allowed with a smile, "but she's fierce and loyal. She's a good herbalist, too, and a healer." She paused, then said, "She would make a good ally on your quest."

Kaden almost dropped the stamp. "What?"

"I've spoken with your friends, Kaden. More than that, I've *watched* them. An elf, a goblin, a fairy queen, and her entourage all working together, at your behest? That's the beginnings of a mighty alliance against Lucient."

Oh, no. No, she didn't understand. "There's no mighty alliance yet," Kaden said, thinking about his failure with Bardicus, how he *would* have failed with Eldrin if Queen Pepper hadn't stepped in to smooth things over. "I'm still gathering my allies, and I still have a lot to learn about how to be a leader. I... it isn't safe to join my company, not for anyone. Not even for me." He gestured at himself hopelessly. "Certainly not for a defenseless girl."

K'Lani raised one eyebrow. "Defenseless? My Ada? She's a good shot with a bow and a better one with a fishing spear. She learned hand-to-hand fighting from her brother, who was training to join his father in the king's army before the war. She has a loyal heart and a wise head for her age and is adept at living off the land."

Kaden backpedaled. "I don't mean to offend you. I'm sure she's very skilled, but... she..." Was there a better way of saying, *She doesn't seem to like me?* Kaden settled on, "She seems like she's not interested in leaving home with a group of people she barely knows."

"She'd pack a bag quick enough if the cause was right."

He shook his head. "I couldn't guarantee her safety."

"No one can ever guarantee anyone else's safety," K'Lani said somberly. "Not even their own. Kaden, I wouldn't bring this up if I thought my daughter could live a good life without regrets here in Whaldalf's Landing, but she *can't*. I've seen it in her, the longing for adventure, the wanderlust. For me to keep her here out of concern for her safety would be for me to condemn her heart to stone. She's just... *destined* for more. Surely you of all people can understand following your calling."

Kaden unconsciously made the symbol of Orealus over his heart. Whenever his faith began to falter, which it felt like happened almost every turn, he recalled his dream of Orealus. *I'm not alone. I'm meant to do this. Orealus guides me, Orealus loves me, Orealus believes in me. I have to believe in myself. I have to believe in my friends. Most of all, I must believe and trust in Him.*

Maybe it was time for him to believe in someone new? Just because Ada wasn't a legendary fighter or the leader of a kingdom didn't make her unworthy of joining them. "She would be welcome. But only if she really wants to come." Because that had to be said—if Ada just felt like she was honoring her mother's wishes or came because she was bored...

K'Lani smiled. "You're at a disadvantage in some ways right now because your recovery kept you isolated. My daughter has spent the last four days listening to your friends talk about your great adventures and speculate on what will happen next. Wanting isn't the issue. Wondering if she might not be accepted is."

"I wouldn't stop her if she really wants this." Kaden was still a bit dubious that Ada *did* want to come, honestly. If she'd been speaking with his friends, then indeed she'd had her fill with danger and near disaster. "But I need to discuss it with the rest of my party as well."

"Of course. Thank you." K'Lani stood up, pulling her shoulders back and keeping her head high. She held herself as elegantly as any queen. "Keep stamping," she advised as she walked away. "You've got a lot left to go."

If that didn't perfectly describe how Kaden felt about the rest of his quest, nothing did. He took a deep breath, centering himself, then stirred the wax and let it drip over the next bundle. *Drip, drip, drip... press.* He pulled the stamp away and looked down at the little blue wave.

Perfect.

CHAPTER 19

The market day began before the sun rose. Kaden woke up as soon as he heard stirring in the bedroom. He'd been mortified last night to realize that he'd taken the only private bedroom in the small stone cottage and had insisted K'Lani and Ada take it back as soon as he found out.

"You needed it," K'Lani had said, but she must have recognized the spark of stubborn pride within him because she didn't insist he keep it. Last night Kaden had bedded down by the fire, surrounded by his companions, and he felt better on the floor beside his friends than he had the night he'd been conscious of being in a bed.

He'd been aware of Ada's eyes on him, on *them*, the way she kept glancing at them through the evening—and the look of... perhaps it was even longing—before she followed her mother to bed. He'd watched her go, then turned to his companions and opened his mouth.

He didn't even get the chance to ask them what they thought of her.

"Ada's great!" Petey blurted from where he crouched by the hearth, Bug nuzzling the side of his face and dotting his green skin with sparkling pink puffs of pollen. "She knows so much about fishing and sailing and the winds... she could be instrumental on our quest!"

"She's not useless, at least," Eldrin allowed. "She has good reflexes and better fighting instincts than you. But she's not nearly as good with that bow as she thinks she is. I'd have to take on training her if she joined us."

"You'd love it, and you know it," Redfern said with a chuckle. "Anything to let you feel like you know more than someone else is something you'd make time for."

"I certainly know more than you," Eldrin retorted.

"I have two centuries on you, *boy*, so I think it's more accurate to say that you only *think* you know more than me."

"Please," Millicent begged. "Not tonight. I spent an hour fishing first one, then the other of you out of the ocean during our stay here, and I really don't want to have to repeat the feat after I throw both of you back in."

Queen Pepper laughed. "I'm sure that won't be necessary," she said gently. Kaden wondered how much of Pepper's ability to get people to do what she wished came from their inability to stomach the thought of disappointing her. "We would have to be blind not to see that Adena is interested in joining us," she continued, crossing her delicate hands on her lap. "But I, for one, wouldn't feel comfortable with that unless she's able to articulate her desire by herself.

"Choosing to take part in a quest like this is a very adult decision," Pepper went on. "This step would mean Adena taking responsibility for her own decisions, her own actions. It doesn't matter if both she and her mother think her destiny is to come with us if *she* can't speak the words to actualize it." She looked into the fire for a moment, the reflected flames glittering brightly in her large violet eyes. "Her future must be decided by her, not by her mother, not by you, and not by anyone else."

"So I should wait for her to bring it up?" Kaden asked, unsure.

"I would," Pepper said. "Adena hasn't shown any signs of being overawed by you—by any of us, really. She ought to be able to do it."

That decided it for Kaden. He wouldn't have anyone with him who didn't want to be there, and in this case, he thought Queen Pepper had the right idea. If Ada wanted to come with them, she would tell them that. She *definitely* didn't seem to have any trouble telling him her mind.

Despite the arduous process of getting things ready for market, packing all the merchandise up, and taking it, it hadn't been bad at all. No doubt seven pairs of hands were much quicker at it than two, and the Davenrich market stall was ready to go well before the market itself was open. Once the market *did* begin, though, the pace became frenetic. Apparently, the Davenriches didn't attend every market day, so it was a notable event when they did. Their stall was swamped with customers, and the central square of Whaldalf's Landing bustled with more people than Kaden had seen in one place in a long time. Even the streets of Lumhagen hadn't teemed so thickly, and there it had been warm and bright, people laughing, loose and fluid. People called the types of products, modest yet functional, that they carried. The market stalls' keepers included a rope maker, a smith, a tailor, a carpenter, a cooper, a blacksmith, and of course countless fishers. The entire village smelled of fish, salt, and low tide, which only became more pungent on market day. Biting through the market aromas now and then was the metallic smell of iron surrounding the blacksmith. The scent overpowered almost all the others, but the smells of burning coal and wood drifted through the air as well. K'Lani had told Kaden how the families of the village often cooked their fish by frying it over an open flame. Their host family had often used this method and served their exceptionally fresh fish with a type of tartar sauce and lemon wedges to complement the smoky flavor.

Whaldalf's Landing was very different from Lumhagen, different from Ashland. This was a challenging place to live, and that tension showed in the face of every person who strode about the streets: part determination, part anxiety. Even the children were quieter than Kaden was used to, less inclined to laugh and play, more of them put to work in the fisheries or running deliveries for their parents' market stalls.

No wonder Ada seems so… grim, Kaden thought to himself as he watched her haggle with a fisherman over the price of one of her mother's salves. Everyone else had returned to the cottage for lunch, their group attracting more attention from the human-majority town than any of them liked, but Kaden had asked to stay with K'Lani and Ada. He had recovered enough to be aware of just how *boring* it was to be confined to the same small place all day, and he was eager to spend as much time as he could outside.

"How do I even know this will really prevent chilblains?" the fisherman demanded, rubbing his reddened hands together theatrically as he inspected the bottle Ada held up. "It wouldn't be the first time I bought something from your mother's stall only to be disappointed in the result."

"You're welcome not to buy anything at all if you think going around speaking lies about our wares will endear you to anyone here," Ada said, keeping her voice level even though her eyes glimmered like green fire. "Our salves offer the best protection against cold and weather along the entire northern coast, and you'll never get a better deal than during the market day. Go buy someone else's cheap, weak product if you prefer, but don't try to blame your folly on us." *Or else,* she seemed to say without speaking at all.

The man backed down and paid for the bottle, muttering the whole time. Ada took his money and gave him an insincere smile before turning to the next person.

"You'll lose us customers with that attitude," K'Lani chided her daughter from the other side of the stall as she handed over a pouch of dried herbs to a heavily pregnant woman with a toddler in her arms. "Take it twice a day until the birth," she added, and the young mother smiled.

"Thank you, Missus Davenrich. You certainly won't be losing *me* as a customer," she added with a wink to Ada. "This is the only thing I've ever found that settles the nausea of carrying little ones."

"It did the same for me," K'Lani assured her. There was a lull in new customers as the woman walked away, and K'Lani turned and looked between her daughter and Kaden. "I can handle things here for the time being," she said. "You two should get something to eat before business picks up again. Ada, you can show Kaden the town too."

"What is there of it to see?" Ada asked with a sigh. "A wharf, a single street along the quay, and the plaza here."

"Get on with you before I set you to cleaning out the pig shed instead," her mother warned.

Ada quickly grabbed the edge of Kaden's sleeve and pulled him to his feet. "We're going!" She led the way out the back and deeper into the market. Kaden didn't have much time to glance at the wares—Ada seemed more intent on getting them out of sight of her mother before K'Lani changed her mind.

"Can we not run?" Kaden asked, breathing a little heavily. It wasn't that he wasn't well enough—he was, he *needed* to be, he was fine, but...

"Oh." Ada immediately slowed down. "I'm sorry." There was no caustic follow-up this time, nothing about how he should be able to handle it, just a simple apology. It made Kaden wonder if she was feeling all right.

"This street leads to the public docks," she said, still holding onto him, only now her grasp on his sleeve had transferred to his wrist instead. Her grip was light enough that he could break it easily if he wanted to… but he really didn't want to. "That's where the merchant ships come in and out. Local fishermen have their own berths farther along the quay."

"Ah." This was actually good information to know since they would have to book passage on one of those ships to get to Westramore. "Do you know any of the captains?" If she could give him a recommendation, it would be an excellent place to start.

Ada looked at him and grinned. She looked so lovely at that moment that Kaden forgot to pick up his feet and nearly stumbled over an uneven cobblestone. "I know *all* of the captains. All the regulars, at least." She pointed at the forest of masts that Kaden could see above the slate roofs ahead of them. "Lots of the bigger ships are captained by folks who used to be part of King Karatheas's navy. They and their ships survived the battle, but with no kingdom to serve, many of them became independent operators."

They emerged onto the street that lined the docks, the briny air coating their skin with salt. If anything, the crowd of people there was even tighter than in the market, compounded by loading and unloading ships, braying donkeys pulling carts, and the strong scent of freshly caught fish wafting in over the salty breeze. Boats of various sizes floated along the docks. A daily fish market lined the boardwalk before the berths. Waves lapped against the docks and boats, which made a creaking sound as people thumped their boots on the wooden walkways. Shoppers could buy fish of various sizes, as well as bait and tackle. Fish for sale included tilapia, swordfish, trout, tuna, bass, catfish, codfish, and many others. Barrels of water contained fish, but also crabs, clams, oysters, urchins, and lobsters. Lobster traps, both empty and full, lined one dock. Men hauled giant nets flapping with ocean life; the silver of the fish glinted in the sun. The sunlight shone with such intensity that a breathtaking reflection of lights danced on the ocean's waves. Ada led the way onto a nearby shop's stoop, slightly elevated, where they could look out over the crowd without being pulled into the maelstrom themselves.

"Captain Herrington's ship, *Dawn's Light*, is here," she noted, pointing at a mast with a blue and red flag flying from the top of it. "And Captain Asiz's *Seaspray* is docked as well. Both of them make regular runs to Westramore."

"What do they charge for passengers?" Kaden asked.

Ada grinned again. "Whatever you can bargain down to."

"Oh." That might be… problematic. Kaden didn't have much in the way of money on him, just what he'd been given in Lumhagen, and he wasn't at all sure what the proper exchange rate was between different parts of the world. He was tempted to ask Queen Pepper to take care of it, but she'd already indicated discomfort with the stares she got from humans who'd never seen a fairy before. Eldrin might be able to do it, but Eldrin might also "accidentally" insult the person he was bargaining with and get them a bad deal.

"Just let me do the talking." Ada stepped back into the crowd, sliding her hand from his wrist into Kaden's palm as she did so. He reflexively held her hand back, warm fingers clasped tightly together, and then they were off, headed toward the ship with the red and blue flag.

"If he's not here, he'll be in the Landing's End tavern!" Ada called over the noise as she led the way. "But he'd harder to deal with once he's drunk, so let's hope he's still unloading!"

"How do you know all this?" Kaden shouted back.

"Captain Herrington's been courting my mother for the past ten years," she replied. "Which means I've had to deliver a lot of poetry from him to her during that time. It's *much* better when he composes it sober, but he's too nervous about sending it to her then," she added. "His last poem compared *her* eyes to the scales of a freshly caught fish."

Kaden laughed. It was a relief to know that there was someone out there who was even worse at paying compliments than he was.

"There's his first mate," Ada said, plunging between two carts. Kaden almost got his foot rolled over trying to keep up, but then they were next to *Dawn's Light*. It was an older ship, Kaden could tell from the color and wear of the timbers and the many outlines of barnacles that had been scraped from the hull, but it appeared to be in good shape.

"Master Sharpey," Ada called out as they walked farther along the dock. "Master Sharpey!"

A burly, broad-shouldered man with dark brown skin and a bald head paused where he was directing the lift and lower of a boom and glanced their way. "Miss Davenrich!" he replied briskly. "Are you here because your mam's ready to put the captain out of his misery?"

"Not yet, I'm afraid," Ada said with a smile. "I'm actually here to find out where you're headed next and whether you've room for any passengers."

"We're bound for Westramore once we get these sacks of feed unloaded," Master Sharpey said, his eyes as sharp as his name as he looked both of them over. "I can't speak to whether or not we've room for passengers, though. You'll need to go to the captain for that."

"Where is he?" Ada asked.

The first mate rolled his eyes and jerked his chin back toward the busy street behind them. "Where else?"

Ada frowned. "Already?"

"He's not had more than an hour to get into his cups yet, though," Master Sharpey replied. "You may yet find him able to negotiate a passage for your… friend?"

"Friends," Ada said, then curtsied. "Thank you, Master Sharpey."

"Aye, you can thank me by putting in a good word for the captain with your mam. You know who he *practices* those poems on, lass?" He pointed his thumb at himself. "Me, that's who. If I have to give one more opinion on whether 'moonbeam' rhymes well enough with 'sea bream,' I'll throw myself overboard."

Ada laughed, and everyone in her immediate proximity turned to look at her, Kaden included. She sounded like a completely different person when she laughed, nothing like the stone-faced girl she'd been selling to people at her mother's market stall. "I'll keep that in mind," she said once she caught her breath, then pulled Kaden back in the direction of the street.

They stopped at the edge of the cobblestones, just out of the flow of people, and Ada pointed at three different buildings lining the street. "That's the Fisherman's Rest," she said, "and that's Landing's End, and that one is the Handsy Kraken. Mother won't let me go in there," she added with a scowl. "She says it's not appropriate for young women. But it's fine because Captain Herrington always frequents Landing's End when he's here. I think the owner is a friend of his. Come on." She glanced slyly at him. "Try not to run into a cart this time."

"That was *your* fault!" Kaden insisted, but he was smiling at her. He was finding it hard *not* to smile at her. They darted across the street together, then went through the broad wooden door of the tavern.

The first thing that struck Kaden about the place was the smell of it, an odd combination of sour beer and oily fish that lodged uncomfortably in the back of his throat. Ada didn't seem bothered—then again, she'd grown up around this scent. He tried to hide his discomfort.

The second thing that struck him was just how *dark* the place was. There were a few windows along the front wall, but the only interior light was a single torch back beside the bar. It was dark and gloomy, cold, and Kaden honestly couldn't see the appeal of it.

Then again, he'd never wanted to drown his sorrows someplace where no one would judge him for it either, so perhaps for these men, it was perfect.

"There he is," Ada said, pointing to one of the few window seats. A handsome but morose-looking older man wearing a light, gold-trimmed red and blue jacket sat there, tankard in one hand, quill in another as he stared down at a piece of parchment. He looked up as they approached.

"Ah, Miss Davenrich!" He smiled at her. "Just who I was hoping to see. I'm almost done with this missive for your honorable mother."

"I'd be happy to deliver it to her, Captain Herrington," Ada said, "but I was actually hoping to discuss business with you first."

The captain straightened. "Oh, really?" Now his eyes found Kaden, and a darkly speculative look crossed his face. "Adena, I hope you're not about to ask me about providing a means of elopement because if you think I'd do that to your mother—"

"No!" Ada crossed her arms defensively. "This is Kaden Sheppard, and he's just a friend."

"Just a friend, eh?" The captain snorted. "Not a friend I've ever seen around these parts before."

"My party and I are just passing through," Kaden said, giving Ada a break before her blush set her face on fire. "We need to find passage to Westramore."

"Westramore, eh? That city is a sty," Captain Herrington said flatly. "A haven for thieves, rogues, and drunkards. What kind of business do any *respectable* people have there?"

"According to your first mate, you sail there frequently," Kaden replied. "What sort of business does a respectable man like *yourself* have there?"

The captain grunted and looked away. "Eh, fair enough. I might be able to find the room for a *small* party on my ship. But we leave tomorrow morning, early."

"That's fine," Kaden said. "There are seven of us. But one is a dog," he added when Captain Herrington frowned. "No berth required for him."

"Hmmph," the captain grunted. "Fine. But you'll have to pay seven Empyrea coins apiece."

"We can do that." He thought they could, at least. If not, then perhaps they could work off their fare on the way there.

"And I can't promise we won't end up at the bottom of the sea," the captain went on, warming to his diatribe now. "The leviathan's been moving about recently, wreaking havoc in the ship lanes. Used to be that the merfolk would help out with that, but..." He paused and took a drink. "They've had more than their share of troubles too, I reckon."

"Perhaps they would be more inclined to help if you flew my family's flag from the mast on the voyage," Ada offered.

Both Kaden and Captain Herrington looked at her. "Why, though?" Kaden asked.

She lifted her chin proudly. "My grandfather was King Karatheas's ambassador to the merfolk during his reign. We have a long tradition of friendship between us, and when my mother took us and fled after the war, a group of merfolk escorted our ship all the way here. We still see them every now and then. If they see that flag, they'll look out for us."

"Seems unwise to fly a false flag," Captain Herrington mused, stroking his chin thoughtfully.

"It wouldn't be a false flag," Ada said. "Because I'm going to be accompanying Kaden and his companions, of course. Not illicitly," she added as the captain's expression darkened. "As a respectable member of their company. You can ask my mother if you doubt me."

"Don't think that I won't," Captain Herrington said warningly, then glanced at Kaden. Kaden knew he looked like a landed fish right now, mouth gaping, but he couldn't help it.

Was this Ada's way of asking to join them? There wasn't much "ask" about it.

"Is this true?" the captain prodded him, and Kaden watched how Ada's spine stiffened, how the firm set of her mouth faltered slightly as the silence extended. She truly wanted to come, even knowing some of the dangers they faced—Kaden hadn't even had to lay them out for her. The captain had done that himself. She was not only willing to brave them, but she also had a means of helping to keep them safe.

There was only one response to that. "It's true," Kaden said, and the smile that bloomed across Ada's face made his whole body feel warm. "She's with us."

"Hmm." Captain Herrington laid down his tankard, packed up his quill and paper, and set a copper coin on the table before pushing to his feet. "Let's see what her mother has to say about that. If she agrees… then I'll give you all passage, and at half price, out of respect for the Davenrich family. And if she *disagrees*?" He leaned in close to Kaden, not appearing at all intimidated by the fact that Kaden was three inches taller than him. "You'll be answering to me, boy," he murmured, and now Kaden could see the captain of a fighting vessel of King Karatheas's navy, a proud and dangerous man.

"I understand," he said, managing to keep his voice level.

"Good," Captain Herrington grunted and then led the way out of the tavern without a backward glance. Kaden and Ada followed, Ada retaking his hand as they walked out into the bright afternoon light. They headed for the market, where her mother would still be at work, and Kaden felt a thrill of excitement go through him.

No matter what happened next, whether they found Weylyn, Son of the Wolf or not, he was confident that their adventure from here on out would be better with Ada along.

CHAPTER 20

To be honest, Kaden had expected a terrible voyage on the Prudent Ocean. Everyone born in Empyrea knew cartographers named the ocean as a warning to seafarers, a suggestion to mind one's actions with constant diligence while traversing the waters. Storms and other mysterious disasters were well known to wreak havoc on ocean trips. Rumors of waves as tall as mountains—which had cracked hulls as easily as hands could snap a twig, drowning entire crews—circulated amongst fishermen and landlubbers alike. Some disaster would have fit with the way things had gone on their quest lately. Something was bound to happen to imperil them—a terrible storm, the leviathan rising out of the depths, or even just some pirates looking to take advantage of a merchant ship.

Expanding impossibly far to the west, the malachite-green, ever-moving surface of the ocean reflected the sunlight, dazzling Kaden's eyes. He felt small on the ship atop the churning waves. Petey couldn't help but voice his concern that the creaking boat would fall apart as it crested even the smallest waves. The rusty iron chain and anchor clanked against themselves, the side of the ship, and the iron loop built into the bulkhead to house this equipment. Wind thrashed against the modest sails, whipping the canvas and tugging the ropes. The water lapped at the wooden hull, as though a friendly dog was greeting the newcomers. The wind whipped their hair and clothes, a cool sensation on exposed skin that helped evaporate the sweat from their bodies.

It was a pleasant, almost unbelievable surprise to have clear skies, a calm sea, and ever-warming winds on the trip south, and only a few other ships appeared in the lane, all of them sporting flags Captain Herrington recognized. The briny air filled Kaden's lungs, adding a weight to the atmosphere, and lingering on his tongue. He felt especially thirsty for fresh water the whole trip. Unfortunately, the boat smelled of rotting wood, expired fish, and vomit.

The worst part about the whole trip ended up being Petey's reaction to the swaying under his feet.

"I hate *boats*," Petey moaned for the dozenth time that day. Considering it was only ten in the morning, that said a lot, but Kaden knew better than to point it out. After all, he wasn't the one suffering from seasickness so bad he had to sleep on the deck at night instead of in the berth set aside for him.

"We should see Westramore soon," Kaden said bracingly, holding himself back from reaching out and clapping Petey on the shoulder. The first time he'd done that since his friend had gotten sick, he'd ended up spending an hour cleaning off his boots. "Then things will be better."

Petey turned bleary, bloodshot yellow eyes on Kaden. "What if they're not, though? What if this cursed boat has broken something inside of me, and I can't get my land legs back, so I can't stay on land, but I never develop sea legs either, and I'm just sick all the time for the rest of my miserable life?"

Kaden could have argued the point, but he was pretty sure nothing he said would make Petey feel better right now. He cast a pleading glance at Queen Pepper, who sat nearby, brushing out and braiding her hair into a tighter style. She smiled with gentle commiseration. "Petey, would you care for some more of my special tea?" she asked.

The tips of Petey's drooping ears turned up a bit. "Yes, please," he muttered. Pepper's special tea, a blend of something she'd brought from Fayspire and ingredients she'd picked up from K'Lani before leaving, was the only thing that gave Petey any relief. The effects didn't last long, unfortunately, and the tea stank worse than the bottom of a troll's foot, but Petey still downed it like King Bardicus drank grog.

With Pepper tending to Petey, Kaden took the opportunity to head to the ship's stern. He could see land in the distance now, the coastline housing the fabled city of Westramore. He'd heard all sorts of stories about it from the sailors on the way here, and at this point, he didn't know whether he should be more excited or afraid to be going there.

Excited! It was hard not to be, despite the city's unsavory reputation… maybe even a little bit *because* of that reputation. Westramore was rife with intrigue and danger, full of mercenaries, thieves, assassins, and more. It was rumored that there never was a moment within its confines where a fight wasn't happening *somewhere*, not even in the darkest hours of the night, and that no matter what sort of entertainment you were looking for, it could always be found—for a price. Men would gamble on anything there, from the outcome of a battle to the size of the next cockroach they saw, and not a woman in town wasn't armed and ready to strike at any time if a man overstepped her boundaries.

Ada joined Kaden. "Are you nervous about entering Westramore?" she asked.

Kaden shrugged. "A bit, I guess. I mean, I hope that we find Weylyn quickly, but I'm not worried about getting into trouble while we're there. Who would want to bother with us?"

"Ha!" Captain Herrington said as he came up to stand beside Kaden. "I think the better question is, how many people will take you for a mark the moment you step through Westramore's gate, and how will you keep them from spilling your guts across the filthy streets before you even find your quarry?"

Kaden and Ada both sighed. Captain Herrington hadn't been pleased that Ada was joining their party, and he had taken it upon himself to chaperone her whenever she and Kaden got within ten feet of each other. It was more than a bit of stifling, but Kaden tried to keep his annoyance under check.

"I think our party is big enough that we won't be seen as easy prey," he said.

"Ha!" the captain said again. "That stain of a city is filled with hundreds of cutthroats, cutpurses, and cut-rate information hawkers. The bigger your party, the more of you they could take advantage of. Nothing short of a fire or flood could cleanse that place of its wickedness. And," he added, "your party will be smaller than you think, for there's going to be no taking those fairies into Westramore if they want to keep their wings."

Ada frowned. "What do you mean?"

"I mean that there are people in there who specialize in trapping the members of all tribes, including those with Orealus-spirited gifts. I've seen them myself—merfolk in tanks, goblins in cages, and don't get me started on the poor centaur I saw last time." He shook his head. "Queen Pepper and her people are too pretty and too rare an opportunity to pass up. You wouldn't make it ten feet past the gate before some fool decided to test their luck, and if that one failed? Someone else would try. Before you know it, there'd be a pitched battle to see who managed to thieve a fairy."

The thought made Kaden ill. "I would never let that happen."

"Then you're best off playing it safe by leaving them here *on board*," said Captain Herrington, stomping a boot against the wooden deck. "If the elf lad and the goblin cover up well enough, they'll probably do all right. You'll pass, of course—be singled out as a mark still, but pass. And *you*"—he pointed the finger at Ada—"will be staying on board as well."

Ada scowled and crossed her arms. "I can handle myself just fine!"

"I promised your mother I'd look out for you, and that promise would be as broken as a brawler's nose if I let you step one foot in that city of, of, of... perfidy!"

"You don't get to order me around! I answer to Kaden, not to you!"

They both turned to look at Kaden, who froze in place. *Uh-oh*. He was going to make someone mad with whatever he said next. "Um." He did want Ada to go with them, of course, he did, but... "I think it's probably best if you stay here."

Ada's look turned into a full-on glare, and she turned and stalked off across the deck, with every inch of her radiating anger. Kaden hated to be the cause of that anger, but he also didn't want to get into a fight in Westramore if there was any chance of avoiding it.

"Turns out you've some sense after all," Captain Herrington said with a grunt.

"I'm not doing it for your sake," Kaden snapped. "I'm doing it for hers."

"Mm-hmm." The captain leaned against the salty wooden rail in front of him. "What *is* her sake, lad?"

Kaden blinked. "What do you mean?"

"What 'sake' are you talking about, specifically? The sake of her modesty, the sake of her safety, the sake of your own conscience when it comes to her?"

Kaden was frustrated to the point of grinding his teeth. "I thought *you* didn't want her to come into the city! You and your crew have been talking of nothing but what a terrible place it is, and you just said she should stay behind!"

"Oh, *I'm* pleased, for sure. For the sake of Ada's safety and her dear mother's heart, I'm pleased, but ask yourself this: What do you expect of her on this quest of yours? Companionship? Assistance at sea, what with her family's flag? A plaything that you can encourage when you feel like it and cosset when you don't?"

The captain turned his eyes out toward the dirty brown cloud hovering over Westramore, which was coming ever closer. "Decide what you expect of her and make it clear to her. Otherwise, you'd have done better for her by leaving her back in Whaldalf's Landing. Clear the deck here," he added. "I have a ship to sail into port." Kaden strolled away, almost tripping over his own feet as he thought about what the captain had just said.

Of *course* he thought Ada could handle herself. It wasn't that. It was that if they had a chance for her not to *have* to do so, why shouldn't they take it? It was no different than Pepper stepping in with King Valymr or Eldrin leading the way along the northern coast. Everyone had their own time to shine, and…

Oh. Okay, I'm an idiot.

Kaden walked over to where Ada stood stiffly at the boat's bow, not far from Petey, who looked greener than ever. "Can I talk to you?" he asked as he stopped beside her.

"It's not like I can stop you, I suppose," she snapped at him. "Seeing as you're the *commander* of this adventure, and everyone has to do whatever you say, even if it's ridiculous."

"That's not the way it is," Kaden assured her. "At all. I always listen to the advice of everyone in our party, no matter what. I wouldn't have gotten this far if I hadn't—after all, it took you and your mother's expertise to cure me of the dark elves' poison. I didn't manage that myself, and Queen Pepper couldn't do it either."

Ada didn't seem reassured. "One life-threatening instance isn't evidence that you care what anyone else can do."

"I do care. And I know you're tough and smart, and probably deadly under the right circumstances," Kaden said.

"Then why leave me behind here instead of joining you in the search for Weylyn, Son of the Wolf?" He could hear longing under the brusqueness of her voice. "I could do it, I *can*, I know I can!"

"I know," Kaden agreed. "But why court danger that we could otherwise avoid? Without Queen Pepper's influence, I might have gotten Petey and myself *killed* by Eldrin when we first got to Kel Tyrion. She led then, and I followed and mostly kept my mouth shut."

Ada smirked. "Hard to imagine."

"I know, it was tough," Kaden agreed, and she chuckled. "The point is, you're a member of the party: a true one, a full one. You don't need to court danger to prove it or let any of us *put* you into greater danger to prove it. I'm going to talk to Pepper and Redfern and Millicent about staying behind too, and it's not because they're not great fighters. It's because I don't want to increase the danger to them for no increase in reward. We're looking for one man, and the less notice we attract while finding him, the better."

Ada sighed and shut her eyes for a moment, the tension leaving her shoulders. "You know," she said, "you're not exactly unremarkable yourself. There are plenty of people in a den of iniquity like Westramore who would see a tall, strong young man like you and start wondering what kind of fight you might give them." She jerked her thumb at his sword. "I suggest wrapping the hilt of that before you go ashore. It's too appealing otherwise. And dirty up your pretty face too." She walked off, leaving Kaden staring after her, knowing his eyes were the size of dinner plates but uncaring at the moment.

She thinks I'm pretty?

"Don't let it go to your head," Petey muttered.

"Oh, whoops... did I say that out loud?"

"You did, not that you needed to." He rolled his bloodshot yellow eyes. "Your thoughts are obvious every moment you're looking at her. You *like* her."

"Keep your voice down," Kaden hissed.

"What did I just say about obvious?" Petey said, then grimaced and let out a huge belch. "Ugh. *Ugh*. You *will* let me go ashore with you, aren't you? Because if I don't get a break from the way my stomach is trying to jump through my throat, I might just die before you get back."

"You and Eldrin are definitely coming," Kaden assured him. "Duke too. Even the toughest footpads will think twice about attacking us with a hunting dog like Duke at our sides."

"Good." Petey forced himself to his feet, standing on wobbly legs. "You tell the others what's going on, and I'll... I'll... oh, not aggghh—" He spun around and put his head over the rail again. The retching was loud enough to frighten off the seagull that had just settled on the rigging above them.

"Right. You... do that, and I'll let you know when we're docked." Kaden hoped it was soon, for all their sakes.

*   *   *

Kaden stepped off *Dawn's Light* and immediately wrinkled his nose. The smell of rotten filth, which had been bad enough from the ship's deck, was ten times worse down on the ground. He could pick out the stench of rotting fruit and floating feces mixed into the pungent miasma of body odors from the people all around him, and for a moment, it was all he could do not to gag. Eldrin seemed similarly affected, pulling his hood tighter about his head with a grimace as his nostrils flared. "I should have remembered to stuff my nose with wax," he muttered.

On the other hand, Petey was happier from the moment his feet hit the slick, sticky cobblestones of the quay. "Oh, praise Orealus," he said, beaming up at Kaden. "The sickness is finally gone, just like that! Ahhh..." He took a deep inhale. "No nausea!"

"How can you *not* be nauseous?" Eldrin demanded. "This place is like a cross between an outhouse and an abattoir."

"Oh, it's a goblin thing, I think," Petey said, shrugging. "It can get very *close* down there in the caves if you know what I mean, and it's not as though we can just throw our waste out into the sea or bury it in the soil. If we couldn't handle all sorts of noxious odors, we wouldn't survive down there."

"Nosegay?"

A small, grubby hand thrust a bunch of wilted flowers under Kaden's nose. "To help you breathe easier, good sir?" The owner of the hand, a child wearing dirty sackcloth and no shoes, continued, "Fights off the vapors, it does."

The flowers were far too tiny and sad to produce their *own* vapors, much less fight off any of the others. Kaden shook his head. "No, thank you." He looked at the gray wall looming in the distance before saying to Eldrin and Petey. "Come on, let's get inside the city."

"Only gonna get worse in there, good sir," the child said, keeping pace with them as they started to walk. "A nice fellow like you will want flowers like these, so you don't get the lungrot, sir."

"Lungrot?" Petey asked in alarm. "Is that real?"

"Oh yes, sir," the child said, switching targets with ease. "Black lungrot, red lungrot, spotted lungrot—that one's black *and* red, sir. They can set in real fast, sir. Nosegye'll help hold back the worst of it until you can get back on board your ship. Unless... are you stayin' here for a while?"

"We're getting out of here as fast as possible," Eldrin interjected, lengthening his stride so that even Duke had a problem keeping up for a moment. The entrance of Westramore loomed in front of them, heavy wooden gates set in a wall made from rough-hewn gray rock that was riddled with divots and pits like it had suffered a round of the pox.

The gates were a violent bustle, guards shouting for entry fees and sticking people with the business ends of their pikes while the rest of the crowd fought either to enter, to exit, or simply for the pleasure of fighting. Eldrin moved like a snake through the crowd, dodging carts and fists with alacrity. Kaden followed him all right but almost lost Petey just a few paces in. He reached down and grabbed his friend's hand, then towed him into the mix, forcing a narrow path into the city through sheer determination—and a few handy elbows.

"Watch who you're shoving!" a gray-haired man with wild eyes and a mouth full of broken teeth howled in Kaden's face. He drew back a hand to strike at Kaden, but the next moment was bumped from the side, which pushed him off balance and back into the press.

"Sorry 'bout that!" the urchin yelled, then winked up at Kaden. "C'mon, sirs, let's get you inside the gate." The child moved just as stealthily as Eldrin had, but Kaden was more ready to follow now, and with only a few more bumps and bruises, he and Petey and Duke made it into the infamous city of Westramore.

"Finally," Eldrin said from where he was standing beside a section of wall a little way down. "I was beginning to think I'd have to go back and rescue you."

"You wouldn't have had to think it if you'd bothered to wait for us in the first place," Petey snapped back.

The child looked at them all and grinned brightly. "What'll it be, good sirs? You want whores? I can get you entry into the finest whorehouses in the whole city. Fights? I know where all the best ones are to be held. Goods? There's everything from precious gems to pickled goblin's ears in the marketplace, and I can find it all in far less time than you'd spend mucking about there."

Kaden smiled. "You're not trying to sell us flowers anymore?"

"Eh, those only work outside the gate," the child said dismissively. "Once you're inside, it's too late for you, so you might as well make the most of it. So, what'll it be?"

"I think we'll start," Eldrin said, coming over and grabbing the child before they could wriggle away, "with taking back everything you just pinched off my companions."

"I never did!" The child writhed in his grasp, scratching and stomping. The few people who even bothered to look over just laughed. "I'm as honest as the day is long! I'm—"

"Your purse." Eldrin handed the leather pouch back to Kaden, who looked at it in surprise. "And yours." He gave the other one to Petey. "Put them *inside* your clothes, idiots," he added, then let go of the child, who stared warily at them, weight already on their back foot as though to run away.

"It's not like I *wanted* to steal them," the child said sullenly. "Times are tough, and I've got a mother and three little ones to keep fed."

"Sure you do," Eldrin replied. The child scowled at him.

Kaden had an idea. "You say you know this place," he said, bending down so he was at eye level with their vendor-turned-guide-turned-thief.

"I do," the child said warily.

"We're seeking a man called Weylyn, Son of the Wolf. He's a great warrior, possibly a mercenary for hire." Kaden pulled a silver coin out of his purse and held it up. It glinted in the dingy gray light. "Do you know where we could find him?"

The child grinned. "You shoulda just *told* me you were interested in the fights! Of *course* I know where to find the Wolf's cub!"

CHAPTER 21

The dark, dungy city buzzed with the sort of excitement born of Kaden not knowing if he was about to be solicited for his next great adventure or stabbed by an assassin. Roiling with scoundrels, thieves, assassins, mercenaries, and other unsavory people, every person in Westramore seemed angry, exhausted, or both. Even in broad daylight, the darkest corners of back allies shifted with shadows, likely criminals concealing their identities. A layer of dust and munge coated not just the surroundings, but the people. Dirt kicked up with every step, making Kaden feel like he needed to bathe even though his party was just passing through.

The whole place's infrastructure had the appearance of a cheap set of playing cards that would topple at the first sign of a stiff breeze. Shanties, inns, and desolate shops lined the streets with no discernable organizational structure. The shanties were little more than scrap wood stacked with tin roofs. Most shops had boarded or broken windows. The tallest buildings, the inns, only stood two stories high. The crumbling façades were riddled with cracked bricks and faulty mortar. Many of the walls were only upright because they leaned on the walls of other buildings. In fact, calling them "buildings" was too generous.

The stench of sewer swirled with the reek of sweaty bodies. With no regard for the environment, people sloshed buckets of putrid liquid out of their windows and into the open sewer drain that ran along the cracked stone street. The smell of feces mingled with that of rotting fruit.

Bodies hustled and bustled, scurrying around one another like a sandstorm colliding with rocks. A burly man bumped into the travelers with no regard for personal space. He did not offer an apology, but only a grunt. Unconscious people, who had overindulged in food, grog, or worse vices, littered the streets. The inhabitants had piled heaps of trash on the corners. Flies buzzed the garbage, but also the dirtier people. Children in bare feet pattered around, playing kick-the-stone or pickpocketing those adults less aware of their surroundings.

A cacophony of slurred speech and angry voices rose up from the city. Irate men pounded their fists on flimsy wooden tables as they argued over the rightful winner of card and dice games. Fed up with a particularly fruitless debate, one man smashed a chair over another man's back, causing the wood to splinter, then crack. People at run-down stalls hawked sketchy items for sale.

The child Led the party to a place apparently called "the Salted Cod," although there was no sign or even a name painted on the side of the building to indicate that. It was a ramshackle old inn, its roof sagging dangerously on one side, and one of its walls leaned especially hard against the building next to it.

"Oh, marvelous," Eldrin said dryly as they stopped in front of the place. "This is just the spot one would expect to find a warrior with the Son of the Wolf's reputation. Yes, clearly only the highest paragons of virtue are to be found within its august walls."

"What's a paragon?" the child asked.

Eldrin's mouth twisted in a grimace. "Nothing within ten square miles of here, I'd say."

Kaden just shrugged. "He works as a mercenary. He has to go where the jobs can be found, I imagine. Anyway, we—"

Just then, a man came flying out the open door of the Salted Cod, sailing clear past them and into the middle of the street, where he came down with a thump flat on his face in the mud. No one walking by paid him the slightest bit of attention, and the child actually laughed.

"Looks like there's a fight happenin' in there already!" Small, bright eyes twinkled up at Kaden. "Nice way to test whether the fighter you're lookin' for has the skills you need, an' without even having to pay for it! Speaking of, sir..." The child held out a hand insistently, and Kaden dropped the silver coin into it.

"Thanks, good sir!" The child darted away into the shadow of the half-collapsed wall, leaving Kaden, Eldrin, and Petey to stare in collective trepidation at the entrance to the Salted Cod. Duke, who didn't look like he cared one way or the other, sniffed a sticky pool on the ground with interest before sampling it with his tongue. One lick was apparently enough to convince him to leave it alone.

When the refuse of a place couldn't even appeal to a dog, Kaden had to wonder what in a troll butt's name was in it.

"I... guess we should go in," Kaden said at last. The noise inside hadn't abated, but they couldn't stand out there waiting for the fight to end. It might *never* end if their young guide was to be believed.

"You go first!" Petey squeaked nervously, his hand rising impulsively to his hood, where Bug was tucked up close to his neck inside the cloth. "I'll just, um... I'll just... um..."

"You can stay out here if you want to," Kaden offered, but Petey shook his head.

"Are you crazy? I'd be robbed, stabbed, and left for dead in under a minute!" Petey hustled in through the door before Kaden could say another word.

"You've finally found the perfect way to motivate him," Eldrin marveled. "Just threaten him with a little indiscriminate violence. I'm happy to provide it, in the future—"

Kaden punched the elven prince's shoulder. "Knock it off."

Eldrin laughed. "We'd better get in there."

Kaden squared his shoulders and walked forward into the dim, smoky light of the… tavern? Inn? Shanty? It was hard to say—there appeared to be plenty of drinking going on, but no one was serving the alcohol. There was a lot of sleeping going on, too, but not in rooms. More than likely, those people were simply passed out in the chairs they were slumped in—or had been knocked unconscious because there was *definitely* a fight going on in there. And the battle was centered around a man in exceptional armor in the center of the room.

He was tall—not quite as tall as Kaden, but he stood above most of the other people in the room, and in his armor, he was simply massive. The metal was silver but hard enough to turn the few blades that managed to make it past the man's guard to strike his wolf-inscribed breastplate. Below the breastplate was a layered metal skirt that almost went low enough to obscure the greaves the man wore on his shins. The armor's pauldrons were so round and bulky that they should have looked ridiculous. Still, instead, they served to set the fighter apart, to broaden his outline into something so intimidating that only a fool would think of fighting him.

Clearly, there were a lot of fools in the Salted Cod.

It's him. This had to be the man they were seeking, and from the look of him, he was every bit the warrior that Bardicus said. His helm was made from the same shining silver metal as the rest of the armor, but the snarling wolf's head it resembled ended just below Weylyn's nose, revealing his own snarl as he laid into the people around him with his sword. His *sheathed* sword, Kaden noticed. The people coming after him were using naked blades, but he didn't match their deadliness.

Crack! A strike with the flat of the scabbard over one howling man's head sent him reeling backward, dumbstruck until he fell right at Kaden's feet. He was bleeding out of both ears and one of his eyes.

Oh.

A bushy-bearded man was standing on a table now, his voice carrying above the roar of the fight as he called out in a sonorous voice, "And the Pig has gone down! Yes, Gundar the Pigsticker has tried his luck for the last time, it seems. Gundar, Gundar, you should have let the embarrassment of the first five tries convince you it was futi—but wait, here comes Rollicking Rock the Destroyer, that's right, the same Rock who's only ever managed to destroy several innocent outhouses and half a brothel in his quest to deserve his title, and he's coming in with a club which—aha, ahaha, has now been *broken* and rammed so far into his gut I think the only thing that's been destroyed here today is the Rock's ability to keep food down for the next week!

"And what have we here?" The little man capered across the table like he was dancing a jig, his brown hat flopping oddly from side to side. "Regan Sharpeyes, by far one of the best fighters in this useless joint, I'm not sure why she's bothering to get involved when Weylyn has *nothing* but respect for her—"

"He stole my last contract!" she shouted. She was a tall woman with thick black hair held back in a coil of braids that wound around her head like a helmet. She had two long, slim daggers in her hands, and she looked very unamused. "Criminally undercut me on price *and* ushered my mark out of here before I had a chance to argue my side. Ruined my reputation with them, and I won't let it stand!"

"Then you won't be standing for long," the little man said gleefully, his hooves stamping out a staccato beat on the table. His—wait, his *hooves?*

"What is that creature?" Kaden asked Eldrin.

"I think it's a..." Eldrin paused, his eyes widening. "No. It can't be. They all perished in the Great War."

"Who perished?" Kaden insisted, keeping one eye on the fight. The woman was clearly experienced, but she didn't have the strength to match Weylyn. He parried her blows twice with his sword and once with his vambraces, then slammed a foot into her stomach, and shoved her back so hard she flipped over a table.

"The satyrs," Eldrin replied. "He... with those feet, he must be a satyr. A manlike creature with the hindquarters of a goat."

"Oh, wow." Kaden looked at the satyr with renewed interest. What he'd thought was a hat were actually long ears flopping on either side of short black horns. Now that Kaden was looking, he could see that the baggy pants were actually furry brown legs. A tuft of thick hair the same color as his fur covered the skin of his arms and sprouted from the collar of his shirt. If what Captain Herrington had said was true, and this place was dangerous for ability-gifted creatures, how was someone as rare as a satyr surviving here?

His question was answered a moment later when, as a frustrated combatant turned to take a quick stab at the little creature, the Son of the Wolf grabbed a chair in one hand, spun, and smashed it against the head of the man attacking the satyr before breaking the rest of it over the back of someone he'd put down earlier who was trying to get back on their feet.

Needless to say, they didn't make it.

Gradually, the fight petered out. The people in close quarters began to back away, tripping over the fallen as they did so, until it was only Weylyn and the satyr still standing in the middle of the room.

"Eighteen!" the satyr cackled as he danced gleefully. "That's a new record! Eighteen down, in under a quarter hour!" He hopped down from the table and reached beneath it, pulling out a mug of... something. "Here, quench that thirst, you champion you," the satyr said, pushing the cup at Weylyn. "You deserve it."

"Wait." As full of fury and battle lust as he'd been a moment ago, the Son of the Wolf was now firmly focused on the three newcomers. "You." He jerked his chin at Kaden. "Are you here to fight or here to pay for a fighter?"

"I'm not here to fight you," Kaden said. He had no interest in ending up smeared across the ground like the rest of these brawlers.

"But what would you do if one of us was?" Eldrin cut in, his voice smoother than silk and sharp as a knife's edge.

The satyr brayed obnoxiously. "What does it *look* like he'd do?" He laughed. "He'd put you in your place under his *boot*. That's what he'd do!"

Weylyn narrowed his eyes. "Do you want to try your luck, elf?" He patted a still-sheathed dagger on his right hip. "I'll warrant I can stick this in your eye before you get a shot off with that fancy bow of yours. If I'm within ten paces of you, I have the advantage."

"Elf?" The satyr paused his capering. "An elf? What?"

"It's obvious," Weylyn grunted. "A man—more like a boy—and an elf, a bear hound and a…" He peered at Petey. "A goblin? You're either very brave or very foolish, coming into a place with a reputation like Westramore's."

"How did you know?" Petey squeaked, shifting nervously on his feet. "There's not enough light in here to see my color."

"It's in the way you hold yourself," Weylyn said flatly. "The language of your movement shouts your heritage to the world. Your allegiances, as well." He looked back at Kaden. "What has a wet-behind-the-ears lad like yourself done to warrant a motley escort like this?"

"I'm on a quest," Kaden said, straightening his back. He'd said it often enough now that he was truly beginning to believe it. "To unite the original tribes of Empyrea against Lucient the Deceiver."

Weylyn stared at him for a long moment, his black eyes glaring, then walked forward until he was less than a hand's width from Kaden's face. The younger man had a few inches of height on him, but Weylyn was far broader. He drew in a long, deep breath. "You don't have the stench of booze on your breath," he said after a moment, "or the stink of wanderweed. Therefore, you've got to be a madman."

He turned to glare at Eldrin. "How much is this milksop paying you to trail after him pretending he's the next King Karatheas? Because whatever it is, it can't be enough to warrant your presence here."

"I'm here because he *is* the next King Karatheas," Eldrin replied, a tiny smirk on his lips. "The next king, at any rate. This is Karatheas's youngest son."

Weylyn looked back at Kaden with renewed sharpness. "No," he said after a moment. "No, I don't believe it. The whole royal family died in the same battle that claimed my father's life."

"Almost," Kaden said. A stricken look came into Weylyn's eyes, so deep and pained that he almost wanted to apologize, even though he wasn't sure what for. "I survived, raised in a small village by a former guardsman and his wife. I didn't even know who my real father was until a little more than a month ago."

Weylyn snorted. "And that somehow justifies you deciding to take off on an adventure to round up the old tribes of Empyrea? Knowing your daddy was a king? You think that *matters?*"

Kaden had been pretty sure this wasn't going to be easy, but he hadn't thought the man would be quite this defensive. He had to keep trying, though. "Of course it matters. Orealus chose my father too—"

"Orealus? Ha!" Weylyn turned and kicked over one of the already broken chairs. "Don't talk to me about that absent god!" he shouted angrily. "Faith in Orealus is useless, and letting yourself be used by Him is *less* than useless. King Karatheas claimed to be guided by Orealus, and look where that led him.

Into the jaws of death! And he took far too many good people down with him at the same time, so don't try to quote holy scripture at me and expect anything but contempt, *boy*."

"Orealus is a joke," the satyr agreed, a grimace stretching his mouth so far down that the corners of his mustache nearly touched his collarbone. "He promised us everything but gave us nothing. You know how many satyrs are left after the war against the Great Deceiver?" He jabbed a thumb at his chest. "Me! Just me! Our great bards, our rangers, our mothers and healers and fawns—all gone! I'm all that's left. What kind of legacy is that?" He took a long pull from the mug he'd tried to push on Weylyn. "Pathetic," he muttered, and Kaden wasn't sure whether he was talking about Orealus or himself.

"You can't expect to live life without facing trials or tribulations," Kaden argued. "Not even Orealus can. Lucient is a trial for all of us, but if you join me in fighting him, we can—"

"Oh, please." Weylyn put away his swords, then crossed his arms. "Now you're trying to bargain with a coin you don't have. Why would Lucient bother with a little thing like you? You know nothing of the greatness that this world used to be, the greatness of men like my father, Khalon the Wolf. You know nothing about the heritage you've laid claim to. Simply calling yourself a king isn't enough to make you one and saying that you're out to fight Lucient doesn't mean the Dark One even knows you exist."

He pulled over a rickety chair and sat down, then kicked his feet up on the table his satyr friend was still standing on. He pulled off his helmet, revealing a chiseled chin, long, thick black wavy hair he had tied back, and a jagged scar that sliced perpendicularly through the skin surrounding his right eye. "I suggest you go home before you attract the attention of someone who'll kill you for free." The satyr laughed and drained the rest of the mug, then turned away from them.

Kaden fought the urge to bite his lip. How would he make Weylyn see sense if he couldn't find a way of appealing to him? Mention of his past wasn't enough. The will of Orealus wasn't enough—

"He's already got Lucient's attention," Petey blurted. "That's why I'm here. I was part of a goblin unit sent by Lucient to murder Kaden. His foster father saved him, but not before taking a mortal wound. I… reconsidered my allegiances and joined Kaden in his quest, first to get the truth from Bhalla, the wizard, then to unite the tribes against the one who'd sworn to kill him."

"That wasn't Lucient's last attempt either," Eldrin put in. "We were attacked just over a week ago by a group of dark-elf assassins. They're finding us wasn't incidental, and elves don't take orders from just anyone." He indicated himself with a hand. "I would know."

"Lucient is after me," Kaden said. He'd never thought that would be an argument to convince someone to join his cause, but it seemed to be the only one that might get through to Weylyn—and it *was* getting through to him. The air of insouciance was gone, replaced with a gleam of hunger in his dark eyes. "He's going to keep trying to kill me as long as I'm a threat, and I plan to be a threat until my allies and I eventually defeat him.

"You want revenge on him for what happened to your father," Kaden went on. "If you join me, you won't have to seek him out. He'll come to you."

"His puppets only," Weylyn murmured, but Kaden could see he was intrigued, on the verge of being hooked completely.

"Only for so long," Kaden argued. "If they continue to fail, then eventually he'll confront me himself. I want to be as ready as possible before that happens." He held Weylyn's intense stare, doing his best to convey his truthfulness.

A moment later, Weylyn pushed to his feet. "All right," he said. "If you can give me a confrontation with Lucient, then I'll join you on your quest."

"Yuh… you… wait!" the satyr shrieked, dropping his mug in his astonishment. "How can you just, make up your mind like *that*? And for a human who's little more than a boy? Why should you believe a word he says?"

"Because I choose to," Weylyn replied, walking over to one of the Salted Cod's thin walls and grabbing a dirty, dun-colored pack off the ground.

"But you, you can't just *leave* me here!" the satyr wailed. "I'll be turned into a stew in a heartbeat if you don't protect me."

Kaden saw Weylyn's hands suddenly still. So there was a sense of morality left in this man after all. "Your friend can come with us," he said.

"What?" Eldrin demanded.

"What!" Petey exclaimed.

"What?" the satyr asked. He seemed stunned. "Really?"

"Really." Kaden shrugged. "As Weylyn said, we're already a motley crew. One more person won't make us any odder than we are."

Weylyn scoffed as he donned his pack. "If Chum here doesn't tip that scale for you, then I'm looking forward to seeing the other oddities you're traveling with."

"Chum?" Petey wrinkled his nose. "Like the fish bait?"

The satyr jumped down from the table and stalked over to Petey, poking him in the chest. Chum, at least two heads shorter than Petey, had to tilt his head up to look the goblin in the eye. "More like 'I'm your chum until you mess with me, and then I'm your worst nightmare!' So don't try and—augh!" A cloud of pink pollen burst out of Petey's hood, catching Chum right in the face and sending him reeling. "What is that stuff?" he gasped.

"That's Bug," Petey said smugly. "And he doesn't like it when beings threaten me, so keep your hands to yourself, *Chum.*"

Weylyn laughed. "This is going to be an exciting quest, I can already tell."

Kaden was sure it would be. He just hoped they all survived it.

CHAPTER 22

Getting out of Westramore was a challenge in and of itself because as soon as it became clear to the street urchins that the infamous Weylyn, Son of the Wolf, was leaving town, Kaden, Petey, and Eldrin were immediately swamped with offers of "cheaper blades, milords, just as fast and deadly as the Wolf at half the price" and "won't get much out of hauling his companion around, sirs, why don't you let ol' Chum stay behind? I reckon he'd make a good stew!"

Weylyn brushed the comments off with the air of someone who couldn't be bothered to reply, but Chum wasn't quite as easygoing.

"Oh, you dolts only *wish* you could taste these haunches!" he shouted, slapping one of his thighs as he trotted along between Weylyn and Kaden, looking out at the crowd smugly. "You could feed a village on me! Satyr meat is the rarest and most delectable of all, and now you'll *never* get your chance at it, you fat-lipped, dunder-headed, dimwitted human miscreants! Ha! Have a taste of that instead!" He kicked a chunk of horse dung with one of his cloven feet and sent it spiraling out into the press of people, which was starting to mutter angrily.

"This little idiot's going to get us jumped," Eldrin spoke from right behind Kaden. "We can't fight all of them, and we're not close enough to Herrington's ship to make a run for it. Even then, he won't leave until he's concluded his business."

Eldrin was right. "Chum, knock it off," Kaden said with quiet intensity to the satyr as they kept moving.

"Or what?" the satyr asked with a sneer. "You'll have your little pal *puff* on me again? I'm not afraid of that! Weylyn doesn't need your help when it comes to protecting his friends. Thank you very much."

"He's not wrong," Weylyn said after a moment, then sighed when three bruisers moved to block their path. "Oh, for the love of—get out of the way, Delios, I've got a contract to fulfill."

"Go on then," the big man in the center said, spitting a gobbet of grayish-brown drool off to the side. He smelled like tar and cheap incense. "Do what you do, but you're leaving the runt with us." He grinned menacingly. "We'll take good care of 'im."

Kaden tightened his grip on Vrangar's hilt. He heard Eldrin grab one of his arrows, and even Petey seemed to be brushing his cloak aside so he could reach Loyal Dwingent.

Weylyn just sighed. "Much as I'd love to stay and give you the fight you're clearly longing to lose, I've got places to go, Delios. So how about you get out of the way before I let Alpheon have a taste of your soul?" He smoothly unsheathed the sword he carried—not even in a threatening way, just like he was about to begin polishing it—and all three men hurried back a few paces.

"Aw, that's not fair," Delios complained. "You can't go bringin' soul-eating weapons into a friendly brawl, Weylyn! You promised the city council not to do that anymore."

"City council doesn't get a say once I've got a contract and am on my way out," Weylyn replied smoothly. "And Chum has never been part of the deal anyway, so I'll defend him how I like. Now move before I move you."

"Son of a—" Swearing a blue streak, the trio of brawlers stepped aside, and the rest of the crowd melted out of the way as well.

Kaden was stunned. How did he... what could he... *what?*

He managed to stay quiet until they were back outside the city and heading for *Dawn's Light* before blurting, "Soul eating? Your sword eats souls?"

"What? *Pshaw*," Weylyn said derisively. "Of course not. Alpheon is unbreakably hard, unbeatably fast, and unbelievably light. It's a light-ability-attuned sword, all right, but it's not a *religious* icon. The soul-eating thing is just a rumor I spread about so that fewer people would bother me whenever I'm in Westramore."

"It's why he fights with the blade sheathed there," Chum added proudly. "The city council passed a resolution that he couldn't use a soul-eating sword against other mercenaries because that just wasn't fair."

"What a ridiculous place," Eldrin muttered.

Weylyn shrugged. "It's an odd spot, but once you know how to bend it to your will, it has its uses. Now. Which ship is yours, and where are we going anyway?"

Kaden had an idea about that, but he wasn't going to get into it yet. "I'll talk to you all about it once we're back on board."

Getting back onto the ship was easy. Captain Herrington had gotten his business done in record time, and he certainly didn't want to linger there any longer than usual. He wasn't taking any more passengers either, something he said he usually did whenever he stopped by the city.

"But I wouldn't want to get anyone else involved with your group before I drop you at your next port," he said to Kaden as his talented crew unfurled the topsail so that they could take advantage of the wind to back them out of the tightly packed port. "Where will that be, anyhow?"

Kaden waited for Queen Pepper, Redfern, Millicent, and Ada to join them back by the stern, all of them glancing curiously between Weylyn and Chum before saying, "I think the next place we need to go is Nethopolis."

For a long moment, no one said anything at all. Then simultaneously, Captain Herrington began to swear as Weylyn started to laugh, a long, loud belly laugh that had him bending over and slapping at his thigh in mirth.

"What?" Kaden demanded.

"You dragged me out of my den to chase fairytales!" Weylyn howled with laughter. "Oh, hells, I should have asked more questions before I said yes but blow me down. Even if I'm on a fool's errand, it's already the most fun I've had in years."

"I don't understand." Kaden refocused on the captain. "We're close to the ancient island where land dwellers used to meet with the merfolk, aren't we? I'm sure I saw it on your map—"

"That island was wiped clean *off* the map by Thálassa the Leviathan, or in sailor world known as the Beast of the Blue, many years ago!" Captain Herrington shouted, both hands grabbing the brim of his captain's hat so hard it started splitting at the seams. "It doesn't even exist anymore! No one knows where the new entrance to Nethopolis is, or even who's running it if it's still around! And even if it is, just *getting* there would—it would—"

He took a deep breath, let go of his hat, then said, "Legend says that Thálassa is controlled by an amulet that hung around the late King Trophorus's neck. Trophorus was killed by his brother Agalus, and Agalus came down on the side of Lucient during the last battle. The heir, Varun, was killed during the war, for all of us know. No merperson has been seen since then, no—"

"That's not true!" Ada said, pushing her way forward and putting her hands on her hips as she faced Captain Herrington. "There have been plenty of sightings of merfolk along the coast!"

"Local legends and the imaginations of drunk sailors at work," Weylyn said, straightening up at last as he regained his breath. "I've traveled far and wide over the sea in my work, and

I've never seen a single merperson or credible evidence that they exist any longer."

"Perhaps that's because you have all the observational skills of a drunken sailor if I were to judge by the way you smell," Ada retorted.

"Where do wenches find such sharp tongues these days?" Weylyn marveled. "Didn't your father teach you not to speak to your elders and betters like that?"

"My father died in battle against Lucient, and my *mother* taught me that no one who would speak to me as though I am a fool is in any way my better," Ada said, crossing her arms across her chest defiantly.

The entire group held its breath for a moment, waiting to see how the confrontation between two of their newest members would play out. Queen Pepper looked ready to intercede on Ada's behalf, and if the way Chum was puffing out his chest was any indication, he was preparing a speech or two as well.

Then Weylyn broke the staring contest, shaking his head. "Perhaps I'm the fool then, to speak down to someone I don't even know," he said. "Your father was killed in battle against the Great Deceiver?"

Ada's posture relaxed the tiniest bit. "He was. My mother fled with my brother and sister while I was still in her belly and made a new home for us in Whaldalf's Landing, but I've never forgotten where I truly come from. And my family has always had a strong connection to the merfolk, the good merfolk loyal to Trophorus. If there are still merpeople in Nethopolis, my flag will buy us entry."

"Bold words," Weylyn said.

"True ones."

"Has anyone forgotten the fact that *I'm* the captain on this bloody ship?" Captain Herrington asked in a snappish voice. "And we won't be going anywhere without *my* say-so, no matter whether this one"—he gestured at Kaden—"believes the impossible can happen because he's got Orealus on his side, or because *you*"—now he was pointing straight at Ada—"think that flying a flag that meant something in a kinder world has any bearing on the cruel place we live today.

"You know who patrols the seas where the entrance to Nethopolis used to be? Ah-ah, no, that was a rhetorical question," the captain said quickly as Ada opened her mouth again. "It's that damnable leviathan, Thálassa! Do you have any idea what it takes to successfully *flee* from a leviathan?" The captain flung his arms wide. "I don't either, because no one ever manages it! And you want us to sail there? Are you *mad*?"

"There *are* still merfolk, and they *are* still our friends!" Ada insisted.

Captain Herrington sighed so heavily Kaden wondered that he still had air left in his lungs to speak. "Even if there are, and they are—apart from the leviathan, that area is shallow and full of treacherous rocks. An entire underground mountain was torn apart during the war, and the pieces of it shift and churn with every tide. It takes a lot of work to safely sail in waters like that, and even then, how would we know where to stop and try for a parlay?"

Listening to the captain was like having a spike of doubt driven into Kaden's mind. *No hope, no hope, no hope.* He could stop looking now, perhaps, stop with the people he had and try to gather a force to fight Lucient with, but... he knew, deep in his heart, that it wouldn't be enough. They needed every strong arm and stout spirit they could gather for the terrors that lay ahead, and it was Kaden's responsibility to bring those people together. But Nethopolis seemed like an impossible nut to crack.

Kaden didn't want to risk his friends, but he had to reach the merfolk. He would borrow a rowboat if he had to and go it alone, ask for Orealus's protection on a solo journey, as long as it meant he was doing his best.

He blinked, startled, as the amulet on his chest suddenly warmed. A brilliant white light burst forth from it, pointing northeast. Underneath the heat, he felt a draw of energy from him, and he knew the amulet was tapping into his Mana, slowly and steadily. The draw felt akin to the energy expended from muscles while walking, but deeper, closer to his soul. Everyone in the party froze, staring at the illuminated path.

Petey was the first to speak. "We should have thought of that earlier!" he exclaimed. "The amulet's always helped us find the right way before. Of course it can help us again!"

Surprisingly, now it was Weylyn who balked. "I don't believe for a minute that that stone is powered by faith in Orealus or *whatever* you're going to try and tell us," he said harshly. "And I won't follow anyone who believes in such blatant ridiculousness. You—"

"The amulet came from Bhalla," Kaden said quickly. It wasn't the whole truth, but it was undoubtedly still truthful. "You've heard of him, I take it?"

"The wizard." Weylyn stroked his chin thoughtfully. "Powerful, from what I recall."

"Very."

"He created this amulet?"

"Yes."

"Ah." The Son of the Wolf's good humor was instantly restored. "Then perhaps this isn't nothing but a fool's errand after all!"

Kaden focused his attention on Captain Herrington. "If you don't want to take us, I understand. But finding Nethopolis isn't optional, and if you don't help us, I'll find someone who will."

Captain Herrington's face sagged for a moment, as though he'd been punched in the gut and had the wind knocked out of him, before firming his jaw once more. "I told that one's mother that I'd see her safe for as long as possible," he said, pointing at Ada. "And I'll be damned before I go back on my word to K'Lani

Davenrich. But I urge your party to seek their own counsel apart from you before they agree to let you lead them into destruction just because you've got a hunch and a magical doodad." He waved his hands at them. "Now get off my foredeck, all of you, I've got sailing to do."

"Ugh, sailing," Petey moaned, already turning yellow around the edges now that he was back on the water. "More sailing. When are we going to get back to traveling on *land*? That's what I want to know."

"Weak-stomached beast, aren't you?" Chum said with a sneer. "Not nearly as hardy as a satyr. Why, I've gamboled through a midden a mile long and come out the other side with a smile on my face and a spring in my step!"

"And that's praiseworthy to you?" Eldrin asked. "That you like to prance through fields of foul refuse?"

"I—what—*no*, that's not what I'm saying at all, you dainty-limbed, pointy-eared—"

Kaden ignored his arguing friends as he concentrated on the amulet. The guiding light was no longer just a light. It felt like a… like a *pull*, an urging, an indelible calling that he knew to be correct. He stayed close to the front of the ship, providing a heading for Captain Herrington, and waited to see if any of his friends would come to tell him that he'd finally gone a step too far—this was it for them, the end of their journey, they would follow him but not into a place protected by the leviathan, not to pursue a city and a people who were as good as lost to time.

No one came to speak to him—not in words, at least. An hour or so into his vigil, Queen Pepper came to him with a mug of tea. The first sip was sweet, almost floral. He recognized it as her unique blend brought from Fayspire, which he knew she was getting low on. He glanced at her, startled, and she just patted his shoulder with a smile.

Eldrin didn't stop by, but he did his part to keep Chum from bothering poor Petey, which was generous of him. He also offered to spar with Weylyn, and the sight of them clashing back and forth on the deck was enough to distract even the most uncertain crewmembers from the future. Eldrin's blade was fast but not as swift as Weylyn's, and the human outweighed him by a significant margin. He held his own for a long while, though, thanks to his own speed and agility, and when Weylyn finally slapped Eldrin's sword aside and pressed Alpheon to his neck, he kept it there only a fraction of a second before stepping back.

"Well fought," he said sincerely, and Eldrin's scowl melted into something a bit less ferocious after a moment.

"Not well enough, but I daresay I'll improve fast if I keep coming for *your* head," he said.

"We'll see," Weylyn replied, and if they were threats, they were delivered with good humor.

A steady wind and a clear sky allowed them to sail by the light of the moon. Captain Herrington had "requested" that Kaden "keep your course where I can damn well see it if you please," so he and Duke stayed at the gunwale while the others gathered around the galley for dinner. It was quiet and calming to stand there, with the wind and the lap of the waves filling his ears while the full moon shone down on the sea, like the sign of Orealus brought to life. Kaden closed his eyes and clasped one hand around his amulet, the other one coming to rest on Duke's head.

I pray that you'll be with all of us on the way forward, to help us accomplish your will and bring together the former tribal leaders of Empyrea and all of the land to defeat Lucient. I pray that you ease the hearts of my companions, even if they're stubborn about believing in you, and give them strength and courage.

And I pray that you save a little for me as well because... I think I'm going to need it.

CHAPTER 23

"**K**aden?"

He startled, dropping the amulet and turning around to see Ada behind him. "I brought you dinner," she said, handing over a wooden trencher. It contained a piece of grilled fish, a generous hunk of fresh crusty bread—something the captain must have bought in Westramore, for there was no bread oven on the ship—and a dollop of boiled green lentils. The container also housed a large piece of fish for Duke, which Ada handed to him with a flourish. He showed his appreciation by scarfing it down in two huge bites.

"You big beast," Kaden said with a chuckle as he scratched Duke's head, then looked back at Ada. "Thank you," he said after a moment. He took the trencher and started to eat.

Ada stayed, joining him at the rail. Standing next to her was beginning to feel familiar. Kaden wondered for a moment if his friends were deliberately leaving the pair of them alone, then dismissed the thought. They had better things to do than try to arrange a romance.

"You believe me," she said after a moment, a statement that nevertheless had a *hint* of question in it. "That there are still merfolk and that they are good."

"I believe you." He did—he had to. "And I'm sure at least some of them are good. Probably some are also bad, but that's the way with every race."

"Bad humans?" she queried with a bit of a smile.

"Bandits, brigands, and thieves. Most of the city of Westramore, probably," Kaden said, rolling his eyes. "Trust me, I got to see that up close."

Ada nodded. "Good goblins?"

"Petey, of course." Kaden thought for a moment. "And his mother. There are probably others too." Not that he had met them, but… there had to be, right?

"Woof," Duke said, as though he could read Kaden's mind. Kaden gave him another scratch.

"And you really think we can find Nethopolis?"

"I have faith that we can." He knew that Orealus was with him, even if he didn't always hear his voice. "I think we're *meant* to, as long as we're brave enough to risk it." He smiled a little. "But I think we should bring your family's flag along, just in case."

"Of course," she said, lifting her chin in the air but not entirely pulling off a haughty tone. "I'll take that back to the cook."

"Oh." He had finished the meal already? "Thank you."

"You're welcome." She walked away, and Kaden had to force himself not to watch her go. He looked out again at the waves instead, drawing his cloak a little tighter around his shoulders. The light from his amulet was a powerful and steady beam guiding the ship on. He would stand here as long as he needed to get them to the entrance to Nethopolis.

Even if it took all night.

*　　*　　*

Kaden woke up to a faceful of sea spray and Duke's teeth in the back of his cloak, jerking him back from the edge of the gunwale. His legs ached, and his face and hands were freezing. Woolly bums, had he fallen asleep leaning here? He glanced around blearily, taking note of the dark sky overhead with just a thin line of red straight ahead. Not yet sunrise. It looked like the ship was running on a skeleton crew, and none of his friends were among the awake.

He felt a little hurt. Why hadn't any of them come to get him to go to sleep?

Why should you need your friends to remind you to be a reasonable person? Kaden shook his head. He needed to take responsibility for his actions, even the dumb ones.

"Kaden!" Captain Herrington's voice managed to stay soft yet travel quite well to where Kaden stood. "Get over here!"

Kaden shook out his arms and rolled his shoulders to warm up a bit as he walked over to the captain. His amulet was still going strong, shooting a steady white beam of light into the distance. "Sir?" he said as he joined Captain Herrington at the wheel.

"Look," the captain said, his voice grim. "Look dead ahead. Tell me what you see."

Kaden squinted into the darkness. "I can't really see anything yet," he said. "It's too dark out."

"No sea eyes," Captain Herrington grumbled. "Then look at what your light is showing you. See it touching out there?"

"I… I do!" It *did* look like the light from the amulet was hitting the water. "That must be it! How far away is that?" It couldn't be too far—they were already here, then, they'd found the entrance to Nethopolis!

"Not more than a few miles," the captain responded. "Now, look at the water beneath us."

Was this some kind of test? The sails were filled, pushing them in the direction they wanted to go. Kaden glanced down at the water and—

Wait a moment.

Wait.

Why was it flowing *backward*? The pull was sluggish for now, barely more than standing still, but the waves were slowly but surely sailing *against* the mighty wind, not with it. "I don't understand," Kaden murmured, but even as he said it, he knew something was wrong.

"There are two options. Either we're headed straight for a vortex, or something big enough to disrupt the ocean's pull is moving in the water right below us." His jaw tightened. "Either way, it's bad news for my ship. That means it'll be even worse on a tiny boat like the one I could send you all off in." He looked straight at Kaden. "You have a choice to make. Either stay aboard and let me take Ada back to her mother, or risk her life and yours rowing a boat into wherever your amulet is leading you."

Kaden glanced at the water again. It wasn't his imagination—it was moving faster now, still in the opposite direction. "Then we have to disembark," he said. "Now."

"If you're sure that's your decision." Doubt and worry clouded the captain's voice, almost enough to make Kaden doubt his own choice. But... no. This was right. This was the only way forward, and he wasn't going to flinch from it just because it looked hard.

Or impossible. And it's not just you that you've got to think about.

Responsibility for the lives of his friends weighed down on him, crushing his heart like a fist. Kaden took a deep breath and made the symbol of Orealus in front of his chest. He had to have faith.

He *did* have faith.

"We're going."

Captain Herrington nodded grimly. "Then wake your people while mine prepare the boat. Sharpey! Levi!" he shouted. "Ready the cutter for launch. We've got to get our passengers lowered down now!"

Kaden ran to where his companions were slowly blinking awake. "Come on," he said, shaking their shoulders one by one. "We've got to go, now."

"We found it already?" Ada asked, sitting up in her bedroll with a yawn. "The entrance to Nethopolis?"

"I think so," Kaden temporized, "but the way there won't be easy, and if we don't leave now, we might wreck the *Dawn's Light*."

Weylyn was already on his feet. "Is it the leviathan?" he asked. He sounded more eager than Kaden had expected, but perhaps that was naïve. Weylyn had already shown that he was willing to fight long odds—and fighting a leviathan were the longest odds out there.

"Maybe. Pack up, quick," he finished, grabbing his own gear and running to help with the boat launch. The hard work was already done, though—the sailors had already prepared the hoist and were lifting the boat into the air. Master Sharpey motioned for Kaden to get in.

Kaden made sure two sets of oars were strapped down tight inside the skiff and tied his pack tightly around his back before getting in with Duke and claiming a spot beside the tiller. After a moment's consideration, he looped a line of rope around his waist, then made a loop for the other end and pulled it tight around Duke's chest. "We're not going to get separated," he promised his dog. Duke licked his face in reply. "*Ugh*, gross."

The little skiff was barely big enough for them all, even considering that Queen Pepper, Millicent, and Redfern could fly. The others joined him quickly, settling on the wooden benches that were fixed to the boat's bottom. Chum was complaining heartily of being woken up so early—"unfair and unjust, and if this is going to become a habit, you'd best beware of snakes in your shoes and scorpions in your drawers!"—but he was the only one. Everyone else was terse and tense, and Petey's ears had drooped so low they almost touched his shoulders.

Ada shared an embrace with Captain Herrington before being the last to enter the boat, taking the seat next to Kaden. She had a bright blue piece of cloth wrapped around her shoulders like a cloak—her family's flag, Kaden realized. She caught him staring and nodded once, a silent affirmation that she was ready.

"This is the next step, then?" Eldrin said, staring down at the water, which was now pulling hard on the ship.

"It is," Kaden said.

"Well, then." He smirked, but it lacked his normal bite. "Good thing I can swim, I suppose."

"Row hard!" Captain Herrington called out to them as his men began to lower the skiff toward the water. "Row as hard and as fast as you can toward that light of yours! Don't stay on the water a moment longer than you have to!"

"Aye, aye!" Kaden called back. A moment later, the boat hit the water, and the sling that had tethered them to the *Dawn's Light* fell away. A moment after that—

"*Whoa!*" Without the bulk of the big ship separating them from the water, their speed was much more noticeable, and so was the turbulence that came with it.

"Get the oars out!" Weylyn ordered. "We've got to row to keep ourselves with the current if we don't want to get turned sideways!" He ripped one set free for himself, then shoved the other set at Eldrin. "Can you keep a count, fey prince?" he asked.

"Can you count beyond the number of your fingers and toes?" Eldrin snapped back, but he immediately set to following Weylyn's orders. Slowly the little boat stabilized as they began to traverse the waves, at ever-increasing speeds, toward where Kaden's light hit the water. Or at least... *primarily* toward it. The boat's tiller was so responsive, the slightest movement from him seemed to send it askew.

"Here," Ada said, reaching out and laying one hand on his. "Let me help you." She steadied their course, and Kaden cast a grateful glance at her.

"Thank you."

"What… is… *that*?" That came from Redfern, who was flying just above the boat, his spear clenched in his hands like a favorite teddy bear. He was staring back the way they had come.

"Oh… Orealus preserve us," Queen Pepper said, pressing one hand to her mouth. Kaden couldn't help it—he turned to look behind them.

In the space between their skiff and the *Dawn's Light*, something that looked like a forest of spears had emerged from the water, bristling and gleaming in the light of the blood-tinged sunrise. "Thálassa," Weylyn said, satisfaction and something like yearning in his voice. "The Beast of the Blue. He's hunting."

The spines swerved back and forth as if debating which direction to go. A second later, a large sea-foam-green dorsal fin parted the water and rose above the surface, attached to a tremendously long, aquamarine, snakelike head framed by two more fins. All three fins looked more like bat wings than traditional fish fins. Three rows of razor-sharp teeth gleamed around its black tongue in its gaping mouth, and its eyes were giant, glowing sulfurous moons with fiery pupils. Even from a hundred feet away, Kaden could see the creature's eyes dilate as it focused on their small boat. The monster must have been larger than a whale.

The head dropped back into the water, and a moment later, the spiny fins of the creature's back turned… toward them.

"Row!" Kaden shouted. They were getting close to the place where his light disappeared, the water pulling them ever harder. "For your lives, row!"

The beast was gaining on them—it didn't even have to *try* to gain on them; Kaden knew that. But the current seemed to displease it, and it surfaced several times, its long, snakelike body writhing as it fought. The worst moment was when Thálassa got close enough to lunge for them—it shot up out of the water at great speed, the front half of its enormous body plunging toward them like a falling tree trunk. Kaden could practically count the vast, blue-green scales as the creature descended toward them.

It missed by less than the length of its head. The splash nearly capsized their boat, but the leviathan didn't seem willing to try again. Instead, it began to pull away, spiny fins vanishing underwater after a few moments.

"It's leaving us alone!" Petey shouted joyfully. "Hurrah!"

"Because we're heading into *that*!" Millicent replied in a frantic shout, and—

Oh.

Oh, Orealus, save them.

The current precisely *resulted from* a vortex, a whirlpool fifty feet across which spun tight and fast, drawing everything into its depths—including their boats. Kaden's light was fixed on the very center of it.

"My queen!" Redfern flew down and grabbed her arm. "We have to fly!"

"No," Queen Pepper replied, afraid but resolute. "I put my faith in Kaden and in Orealus."

"My *queen*—"

"I will not abandon my companions," she said sternly. "And they don't have the option of escape now."

It was true. They were well and truly caught in the vortex's draw, the skiff beginning to spin in an ever-tightening circle. The sound of the water went from a rush to a scream, the terrifying force surrounding them, encompassing them. Kaden could barely breathe for all the spray that flew around him, and soon the boat would hit the center of the vortex, and—and—

Was that *another* light down there? Bright and blue? Where could it be coming from?

Kaden couldn't voice what he'd seen before the water suddenly consumed their boat, closing over his head and blocking out all light.

They were lost.

CHAPTER 24

Kaden came back to consciousness slowly, drifting up from total darkness through gray light and finally into something that left the dream world behind in favor of reality.

I'm alive. I survived. Orealus be praised, I'm living.

But was anyone else?

Kaden, eyes closed, lay still for a long moment, cold, sore, and utterly drenched as he worked up the willpower to confront what could have happened to the rest of his group. It was hard to breathe for some reason, and he couldn't think of why until he remembered he looped a line of rope around *his waist* then made a loop for the other end and pulled it tight around Duke's chest.

"Duke!" Kaden bolted upright, coughing out the last of the water in his mouth as he looked around desperately for his dog. Duke lay a few feet away from him on his side, unmoving except for the slow rise and fall of his chest. Kaden carefully patted Duke down, feeling for wounds... but there was nothing. A lot of wet hair, but his lungs seemed clear. What was wrong, then?

And it wasn't just Duke. Everyone in his party was lying on the same coral-colored floor, all of them breathing but none of them stirring. Kaden rolled onto his hands and knees in preparation to get up—his legs were shaky, but he'd get to his friends if he had to *crawl* to them—when suddenly—

"Kaden?" a voice asked from behind him. He turned with a pained grimace—he was alive, but *ow* was he bruised—and let out a great sigh of relief when he saw Ada, awake!

"Ada!" It took a moment for the dim light to resolve and for him to realize that she was no longer wearing her flag—and that her hands were bound together. "What—oh no." He glanced around again, and for the first time, it occurred to him that the place they were in could be a cell. The room was shaped like a dome, gray and pink and pitted. Light percolated through the material, giving it a soft blue glow that was barely enough to illuminate Kaden's friends. Only one of the sides of the room was open, and it seemed to open onto... onto...

With clumsy fingers, Kaden untied the knot that kept him attached to Duke, then got to his feet. He staggered over to the open wall, reaching a hand out to touch it.

Water. Cold, dark water.

Kaden drew back, shocked. "What... how is this possible?" He looked at Ada, who seemed somber. "Did Agalus take us prisoner?" he asked quietly.

She shook her head. "Not Agalus. Varun, the king's son."

"Wait." Then this made less sense to him now. "Why has *he* imprisoned us?"

"They haven't told me much yet," Ada said with a frown. "But they woke me up first because of my family's flag, and while I was coming to, I heard them talking about how we shouldn't have been able to get this far, especially not with Thálassa on patrol. They're afraid of the leviathan, *really* afraid of it."

"What else?" Kaden asked.

"They asked me who I was and why we were here. I told them about us and about your quest. The guards agreed to go and tell King Varun, and one of them said they'd lift the..." Ada looked around at the room they were in. "Energy in here? Mysterious power? Whatever it was that kept us all asleep. The others should wake up soon."

Kaden reached out toward her wrists. "Why did they bind your hands?"

She rolled her eyes. "To 'send a message' to the rest of you, apparently." She tugged at the binding. "They don't hurt, but I can't break them. I even tried cutting them, but it didn't work."

That was no good. "We can try Vrangar, let me—"

"No," Ada said firmly. "That would only make them suspicious. Besides, we have other things to deal with right now."

"My *head*," Petey moaned from behind Kaden. He turned immediately to help his friend. All around them, the others had suddenly begun to stir, and Kaden and Ada did their best to orient them on where they were and what was going on.

Before they had time to discuss their options as a group, two bright green lights appeared in the distance through the water wall. As they neared, the light was resolved into the glow of two tridents, each held by a merman.

Kaden was awed by their appearance. The top halves were those of men, although men who had been tattooed with markings across their chests and arms that he'd never seen the like of before. Their hair was long and varied from pale sea green to midnight blue. But their lower halves were... to say that they were shaped like fish would be inaccurate because Kaden had never seen a fish so muscled and sinuous, so finely scaled and brilliantly colored in hues similar to their hair. They looked absolutely amazing.

"Oi! Fish butt!" Chum shouted as he bulled his way to the front of the group. "What sort of cowards lock their guests away in an overgrown sea urchin, huh?"

Weylyn smacked his friend's forehead with the palm of his hand. "Chum..."

"No, really! I want to talk to these, these *buffoons*, and tell them exactly what I think of their manners!" Chum waved a fist. "But I can't because they're swimmin' around out where they know they're safe and don't have to talk to us because they're cowards! That's right, I'm calling you cow—whaaaa!" He darted behind Weylyn as one of the mermen swam right up to the water wall, then *through* it, and—

His emerald-green tail disappeared, leaving muscular, bare legs where it had been. Very bare… legs. And everything else. Kaden resolutely kept his eyes on the merman's face, which was actually an inch or two higher than his own. He made an enormous person in this form, with shoulders broad enough to sit a child on either side with room to spare, his dark torso covered in black lightning-shaped tattoos. His shoulder-length, pale sea-green hair framed a rugged, wide jaw, and as Kaden watched, the feathery gills on either side of his neck retreated into pockets in his skin. The blue of his eyes roiled in a way similar to the ocean behind him.

"You dare to threaten us?" the merman asked, his golden, gem-studded trident gripped defensively in both hands. "You who intruded upon *our* realm?"

"I told you, it wasn't an intrusion!" Ada protested. "We seek an audience with your king. No more, no less."

"You riled the beast," the merman said as though she hadn't spoken at all. "You strained the barrier that protects our people from its rampages. You came uninvited and unasked. Why shouldn't we treat you as nothing more than prisoners, or worse—spies?"

"We aren't spies," Kaden said. "Who would we spy for?"

The merman's bright blue eyes narrowed. "Lucient, of course."

Weylyn interrupted the conversation with a guffaw. "Lucient! Yes, because Lucient is so good at inspiring the loyalty of the races of men, elves, fairies, goblins, and satyrs all at once! Ha!" He shook his head. "If Lucient could do that, he truly *would* be worthy of the title 'the Great Deceiver,' but he's not."

Weylyn took a step forward, one hand resting not-so-casually on the hilt of his *own* weapon. "And I stand by what my little friend said. If your king won't meet with us after what we went through to get here, then he's a coward who doesn't deserve the help we're here to offer."

The merman raised his chin arrogantly. "And what help could a ragamuffin group like you offer to the king of Nethopolis?"

Weylyn grinned. The way he bared his teeth made Kaden think of a shark. "He'll have to meet with us to find out."

"Or he could leave you here to rot under the sea," the merman suggested.

"Thereby confirming that he's a coward," Weylyn replied. "Not to mention, he'd be trapping a sovereign monarch, a prince, and the heir to King Karatheas here. You think they won't be sought out? You think their people won't come for them and bring a new wave of war to your kind if you do them harm?"

That was *not* how Kaden would have put it, at all, but the argument seemed to have some effect on the merman in front of them. "Supposing I take you to see the king," he said after a moment's pause. "Do you swear to accept his judgment upon hearing your request, no matter what it is, and leave this kingdom in peace?"

"We didn't come here to make trouble," Ada said quietly. "We came here to make allies."

"We will leave in peace," Kaden affirmed. "But only if the king hears us out."

The merman hesitated, then shrugged one massive shoulder. "Very well. I'll take you to the king, and he will hear what you have to say. But know this." He brandished the trident menacingly. "Anyone who threatens him, or this realm, will regret it."

"We understand," Kaden said before Chum could release whatever nonsense was causing his chest to puff up. "Thank you."

"Come." The merman turned and stepped through the watery portal. A second later, the water belled out, like a bubble of air being pushed out ahead of them, only it didn't stop. It stretched into the distance, leaving a tunnel—with a damp, sandy floor and water on all other sides—for them to pass through. The two mermen swam on either side, tridents at the ready.

With no other option, Kaden moved into the tunnel. It was *bitterly* cold in there, the warmth of their cell vanishing in the space of a heartbeat and replaced with the chill of the deep ocean. He could see his breath in front of his face. Duke shook his fur hard, then joined Kaden. Petey followed—Bug looking rather sad and bedraggled where he sat on his shoulder—then Eldrin, then Weylyn, and Chum.

"Astonishing," Queen Pepper said, stepping into the tunnel last as she shook a few droplets of water from her wings. "There is a very subtle power at work here. It's been... tuned, somehow, so that the forces are held permanently in place. I think it uses energy from the earth itself to power it."

Millicent frowned as she moved up beside Pepper. "How can an ability's effect be maintained for such a long time?"

"Carvings, perhaps," Pepper mused. "Glyphs, time-tested over the centuries the mermen have lived here. It is interesting, don't you think, that Varun is in command of Nethopolis while his uncle Agalus, who controls the most terrifying monster in the seas, is not?"

"If we really *are* going to meet with Varun," Redfern grumbled. Of all the fairies, she seemed to hate being on the ground the most. She tried to lift off, but the cold temperature and the slender tunnel they had to traverse made flying impossible. "If it's not Agalus playing with us all."

"We were unconscious, and they left us our weapons," Queen Pepper reminded him. "I think a person of Agalus's ill repute would certainly have taken them if he didn't have us killed on the spot." She smiled at Ada. "I'm sure it helped that you wore your family's flag. The sight of an old ally might have stayed their hands."

"I hope so," Ada said. She'd tucked her hands under her armpits, and Kaden could see she was shivering. He wished he had something dry to offer her, but everything in his pack was as damp as the rest of him. "I confess that I'd hoped it would do *more*, though."

"Like what?" Weylyn asked, sarcasm heavy in his voice. "You came with a symbol but no abilities. People with yah'zaval only respect others who have it. Remember that when it comes time to negotiate with Varun," he added to Kaden as he dodged around a crab crawling across the sand.

Chum didn't bother to dodge. He just picked it up and bit right into the still-flailing crustacean. He chewed noisily, then spit out a mouthful of the shell. "Delicious!" he said, grinning at all of their dumbstruck expressions. "Nothing like getting it fresh from the source!"

"You're appalling," Petey informed him, his ears twitching with disdain.

"Hey, if you knew how good it was, you'd be biting down too instead of mocking me. After all, we don't know when we're gonna get another meal."

Kaden figured he'd have to be a *lot* closer to starving to eat a raw crab, but he refrained from joining the argument and walked on. He could see something in the distance now—another light, this one much brighter and broader than the little glows from the tridents. This one looked like a dome, expanded weblike around a gigantic central structure. "That must be Nethopolis," he murmured.

The land walkers had a fantastic view of the castle, the central structure to a dazzling city. The building was made entirely of coquina and nestled into the surrounding coral, organically grown from the reef, working with the sea life rather than against it. In fact, all of the city's buildings were built directly into this reef, which was brilliant in bright shades of blue and pink. As the party walked closer, Kaden realized the coral and even the seaweed growing from the streets glowed due to the bioluminescent quality of these plants. Jellyfish and angler fish floating around the city also had a natural glow to them. These creatures acted as streetlights would in a land city. Sunlight sparkled down in glimmering shafts from the surface of the sea. Countless species of aquatic animals moved in and around the windowless palace. Throughout the city, the multicolored merfolk rode dolphins and giant seahorses like humans riding horses.

"Wow. It's beautiful," Petey said, brightening a little. "It kind of reminds me of Shroudscar."

"Beautiful? Shroudscar?" Eldrin shook his head.

"It can be! When my mother sat on the throne, she mandated a festival of lights every year. All the torches are extinguished, and the soot is wiped off the walls. After a while, the luminescence comes back, and everything in the city glows in a dozen different colors." Petey smiled. "Beautiful."

"I'd like to see it someday," Kaden said. His friend beamed at him.

"And the odds are likely that you will!" Weylyn announced, slapping Kaden on the back. "Given your hopeless fight against Lucient and the fact that you're a madman, that is."

"Hey, you didn't have to come along," Kaden pointed out.

"I never said I didn't like madmen, did I?" Weylyn pointed ahead of them. "We're here, I think."

They had reached the tunnel's end, passing straight through the wall of weblike energy and into a hall crafted from rock and living coral. It was naturally beautiful in the same way that Fayspire had seemed to Kaden. Rocky sconces held pools of glowing yellow light, and the path ahead of them led the way to a great, gold-colored throne room.

Shells and sea life featured predominantly in the furniture. Kaden could feel the pressure of the water around them, but the tunnel was sturdy, and he knew it had withstood the test of time.

Both of their guards emerged from the water and changed instantly, legs forming where their tails had been a moment ago. One of them moved quickly ahead while the other, the one who'd spoken to them already, gestured down the hall with his trident. "This way to meet with King Varun."

He led the way, and as he walked, he was met at every intersection by another merman or mermaid bringing him something—one came with a loose, flowing robe sewn with a thousand pearls, another came with a goblet that he drained in one long gulp as he kept walking, then handed back to the waiting attendant. The final one who approached did so with her eyes down, carrying a fluffy, kelp-like pillow in her hands. On it was a golden crown, decorated with gleaming abalone shell and, set on top of it, the greatest, blackest pearl Kaden had ever seen.

The merman put the crown on, then moved up the steps to the throne, turned, and sat down with an air of authority.

Ah. Kaden should have guessed sooner that they were dealing with the king himself, but Nethopolis was very distracting. Nevertheless, he bowed, and the murmur of movement behind him indicated that most, hopefully, all of his companions were doing the same.

"Rise," King Varun said shortly, his voice echoing in the dome room. "Rise and tell me what you expected to find by venturing into my kingdom and what you hope to extract from us. And *do not* lie to me. One word and I can flood this chamber with water and drown all of you before you can do more than raise a blade in my direction."

Well. That wasn't the tone that Kaden was hoping to strike in the very beginning. "We did come here hoping to find your kingdom, it's true," he said cautiously. "We were seeking

Nethopolis, and anyone within it who wishes to strike back against the Great Deceiver, Lucient."

"Strike *back*?" Varun raised a green eyebrow in a show of skepticism. "Who do you know who has ever managed to strike *back* at Lucient? That snake always makes the final blow himself and makes it so powerful that it can't be overcome. Look at this place." He gestured around with the hand not holding the trident. "This is the old home of my people, true enough, but my siblings and I once ruled *all* the provinces of the sea under the guidance of our father.

"Trophorus was a great king, a wise and a just king, yet he didn't even see Lucient's vicious blow coming in the form of his own brother. Lucient's forces we could have stood against, but my uncle Agalus? Who knows the ways of the waves and commands the terrible Thálassa?" Varun shook his head. "There was no hope of winning that fight. No hope of keeping what we had. It was all I could do to get the remnants of my people into this place, where Thálassa can't reach us, and seal it against my uncle."

He looked at Ada. "We have emerged infrequently since the fall of our ancestral kingdom. There are other merfolk out there who have sworn fealty to my brother, and when we meet them, the water turns red with blood. Very rarely, we check in on those we used to know. It's how my people recognized your flag when we found you, Adena Davenrich."

Varun turned his attention back to Kaden. "Your quest be damned, what I want to know is how you and your people escaped the vortex and ended up not only within my kingdom's barrier but also with no drowning deaths. By the time I had you transported to the cell where you woke up, a quarter of an hour had passed since we found you, yet you are all not only alive but well recovered."

Hope surged in Kaden. "It was Orealus," he said, firm and sure. "The power of Orealus saved us all. He guides me through my journey, helping me and my companions do his will to bring the leaders of the tribes into accord. That's why we're here—not to ask your presence on our quest, but to elicit a promise from you that when the time comes, you'll help us strike back—strike first *and* last—at Lucient."

Varun stared broodingly at the space just above Kaden's head. "You speak of impossibilities," he said at last. "The power of Orealus isn't something that can be relied upon. He may have saved you—for reasons of his own—but he didn't save your father. Yes, I recognize Karatheas's blood in you," he added when Kaden looked surprised. "I'm glad one of his children survived, but consider that: only *one* of his children lived. You had siblings, and they are dead. You had a mother, and she is dead. You had a father, a truly great man, and *he* is dead. Orealus didn't save them, and many, many others lost their lives fighting in that war. Orealus didn't stop Thálassa from becoming Thálassa, a vile tool in a vile merman's fist.

"No." Varun sat back on his throne. "We cannot help you, not with that beast patrolling the seas above us. My people are already too few, and a confrontation with Thálassa would be the end of us."

"What if we could kill Thálassa?"

Kaden turned in surprise to Weylyn, who had his arms crossed pensively. "What if we could take the beast out?" he continued. "Then would you support the fight against Lucient?"

Varun chuckled, but it was an ugly sound. "What did I tell you about *lying*?" He waved a hand, and a booming sound began to echo through the room. Water poured around their feet, then rose up to their calves.

"I did not lie! I merely asked a question," Weylyn shouted. "Are you so afraid of the answer that you would kill us to keep from having to confront your own fears?"

Varun held up his hand again. The water stopped at the level of Kaden's thigh. Duke's head was barely out of the water, and both Petey and Chum were soaked up to their chests.

"You can't destroy the leviathan. No one can," King Varun replied after a long pause. "I've tried. My strongest swimmers, my greatest warriors, have tried to kill it, and all of them have ended up a meal for the beast. Our protections, our energy shields, they keep us safe best if they're stationary—they don't work well while mobile, and Thálassa, as I'm sure you noted before you fell into my kingdom, is highly mobile. It's impossible."

"It's not impossible. Anyone—*everyone*—can be killed," Weylyn replied firmly. "You just have to have the right weapon and the right tactics. And I'll make you a promise, king of your single city: if you swear to come to the aid of Prince Kaden when we move against Lucient, I will slay your nemesis before you have to set one fin in open waters."

What? How? Kaden wanted to ask, but he also knew better than to interrupt right now. If he threw off negotiations, King Varun might just decide to drown them after all.

"You would ensure Thálassa is dealt with *before* my people and I were required to assist you?" Varun stroked a finger across his chin. "It would be a more than fair offer if you didn't speak the words of a fool."

"You have nothing to lose by it," Weylyn pointed out. "You can agree and preserve your honor whether I'm a fool or not, with the hope of someday regaining your father's fractured kingdom, or refuse and wonder for the rest of your long, isolated life whether or not I, the Son of the Wolf, could have done the impossible."

"Hmm." Varun was silent for a moment, then smiled at last. The water that had flooded the room began to recede. "Very well. You have an agreement, Son of the Wolf, and Kaden, son of Karatheas. Destroy Thálassa, and I will lead my people to your aid in the fight against the Great Deceiver. But until the beast is gone, you'll see nothing of us." He glanced at Ada. "Flags of friendship or not. Understood?"

Weylyn looked at Kaden, silent for once. Kaden stepped forward. "Understood," he said. "Thank you, King Varun."

"Don't thank me until you complete your half of the deal," Varun said. "I'll lend you a means to get back to shore and a merman to pilot it, but once you are gone, you will *not* return to Nethopolis until the leviathan is dead. Now." He nodded to someone they couldn't see, and suddenly the other guard appeared from the water behind them. "Get them out of my kingdom."

CHAPTER 25

Kaden and his friends were deposited at the edge of the vast grassland that led to Wildepointe by one of Varun's underwater boats. It was a fascinating craft, one that carved through the water like a fish but held enough air for all of them to breathe comfortably during the journey, all while allowing them to look out at the dark but beautiful aquatic world surrounding them. Kaden wished he could have taken the time to appreciate it more, but his thoughts were on Weylyn. Eventually, he couldn't keep them to himself any longer and sat down next to the other man as the water outside the craft slowly grew lighter.

"Do you really think you can defeat something like the leviathan?" Kaden asked in a low voice. The hum of the craft and Chum and Petey's bickering likely covered the sound of his question, but he wanted to be careful anyway.

Weylyn smirked and looked up from where he was, inspecting the edge of his sword. "Why? You afraid I'll make you look bad if I don't win?"

"No, I'm afraid you'll *die* if you don't win," Kaden said.

Weylyn shook his head. "You are the weirdest person I've ever worked for, bar none, and I once took a contract to help a man hunt down a *sheep* that had eaten his favorite rosebush." He shrugged, his massive pauldrons moving like they weighed nothing. "I'm a mercenary, Kaden. I go into every job knowing it could be my last. That comes with the territory, and while

I'm not reckless, I'm not afraid of death either. I'll take on the leviathan when the time comes—if I last that long. If I don't, then you'll probably be the one to handle it. You or that elf, but I think your blade is probably better suited for the job," he added. "Weapons infused with the blessing of Orealus tend to do better in dire circumstances."

"Are you really not afraid of dying?" Kaden couldn't imagine it. Even with the blessing of Orealus, he still felt afraid every time he thought about all the ways that he—or his friends—could perish.

"No. My fears tend more toward the esoteric at this point." Weylyn inspected his sword one last time, then resheathed it. "I came with you because you're the first person in a damn long time who's been brave enough to even mention the name Lucient to me. No one wants to tackle the big problems anymore, and there's no bigger problem than that serpent. I can't blame them for not wanting an all-out war again, but nothing will ever change if fiends like Lucient stay in power. I don't want to live out a safe, comfortable life knowing that the creature who killed my father is still drawing breath. That would be worse than death."

"I'm afraid," Kaden confessed. He didn't really want to— he wanted Weylyn to think he was brave, but he also knew it was essential, to be honest. "Not just of dying, but... that's up there."

"You *should* be afraid. You're the leader. You've got a lot more to worry about than I do," Weylyn said, an odd little smile on his face. "Don't be ashamed of fear. Only be ashamed if that fear keeps you from doing what you think is right. And in the meantime, use us." He nodded his head toward the rest of the group. "We're not here to be ornaments, pretty as some of us are."

"Did I hear someone say 'pretty'?" Chum asked, abandoning his halfhearted quarrel with Petey as he sidled over. "Are we all finally acknowledging that I'm the most breathtaking member of the company?"

"You're *breathtaking*, all right," Petey said. "You stink so badly that most of us would rather hold our breath than subject ourselves to taking your putrid odor into our nostrils."

"You're just jealous that I have a signature aroma," Chum snapped back. "Better than a generic goblin funk, which is all you have going for you."

"I—"

"We've stopped," Queen Pepper said, rising gracefully from her seat. "I believe it's time to disembark."

The craft surfaced, and after a quick climb to the top of it and a short walk down a retractable ramp, it was gone again in less than a minute. Kaden watched it disappear in a froth of bubbles, then turned back to see where they'd been deposited. A vast grassland spread out in front of them, punctuated here and there with copses of trees. A few bright shafts of sunlight split through the clouds above, turning the dun-colored stalks into a wave of gold.

"Why aren't there any villages or towns?" Kaden asked.

"We're too close to Wildepointe for Cimetes to tolerate encroachment," Queen Pepper explained. "His tribe might be nomadic, but they maintain a city of sorts to make it simpler to interact with the outside world. Wildepointe moves about, but it's always close to good forest hunting grounds and the Junagi River that flows through this part of Empyrea."

"You don't want to get on the bad side of a centaur," Chum added. "You think I'm fierce? Take me and multiply me by ten, and that's the ferocity of a centaur."

"Don't delude yourself," Petey said, settling Bug on his head as he hoisted his pack into place. "No one here thinks you're fierce."

"That's your first mistake," Chum countered.

"How do we find Cimetes?" Kaden asked Queen Pepper, doing his best to ignore the squabbling behind him.

"Probably the best thing to do is simply to start walking," Pepper suggested. "I daresay he and his people will find us soon enough. Millicent, Redfern, would you mind scouting ahead for the river? That will help us orient ourselves."

Millicent nodded and took off, but Redfern balked. "I'd rather stay close," he said firmly.

"You will be close," Pepper assured him. "Stay close enough to see us, but fly high enough to get a feel for the land. I'll be safe here with Kaden and Eldrin and the others." Redfern didn't look totally convinced, but he bowed and took off.

"He's rather inclined to cling, isn't he?" Eldrin asked with a half smile.

"Watching your monarch get sucked through a vortex into what you believe will be a watery grave will do that to some people," Pepper replied evenly. "Shall we, then?" She alighted as well, but not too high, smiling and stretching her wings as far out as they could go. Her white hair glowed in the sunlight, and her violet eyes sparkled. "It feels lovely to be in the open air again."

It really did. Kaden had to agree. Duke did, too, if the way he was bounding ahead through the grass was any indication. A few seconds and a brief snarl later, and he ran back with a rabbit clenched between his jaws, hind legs twitching in its final death throes. A second later, he was crunching it down: fur, bones, and all. Ada made a face, but Kaden just laughed. He was used to the way Duke liked to hunt.

"What, the fish wasn't enough for you?" Kaden asked, scratching his dog's head as they moved along. Then again, it had been quite a while since any of them had eaten a decent meal. Varun certainly hadn't supplied anything. He glanced at Eldrin. "Keep your eyes open for game along the way. I think we could all use a little more than stew tonight."

"Maybe the centaurs will come to us before that and offer us something from their table to eat!" Petey piped up. He seemed happy—so did Bug, who was trailing a faint cloud of pink spores and appeared to be nodding his little head in time to

Petey's footsteps. Small wonder, too, with how badly his body had reacted during their time on the boats.

"Or maybe they'll throw a bunch of spears at us from a distance until we're perforated like pincushions and snicker to each other, ever think of that?" Chum replied. He looked downright grumpy. "Centaurs, *ugh*. Stuck up, boneheaded brutes who think just because they're big, they have the right to look down on you. Freaks, too, running around on a single toe like that, whining like babies if they get so much as a bruise on their foot. Never trust a hoof that isn't cloven!"

"I take it you've met them before," Kaden said.

Weylyn chuckled. "Chum's met members of every tribe in the whole of Empyrea and loathed most of them on sight. Don't take his word for anything."

"I'm not making this up!" Chum snapped. "Chief Cimetes is a tricky one, and if we don't make him happy, he won't have the decency to just *drown* us like King Varun was going to. He'll wrestle some sort of concession out of us, *then* get us killed, then expect us to thank him for his hospitality. I told you—tricky!" He turned and glared at Kaden. "Don't trust him, don't make any deals with him that aren't signed in blood, and even then, it's probably not good enough to keep him from turning on you if things aren't going his way."

"I'll keep that in mind," Kaden said. They walked on for a while, the light of day slowly dimming before Redfern and Millicent flew back down.

"No sign of Wildepointe or the river yet, but there's a nice spot for a campsite in a little forest up ahead," Millicent said.

"It's certainly better not to continue into unknown territory as night falls," Queen Pepper agreed. "What do you think, Kaden?"

He glanced around, looking from the setting sun to the terrain ahead. He could make out the trees in the distance, but everywhere else was either grassland or the sea, vanishing into the space behind them. "It sounds good," he said. "We can set some snares when we get there, see if we can't catch anything to go with dinner."

"Snares," Petey said with a chuckle. "We won't need snares. I can see in the dark—I'll hunt something for us!"

"If dinner rests on your prowess, then we're all sure to starve," Chum quipped. Petey knocked into Chum's shoulder with his backpack as he marched ahead, and Bug sprayed a small, highly concentrated cloud of yellow spores at the satyr that made him start to cough uncontrollably.

"Murder!" he choked out. "I've been poisoned!"

Queen Pepper patted his shoulder. "Don't be so dramatic, Chum! It just causes a minor itch, which should be gone in minutes," she assured him. "Drink some water, and you'll be well."

"And I know this is rich coming from me," Weylyn said as he handed over his waterskin to his gasping friend, "but maybe learn to pick your battles a little better."

They made it to the forest before night set in, and Eldrin and Petey left to hunt while the rest of them prepared the camp. Kaden felt oddly on edge—this forest was different than any he'd been in so far, with tall, almost smooth-trunked trees that had spreading canopies up above, but very little below that. There was practically no firewood to speak of, no branches or twigs lying around. Eventually, he and Weylyn found an old stump and hacked off enough of it to use for a fire, but it certainly wouldn't keep them warm all night.

"I don't know much about this place," Ada admitted when Kaden brought up the strangeness of it all to her. "I was always more concerned with the realms of the sea. From what I understand, the centaurs fared better than many other tribes after the war against Lucient. Maybe it's because they're nomadic. They didn't have a city to hunker down and defend—they could just pick up their tents and make a new city somewhere else."

"That's a pretty good trick," Kaden admitted.

"It always pays not to set down roots," Weylyn said from the far side of the fire. He and Queen Pepper were tending to the pot—he'd volunteered to help cook, and she'd seemed pleasantly surprised by the offer. She hadn't even gently corrected him yet either, so he must actually be pretty good at it. "Keep yourself mobile. Give yourself the ability to move on when things start to go bad."

"That sounds like an unsatisfying way to live," Ada said. "What about doing the things you love? Gardening, sowing crops, building something that lasts?"

"The thing that most folks love best of all is *staying alive*," Weylyn replied. "Being prepared to drop everything at a moment's notice in pursuit of that goal is something too many people overlook. The weight of your personal history can get you killed if you let it."

"Well, I think—"

Suddenly, Duke stood up on all fours and began to growl, glaring out into the darkness of the woods. Everyone fell silent. The hairs on the back of Kaden's neck began to prick with tension. Was it another ambush by dark elves? Another pack of grawlers?

Suddenly a figure appeared at the edge of the firelight. At first glance, he looked like a man with long shaggy brown hair on horseback. It took Kaden a moment to realize that no, this was a man's upper body, complete with elaborate, angular tattoos, but a horse's lower body of chestnut color. And the powerful arms of that human body were holding a spear in a ready position. For all that he was poised to harm them, though, the centaur's face was calm, even curious.

"You are all very surrounded," he said in an accent that Kaden had never heard before. "You have been watched from the moment you stepped onto our land. If you are wise and do not struggle, things will go better for you now."

Kaden stood up slowly. "We came here to meet with Chief Cimetes," he said, leaving his hands where the centaur could clearly see them.

"And you shall," the centaur said affably. "But his given name is for friends and allies only. Chief Gallopfoot, as you should call him, will be pleased to enjoy a new fight from you and your people. But if you choose to fight against us now, we will have to kill you rather than take you to our chief. That would please no one."

"We didn't come here to fight," Kaden said with a frown.

"You shall fight anyway," the centaur said. "Your hunters have already been subdued by us. Gather your things quickly, and we shall take you to join them."

Kaden glanced at Queen Pepper and Weylyn. They both seemed unfazed by what amounted to their arrest. "It's all right," Queen Pepper said as she caught Kaden's eye. "This is as good a way as any to get an audience with the chief. Hopefully, he'll be ready to listen to what you have to say." She then looked at the centaur and said something in a fluttery, rolling sort of language that Kaden didn't understand, but which made the centaur's severe face light up with a smile. He replied in the same language, then set aside his spear and began to take down one of the tents.

"How in all that's holy did you manage that?" Weylyn demanded.

"I simply asked for his assistance," Pepper explained. "I speak a little Waptoo, which is their language, and apparently it was enough to endear us to him."

"But not enough to get them not to fight us?" Kaden asked.

Queen Pepper smiled apologetically. "I doubt it."

Breaking down camp went fast, and Kaden shouldered both his pack and Petey's before they set out through the forest. He was nervous, wondering if the centaur was telling the truth about Eldrin and Petey, but more than that, he was tired. Tired down to his very soul. He felt like they'd been careening from one danger to another ever since leaving Whaldalf's Landing, and even then, the break had been because he was recovering from poison, not really a time to rest. Finding Weylyn, getting sucked into Nethopolis, being captured by centaurs… Kaden felt like many things—perhaps too many—had happened as a result of him reacting in the face of danger.

This is the life of an adventurer, he reminded himself. This is the path you've chosen for yourself as you bring the tribes together to defeat Lucient. Orealus is with you. It had been a while since he'd felt the presence of Orealus, though—Kaden was so exhausted at night he didn't even remember his dreams.

He was drawn out of his morose thoughts by the welcome sight of Petey and Eldrin in the clearing up ahead, both of them passive in the face of half a dozen spears pointed at them, and neither of them happy about it. The centaur who had captured the rest of them said something in Waptoo, and the others lowered their weapons.

"We will be there soon," he said, then moved to the head of the party to lead the way back into the grassland.

"I see they got you too," Eldrin murmured as they rejoined the rest of their group.

"Apparently, we're going to meet Chief Gallopfoot," Kaden said. "And fight someone."

"Naturally."

"I don't want to fight," Petey said worriedly.

"It won't be you," Weylyn said from behind them. "If anyone here is going to fight a centaur, it'll be me."

"I could do it," Kaden said immediately. He felt shifty in his own skin, ready to burn off his strange, latent anxiety. "You don't have to—"

"You're the leader," Weylyn reminded him. "I'm the mercenary. It doesn't make sense for you to risk your life in single combat when I'm here for that express purpose."

Kaden wanted to argue, but then he caught sight of torchlight in the distance. It took a bit more walking for him to get close enough to make out where they were headed, but when he did…

So, this is Wildepointe. The tent city, alight with campfires and torches stuck into the grass, blended into the grass at the edges, but as they stepped inside its boundaries, it felt... well, like an actual city. The grass had been trampled down to lie flat, and there were streets between the canvas tents, true thoroughfares that centaurs of many different sizes and colors, from palomino to black, walked along. Some tents were clearly larger for communal gatherings while the private homes were smaller, but the tents had larger dimensions than average human tents to accommodate the size of the creatures. The whole place smelled of fresh grass and dried hay, and here and there, the scent of roasting meat wafted to them, making Kaden's mouth water. The camp rested near a pond for water and fishing. The backdrop of the plains, dotted with lakes, was a verdant forest where the centaurs likely hunted. Within the open armory tent they passed, Kaden could see weapons with refined spears, bows and arrows, and swords. He guessed there were enough weapons for every single person in the tribe, young and old alike. Many young male centaurs held spears or bows and arrows. The travelers witnessed female centaurs whittling detailed figurines and carvings tools or furniture. Tall tables, placed in the open air and built to accommodate the people's height, did not have chairs because the centaurs stood to eat. The tables were expertly crafted by this carpenter nation. The centaur's swift hooves made a sound on the grass but clopped on harder surfaces, such as when someone walked on stone.

All of the adult centaurs he saw were tattooed, with some across their face and necks, others more on their arms and torsos. The women wore crisscrossed strips of cloth across their breasts, but the children were all bare chested and unmarked. All of them, men and women, boys and girls, carried weapons—spears and bow and arrow sets for most of the males and long knives for all of them. They stared at the incoming prisoners with open curiosity, chatting at each other in smooth, flowing

Waptoo and occasionally laughing at each other. The sound was startlingly similar to a whinny, despite their human faces.

Their centaur escort led them into a large circle where enormous fires burned on either side of a massive tent, stitched with tribal patterns around the edges of it and pierced with cutouts in the shape of tree trunks topped with a crescent moon instead of leaves. "The symbol of the Gallopfoots," Queen Pepper murmured. The centaur who had taken them captive in the forest clopped forward and banged the base of his spear against the ground. "Chief, we come to celebrate this fair night with trespassers and a fight for glory!"

"We're not—" Kaden didn't have time for more than a token protest before the crowd of centaurs who'd been gathering around them roared in approval, stamping their hooves and whickering and neighing. There was a sound from inside the tent, and then the flaps of it were thrust aside, and another centaur emerged.

At first glance, Cimetes muscular form didn't look very different from any other male centaur. His horse haunches had buckskin-colored fur. He had angular features accentuated with black tribal markings similar to his people's, with the tree and crescent-moon featuring prominently on his neck and chest. His brown hair was dark, long, and coarse, and his brown eyes shined like polished coal in the light of the fire. He was solidly built, and when he'd finally had his fill of looking at them and spoke, his voice was bright with interest and authority.

"We may indeed have a masterful fight for glory on our hands," Cimetes said, his gaze darting from person to person. "But we are not without mercy either. Welcome to Wildepointe, strangers. Have you sought us out?"

Kaden stepped forward. "We have," he said firmly. "And we didn't come here to fight you, Chief Gallopfoot. We came to implore you to join us in our fight against Lucient, the Great Deceiver."

"Ah." Rather than protesting or asking questions or any of the dozen things Kaden had thought he might do, Cimetes brushed his words aside entirely. "So you came deliberately, not out of ignorance of our ways."

"Well, we—"

"To ask anything of us means accepting the cost," the chief went on pleasantly. "And that cost is single combat with one of our warriors."

Kaden's eyes narrowed. "Wait, we can't even ask a *question* without a fight?"

"You aren't known to us," Chief Cimetes explained. "If we had a history with you, we could take your honesty at face value, but we don't. The good news," he added, "is that whether or not your fighter wins or loses, I shall give your question careful consideration and an answer afterward."

"Oh." Kaden looked at his friends. Their expressions mainly were resigned; Eldrin shrugged, and Millicent and Redfern both shrugged as well. Only Queen Pepper looked distressed.

"I fear there's something we don't know," she said quietly. "Something that we *ought* to know before entering into a trial by combat."

"If they won't even answer our questions without a fight first, what choice do we have?" Kaden replied just as quietly. "We have to seek their help. We'll *need* it in a war, especially on an open battlefield." She nodded uncomfortably, and he turned back to Chief Cimetes. "Very well, we agree to single combat in exchange for your response to our question."

"Excellent!" Chief Cimetes clapped his heavy hands together. There was movement from somewhere behind his tent. "A bold choice. I applaud your bravery." There were whicker-snickers from the crowd, and after a moment, Kaden saw why. The centaur who emerged from the shadows was... *immense* was the only word Kaden could think of. He stood a head taller than his chief, on four thick legs that could have doubled for tree trunks. His chest was approximately the shape and size of one of Bardicus's massive grog barrels, and his body was cruelly scarred. He held a long spear with leaf-shaped blades on both ends in his hands.

"Choose your representative," Chief Cimetes went on. "Let them step into the Woo'apma and fight a glorious battle to the death!"

CHAPTER 26

"The *what*?" Kaden exclaimed. "You didn't say this would be a battle to the death!"

Chief Cimetes smirked. "How else can we judge your sincerity? If you're too afraid to commit to a fight with *us*, then you would make a poor ally in any fight we might undertake together. Choose your champion, whoever you think is the closest thing to a match for the mighty Muk Muk, and let the battle be fought."

Chum immediately stuck a furry hand into the air. "Not me!" he shouted. "Don't even think about it!"

"I wasn't planning to," Kaden snapped, then stopped and took a deep breath. It wasn't productive to feel angry right now, not when he had so much left to accomplish, but it was also very hard *not* to feel angry when the price of just being listened to threatened one of his people with mortal danger. It made him *sick* and furious, and to hell with passing on the threat to someone else, he was going to fight this time. He firmed his jaw and reached for the hilt of Vrangar—

Only to have Weylyn's hand grip his wrist just before he could grab his sword. "Don't," he said, quiet but quelling. "You're the leader of this party, not me, and besides, you are no match for him. If you go and get killed in a fight with Big Boy over there, then it all falls apart."

"I won't keep asking others to take all the risks while I stand aside," Kaden insisted.

Eldrin stepped up next to him. "Since when have you ever stood aside?" he asked with mock disparagement in his voice. "All you've done since I've met you is charge headlong into danger. Weylyn's right, though—this isn't your fight." He squared his shoulders. "I'll do it."

"No, I'll do it," Weylyn said. Eldrin objected, but Weylyn spoke right over him. "I'm the one with experience when it comes to taking on centaurs, and I know something about Muk Muk over there specifically. I'm here to fight for you, so let me fight."

"It doesn't seem fair," Kaden said, soft but as earnestly as he could manage.

Weylyn grinned at him. "Life's not fair, Your Highness. The sooner you wrap your head around that and stop letting it knock you off balance, the sooner you'll use your people to their full potential. They'll thank you for it, believe me. Now"—he inclined his head to them—"I've got some business to attend to." Then he turned away and walked toward Chief Cimetes and Muk Muk, his gait relaxed, his expression pleasant verging on insolent.

"Muk Muk, eh? I've heard of you," he announced, staying just out of attacking range as he spoke. "They say you're a force to be reckoned with on the field. A devastating fighter whose blows are too powerful to withstand."

Muk Muk laughed. His voice was so low Kaden felt the rumble of it in his chest. "You can't have spoken to anyone I fought against," he said. "Because none of them still live."

Weylyn tilted his head slightly as he sized up his opponent. "You're quite confident."

"It is our way," Muk Muk boasted. "The strongest survives the conflict. The weak are culled from the tribe. Wildepointe is a place of great peace and prosperity because of this tradition.

No petty fights are ever fought because every fight might be for your life."

"You don't think those lives are wasted?" Weylyn pressed. "That good people of your tribe haven't had their lives cut short because they were slightly less skilled?"

Muk Muk glowered at him. "What would you know of our ways, *human*? What would you know of what is right for a centaur?"

"What would *you* know of what's right for a human?" Weylyn asked.

"The questions are irrelevant... and you'll be dead soon enough!" With that, Muk Muk raised his spear and leaped forward, stabbing it with such ferocious intensity that one tip of it went into the ground, causing the earth to violently shake.

Unfortunately for him, Weylyn had already shifted to the side and leaped in the air, catlike quickness coming to the fore as he evaded the strike and lashed out with his sword. The edge of it came down crashing against the spear, right at the haft, and in one ferocious strike lopped off the leaf-shaped blade.

Muk Muk stared at the shorn end of his weapon for a moment before rearing back and bellowing with pure rage. He whirled the spear over his head to reorient it, bringing the other point to bear, but he didn't charge in again. Instead, he fired strikes forward with lightning speed, brutal stabs that had enough power behind them to penetrate armor. Kaden couldn't even *see* the tip of the second blade without relying on the firelight glow of it, and by the time he figured out where it was, it had already found another position.

This was where Weylyn's experience looked to stand him in good stead. The spear tip never touched him, sliding off the edge of his sword or jutting into nothing but air with every strike. "Watch him move," Eldrin whispered to Kaden, somehow able to make his voice heard over the roar of the crowd. "Keep your eyes on his feet. See, there? Mobility is the most important thing for a fighter like Weylyn. It's what gives him an edge over almost all his opponents."

"But Muk Muk is so strong!" Kaden replied. "And his strikes are so fast! How does Weylyn stay ahead of them?"

"He's not watching Muk Muk's spear," Eldrin explained. "He's watching his body. Look at his shoulders and chest—you can see how the muscles bunch before every strike. Weylyn understands how to use the distance between them, but Muk Muk's no fool. He could try to charge in and trample Weylyn into the ground, but he knows he's not as fast, so he's trying to wear him down. I think they're both trying that, actually." And it wasn't clear who was doing it better.

Weylyn had done what he could early to even the odds by reducing the spear's dangerousness. But the spear was long, the point that remained was terribly sharp, and Muk Muk was skilled in using it. At one point, he appeared to overextend, thrusting too deep, and Weylyn went to slice at the shaft again. Before he could, though, Muk Muk swept the spear sideways, hammering the hardened wood shaft into Weylyn's chest and nearly knocking him down.

"Not fast enough!" Muk Muk roared as Weylyn staggered out of the way. He followed his boast with a strike from the spear, but somehow Weylyn parried it, then laughed.

"Still fast enough," he said mockingly, then all of a sudden, he was closing the distance between himself and the centaur, charging forward and thrusting with his sword. Muk Muk danced back, but the tip of Weylyn's blade caught his flank, leaving a long, bloody gash that darkened the chestnut hair of his front left leg.

Muk Muk reared onto his hind legs, trying to crush Weylyn beneath his hooves, but again the expert fighter evaded the centaur's attack, pivoting and dodging until he was out of range of both hooves and spear.

"At this rate, you might as well try throwing that thing," Weylyn taunted him. "You have a better chance of hitting me that way than you do with your hands still on it."

"Coward!" Muk Muk accused him, stomping forward slowly but inexorably. There was only so far back that Weylyn could go before he ran into the edge of the Woo'apma, and in a few more steps, he would be at his limit. "Stand your ground and face your death with honor!" Muk Muk darted forward the last few feet, the spear raised for a tremendous blow. He struck—

And Weylyn somehow rolled beneath the blow, all while grabbing something off the ground. What was it? Kaden couldn't see until Weylyn got to his feet and—

Oh, praise Orealus! It was the other end of Muk Muk's spear, the blade that Weylyn had cut free in the very beginning and then ignored for the rest of the fight. Until now. He had grabbed it by the bit of shaft left attached, and as he used his sword to block Muk Muk's attempt at another devastating body blow, he simultaneously used the daggerlike spear end to cut a line across Muk Muk's right arm.

Muk Muk bellowed with pain and rage and dropped the spear. Kaden tensed, thinking that this was it, Weylyn was about to strike the killing blow, but almost faster than he could see, Muk Muk spun on his front legs and lashed out with a powerful kick. Weylyn dodged the worst of it, but one of the hooves caught the edge of his breastplate, sending him sprawling five feet back.

"Weylyn!" Kaden shouted. He tried to go to him but found himself held back by Eldrin—and Chum, of all people. "Let go of me, I—"

"You *can't* interfere," Eldrin insisted tensely. "I know it's hard when all you want to do is run out there and protect him, but you *cannot*. This is a formal challenge, and any interference from one of us might invalidate it. Do you want Weylyn to have to do this all over again with a new, fresh opponent?"

"It might look bad," Chum added, his jaw flexed pugnaciously, "but the Son of the Wolf's been in and lived through worse. Don't cheapen his abilities by doubting him the first chance you get."

When he put it like that… Kaden subsided, but his heart hammered in his chest as he watched Weylyn blink up at the stars for a long moment before finally pressing back to his feet. Miraculously, he'd held onto both of his weapons as he fell, but he was moving a lot more slowly now.

Of course, so was Muk Muk. The centaur hadn't capitalized on his attack by running Weylyn down. Instead, he'd backed off and picked up his spear, keeping it well in front of him, as though he were afraid of Weylyn being the one to run in first. He was limping, and the wounds on his arm and flank were bleeding badly. There was no quit in his eyes, though, no quarter given as he returned to a slow, steady progression forward. They were clearly both tired, but just as clearly, they were both determined to see this battle through.

Muk Muk thrust forward with the spear, targeting Weylyn's wounded side, perhaps expecting him to jerk it back out of reach. Instead, Weylyn stepped forward *with* that side to the front and used both his blades to make a powerful, X-shaped block. If he had missed the spear or if he had moved a fraction of a second too slow, he could have been run through.

Weylyn didn't miss it. He drove the spear straight up into the air, twisted with his blades to keep them on top of it as he pinned it to the ground, then stomped on the spear shaft. The wood was solid, but so was Weylyn. He broke the spear in two, the far end of it clattering to the ground. Muk Muk could only stare for a moment, stunned, at the shattered weapon he held, and that was all the time Weylyn needed to close the distance.

His first strike cut across the back of Muk Muk's hand, slicing to the bone. The second saw his sword at Muk Muk's throat even as the double-edged spear blade pressed beneath his forelegs, where one swift motion would drive it into Muk Muk's guts.

The centaur, bleeding and dazed, nevertheless managed a laugh. "You're stronger than you look," he said admiringly to Weylyn. "It is no shameful thing to lose at the hands of a warrior like yourself." He straightened his massive shoulders and lifted his chin. "I am ready to die."

"That *is* a shame," Weylyn said, his words strong and clear even though he was panting for breath. "Because I'm not going to kill you." With that, he lowered his blades and stepped back.

There was an immediate outroar in the crowd. Chief Cimetes looked stunned, but his expression was nothing compared to the look on Muk Muk's face. His stolid countenance had cracked wide open, replaced by disbelief, then anger. "You have to!" he roared. "To deny me my honorable death is outrageous! *No one* who enters into single combat in the Woo'apma is spared!"

"Do I look like a centaur?" Weylyn snapped back. "Do I? Because where *I* come from, good fighters are valued for more than the length of a single battle. You fought well. You can teach others to fight well, and killing you would be an absolute waste of your skill and my time! *Do you understand me?*"

He turned and glared at Chief Cimetes. "I won't do it. If you really want him dead, kill him yourself."

Muk Muk snorted, then turned and looked at the chief. Cimetes stared at him for a long moment before finally shaking his head. Muk Muk exhaled, long and slow, and Kaden saw his anger and readiness turn to relief. "As my chief commands." He limped out of the circle of light, and Cimetes stepped forward.

His heavy hooves made almost no sound on the hard-packed, bloodstained grass. He held a spear of his own, and while it wasn't as long or as heavy bladed as Muk Muk's, it seemed to glow with its own inherent light. *Another weapon infused by the power and glory of Orealus? Is he going to fight us himself now?*

Kaden stepped forward, shrugging off Eldrin's attempt at restraining him. He wasn't going to let Cimetes attack Weylyn while he was wounded.

"Your man fought well," Chief Cimetes said at last. All of the centaurs had quieted, listening intently to their leader. "But as generous a gesture as sparing Muk Muk is, it invalidates the results of the fight."

"You're going to *punish* us for showing your best fighter compassion and mercy?" Kaden demanded. "Are you serious?"

"Those are our tribe's rules," Chief Cimetes said firmly, a slight smile playing about his lips. "But out of deference to your sensibilities, I'll make the second fight a little more interesting." His smile widened to a grin.

It was all Kaden to do to keep from protesting. *I'll make the second fight a little more to your liking!* "I doubt you can."

"You haven't even heard my offer." Chief Cimetes extended a hand toward the edge of the circle. "But if you'd rather not hear it and take your people and leave, then you may do so now with no repercussions."

Kaden wanted to. At that moment, he genuinely wanted to step away, to lead his friends, his valiant friends, away from those who seemed to want nothing more than to toy with them instead of dealing honestly. It hurt, the thought of staying here and letting Chief Cimetes play his games with them. But he also couldn't walk away. He simply couldn't—Orealus had set him a tremendous task, and Kaden had known from the very beginning that it wouldn't be easy.

He hadn't anticipated it would be challenging in such a humiliating sort of way, but clearly, he should have. "Fine. Tell us your terms."

"A forest elemental named Gangor recently entered our forests." Chief Cimetes's smug look had turned stiff and displeased.

Kaden had never heard of it before. "What's a forest elemental?"

"A type of golem," Queen Pepper offered. "They were originally thought to be divine constructs set in the world by Orealus himself, but whatever benevolence they originally contained has been infected with the evil of Lucient. They're enormous, mighty creatures."

"Too powerful," Chief Cimetes agreed. "This one has claimed too much of our wildlife and hunting grounds to leave alone, but it's proven... difficult to eliminate. Many of my warriors have gone after it and not returned. I want you and your people to hunt it down and destroy it. In exchange, I will look favorably on any request you have of me."

Kaden didn't trust Cimetes, but he had to admit this was better than fighting another one of his centaurs to the death. "When do you want us to do this?"

Chief Cimetes's broad smile was back. "Why, right now!"

CHAPTER 27

Walking along the path to the forest with an armed four-centaur escort would have been more tolerable if Chum hadn't insisted on talking the whole way. Even that would have been all right if every word out of his mouth wasn't dripping with smugness.

"What did I tell you?"

"Shut up, Chum."

"You can't trust 'em. I told you all not to trust 'em, and now here we are, marching to our doom in their Orealus-forsaken forest to have a battle with a Lucient-corrupted golem—"

"Shut *up*, Chum!"

"—and I just want you all to know that *this satyr*?" He jerked his thumb at his own chest. "Won't be acting as a lure, or bait, or doing much of anything at all in this fight, because I told you, I *told* you, what would happen. Weylyn is exhausted, so it's going to be up to *you* people to take on Gangor while I look after my friend. Got it!"

Part of Kaden wanted to argue, but a vast amount of him just wanted to get all this over with. It didn't help that he knew Chum was right. He should have asked more questions of Chief Cimetes and his people before entering into any kind of bargain with them... but they wouldn't answer any questions without a fight. What was Kaden supposed to do, just pack up and leave?

Maybe yes, if that means your friends would all be safe and sound instead of walking into a fight with a creature you've never seen before and have no idea how to battle.

Well, that was as good a starting place as any. He moved closer to Queen Pepper. "How do we fight a golem?" he asked.

"It depends on the golem," she replied, and Kaden sighed. That... wasn't as helpful as he'd hoped. "The force that powers each of them is concentrated in a specific part of their body," she went on, and okay, this was better. "For some, it's the head—specifically the mouth. For others, it's the center of the chest. I once found the remains of a golem in Fayspire Woods whose power had been focused in his right hand. Unfortunately, that hand had been removed, and the rest of its body simply... lost its life. It became unmoving and still, like a tree cut off from its roots."

She shook her head, and actual tears were glittering in her violet eyes. "They were once so beautiful, so gentle. My family has kept long records, and in the oldest of them, there are tales of interacting with the forest elementals, learning from them, and even traveling with them. But once the poisonous dark spiritual mist of Lucient was introduced to their systems, it quickly overwhelmed them."

"I'm sorry," Kaden offered because the thought clearly pained her. "I wish we didn't have to do this."

"Oh, Kaden." She patted his shoulder. "I wish that as well, but I feel as though we may be doing this poor creature a favor. Nothing that has known the favor of Orealus should be left to founder in the darkness of the Great Deceiver for the rest of eternity."

"Keeping that in mind, let's talk strategy," Weylyn said from a few paces back. "I'm not going to be terribly useful in this fight"—the scowl on his face readily conveyed how he felt about that—"and I've got the feeling that our escorts are here more for show than to actually assist us, at least until Gangor is near death. Eldrin and Ada are our distance fighters—let's see if they can't weaken the brute before the rest of you charge in for hand-to-hand combat."

"Arrows against a massive construct like this?" Eldrin shook his head. "I don't think that'll be very effective."

"It won't hurt to try, though," Queen Pepper said before Weylyn could take some sort of affront. "After all, some creatures touched by Orealus respond especially badly to iron and steel."

Weylyn nodded. "If it doesn't work, Redfern and Millicent should work to harry and distract it from above with their spears while the rest of you go low and cripple it enough for you to strike at it with your swords," he finished, then looked at Kaden. "Sound reasonable?"

Kaden thought about it for a moment, then looked at Pepper. "Do you think your yah'zaval would work against it?"

"I can't say for sure," she replied thoughtfully. "Our abilities are based in the same natural realm. It might be immune to my influence, or it might be very vulnerable to it. I won't know until I try."

"Please do so," Kaden said, and she nodded. "Now I think we're ready."

"That's good," Petey said with a gulp as he pointed a trembling green hand ahead of them. "Because I, um, I think we're getting close." They'd reached the edge of the forest, and just inside the outer layer of trees was an utterly ruined swath of foliage. Tree trunks had been shattered, branches ripped to splinters, and the undergrowth thoroughly trampled. There were spots of blood here and there as well, and the pervasive scent of rot and the buzz of carrion flies made Kaden wince and wish he could plug up his nose.

"It seems quite powerful," Weylyn noted. "Don't let it grab you."

"Brilliant advice," Eldrin said, rolling his eyes. "*Do not get grabbed by fierce, Lucient-driven forest elemental.* That's going on the top of my list."

One of the centaurs prodded Kaden in the back with his spear. "Gangor likes to settle in less than a hundred paces deep," the centaur said, pointing into the woods. "It's made itself a nest, of sorts. Follow the broken path, and you'll find it quick enough."

"Not coming along, then?" Eldrin asked. "What noble creatures you are, letting others fight your fiercest battles for you." The centaur scowled and began to lift his spear in Eldrin's direction.

"That's not necessary," Kaden said quickly, stepping between the centaur and Eldrin. "We're going, just stop, we're going." He turned and chivvied Eldrin along the path of broken undergrowth.

"My hero," Eldrin said, laughter in his voice. "Honestly, though, I could have—"

"Could have what? Could have provoked him into attacking you before we even get started on Gangor? Yeah, that sounds like a great idea." Without thinking, Kaden smacked Eldrin up the backside of his head. "Stop acting like a child."

"I... you... hey!" Eldrin seemed somewhere between annoyed and amused. "Did you just—I'm a *prince*!"

"Right now, you're a member of my party, and a friend, and also kind of an idiot," Kaden said. "Seriously, we're about to go up against an enormous forest elemental, and you want to pick a fight with a centaur? How is that smart?"

"If I didn't pick fights, I don't think I'd know what to do with myself," Eldrin replied. Kaden was a little surprised at the honesty in his friend's voice. "But I'll try to restrain myself right before we head into battle in the future."

"Thank you." Kaden looked around and found all of his friends staring at him in the torchlight. Petey was smiling, Queen Pepper looked downright misty, and even Redfern wasn't scowling anymore. "What?" he asked.

"Nothing," Queen Pepper said, smiling at both of them. "Nothing at all. Come. We're close." She flitted ahead, Redfern and Millicent staying right on her wingtips.

It was slower going for the rest of them since they had to climb over the fallen remains of dozens of trees, but after less than five minutes, they arrived at the edge of what *should* have been a clearing. There were no trees here, and the break in the canopy overhead afforded them more light from the bright full moon.

It wasn't a clearing, though. Instead, there was a giant lump of broken branches and brambles taking up almost the whole of it, stacked in a messy, haphazard way.

"Great," Chum muttered. "Where are we supposed to go now, then? Is the damn golem *behind* the pile, is it on top of it, did it bury itself under all those branches like they're some sort of blanket?" He stumped forward and kicked the edge of the pile with one of his hooves. "Useless pieces of—"

Petey pulled him back and clapped a hand over Chum's mouth. "Stop!" he hissed intently. "Don't you get it? This *is* the golem!"

Wait... this was Gangor? Kaden looked at the twisted pile in a new, stomach-churning light. It had to be fifteen feet high! Now that he was paying closer attention, he noticed that the buzz of flies was thicker here, focused on the middle of the elemental, where the darkness within the branches appeared to be due to more than just the shadows.

"It feeds," he said softly. "It doesn't just kill creatures. It *feeds* on them. Why? It's made of plants, of—why would it try to feed on animals, on people?"

"Power," Queen Pepper said. Her white hair was beginning to glow, flowing back from her head like a silvery wave. She raised her hands, and they too began to glow with the power of yah'zaval. "The dark magic or dunntaika of Lucient is a corrupting force that twists the natural order of things into behaving in foreign, damaging ways. The forest golems were meant to subsist on nothing more than light and water and good, rich earth. And now…" She shook her head. "Gangor is deeply infected with the evil of Lucient."

"Then to destroy him will be a mercy," Weylyn said with a cough. "Ah, curse these ribs."

"You stay back," Kaden commanded him. "Use your spare bow if you can without hurting yourself, but leave this fight to us." He looked at Pepper. "How do we wake it up?" The golem was utterly still, unmoving even with them right in front of it.

"How about we set it on fire?" Chum asked, hefting his torch. "Stand back and watch it burn, problem solved!"

"And set the forest on fire and then have to fight a creature on fire as it flails around trying to kill us?" Millicent shook her head. "You're hopeless."

"I can wake it," Queen Pepper said. She shut her eyes and made a curious gesture with her hands, almost as though she were cutting something in two. It seemed a strain, and Kaden wondered what she was attempting that made her grit her teeth like that when—

The ground beneath the golem opened up in a rush, burying it five feet deep in the earth. Roiling dirt churned around the base of it, moved aside by the strength of Pepper's yah'zaval, and just as quickly settled back tightly against the golem, doing its best to hold the elemental in place as it slowly, ponderously, came to life.

Kaden had expected to see… well, a *head* of some kind. What was it eating with? It was not a head? But instead, a dark-red light began to emanate from the very center of the golem, right where the swarm of flies buzzed the loudest, where the smell of rot was the strongest. He couldn't make out any eyes—what use did a creature of the forest, a creature intimately connected to everything around it, have with eyes? The light was a glow of twisted sentience, not vision.

That's where we have to strike. That's where its power resides. Kaden gripped Vrangar more tightly, then reminded himself of the plan. *Ada and Eldrin attack first.* Even as he thought it, twin arrows flew through the darkness behind him into the center of the golem, right amid the vile red light.

The golem wasn't even fazed. Two enormous appendages emerged from the hulking body, one thick and rigid and studded with broken branches like a mace, the other thinner and far more flexible, twisting and curling around in the air like a whip. Individually they would have been intimidating—together, they were nearly paralyzing.

"Fairies, stay out of range of the smaller one!" Weylyn called out. "Eldrin, get your blade out! Kaden, time to *move!*"

Kaden struck at the nearest part of Gangor he could reach, one of the—legs? Trunks? It hardly mattered—his blow had no effect. The wood was old and tough and suffused with power pulled from blood and death. Gangor tried to kick Kaden, but the movement was ponderously slow, and he was able to dodge it easily.

Thank goodness for small favors. "Try to get to the center of it!" Kaden called out. "We need to cut out its core!" He took a step forward, and—

—found himself suddenly wrapped up in the long, whippy wooden limb. It lifted as it squeezed, and soon he was ten feet in the air. Kaden's arms were still free, but Gangor used the branch to fling him toward the trees before he could strike at it.

Oh no! If he hit a tree, his bones would be shattered.

Millicent caught him just before impact. Unable to stop Kaden's momentum, she used hers to redirect him, and a moment later, they careened into the slender branches, not the rigid trunk, of a tree. Kaden earned some scratches from it, but nothing as much as he'd feared. Millicent, however…

"*Ah!*" She clung to one of the lower branches, her right-wing pitifully crumpled. Kaden dropped to the ground, then supported Millicent's feet so she could let go of the branch. He helped her down, but she blanched when she tried to fly.

"Millie!" Redfern shouted frantically. She tried to fly down to her, but the same whippy branch that had grabbed Kaden blocked her.

"Are you—" Kaden began, but Millicent pushed at his hip. "I'm fine, go, go!"

Kaden ran back into the fray, determined to be more careful this time. Eldrin seemed to be making some headway. With Petey and, to Kaden's surprise, Chum drawing the attacks from the heavy, mace-like branch, Eldrin had slid close to the center of the golem and was hacking at the blood-red glowing heart of it. Splinters flew, some of them bigger than Kaden's hand, and it seemed for a moment like Eldrin was about to break through.

"Wha—whoa!" The whippy branch wrapped around his middle as Gangor groaned, a sound of dark, abiding rage. It began to pull Eldrin away from it, probably to throw him like it had Kaden.

No! Kaden wasn't going to let another of his people be hurt. He raised his sword and leaped, and as he did, the crystal amulet around his neck pulled from his Mana and blazed with white fire. The fire raced down his arms and along the blade, and a second later, he struck the branch just above where it held Eldrin.

It sheared away cleanly, the severed end and the elf prince both falling to the ground. Eldrin looked up at him, a savage grin across his face. "Do that to the core!" he shouted, and— yes, of course. Kaden turned, chopped at the nearest trunk, and was thrilled to see Gangor flinch back. The fire didn't hurt Kaden, didn't feel like anything but a tingling warmth alongside that internal draw from his energy, but it clearly bothered the elemental.

It must have *really* bothered it because, a second later, the mace-like limb swept across the front of Gangor's body like a pendulum. Kaden was barely able to jerk himself out of the way in time, and the strike succeeded in ripping his sword from his grip. It flew off to the side, the fire dying out. Gangor made another noise this time, a sound of dark satisfaction as it raised its heavy limb above its head, ready to crush him.

Gangor faltered as Petey's faithful Dwingent flew right into the golem's center of mass, smack dab into the middle of the roiling red core. Petey dashed in after it, turning to Kaden as he went to shout, "Go get your sword, quick!"

Kaden pressed to his feet, a slight challenge countered by his excitement, and ran to the sidelines. Where had it—

"Behind the big oak!" Millicent called out, jabbing at the nearest edge of the golem with her spear. It seemed like it was trying to climb out of the hole Pepper's power had created—not good, not good. Kaden ran over to the oak tree and—ah, there! He grabbed his sword off the ground, then turned back toward the fight.

The tide of the battle had turned in their direction, it seemed. Queen Pepper was glowing brighter than ever, both hands lifted above her head. Thick roots had sprung up out of the ground, tethering themselves to Gangor and keeping it from excavating itself, as it seemed so desperate to do. Even its dangerous mace was immobilized, although it was fighting that, fighting it hard, straining against roots to bring it down on... on...

"Ada!"

Kaden moved faster than he'd ever run before in his life, flinging himself at her just in time to push her out of the way as Gangor finally freed itself and smashed the limb down hard right where she'd been standing a moment ago as she fired arrows into its core.

"Kaden," she said with a cough from beneath him. "What—"

But there was no time to talk now. He had to finish this before the golem could recover, before Pepper was too tired and more of them were too injured to fight. Kaden climbed to his feet, dodged around the thick, studded limb that was rising up for another strike even now, jumped so that he was on a level with the dark red core, and plunged Vrangar into the very center of it.

Gangor screamed. There was no other word for it, for a sound like thousands of branches suddenly snapping, twisting in on themselves, and shivering into splinters. The golem shuddered beneath him, quivering as it tried to gather itself for another attack, and then... and then...

Suddenly it was nothing more than a heap of dead branches falling in on itself, and Kaden fell with it. He had just enough presence of mind to fling his arms over his head before the crumbling pile of wood covered him completely, blocking out the dim torchlight.

It should have been terrifying, he should have been fighting with every breath, afraid for his life, but instead, he felt strangely calm. He was inside of it, he realized—inside of the golem's core. The wash of red had vanished, and as he watched the palest blue-white filament spread over the wood closest to him, like fire appearing on the surface of a piece of coal.

It was a beautiful sight, soothing somehow. Kaden's breath caught in awe as he watched it, and in his head, he suddenly heard, Blessed, are you, Kaden, son of Karatheas. Blessed is your line, and glorious is your fate. May you free these lands from the power of Lucient as you have freed me. Blessings of Orealus on you, forever. The blue-white light faded then, and so did the soothing presence. A moment later, Kaden knew he was entirely alone.

Alone, but not for long. A second after that, the branch just above him was pulled off, torchlight illuminating his rescuer. It was Ada, open-mouthed and wide-eyed, breathing hard. "I've got him!" she shouted, and then more hands joined in, and a few minutes later, Kaden was pulled free of the remains of Gangor the golem.

"Are you all right?" Ada asked frantically, her hands clenching and relaxing as though she stopped herself from reaching out and grabbing him again. Kaden kind of wished she would.

"Are *you* all right?" he asked. He could see that she was, she was less than a foot away from him, but he felt the need to verify after what they'd just been through.

"I'm fine, don't worry about me, worry about yourself, you... you..." She shut her eyes for a moment. "I thought you had been *killed*. You jumped right into the middle of this thing, and then it collapsed, and none of us could hear you, and you weren't saying anything, and you had just saved my life, again. Again! Let someone else do the saving for once, Kaden!"

"You can save me next time," he quipped, and he was relieved to see a smile spread across her face.

"Don't think for a minute that I won't," she replied.

"If you two can take a moment away from each other," Weylyn called out dryly, and they jerked apart as though lightning had just touched down between them. "Grab something close to identifiable in that creature, and let's get back to our escort before they give us up for lost."

Right, right, they still had to... of course. Kaden turned back into the pile and looked for something, anything, that seemed suitably representative of Gangor instead of just a piece of wood. He found the end of the whippy, clearly manufactured branch that he'd chopped off earlier and cut it short enough to comfortably carry, then straightened up. The moon had moved behind a tree, and he could barely see his friends in the gloom, but no one seemed to be in terrible pain, so that would have to be good enough for now.

"Let's head back." Kaden led the way through the woods, exhausted but determined not to show it in front of the centaurs. They emerged from the trees into the welcome light of the moon, and their escort looked genuinely surprised to see all of them. Cimetes was there as well now, dressed for a fight, and a host of other centaurs were right behind them.

"We heard the sounds of a great battle," Cimetes said, looking downright stunned to see them. "We thought it would take more… *effort* to subdue Gangor. We were prepared to assist you."

"You thought you were sending us to be slaughtered and were prepared to finish off the golem once we had softened it up," Kaden said flatly. "I know. Yet here we are." He hefted the elaborately wound-up piece of wood, then threw it onto the ground at Chief Gallopfoot's front hooves. "We killed the golem, and here's our proof. Now, we've done a great service to you. Will you swear on your honor to do the same for us? Will you be our ally against Lucient and fight for the freedom of all people?"

Cimetes stared at the twisted wood, then at Kaden. His dark eyes shined brightly in the moonlight. "You truly think you have a chance against Lucient?"

"I do." Orealus was with them. The true spirit of *Gangor itself* had blessed them. "I know that together, we all do."

Cimetes bowed his head. "Then you can count on the centaurs of Wildepointe to come to your aid."

Kaden was almost dumbfounded by the chief's agreement. That was that? It seemed so simple, so…

"What's that?"

Kaden followed Chief Cimetes's gaze down toward his foot, where Bug was hopping anxiously up and down by his foot. The little creature glowed a pale orange color. "Bug? What's wrong?" Kaden looked around, but he didn't see…

"Where's Petey?" They all looked around, but he wasn't there.

"Did he get hurt?" He had to be hurt. And Kaden had just run off and *left* him there in the wreckage of Gangor after Petey had saved him from the golem! He picked up Bug, then turned and ran back into the forest. He was quickly passed by Queen Pepper, whose glow lit the way for the rest of them. "Petey!" Kaden shouted, running around the edge of the ruined elemental, searching for any sign of his friend. "*Petey!*"

"Over here!" Kaden ran toward Redfern, who was hovering beside a thick tree a few feet back from the mess of battle. "Look," he said grimly, pointing at the trunk. Even leaning close, it took Kaden a moment to see what he was pointing at.

Loyal Dwingent was stuck in the tree. The blade glowed from the reflection of the direct light. Drops of dark red goblin blood, nearly black in the moonlight, speckled the sharp edge near the hilt. Directly beneath them, flush to the tree, was a slip of parchment.

Kaden pulled his friend's blood-smeared dagger free with a grunt—it had been stuck deeper than he'd expected. Just watching the droplets of the blood leave the blade made him fear the worst for his friend. He grabbed the parchment before it could fall, but he couldn't read the writing on it.

"It's in the goblin language," Eldrin said, holding out a hand. Kaden gave it to him, anxiety for Petey making his heart pound like a drum inside his chest.

"What does it say?" he demanded.

Eldrin scowled. "It's an ancient dialect, but I think it says… If you want the runt back, you must come to the fallen bridge on the outskirts of…'" He shut his eyes for a moment. "Oh no."

"Where?"

"Shroudscar," Eldrin muttered, despair in his face. "They're taking Petey to Shroudscar."

CHAPTER 28

The only good thing about the time it took for their party to make it to Shroudscar was that the walk gave Weylyn and Millicent space to heal and Queen Pepper time to rejuvenate after expending so much of her abilities.

Kaden had been insistent, at first, that they set out immediately and possibly even run down the goblins who'd kidnapped Petey, but Chief Cimetes had quickly dashed his hopes.

"The grasslands are a good place for ambushes," he said, his formerly amused eyes dark and determined. "That's one of the reasons my people like them, of course, but beyond the borders of Wildepointe and our hunting grounds, we can't guarantee your safety against intruders. That includes goblins. There could be as many as a hundred hiding in the grass, and unless the wind shifted and brought their stink our way, we'd never know it until it was too late."

"It seems like you weren't interested in guaranteeing our safety even *within* your borders," Eldrin groused, but Cimetes had just shrugged.

"Before you defeated Gangor, we weren't allies. Allies get much more consideration than mere travelers."

"How gracious."

"Eldrin," Queen Pepper had chided him wearily. Chief Cimetes had looked at her with concern and said something in Woo'apma. She replied in the same tongue, then told the rest of them, "He's offered us tents, food, and the services of his healers. I suggest we accept and start fresh in the morning."

Kaden wanted to shout, to scream. He wanted to go *now*, to go after Petey and get him back before the goblins were able to do anything worse. It hurt, knowing that he'd failed to notice that his friend was missing. Yes, he'd been tired, yes he'd had wounded to worry about, but he should have known that something was wrong. He *should* have. Petey had been with him longer than anyone else, except for Duke, and stuck with him through the worst trials of Kaden's life. Petey was faithful, and how had Kaden repaid that faith? By letting his friend be spirited away by the goblins and being tortured. It was unconscionable.

Weylyn had laid an arm across his shoulders. "Think about who you can help right now," he said in a low voice. "Measure the needs of your party and do what's best for the greatest number of them. Petey's a tough one. He'll be all right for a while."

Weylyn was right, Kaden knew it, but that didn't make this part any more manageable. "Okay," he said at last. "We'll stay here tonight. But we leave at first light tomorrow morning!"

"Agreed," Queen Pepper said, her voice full of compassion. "You know I'm worried about him too."

"I know." He did know that, but no one was worried the way Kaden was. How could they be?

Still, there was no doubt that the food and rest helped, and so did time with the healers. Weylyn had bruised ribs, but none broken, and a powerful and pungent salve rubbed over his chest soon had him breathing easier. Millicent's wing was more worrying, but Queen Pepper tended to it herself, straightening it with great care before wrapping it in a thin gossamer bandage.

"It only needs time now," she said, kissing Millicent's sweat-drenched forehead once she was done setting the wing. "Time and rest. No flying for you right now, my dear. You might consider staying here until we—"

"Absolutely not," Millicent insisted immediately. "My place is by your side, protecting you, whether I can fly to do so or not. And if I wasn't protecting you, I would feel honor bound to be there for Kaden, so one way or another, I'm going." She blushed slightly. "Your Majesty."

"*Now* you remember your manners?" Pepper shook her head, but her voice was fond. "Very well, then."

Millicent caught Kaden's eye. "I won't slow you down," she said, and Kaden could tell that she meant it.

"Thank you," he replied, a wealth of meaning in those two words. He looked at the rest of their group, all of them clustered within the same tent even though their party had been given three by their newly gracious hosts. "Thank you all," he said again.

No one spoke, but no one had to. They were bound together now, joined by mutual respect and the bonds that came from shared hardship. They all wanted to get Petey back, and just seeing the fierce intent in each of their faces made Kaden feel a little bit better about what was to come.

He wasn't alone. He'd never had to do any of this quest alone. Orealus willing, he never would.

*   *   *

Reprovisioned, they headed out the following day. Centaur scouts had followed the tracks of the goblins to the edge of Cimetes's territory, and they graciously offered to give Kaden and his friends a ride that far.

It was *very* odd riding a centaur. Nothing like riding a horse, partly because there was no place Kaden really felt comfortable putting his hands. He ended up holding onto his mount's shoulders, and it was still a bumpy, nerve-wracking ride that he was more than happy to see the end of.

"There." The centaur—one of the ones who'd accompanied them to Gangor last night, Kaden realized—pointed with his spear at a faint trail in the tall grass. "There are at least five of them that we could tell, including your friend. They are fast," he added. "We thought we might catch them before they passed our borders, but they're running as though the Dark One himself is driving them on."

He may be, Kaden thought with a shiver. He didn't like to contemplate how aware of him Lucient might be, how much he might know about Kaden's existence so far. It was clear from the attacks on them before this that Lucient knew *something*, but he seemed content to work through puppets for now.

They would vanquish him. Kaden believed that with all his heart, but he wasn't going to do anything without getting Petey back first.

The prairie was eerie in a way Kaden hadn't expected, the grass just tall enough to obstruct his view and dense enough that he really had to push to make his way through it. Even cutting at it with Vrangar only seemed to clear a path for a moment before the wind pushed more into his path, always more, a never-ending wave of green and brown, purple and gold. It was beautiful, but ever since the centaurs had mentioned ambushes, all he'd seen when he looked out at it was potential places for goblins to be hiding, waiting for them to get close before striking.

It didn't help that the trail the goblins left behind was a wavering thing, vanishing into the springy, resilient grass here and there before popping up ten, twenty, or even fifty paces further along. Kaden became extra grateful for Eldrin's tracking expertise. Even though he was far more used to the forests than vast plains like this, he was trained to recognize the slightest detail that might indicate the passage of a person or animal. He—and Bug, who seemed to have a sixth sense for where his master was heading—not only managed to keep them on the trail of the goblin kidnappers, but he also helped to find game to eat along the way.

"We'll be grateful for the fresh food while we can get it," Eldrin said the second night of their journey. They'd mashed down a circle of grass just big enough for a campsite and had a small fire going in the center of it, where two jackalope were roasting over spits. "I've never been to Shroudscar before, obviously, but I know enough about it to know that I'm not going to touch anything that looks even mildly edible down there."

"Petey never talked about it much," Kaden said, staring at the flames like they might show him something if he just looked hard enough. "I know he was mistreated there, and the goblins who came after me before were..." *Filthy, horrible, merciless brutes.* "Nothing like him," he finished after a moment.

"Petey is the least goblin-like goblin I've ever encountered," Weylyn put in, reaching out to turn the spit. "Which doesn't say much, since the only goblins I've ever met have ended up impaled on my blade."

"Petey is lovely," Ada said, sounding almost defensive. "He would be lovely no matter what tribe he was a part of."

"Sure, but the point is, he's part of a tribe where that sort of attitude would normally get you dead," Chum replied. "It can only mean he was cosseted as a child, maybe raised outside the normal order of things."

Kaden glanced at Queen Pepper. He wasn't sure about telling the rest of them about Petey's royal history—it didn't seem important at the moment, and it wasn't his story to share. She shook her head minutely, then said, "What we know about Shroudscar isn't much, but it will hopefully allow us to be as prepared as possible. I know it's an underground city—"

"An underground *shanty*town," Eldrin interjected. "There might once have been a grand plan for Shroudscar, but that aspiration died alongside the king and queen. From what I've heard, nowadays the place is little better than a collection of hovels stuck together with swamp glue and grit."

"Ugh, who'd want to live in such a place?" Ada asked, toying with the end of one of her braids with a disgusted look on her face.

"Someone who didn't want to worry about having to fight too hard for it, maybe," Weylyn suggested. "The dwarves are constantly on alert because everyone in the land, and probably the sea too, knows that they're sitting on a pile of treasure in that mountain of theirs. It draws others to the attack, and they have to battle constantly to keep what's theirs. But an underground cavern that never gets natural light or fresh air, one where even a salamander would think twice about settling in—that's a place someone hardy enough could claim with little fear of it being stolen."

Kaden thought about his village, small and hardly noticeable beside Ashland Woods. He thought of how bored he'd been there at times, how much he'd wanted to move away, move on, do anything other than stay in a place where nothing ever changed. Now he realized that the whole reason his village had survived the great war was *because* it was small and dull, not worth the conquering by anyone larger and more powerful.

I hope it stays that way. Blessed Orealus, keep my mother and my home safe. The fewer people who knew where he came from, the better.

They didn't camp for long. Even recognizing that rest was necessary for all of them to stay at their best—that Weylyn and Millicent *needed* rest if they were going to be in fighting condition once they reached Shroudscar—Kaden had a hard time falling asleep. He tugged Duke close to him in the night and buried his face in the big dog's fur, trying to block out the terrible images of his friend he kept imagining. It rarely worked.

Was Petey scared? Did he miss Bug? Did he miss Kaden? Were they hurting him or sticking to teasing and taunts for now? If they got tired of him, would they just kill him and throw him aside? What if he was already dead, buried in a shallow prairie grave that would be dug up in no time by the long-snouted coyote scavengers, hooting and howling into the night even now?

Don't go borrowing trouble. He had to assume that Petey was still alive and was doing his best to stay that way. He knew that Kaden and the rest would be coming for him. He only had to last a little bit longer, and then…

Then Kaden and his group would have to break into a goblin stronghold, get Petey, and try to make it out again.

They kept up the challenging pace all the way to the edge of the grassland, which turned into craggy granite and patchy forest quicker than Kaden thought possible. Redfern spotted the first trap, a line no thicker than a spider's silk strung taut between two trees.

"Wait," she said, flying to the front of the group, then carefully severing the line with the tip of her spear. A series of darts exploded from just behind one of the trees, embedding themselves and, in one case, bouncing off the opposite tree. Weylyn bent down to retrieve the dart that had missed its mark.

"Poisoned," he commented as he closely inspected the tip. Kaden moved in to look for himself, and—*ugh*, there was a thin, glistening layer of orange on the end of the nasty metal dart. "Heart's Woe, from the smell of it."

"That is not good," Queen Pepper said somberly. "I can't purge Heart's Woe."

"What is it?" Ada asked, craning her neck to see the dart for herself.

"It comes from a mushroom grown deep in the earth," Pepper elaborated. "Legend says it only grows in a spot where a dragon died. I don't know if that's true or not, but the effects are just as deadly as any dragon. Once the poison is in your body, it races to your heart and sets it to beating so fast that eventually, it gives out entirely. It is almost always fatal." She shook her head. "I will use the power of yah'zaval to create a shield for us from here on out."

"Majesty, you can't," Millicent objected. "It will drain you too quickly!"

Pepper put her hands on her hips. "Better than one of us dying such a horrible death."

"We won't. We just need to be more careful," Redfern said. "Clearly, the goblins are more comfortable now that they're back on their home turf if they're taking the time to arm traps like this. We can't be far behind them, though. That thread wouldn't have held for more than a day." She flitted into the air again. "I'll scout from above."

"I'll lead down below," Weylyn added. "It makes sense," he said to Kaden before he could voice his objection. "I've got the best armor by far. Little darts like this won't give me any trouble." Neither he nor Redfern moved, though, waiting for Kaden to speak.

It warmed him to feel so respected by his friends and straightened his spine. "We'll do it your way," Kaden said, "but go very carefully. We all want to save Petey, but not at the expense of losing more of us to poison and traps." He hated to say it so bluntly, but he knew he was right. Moreover, he knew Petey would feel precisely the same way. Bug trembled on his shoulder, and he reached up and gave the hopping toadstool a little pat. "Let's go."

They moved at an earthworm's speed compared to what they'd been doing, triggering two more deadly traps over the next four hours. As the sun began to set, Kaden contemplated stopping them for the night. They had to be close, but he didn't want to risk anyone's injury or death in the dark. Then again, it would be difficult no matter what they did because the goblins could undoubtedly send a party out after them to attack, and with their night vision, they would have an advantage. Should they retreat to a safer area and come back tomorrow? But that would waste so much time—

"*Aha!*" Weylyn called out from up ahead, quietly but with satisfaction. "We've found one of their holes." He was standing in front of a boulder that looked quite solid to Kaden. It had a small crevice in the top of it that a gnarly pine tree was growing out of, twisted so that it hung down instead of up, but apart from that...

"Look." Weylyn lifted the heavy boughs of the tree, and there beneath it was a jagged hole in the rock itself, a passage that disappeared into the earth. "What say you? Shall we see where it leads?"

"It'll be watched," Eldrin cautioned even as he stepped closer.

"Of a certainty," Weylyn said. "But we'll be on guard too. And I think between all of us, we can come up with some tricks to get us in there undetected."

Kaden felt Bug begin to hop excitedly on his shoulder. He felt that same excitement rising within him. "Let's do it," he said. "Let's go in and get Petey back."

CHAPTER 29

The tunnel was surprisingly clean, given what Kaden had been expecting of anything goblin-made and maintained. That didn't mean he could go more than a step without worrying he was going to fall into some sort of trap, and the darkness slowed them all down considerably.

It was enough of a problem that Queen Pepper, after leaning in to consult with Bug for a moment, moved to the front of the group. "We need light if we are to vanquish the darkness," she said simply.

Weylyn shook his head. "We can't risk it being seen. Something tiny, perhaps, that could be concealed by—"

"I've thought of that." She nodded at Bug. "Our little friend has graciously agreed to help me."

Chum scoffed. "And how's a walking mushroom supposed to help with that?"

"Hopping toadstool," Pepper corrected gently. "And I'll show you. Just trust me." She looked at Kaden, and he nodded.

"As long as you can do this without exhausting yourself, please." *Anything to get us to Petey faster.*

"Thank you for your faith," she said, then looked down at Bug. "All right, get ready. On the count of three..." She raised her hands, and Bug hopped up and down a few times. "One." His cap began to expand, turning bright blue. "Two." It thinned and got even more extensive, and the glow turned into a shimmer that seemed to rise into the air. "Three!"

The shimmer puffed off the top of the mushroom and instantly changed color, becoming a moving shroud of darkness even blacker than the tunnel walls. Queen Pepper used her power of yah'zaval just a half-second after, which made a bubble of light behind the veil yet kept it intact, perfectly fitted to the tunnel. It moved ahead of them slowly, and she smiled triumphantly.

"That particular ejection of spores is known as Nightshade," she explained. "Hopping toadstools use it as a form of defense, to cover their escape. It's penetrable to sound, and obviously, someone could walk through it, but it captures the light quite well. And my power will hold it in place for the length ahead of us."

"Clever," Eldrin said admiringly. "I had no idea those little creatures were so useful. I always just ignored them whenever I was in Brightshire."

"I'm thrilled Bug is here, but shouldn't we be catching up to the shroud?" Ada asked. It *was* getting rather far ahead of them now. Weylyn went first, still checking for traps in the now well-lit tunnel and triggering the ones he found with no ill effects to their group.

It was Eldrin who first realized that things were changing. "I hear new sounds," he said lowly. "And the scent is getting wetter. I think we're close to the end of the tunnel."

"Weapons at the ready and lights out, then," Kaden said, putting one hand on Vrangar. There was no telling what was waiting for them and then just beyond the tunnel, and he wasn't going to be unprepared. Queen Pepper nodded, and as soon as everyone had armed themselves, she let her power go. The Nightshade vanished, and instead of more darkness, now they could see the faintest hint of a sickly green light up ahead. They moved forward in near silence, with Weylyn and Eldrin at the front, Kaden, Ada, Bug, and Pepper in the middle, and Chum and the other fairies at the rear.

Kaden's hands shook, and he wasn't sure whether it was more from fear or rage. They were about to walk into a goblin's lair, into the home of the people who had killed Daneyel, who had stolen Petey. He hated them, *hated* them, hated the fact that they'd taken away not one but two people he cared for and that they had been the reason for the end of his old life. He knew now it would have come to an end one way or another, but his violent transition from innocent and ignorant to knowing more than he'd ever wanted to had left him scarred.

The only reason he was still alive now was because he'd found people to help him along the way. Kaden wasn't going to lose Petey to the evil creatures who'd changed his life with such deadly finality the first time around.

They reached the end of the tunnel, and everyone in the entire party grimaced as the stench of Shroudscar wafted in to mingle amongst them. "Ugh, are we standing right over their sewage?" Ada asked, clearly trying not to gag.

"More like we'll be wading right into it once we head down there," Weylyn murmured, nodding his head toward the middle of the vast space they'd just entered. "Take a look at that."

They were able to take a better look than Kaden had anticipated. The tunnel they were emerging from gave them a bird's eye view of what they were about to get into. There was no guard at the base of the tunnel, which struck him as odd at first, but as his eyes adjusted to the strange new light, he realized why they didn't even bother.

Shroudscar, situated in the deep, concave center of the immense cavern and lit mainly by the pale green phosphorescence of a scab-like fungus that seemed to grow on everything, was a fortress. It was a *single* fortress, not a series of buildings out in the open, nor built into the rock itself as the dwarves had done. The fort had strong wooden walls built along a rectangular perimeter that housed a village in the fort's courtyard. Just inside the fort, a wooden boardwalk, walled in for protection, rimmed the top of all four walls. Wooden watchtowers, stationed with archer goblins, stood tall at the four corners of the fort. Heavily armored guards patrolled the dirt street with growlers on chain leashes. They wore layers of leather and cotton with rough, well-used boots covered in filth. Some had expensive jewelry, likely gained as loot from pirating, and all wore tricorn hats. The fort squatted like a festering boil in the middle of the landscape, long and vaguely rectangular, made from thick, rough-hewn pine logs that looked as though they'd been hastily painted over with something thick and clotted.

"They're at least smart enough to take pains to cover the place in chemille. It's a special type of mud," Weylyn explained, "that makes it harder to set the wood on fire. Which is a bit of a shame because nothing gets people's attention like fire."

Kaden shook his head. "It would have been too risky to Petey anyway," he said. "I count four watchtowers."

"Each with two guards," Eldrin confirmed. "But only the one gate, right there in the middle of the long wall facing north."

"How do you even know which way is north after all this time underground?" groused Chum.

"Because I pay attention, unlike some people," Eldrin replied, then pointed. "Grawler patrols along the outside walls, look." True enough, at least two teams of goblins were walking with pairs of grawlers, the big beasts both hobbled and muzzled, presumably for the protection of their escorts. Kaden bet that the moment they caught a rogue scent, the goblins could rip the grawlers' chains off and set them loose at top speed.

"We'll have to disguise our scents," he said. "Preferably with something not too foul, but it's going to have to be thorough *and* dirty if we're going to get around their noses, not to mention the guards' eyes." He bent and scraped a hand along the floor, coming up with a wet, gritty substance. Duke sniffed at his hand and sneezed, then pawed at his nose. "This might do it."

"How do you know this?" Redfern asked, looking a little boggled.

"I was a farmer." Everyone still looked blank. "Have you ever tried to get close enough to help a birthing cow who bolts at the smell of people?" Kaden asked impatiently. "Because I have, and I would have gotten my face kicked in if I hadn't taken some precautions." His foster parents had taught him that much.

"That's good for getting close," Weylyn agreed, "but we'll still need a place to go once we're in there. And we don't know how we're going to get in there at all yet."

"Let me fly a little higher," Millicent offered, flexing her wings. She'd been doing her best not to overtax herself, but the bandage had finally come off yesterday, and Kaden knew she was eager to be in the air again. "I'll see what I can make out."

"Don't get much closer," Queen Pepper warned her worriedly. "I can disguise you from far away, but..."

Millicent patted her queen's hand, then set down her spear. "I can cover myself for this much," she said and then rose into the air. A moment later, her colors blurred and faded, leaving her the same dull, murky grayish green as everything else in here.

Kaden watched her fly, unwilling to take his eyes off her for fear of losing sight of her vague outline entirely. She went up high, nearly to the top of the cavern, and flew a few hundred feet closer. There she hovered for a few minutes, and Kaden felt like he could barely breathe the whole time he watched her.

Someone down in Shroudscar shouted, loud and long, and Kaden jumped. Ada covered her mouth with her hands, eyes wide as they glanced anxiously at each other. But—no, the goblin in question had just been head-butted by his grawler, which knocked him onto his rear. His companion laughed at him, and his shouts had turned into vehement curses. The strain in Kaden's shoulders slowly faded, and when Millicent touched down again a minute later, he was almost breathing normally again.

"I could see him," she said, and instantly Kaden felt all knotted up again. "Near the back of the fortress. He's in a cage on a platform, right next to what looks like some sort of throne, and there's a huge goblin in it. There are what seem to be traditional fights going on—goblins fighting goblins. I counted at least a hundred of them out in the open and plenty of grawlers. I didn't see any way in other than the front gate," she finished in a tone of mild apology like it was her fault that the goblins were paranoid enough to create only one entrance and exit to their fortress.

"Well." Weylyn stroked his chin as he stared down at the fortress. "If you saw a hundred in the open, then we double that number to estimate how many might truly be there. Shroudscar isn't the only goblin city out there, but it's the closest to the surface and where their heartiest warriors reside if I remember right. A few hundred tough, battle-worthy goblins are a hell of a thing to try and workaround."

"You're not saying we should give up, are you?" Kaden asked.

"No, but we do need to consider how we do this very, very carefully," Weylyn said. "Remember, they expect us to come. I doubt they run these kinds of patrols or waste torchlight like this during normal operations. They left us a challenge, and we'll have to answer it one way or another. But remember," he added, "that the last thing Petey would want is for you to give your life needlessly."

"We need to find a way to confuse or bottleneck the goblins," Eldrin said slowly, still staring at the fortress. "A way to keep them from being able to attack us in the open. In a small space, we'll have an advantage—we know how to fight around each other. Goblins learn that with their patrol groups, but all together like this? When they're already being exhorted to fight one another? There's no chance of that kind of cooperation."

This was sounding promising. "There are plenty of buildings in there," Kaden said.

"We can't risk blockading ourselves someplace we can't get out of," Redfern pointed out.

"True, but—"

"You know, the inside buildings aren't covered with mud," Ada said suddenly. "Not like the outer walls. I bet they'd burn pretty well." Everyone looked at her. She shrugged. "What? There's a reason we built with slate in Whaldalf's Landing, and it's not because it was warm—we needed to be fireproof. If a few of us can set fires to create a distraction, that will help get the goblins off our backs."

"I can try to make sure they burn hot and bright," Queen Pepper added.

"That brings us back to the trouble of getting inside in the first place," Weylyn said. "We might be able to kill both patrols, even simultaneously, but the watchmen will surely see us if we do."

"That's not the only entrance. It can't be," Eldrin muttered. "It's strategically unsound, and these goblins aren't all stupid. There's a rhyme... my father told it to me when I was just a child, asking about the other tribes..." He closed his eyes for a moment, his lips moving soundlessly before he finally said, "In the depths of darkness Shroudscar lies, deep below the shadowed skies, a breach to the east, a breach to west, one on the ground, one 'neath the rest..." He trailed off.

"What does that mean?" Kaden asked.

"I asked my father when he told it to me, but he didn't know. It's an old rhyme, but then Shroudscar is an old city, for all it looks like a clump of dung." Eldrin stared out at the fortress. "A breach to the east, one on the ground... that could refer to the big gate that we're looking at. A breach to west, one 'neath the rest... perhaps there's another way into Shroudscar after all. And the western side of the fortress is where the largest buildings are, probably where their leader lives." He shrugged. "It would make sense, is all I'm saying. No leader would leave themselves without another exit if they could help it."

"Do you think there might be a tunnel or something?" Well, if nothing else, Kaden had learned that goblins were expert tunnellers. "We might as well go and check it out," he said to the others. "Our only other option is a frontal assault, and the way things are now, the odds of that working don't look so good."

"Then..." Queen Pepper sighed and looked at the mucky ground. "I suppose it's time to get dirty."

They all made quick but thorough work of covering themselves in grime. It smelled more earthy and metallic than foul, but it still wasn't a pleasant state to be in. Kaden smeared the last bit across his nose, then turned to look at the rest of his group.

"Wait," Ada said. Reaching out, she rubbed her thumb against his cheek, just under his right eye. Her skin was soft and warm compared to the dirt she was spreading across his skin. "There," she murmured. Kaden swallowed, unable to look away.

"Ex*cuse* me," Chum interrupted just a few decibels short of a bellow. "If you two are through *ogling* each other already, we might actually get something done!"

"And if you get us caught because of your shouting, we won't get anything done!" Redfern hissed back. "So close your braying mouth!"

"Both of you," Weylyn said before Kaden could, "need to stop. Right now. If you don't think you can keep yourself under control for this, Chum, then stay here. There are some times and places where you can get away with being insubordinate, but this isn't one of them."

Chum frowned, looking hurt. "But we're a team!"

"And to stay a team, we both need to stay alive," Weylyn replied. "So. Are you in, or out?"

"In," Chum said, sounding unexpectedly profound. "I'm in."

"Good." Weylyn looked between Kaden and Eldrin. "So. What next?"

"I guess we leave our packs here, then head for the east side of the fortress and see what we can find," Kaden said.

Eldrin grimaced. "It won't be easy to discover a goblin bolt-hole if it's even there."

Kaden smiled at him. "Actually, I've got an idea for that."

Getting around to the east side of the compound took time. The rock beneath their feet was loose like scree, and if they tried to move too quickly, a shower of it would fall down the side of the hill. Twice they almost alerted goblin patrols to their presence with the noise. The second time, the goblins and their enormous, red-eyed grawlers came so close to the jutting outcrop of dark, dank stone they'd hidden behind that Duke had started to growl. Luckily for Kaden, he felt the rumble build in his hound's chest before it came out and clamped Duke's muzzle firmly shut before any noise could emerge. After a few more seconds of peering into the green-tinged gloom, the patrol moved on.

"That was close," Redfern said softly.

"We could have taken 'em," Chum opined. Now that he'd come down on the side of action, he seemed to be bristling with energy for it, holding Petey's dagger like it was a broadsword ready to chop off goblin heads. Kaden had *hated* letting someone else use Loyal Dwingent, but it was one of the best weapons they had and shouldn't be left to sit idle in his pack when it could be put to good use.

"We could have gotten into a big loud fight and alerted half the goblins in this damn cavern to our presence too," Weylyn said, giving Chum a little shake. "Save it for when we've got no choice." Chum came the closest to pouting that Kaden had ever seen on his goaty face, but he obliged, and they made it the rest of the way to the east side of the fortress without incident.

"So," Queen Pepper began once they found a place to hide behind that offered them a view of the whole eastern wall. Thankfully, it was one of the smaller walls but still several hundred feet long. "How do you propose we find the secret entrance?"

"Simple," Kaden said, hoping that it really was. "I'm going to get Duke to do it."

Everyone—absolutely everyone—looked confused. "You mean, he'll sniff it out?" Eldrin asked.

"Yes."

"But you'll have to lead him to every spot to check. That'll take hours," Millicent pointed out. "You can't simply let him run off on his own, or he might go after the grawlers."

"Duke is a farm dog," Kaden said, scratching his big hound behind the ears. Duke leaned into the petting, his tongue lolling out. "A working dog. You can't justify feeding an animal this big on a farm that doesn't do any work. One of the things he did for us helped drive off any rabbits or gophers that tried to make inroads into our fields. It's a special skill, and it'll work for this." *I hope.* Kaden lifted Duke's face so that the dog was looking straight at him and said, "Duke, *rabbits*! Go get the rabbits!"

Duke turned and took off at a crouch, nose to the ground, sniffing all over the rocky ground, searching for a scent that stood out. Kaden kept his eyes on him, ignoring everyone else for the moment so he could make sure his dog didn't stray too close to the wall and any potential patrols that might be passing by there. *You can do this, you can do it...* It felt like it had been forever since Duke spot-hunted rabbits like this, but he seemed as confident as ever.

It took almost a quarter of an hour, during which the group at Kaden's back seemed to get louder and more doubtful with every passing minute, but then Duke suddenly laid down and put his head on his paws about a hundred and fifty feet away, and a little bit downslope. Kaden moved over to him quietly, whispering praise as he came to see what Duke had found.

At first, it looked like nothing at all—not surprising, since the goblins had already proven adept at hiding their tunnels. But a bit of brushing away the debris there revealed the ragged edges of the large, flat rock that was being used as a cover. With Weylyn's help, Kaden pushed it to the side. The hole the stone had been covering was pretty large, and the smell of smoke, along with cooking meat, wafted up from it. Perhaps it led to someone's private home?

"It's actually here." Eldrin sounded surprised that his riddle had turned out to be true.

"Good thing too," Weylyn said, glancing downslope again as another goblin patrol passed. The noise from inside the fortress was getting louder, more raucous—that probably didn't bode well for whoever was taking the brunt of that attention. "All right. One of us should go in and check it out first, then report back and—"

"No." Kaden shook his head. "We need to stay together and get Petey out as soon as possible."

Weylyn raised an eyebrow. "That's not good tactics, Kaden."

"I know, but…" He looked over toward the fortress. "It's just a feeling I have. We need to move fast, or soon it'll be too late."

"A leader shouldn't base his actions on feelings."

"And I'm not saying we're just going to run down there and pop out into whatever we find at the other end," Kaden replied. He didn't know why he was arguing about this, but he knew in his heart it was vital that they move as one and quickly.

Orealus, guide me. "We'll be careful, but I want us to be ready to move. Eldrin, you go first," he said, stepping back. "You're good at locating traps, and Queen Pepper can provide you with a light to help see them by. Check at the far end and make sure it's all right for us to emerge."

Eldrin smiled and nodded. "As you command." He waited for Pepper to send a glowing ball of light into the hole, then dropped down himself. Kaden turned to Weylyn again.

"I understand if you're uncomfortable with this and would rather remain here," he said earnestly, looking at all of them—his comrades, his friends. "But I'm asking you to trust me. Please."

Queen Pepper smiled. "Of course I'm with you." Her guards nodded firmly. "We're safer together. I'll do my best to make sure of it."

"I'm going," Ada said firmly, locking eyes with Kaden. He felt his face heat and was a little grateful the darkness hid his flush.

"It's not the dumbest order you've ever gotten," Chum pointed out to Weylyn with a shrug.

Weylyn sighed, then nodded. "I don't have to agree with it to do it," he said. "For what it's worth, I do trust you. You're the leader, Kaden. You make the decisions. You decide if you can live with what might happen as a result of those decisions."

The weight of that responsibility made Kaden feel like he'd just shouldered a mountain, but he held firm. "I understand." He turned back to the hole, dropped inside, and then motioned for Duke to follow him. The big dog jumped down quickly. Kaden turned and looked at Eldrin, already fifty feet away and moving slowly but smoothly, accompanied by the glowing light ball. "Let's go."

To everyone's surprise, there were no traps in this tunnel, and despite the reasonably tight fit and the slippery, mold-drenched floor that threatened to tumble them with every step, they made it to the far side in good time. The smells got more robust as they closed the distance, and more sounds began to penetrate the rock—yelling, whooping, and hollering—but none of it right above them. Once they were at the far end, Eldrin put his shoulder to the rock above him, then hissed and dropped down again.

"It's sweltering," he said. "I think the tunnel is part of a fireplace. Something is cooking up there."

Oh, no. Were they stymied already? But now Weylyn moved to the front of the line, flexing his gauntleted hands. "All of you, stand back," he said, then set his armored hands and arms to the stone and pushed. A shower of sparks rained down, but he didn't hesitate, and a moment later, the stone was pushed aside, and so was much of the heat. Weylyn stuck his head out, then retracted it.

"We're lucky," he said quietly. "It's a kitchen all right, but the fire's down to embers, and the spit is empty. The food's already been moved."

Kaden exhaled heavily with relief. "Thank you," he said. "All right, let's head up—carefully. As soon as we locate Petey, we start creating distractions so I can get him."

"What do you want us to do?" Ada asked.

Kaden told her.

CHAPTER 30

The air was filled with sounds: goblins throwing darts at a target pinned to the wall, guffawing or groaning as they struck home; grawlers gnashing and howling, cut off by sharp strikes from their impatient masters; the moans of the injured, sometimes dying as goblin bodies were carted off the field of combat in front of the makeshift throne in the plaza just in front of Kaden, where they competed for the favor of their master, Garth.

Garth was twice as big as the average goblin, more prominent than most men, and he sat on his throne of wood and iron and ruled over his people with a deadly fist. No one who jeered at him went away unpunished, and some of them didn't survive his attentions, forced into the ring to fight for his amusement.

Kaden hated him on sight. He wasn't sure whether it was the fact that the goblin was clearly a bully, so used to forcing people to give him what he wanted that he didn't care if he killed them on the way, or if it was because he had Petey in a cage beside his throne, but Kaden burned with a fire that few had ever roused in him. His first priority was to get Petey out of there, but after that... oh, if he got the chance, he would love to see Garth fall.

Focus. This isn't about him. It was about Petey, not Garth, and definitely not Kaden's wild dreams of fighting him. This wasn't the place for a confrontation, and they didn't have the numbers for it anyhow. Right now, the priority was causing chaos and getting Petey out of there safe.

The chaos was up to other people. The rest of Kaden's party, except for Duke, was already making their way through the dark spaces along the edges of Shroudscar, ready to wreak chaos. As soon as the first flame was lit—and Kaden knew it would be a big one, with Queen Pepper on hand to stoke the fire with her power—goblins would begin to panic. If he was any kind of leader, Garth would go see what was going on, try to get a handle on it, and get things under control.

That was when Kaden would free Petey, staying low in the dark cloak he'd found near the kitchen they'd emerged from and cutting through the cage Petey was bound in with the help of Vrangar. Then they'd return to the tunnel, and once everyone was accounted for, they'd make their escape with none of the goblins the wiser.

Kaden *hoped* it worked out that way. There were too few of them to take on all of Shroudscar, and he wasn't here to start a war.

Still, it was hard. Hard to watch the goblins behaving so terribly to one another, harder to watch them kowtow to their brutal leader Garth, most problematic of all to see how he treated Petey.

"Enjoying the show, runt?" Garth shouted with glee after a particularly fierce battle, where one goblin ended up decapitated, his life over despite the way he'd begged and screamed for mercy at the end. "Should put you in there, eh? At least that way, you could die as one of us, rather than the lickspittle lackey of a human. A *human*."

Kaden was close enough to hear the goblin leader spit at Petey, who shrank back. "Of all the filthy things. A goblin, offering his fealty to a human? You've been cursed and—no doubt, little Petey—condemned since birth. But we'll give you the cure for that curse as soon as your little friends show up.

"Will watching him die fix you, do you think?" He leaned over toward Petey, yellow eyes gleaming in the torchlight. "Or will it only break you further?" Garth laughed and sat back on his throne and then gestured for the next fight. "Either way, I'm looking forward to seeing what happens next."

You won't be for long, Kaden promised himself. He longed to draw Vrangar from its sheathe along his back, longed to leap out of the shadows and stick it straight through the goblin leader. He didn't care about an honorable battle, not right now. This was about culling cruelty from the world, and he was more than ready to do that in the case of the goblin leader.

But it wasn't time yet—he would be seen. So he stuck to the shadows, pulled back whenever a grawler came near, and waited for the perfect moment to strike.

Every second seemed to crawl, but Kaden knew it didn't take as long as it felt. One moment he was crouched beside the doorway of the kitchen they'd all emerged from, wondering whether or not his friends were all right, whether they were accomplishing their goals, and the next, he heard a scream, and then an off-key bell began to clang.

"Fire!" someone shouted, and goblins began to emerge from every building, all of them running about in a frenzy as they tried to find the source of the flame. "There's fire here! Fire!"

Garth stood up, his gray-green skin glistening in the dim torchlight. He had a broadsword attached to his belt, and his jagged-toothed mouth gaped wide as he called out, "Find whatever fool let a fire get away from them and bring them to me! I'll flay the skin from their bodies and stake them out for the worms!"

"Another one!" a new voice wailed from the opposite side of the fortress. "Fire, right next to my shop! Help me settle the flames, or go without my store of Bardicus's grog!" There was practically a stampede in the direction of the voice, and after a moment, Garth followed them, jumping down from his throne with a fierce grimace and beating his frantic subjects out of his way as he pushed toward the source of the complaint.

Now. Go now! Kaden knew he would never have a better shot to get Petey, even with all the goblins still running around in the streets. He signaled to Duke to follow him, then darted out from his hiding place toward the cage, dodging the chaos as best he could. The air was slowly filling with smoke, and it made for decent cover, but—

"Hey! You, there!"

Not quite decent enough. Kaden was almost twice as tall as many of these goblins, and the creatures who had seemed so fiercely intimidating to him just a few months ago when they'd attacked him in Ashland Woods now seemed… small. Still ferocious, but small. A pair of them, with a grawler out in front, had caught sight of him. The one holding onto the beast's reins released it with a shouted command, and the creature lunged toward them, jaws slavering as it dug its paws into the grimy, dirty ground, preparing to leap.

Duke got to the grawler, his armor appearing just as the big beasts clashed. The grawler tried to get its teeth into Duke's shoulder, but it was no good—the blessed armor protected him, and it was light enough that Duke kept both his speed and his agility even when it was activated. He twisted his head and got one of the grawler's ears between his teeth, then jerked his head and shredded it, leaving nothing but wisps of bloody tissue behind.

The goblins were stunned to hear their grawler howl in pain, shocked further to discover that what they'd thought was an alpha beast was really only good at taking advantage of the weak. A few more snaps and snarls, and the grawler began to back away, straight through its befuddled handlers. Sensing a predator turned to prey, Duke pursued the formerly vicious beast.

Kaden would have called him back, but even without their grawler, the goblins weren't about to let him walk off. The one whose hands were free the whole time had already drawn a long, curving blade, and he ran at Kaden with the sword held low, ready to gut him.

Kaden pulled Vrangar free while simultaneously using the sheathe to block the incoming strike, then hammered down with the flat of his blade on top of the goblin's head. The wiry goblin staggered, but the second one was charging in now, screaming for blood. Kaden blocked, blocked again, and realized that the first goblin was getting up.

He was both surrounded and alone. He'd never get Petey if he didn't finish things.

It hurt to think about what he had to do now, about the step he had to take, but he gritted his teeth, turned his blade, and struck again. This time, Vrangar's keen edge found the back of the goblin's neck and bit deep, sending him to the ground in a mess of spreading gore. This time, he didn't get up again.

"I'll have that blade from your corpse," the second goblin hissed. He was dual-wielding a pair of long, nasty daggers, and he feinted low with one before striking toward Kaden's unprotected side with the other. Kaden managed to block it, but the goblin parried Kaden's next two strikes, seeming to know where they were coming from almost before Kaden did.

"Little human pup," the goblin said with a sneer as he backed Kaden toward Petey's cage. Kaden didn't dare look at his friend yet—he couldn't afford to get distracted. "I've three times your experience, at least. You think you can dance with my blades for long?" He attacked again, and while Kaden was still able to hold him off, he couldn't break through with any of his own attacks. Worse, the goblin controlled where he went, forcing him to move backward until he actually ran right into the cage.

Kaden dodged the next two strikes, lashed out with Vrangar hard enough that the goblin had to duck, then darted to the side to give himself more mobility. The goblin sneered and took a step forward, then was hauled back abruptly by the edge of his ragged cloak.

"Now, Kaden!" Petey shouted from the other side of the cage. He'd grabbed the cloak and pulled it as hard as he could, knocking the other goblin off balance. Kaden struck before his opponent could right himself. Vrangar sank into the goblin's heart, and with a puzzled frown on his gruesome face, the goblin collapsed to the ground.

"Kaden! What are you doing here?" Petey demanded as Kaden turned toward the cage, determined not to look too closely at either of the people he'd just killed.

"I'm getting you out of here, of course," Kaden said, breathlessly looking over the cage for a weak spot. There, a vast, rusted lock… he smashed it with Vrangar's hilt as hard as he could manage, and the lock shattered satisfactorily.

"You shouldn't have come!" Petey scolded Kaden even as he helped push the heavy metal grate off the top of the cage and climbed out the open corner of it. "The things Garth wants to do to you—he said that if you showed up at the front gate, he'd have you lamed with arrows, then cut every tendon in your legs, then every tendon in your arms, then he'd cut off your ears, then he'd—"

"I get it." Kaden could imagine it very well on his own. He didn't need Petey to lay it out for him. "But that's not how we came here, and it's not how we're going to leave." He crouched down to disguise his height a bit better from the passing goblins. "As soon as we get our chance, we'll—"

"*Intruders!*" the stentorian voice echoed over the ramshackle city like a pronouncement of divine doom. "Drive them toward the center! Drive them into the arena!"

Petey blinked his big eyes in startlement. "Wait. Did you bring—"

Kaden didn't have the breath to answer, though—he looked past the cage into the place where goblins had been battling each other for their leader's sadistic pleasure and saw Ada stumble across the blood-soaked stones, her bow drawn but her arrow vastly outnumbered by the goblin archers herding her. Eldrin was next, followed closely by Weylyn and Chum.

A moment later, Queen Pepper and her guards flew into view, and Kaden felt his heart pang even worse. They could have gotten away… but he knew Pepper never would have left him and the others. She hadn't on the way to Nethopolis, and she wouldn't here in the stone-walled pit that was Shroudscar.

Kaden and Petey might be able to run now… they might even be able to make it out. But he couldn't leave his friends any more than they could leave him. Firming his heart and readying his sword, Kaden stepped out from behind the cage, with Petey nervously trailing him. The fires, no matter how hotly they'd burned just minutes ago, seemed to be going out. That gambit had failed. There was only one way he could see that he might be able to get him and his people out of here now.

"Garth!" he shouted, doing his best to match the volume of the goblin leader. To his surprise, his voice carried well, and the shouting rabble slowly quieted as they realized the human boy wasn't just yelling but was making himself heard. "I challenge you to a fight! You and me, one on one. Winner takes all."

"Kaden, no!" Weylyn shouted helplessly, but Kaden stood his ground. Now wasn't a time for him to let someone else step in and take the brunt of every attack, and he had the feeling his friends needed to save their energy for whatever came next. If he lost…

A moment later, the enormous goblin he'd seen before from a distance stepped forward, and Kaden swallowed hard. All of a sudden, losing seemed a lot more possible than he wanted it to.

The goblin had at least a head on him and was massively muscled as well. He carried a long sword with a jagged section in the blade close to the hilt, which had spikes jutting from both sides of it. He was wearing bulkier armor than most of the other goblins, more than just leathers and metal studs—his hands were gauntleted, his shins were covered, and he appeared to be wearing a mail shirt. His eyes were narrowed so close that Kaden almost couldn't see the gangrenous yellow-green color of them, and his broad ears were notched and scarred.

"So you came after all," Garth said, smiling a terrible grimace of a smile. His teeth were dark with rot, and Kaden could practically smell the foulness of his breath from twenty paces away. "Our lord said you would. Said you were weak enough to be moved by the plight of a friend, even when the friend is that useless little runtling." He lobbed a gobbet of spit in Petey's direction. "And now I've got you all right where our lord wants you. I don't even need to fight you now—you'll do what I want, or I'll slaughter your friends in front of you."

Kaden laughed. It was a slow, deep laugh, haughty and mocking—the sort of sound he didn't know he could make until now. Inside, he was shaking, but he showed nothing but confidence on the outside. All their lives depended on it.

"Of course you don't want to fight," he said. "Not when you're afraid you might lose. You sit here on your throne and watch your people kill themselves for your amusement, but when it comes to stepping up and proving that you're tough enough to do the same, you refuse. Because you know you won't win." He laughed again. "Look at you, afraid of a human like me. And you should be, because if you *don't* fight me, you're proving to everyone here that you're nothing but a coward at heart, and one of your braver followers will stab you through the back the second they get a chance. And it'll be what you deserve."

Garth's expression got darker and darker the longer Kaden talked. By the end of his speech, the goblin chief was practically foaming at the mouth with fury. "I'm the best there is!" he roared. "The biggest, the strongest, the most powerful! Our lord Lucient knows it, all my people know it, and soon you'll know it too, you human stripling!" He shook his massive sword in Kaden's direction. "We fight! Now!"

"Not until you agree to my terms," Kaden pressed. "If I beat you, that's a sign to you and everyone else that Lucient has deserted you. That means that my people and I go free."

"And when I beat you," Garth grunted, a line of drool sliding out from between his sharp bottom teeth, "I'll tie your friends to spits and roast them over an open flame." He grinned. "What do you think fairy wings look like when they burn?" Garth stepped forward into the cleared space between them. Kaden went to join him, but Petey suddenly caught the edge of his tunic.

"Don't get too close," he whispered as he stared up at Kaden, his eyes huge and frightened. "He's as good a grappler as he is with a sword. If he gets his hands on you, he'll crush the life out of you!"

"Thanks," Kaden whispered back, then steeled his spine and stepped forward toward Garth. He took a moment to grip his amulet. *Orealus protect me, and I'll cover my friends.* Then he gripped Vrangar's hilt with both hands and moved it to a ready position. "What, are we going to stare at each other all day, or are we going to fight?" he asked with a sneer.

Garth roared, and his goblins roared with him. The sound echoed through the underground cavern, bouncing from rock to rock and almost deafening Kaden. A moment later, Garth charged forward. Kaden raised his sword to defend himself, and the resulting clash was so tremendous it drowned out even the goblin horde. Sparks flew as the blades slid against one another, and in the very last moment, Kaden remembered to pull back, just as Garth freed a hand to reach out for him, his thick, clawed fingers grasping greedily.

"Now, who's a coward?" Garth taunted, then struck again. And again. Every hit felt like being whacked by the forest golem, only with more speed. It was all Kaden could do to block, much less think about striking back. He gritted his teeth and maintained his control, waiting for an opening, for a moment to take his shot… but there wasn't one.

"I'll kill you," Garth said. "Roasting your friends is only the start. That pretty little girl over there?" His eyes gleamed with an evil light. "She'll get to watch it all, then be dessert."

"*No!*" Kaden attacked with everything he had, horrified and infuriated by the vision that the goblin leader had put into his head. It wouldn't go like that. It *couldn't*. He had the favor of

Orealus. He had faith in him. He would *not* fall before his quest had been completed.

He fought hard, and for a moment, he put Garth on the defensive—then his foot slipped in a pool of something foul and sticky, and the goblin took immediate advantage, hammering down with his terrible serrated blade so fast that it took everything Kaden had to pull off blocks.

One minute in, Kaden was breathing heavily. Before long, his sides ached with every twist and turn he had to make to keep Garth from cutting him in two, and his hands were nearly numb from blocking such powerful blows. Vrangar was keeping him protected, its edge staying strong even as Garth's grew more and more notched, but he couldn't match the goblin's power or speed.

Garth knew it, too, if the wicked grin creasing his face was any indication. He swept his sword up in a powerful horizontal cut that batted Kaden's blade to the side, then roared and swung down without a second's pause, knocking Vrangar clean out of Kaden's hands after his hasty block.

"No!" Ada screamed. Kaden sensed his friends moving to help him and knew they were all held back. He faced the goblin leader empty-handed, looking frantically for his sword—but it was too far away for him to get to without being skewered. Weylyn was shouting something now, and there was a burst of light from Pepper that was quickly smothered in a wave of darkness.

"Now die, whelp." Garth raised his sword for a final blow, one that Kaden wouldn't be able to avoid or outrun. He wanted to do something, but his mind was empty of everything but fear.

This was it.

A second later, Kaden was forcefully thrown onto his side. Someone screamed, and then there was a wave of dark laughter from the crowd. He picked his head up dazedly to see what had happened, expecting the sword to descend any moment.

But Garth wasn't looking at him. He was staring from the body in front of him to the dagger embedded in his sword hand. "This didn't come from you," he snapped at the person he'd just cut down, then jerked the plain, unremarkable blade out of his skin and turned to roar at the crowd, "Who did that? Show yourself, you filth!"

Kaden was too focused on the person fallen at Garth's feet to care what he was talking about. He crawled over, his lips forming the word "no" over and over again even though he didn't make a sound. He got to the body—small, so small—and rolled it over so that he could see his rescuer's face.

It was Petey. Of course, it was. Blood trickled from his mouth, and when Kaden looked down, he wished he hadn't. Petey's stomach had been ripped open by Garth's blade, and glistening pink and red coils bulged through the slice in his filthy tunic. "Petey," Kaden managed at last. "No. No, why did you… you shouldn't have…"

Petey smiled. It was ghastly, blood coating all his teeth, but he looked genuinely happy. "You're my friend," he said, his voice barely a whisper. "My brother… my family." His big golden eyes closed, and Kaden felt like his heart had dropped out through the bottom of his chest.

"Petey?"

His friend didn't respond.

"Petey, please don't." There had to be something he could do, something, *anything*. "Don't die." He couldn't have come so close only to fail so badly. Anger and heartache warred inside of him, and the urge to cry was almost overwhelming. It would be so easy to give in to that anger right now.

He didn't want that. Kaden fumbled his hand onto the amulet. *Orealus, guide me. Please, help me to do your will. Help me find the strength to defeat my enemies.* To his great surprise, the amulet pulsed in his hand. There was no light, and yet it felt as though the light was inside of him, growing and glowing and filling him with righteousness, restoring his soul and, by extension, his Mana.

I AM WITH YOU.

The shadow of a monster fell over him from behind. It held a blade in its hand. "The little runt had it coming," Garth scoffed, then began to laugh. "A fittingly useless end for a useless life!"

Kaden spasmodically clenched his fists. He let go of the amulet and turned to face Garth, picking up Vrangar as he went and holding it in a ready position.

"No more friends to sacrifice themselves for you now," Garth said with a leer. He held up his hulking blade—only this time, facing it, Kaden felt no fear. "Now you die!" Garth lunged forward, sword scything in a tremendously powerful arc. And Kaden…

The restoring light he carried within him shot forth in a brilliant white wave, washing over Garth, the goblins, his friends, and lighting up the entire cavern like day. Garth stumbled, his eyes unable to take the sudden brightness. His sword fell, and a second later, Kaden attacked with Vrangar.

One blow was all it took. His sword was an instrument of the light he carried within him, and a focused beam of this expended energy sliced through his enemy without pause, cutting a swath through the goblins in front of him straight through to the reinforced wall of Shroudscar, which blasted apart. Debris flew everywhere, raining down on the terrified goblins and Kaden's awestruck friends.

Kaden spoke at last, quiet yet booming, the power of his faith infusing every part of him. "If you want to live," he said, "run."

Every goblin and grawler scattered like ants into the slowly encroaching darkness.

CHAPTER 31

It hardly felt real.

It was, Kaden knew that—he'd just lived it, after all, lived the fires and the fight, lived the explosion of light from within himself that had ended the threat with such finality. It had all happened, and now it was done... and Petey was still dead, on the ground not five feet behind him. Kaden knew it and knew he should do something about it, but he couldn't bear to look at his friend's body and admit that, despite everything, he'd still done too little, too late. Suddenly, he felt exhausted. Completely drained, yet he knew he needed to pull himself together. His sword felt so heavy, his arms heavier.

The others slowly gathered around him, lit by the light of Queen Pepper's delicate elemental ability, a ball that floated in the air like a miniature sun. Only Bug went straight to Petey, hop-hop-hopping dejectedly but with determination.

Kaden jolted when Weylyn clapped a hand on his shoulder. "It never gets easier to lose a comrade," the mercenary said, uncommon compassion on his face. "But it's a part of leadership. If you want to lead a rebellion against Lucient and win it, really win it, then this is something you have to learn to live with."

"I can't stand it," Kaden confessed. A calm, delicate hand slipped into his—Ada.

"You don't have to do this alone," she said. "We're here to help bear the weight, after all."

"You shouldn't be." Kaden didn't know these words were going to come out of his mouth, but he let his new, frenzied thoughts loose, unable to hold them back once they started. "Petey was my first friend on this journey, he stuck with me through the worst of things, and I still wasn't able to save him. How could I hope to do the same for you? I—perhaps my faith in Orealus isn't enough to—"

"It's not about faith in Orealus." Eldrin's voice was firm. "We're not following you out of faith in anyone other than yourself, Kaden."

There was a startled peep in the distance, but Kaden barely heard it as Queen Pepper began to speak. "Even if this were about faith in Orealus," she said soothingly, "*your* faith isn't lacking, my dear. Look at what you accomplished here. That was an act of pure yah'zaval, which unlocked a dormant ability deep within you that comes directly from such faith, and it was one of the most impressive displays that I've ever seen. Something like that could only be accomplished by a person who has great faith in Orealus. You're not alone, Kaden, in so many ways.

"None of us will ever replace Petey"—there was another peep, louder this time, but Kaden couldn't look away from Pepper—"but we're with you on this quest, to the end. No one can know their fate, but I look at you, and I know I'm not afraid of what lies ahead."

"I am," Chum said candidly. "I'm about to shake out of my fur, I'm so damn afraid, but I'd rather be on the side of the guy who can cut a goblin in half with a sword made out of light."

"I don't know if I can do it again," Kaden confessed.

"You'll figure it out," Weylyn said, squeezing his shoulder before finally pulling back. "Now, much as I like gloating over a fallen enemy, we should get out of here before the goblins think about regrouping. We need to get Petey's body and—"

"PEEP!"

All of them turned toward Bug, who was hopping up and down around Petey's head and glowing a soft pink color. His cap expanded like a fan and rained sparkles down on Petey.

Who... was... *moving?*

Kaden darted forward so fast his feet skidded, falling to his knees beside Petey a second later. "More light!" he called out, and Pepper's sun illuminated his friend, whose lips were moving and whose eyes were slowly opening. Kaden looked disbelievingly at the wound in Petey's gut... which had somehow closed up, the fabric around it still bloody, but the big gash itself completely healed.

"Petey?" Kaden reached down and grabbed his friend's hand. "*Petey?*"

"Hmm... Kaden?" Petey's eyes opened all the way, and he stared blearily up at Kaden, slowly panning around to take in everyone else as they clustered in close. "What... happened?"

"You died," Kaden said, and tears poured from his eyes as he realized the gift he'd just been given, that *all* of them had been provided. "Orealus brought you back." Whether it was for their faith or simply a beneficent act from him, Kaden could never thank Orealus enough for returning his friend to him. "You're back!"

"Impossible," Weylyn murmured, his eyes wide. He backed away slightly. "He must not have really been dead."

"He was, though," Eldrin said, his own gaze sharp as it lingered on the slice in Petey's jerkin. "He really was."

"Then this is some type of magic. It is *not* some miracle from Orealus. It must be Kaden's wizard magic, or Queen Pepper's magic, or—even the mushroom's magic!"

"Hopping toadstool," Millicent corrected quietly.

"Whatever! It can't have been Orealus," Weylyn insisted. "Orealus is nothing but a story, and no God goes around bringing people back from the dead just *because*. I'm... this..." He abruptly turned and marched away, out of the light.

Redfern and Eldrin exchanged a glance, then got up as well. "We'll keep him from running off," Eldrin said and loped off after the Son of the Wolf.

Ada helped Petey sit up, fussing a little over the blood. "You'll need a replenishing potion," she said, looking carefully at his eyes. "You might be healed, but that doesn't mean you didn't lose a lot of fluids. I've got just the thing to help in my bag."

"Thank you," Petey said, a little dazedly, then looked at Bug, who was still hopping about joyfully. "And thank *you*, little one." Bug nuzzled him, leaving a pink smear across Petey's hand. Kaden laughed.

"Bug was the first one to notice. Of course."

"Nothing gets past him," Petey said proudly.

"No." Not like it did Kaden. "You should have saved yourself," he said quietly, in a voice meant for just the two of them. "Not stopped Garth's sword with your body."

"I'd rather stop a thousand swords with my own body than let any of them touch you," Petey replied, just as quiet, just as sincere. "I would protect you over and over again. You're too important for anything else. Although," Petey added a bit louder, "we really ought to think about getting some armor for you."

Kaden laughed. "Yeah, we really ought to do that." He slung an arm around Petey's back and helped him stand up. Once he was sure his friend was steady on his feet, he looked around for Duke and saw him in the process of—"Ugh! No! Bad dog, don't lick that! Come here!" Duke obediently left Garth's corpse behind and trotted over to Kaden, who grimaced but petted his head anyway. "Let's get out of here."

"Let's," Queen Pepper agreed. Millicent went to get Weylyn and the others while Queen Pepper flew above the wreckage, lighting a path for Kaden, Petey, Ada, Duke, and Bug that would lead them out of the ruins of Shroudscar.

"What do we do next?" Petey asked quietly as they climbed over thick, broken logs, averting their eyes from the occasional corpse of a goblin or grawler who could not escape Kaden's attack.

"I…" Kaden shook his head. He'd visited all the tribes of Empyrea and done his best to secure them as allies, but was he really ready to confront Lucient? He'd managed to break the goblin stronghold, but that felt more like luck than fate to him. He wouldn't even have come here if Petey hadn't been captured. "I don't know," he said. "I guess I'll have to think about it."

"We'll help you figure it out," Petey promised him, and Ada nodded firmly. Kaden smiled at his friends.

"I know you will."

By the time the group finally made it up and out of the tunnel, they were all exhausted. The sky was dark but still lighter than Shroudscar had been even with the luminescent moss and the torches. They made a rudimentary camp a mile away from the tunnel, just in case stragglers followed them up and decided to take revenge. Pepper made a basic but hearty stew, and once everyone had eaten, people began to head for their bedrolls.

Kaden, who knew he ought to feel utterly exhausted, was instead tense to the point of barely restraining himself from getting up and pacing. "I'll take the first watch," he said and wouldn't hear of someone stepping in to handle it instead. "I won't be able to sleep now anyway," he assured them all, and finally, they acquiesced, Ada, putting up the most resistance until she finally bedded down near him.

"Promise to wake one of us if you start to tire," she insisted before pulling her thick, mountain-sheep-wool blanket up to her head.

"I promise I will." Kaden watched her close her eyes, and despite her readiness to sit up with him, she was asleep in moments. He sat down cross-legged and breathed deeply, trying to center himself enough to focus on his surroundings, but it was so hard. Not knowing what came next was preying on his mind now that he had time to think again.

He thought about it. He thought for hours, through when his watch should have ended, through the night calls of mysterious animals and the hooting cries of soot-colored owls. He sat, outwardly calm but inwardly in turmoil, as he contemplated his warring emotions and considered what to do next. What, what, what was he supposed to do next?

He needed to make a plan. How could he keep everyone together if he didn't have a plan? What was he going to do, start marshaling troops and going after Lucient when he didn't even know where to point them? He had no experience as a general and no experience gathering intelligence, which he knew he would need if he would be successful. He didn't even have *armor* for crying out loud, so how was he going to keep things like what had just happened with Petey from happening again? There was only so much a good offense could do, and Kaden's wasn't even all that good yet. He knew the best warrior. Weylyn also had some of the thickest armor.

What was Kaden going to do? What could he possibly—

"You look like you're thinking hard."

Kaden jerked his head to the left. "Bhalla?"

The wizard chuckled from where he stood between the trees a few yards away. "In the skin, so to speak." He tilted his head a little. "It seems like you made quite an impact on the goblins of Shroudscar."

"It was just luck." As happy as Kaden was to see Bhalla, he also knew he hadn't exactly covered himself with glory down in Shroudscar. "We were hardly able to—" He paused and glanced back at his sleeping friends. He didn't want to wake them.

"They won't hear us unless you want them to," Bhalla assured him. He came over and sat down beside Kaden. "Go on. Tell me all about it."

So Kaden did. He spoke about their quest after leaving Lumhagen, their journey back into Brightshire Forest and their meeting with Valymr, their failure with Bardicus Blakenshield, the dark elf attack on the way to Whaldalf's Landing, sailing to Weylyn and Nethopolis, and the fight to get the centaurs on their side, and finally Petey's capture and their journey to Shroudscar.

"He died for me, and I hated it," Kaden confessed. "I— Orealus brought him back, but I know in my heart that it's because Petey is such a good person, not because I deserved it. My faith is strong, but…"

"It's hard to reconcile, isn't it?" Bhalla said calmly. "Why one person is saved by such miraculous means when there are so many others who deserve saving. I pondered the question for a long time after we lost your father. Why Karatheas? Why, after all his great deeds in the name of Orealus, why should he and his family be victims when they seemed destined to be saviors? I know some of your friends feel the same way about the people in their lives."

Kaden thought of Weylyn, about how he wore his father's armor even now and how he refused to accept that it was Orealus who had saved Petey. He thought about Eldrin's reluctance to leave his own father, about Queen Pepper's great faith even though she had lost her husband of centuries to a doomed war. He thought about the father he had known his whole life and how Daneyel had died in his arms at the beginning of this quest. Why hadn't he been saved? Why wasn't he worthy of that grace? In the end, all he could do was nod.

"Eventually, I came to the belief that the only one who can see all threads, and knows which should be extended and which should be cut short, is Orealus," Bhalla said, gentle but firm. "We can wonder, we can praise, we can rage, but we can never fully know the mind of Orealus. All we can do is our best to act on his will and create a better world for all the tribes of this vast land. Including those we must first fight against." He looked up at the moon, a slender crescent above them. "Who can say where the refugees of Shroudscar will go and how they will be treated? Perhaps freeing them from that place was a beneficial act. Either way, you did all that you could, and to feel guilt over the return of Petey, a great demonstration of the power of faith, is illogical."

"But what do we do now?" Kaden asked. "We're not ready to fight. I need a battle plan, I need... I need to know more, I can't just..."

"Mmm. I would suggest that, now that you've looked after others, the next step is looking after yourself," Bhalla said. "You have a mighty sword to protect you, and a sword is what you've forged with the alliances you've made along the way. Your next step is to find an even more powerful sword and a shield, to surround yourself with armor. Even the most powerful sword can be turned aside by a strong defense."

"Is this a metaphor?" Kaden asked suspiciously.

Bhalla laughed. "It's literal *and* figurative! The sword that your father carried and armor that he wore was that of Orealus and has been scattered worldwide after his death. Wearing it all would provide the people who follow you with a symbol that you are more than just a man who claims to be his heir—you are acting as he would have, acting for the good of all. Plus, it's a magnificent sword and armor," Bhalla added. "Quite wonderful, quite powerful. You'll need it before you battle Lucient."

"Where is it?"

"I'll tell you all about it," Bhalla said, then looked at the sky again. It was beginning to lighten, the silver gold of dawn breaking up the edge of the solid, midnight-blue expanse of sky. "Over breakfast, with your comrades."

Kaden grinned. "Thank you."

Bhalla grinned back. "Oh, don't thank me until you know where you've got to go, lad! You thought Nethopolis and

Shroudscar were hard to reach? Ha! You've got an adventure ahead of you, full of treacherous paths, vile creatures, unstable climate conditions, and forces of evil that will stop at nothing to devour you."

Another adventure… another leg of the quest. A *plan*. Even if it was a hard one, and he knew it would be, Kaden was excited to face it with the rest of his friends.

Thank you, Orealus, he thought as he stood up, ready to wake up the rest of his party. Thank you for my friends. I believe that together, we can do your will.

Together, they had everything they needed.

*   *   *

From half a mile in the distance, a treetop swayed. The man within it, wiry and fast as a weasel, folded up his looking glass.

So, the wizard had come after all. Good. Perhaps he would do more to protect Kaden this time than giving the boy a sword he could barely use and sending him off into the wilds with a dog and a *goblin*, of all the creatures. Kaden was going to need much more than that if he was going to survive this fool's quest of his.

You're just jealous it's not you, the voice in his head hissed. *You're just upset that you weren't the one given credit for saving him.* The man had to acknowledge the truth in that—he'd long ago stopped lying to himself about his own motivations. He'd thrown the dagger from the shadows of Shroudscar that had prevented the goblin behemoth from striking Kaden down before he could fight back. He'd saved him, as indeed Petey had, but he'd never get recognized for it.

You don't want recognition. He didn't. All he wanted was for Kaden to be safe, with a silent watcher guarding his back when he and his friends were too hasty to protect it themselves.

The man began to lower himself out of the tree. His companion, a familiar black crow, cawed hoarsely and flew into the air, only alighting back on the man's shoulder once he reached the ground. The man passed the crow a morsel of meat, which the bird snapped up greedily.

"We must continue to follow and watch," he told the bird. "We must keep him safe. Go. Stay with him until they move out, then return and show me where they've gone."

The crow nodded its slender head, then cawed again and took off through the trees. The man watched her go, idly snatching a small black feather out of the air as she flew away.

He would follow, as he had. He would guard, as he had. He would be there for Kaden, even though Kaden didn't know he existed.

It was what family did, after all.

ACKNOWLEDGEMENTS

Writing a novel is much easier than pushing toward the finish line of completing one. None of this would have been possible without the support of those around me. I am grateful to Cath for her wisdom, attention to detail, and uncanny writing skills. She was an invaluable asset to me! A salute goes out to Kyri for her creativity and helpful suggestions. Her skill as a wordsmith is impressive. To Jude, thanks for helping my mind meld and fine-tune my vision at the early stages of writing this novel.

Thanks to my mother, Otherine, who has always been in my corner. She always taught me to chase my dreams and never give up. She taught me discipline, tough love, manners, and respect and has been essential in pushing me to succeed. She has always encouraged me in my life.

Writing a fantasy novel has been so exciting for me. I never thought I could write a book, let alone complete one. Thank you, Nathan and Marcell, for convincing me to write a novel.

A thanks goes out to my brother Erik for his support. To my sister Monica, thank your for your kind words during this journey. P.S. Monica, please edit and publish your completed manuscripts.

Finally, I thank all who have been a part of helping me get to this point: Skye, Zach, Chnice, and many others. Last but not least, I must thank Yahweh, for everything was possible through Him!

ABOUT THE AUTHOR

B.H. Preston was born in 1983 in Harvey, Illinois. Growing up, reading fantasy fascinated him, and he frequented the local public library. While dabbling in a few fields, from website implementation specialist to life coach, Bryant has spent several years writing his first novel. He is the father of a young 6-year-old boy and friend to his trusty 16-month-old Goldendoodle. As an avid fantasy novel reader of J. R. R. Tolkien's *Lord of the Rings* series and C. S. Lewis's *Chronicles of Narnia*, he inspires to replicate that level of world-building in his novel. Bryant loves to create an immersive world that readers could really be a part of in his writing. When he is not writing, Bryant spends his free time watching movies, listening to music, and playing video games. He is the latest new author behind the fantasy novel *A Hero Forged in Blood*, the first book in the *Chronicles of Empyrea* trilogy. He currently lives in Duluth, Minnesota.

CHRONICLES OF EMPYREA SERIES

APPENDIX

Protagonists

Kaden Sheppard

– The Hero

Kaden has a strong, determined will, together with perseverance. His level of endurance and courage against adversity is second to none. Although he is passive at first, he has an unbroken spirit waiting to be discovered. He is not perfect, and while struggling with bouts of selfish and vengeful behavior, he learns that he must share responsibilities with his loved ones. Nonetheless, he has a strong innate sense of good and doing what is right.

Petey Elvenshire

– Awesome Sidekick

Petey exhibits zany, kind-hearted behavior. Petey will commonly crack jokes when he is nervous or afraid. Petey can be cowardly but is known to be brave when his back is against the wall or protecting loved ones. He is very energetic and often talks too much, annoying people. On the other hand, Bug is a frockling mushroom that is a nuisance to Petey. The gentle, rare creature hops around while shooting phosphorescent spores in the air, often on Petey's face.

Adena "Ada" Davenrich

   – Hero's Friend

A lot can be assumed when you first look at Ada, but those close to her know she's a strong and capable hunter. Of course, she's also caring, compassionate, and loving toward others. Still, many can perceive her as being hardened on the outside. Her protectiveness for those she loves, at all costs, can cause her to exhibit stubborn, rebellious behavior. Inside her core, Ada is kind and has yearned to join someone on an adventure outside her average life.

Bardicus Blakenshield

   – King of the Dwarves/Drinker of Grog

Bardicus is brave and strong, yet arrogant. He lives underground in a rare material mine known for its famous grog. After the Great War, he spends time sitting on his throne drinking grog and having grand celebrations full of food. The countless parties could be due to shame from betraying the late King Karatheas. Maybe he will have an opportunity for his tribe to be redeemed.

Eldrin Tolbarg

   – Elven Prince

Eldrin is the prideful prince of the elven King Valymr. As regal as his background, he has a good heart underneath his narcissistic behavior regarding his handsome looks and advanced skill with a bow. He is adept at hand-to-hand combat and the use of daggers. He went through elite training as a longbow sniper before receiving his trusted bow, Driftwood.

Cimetes Gallopfoot

   – Honorable Chief

Cimetes is a strong warrior and leader of the centaur tribe. After the Great War, he placed his focus solely on his tribe. He wields a mighty spear named Wind Piercer that his father passed down to him. Although brave, he now secretly fears Lucient and his army after the war.

Pepper Shinyfawn

– Queen of Fayspire

Pepper is the gentle wife of her late husband, the powerful Faedner Shinyfawn. For most of her life now, she and her kingdom have strayed from anything that is not peaceful, especially war. Even though Pepper is friendly, she is a powerful fairy capable of defeating many creatures in combat. Using the forces of nature through the blessing of Orealus, she can assist her allies in a time of need.

Varun Gadar

– Protector of the Prudent Ocean

Varun is the merfolk king alongside his wife, Dinereus. Varun became king shortly after his father, the great King Trophorus, was assassinated by one of his brothers Agalus, the traitor. Many merfolk warriors defected to Lucient's army out of fear of Agalus. They waged a terrible war against the sea kingdom during the Great War. Varun was defeated along with many of his siblings, and Varun was broken. Many lives of the united sea kingdom of warriors and civilians were lost.

Weylyn Echethier

– Son of the Wolf

Weylyn, "son of the Wolf," is a wandering mercenary for hire that belongs to no one. Weylyn is a sworn enemy against Garth and the goblin clan. He abandoned his faith in Orealus, often blaming Him for not intervening and stopping his father's death. After the death of his mother from old age, he wanders the world in search of Lucient to avenge his father's death even though it would be sure death. He works with Chum to get information on the hit targets that he is seeking. Maybe it is destiny for Weylyn to take up his future to protect Kaden and avenge his father.

Duke

– Furry Friend

Duke follows Kaden off on his quest as his loyal companion. Duke was found as a puppy by Kaden near Ashland, and they have been inseparable since.

Bhalla Bristlekamp

– The Bright/Protector of the Light

Bhalla is the eldest of all wizards and a blameless servant to Orealus. He oversaw the Tower of Enlightenment and now lives in Lumhagen. Many of his followers and fellow wizards do not understand his deep devotion or trust in Orealus after the Great War. However, they still follow him as he is deeply revered in the city. Bhalla is a powerful wizard capable of healing, raising the dead, causing storms, and protecting others through shields and other magical feats. Bhalla is a wise spiritual person who relies on all his knowledge from Orealus. He often calls on his closest friend, a giant eagle named Ga'noole, when needing help.

Chum Scruffenhoof

– Clever Thorn in the Side

Chum is rumored to be the last of his kind. He ventures almost daily to Kugdor to steal grog. He is often caught and thrown out. He is known as a gatherer of information and procures rare or unique items for something in return. Often the things he steals are to trade for more grog.

Antagonists

Lucient

– The Great Deceiver

Lucient is the king of the Serpent Army and leader of the Four Horsemen of the Apocalypse. Not much is known about Lucient other than tales that he was once a top general in Orealus' army and his closest advisor until he attempted mutiny. After manifesting himself as a serpent, he tried to defy Orealus by corrupting his fond creation and its other tribal leaders.

Garth

– Scourge

Garth is the tribal leader of the goblins because of being the largest and strongest of them. He is cruel and only cares about loot and the misery of his brother Petey. Garth has loyalty to only his clan. Promised riches by Lucient, he sends members of his clan to destroy Kaden but, at times, will make an appearance himself.

Omak

– The Grinder of Bones

Omak became the leader of his ogre tribe by besting the last alpha leader Og, in battle. He wears the skulls around the of those he beat in a match. Omak is fast for his size and does bursts that help cover a short distance swiftly. Although primitive in thinking, Omak was crafty enough to create a morning star from the material of past foes. The Morningstar named "Smasher" is strong enough to break through rigid walls and too heavy for most creatures or humans to carry.

Other Characters & Misc.

Millicent

– Queen's Guard

Millicent has a fiery personality and is usually serious. She is sometimes overprotective of Queen Pepper as her guard. At times she can loosen up, but usually, that is brought upon by her friend Redfern.

Redfern

– Queen's Guard

Redfern has a strong, proud personality. Usually, she has a cooler head than her friend Millicent and can cool her down. Redfern is loyal to Queen Pepper and fiercely protects her. She often quarrels with Millicent because they are both hot-headed.

Frockling Mushrooms

Kaden and his crew encounter a frockling mushroom named Bug during their journey. These gentle, curious creatures look like a cross of a capped mushroom and a rabbit. When they hop around, phosphorescent spores are released into the air.

Muk Muk

Muk Muk has a strong, proud, arrogant personality. He is fierce and feeds off the fear that others have of him. Rage and fearlessness feed him. Muk Muk is loyal after a defeat in an honorable battle.

Growlers

Growlers are a type of wolf breed stricken with a disease from the curse of sin that Lucient unleashed from his dark aura. These creatures are known to have been tamed by goblins to mount and ride into battle or hunt prey. Their strong sense of smell and heightened vision make them perfect hunting companions for goblins when trying to track a target.

Dark Elves

Dark elves are rumored to be a mutated, cursed off-breed of wood elves. Dark elves have an intense hatred for distant relatives in the wood elves. They possess some of the same physical attributes as wood elves but are more dangerous. The arrowheads on their arrows are coated in poison. Dark elves have the same ageless look as wood elves but are hot-headed. They have deceitful, evil intentions.

Gangor

Gangor is a forest golem that is 9 feet tall and over 2,000 pounds but could expand its height and size to be even larger. It is unknown how Gangor came to be, but old rumors say that the dark-infused seed from a flower in the land from which Lucient was sent traveled through the air and landed near Wildepointe. Once germinated, the seed may have grown into this beast.

Pixies

Pixies are mysterious, small creatures full of light whose appearance is unknown. Although, it is suspected that pixies are distant relatives from the same family as the fairies.

K'Lani Davenrich

K'Lani is Ada's mother and a healer. She is a compassionate mother, quick of wit, and with a caring bedside manner.

Captain Marcus Herrington

Captain Harrington is more comfortable on a ship deck than on land, having earned his sea legs at a young age. He is a captain for hire of the ship Dawn's Light and ex-royal Empyrean naval officer. While he has a dark past, he views the world with undeniable optimism.

Captain Asiz Seaspray

As Captain Harrington's most trusted supporter, his loyalty is legendary. He cares about making Harrington proud and living on the sea. He prefers to keep to himself when not with Harrington. He can only speak about returning to the boat whenever he ventures on land. However, the man never seems happy, only content with sea travel's solace.

Lieutenant Reginald Sharpey

Lieutenant Sharpey is the first mate of the ship Dawn's Light. He is interested in traveling the world by sea. He wants to leave no stone unturned. His friendly demeanor and approachable manner lead to his friendship with most. He has an incredible singing voice and loves a good sea shanty. His laugh, always close to his lips, booms. He is an excellent storyteller.

Daneyel

His tragic loss marks the beginning of Kaden's adventure. At the request of Bhalla, he and his wife raised Kaden, keeping the heir of Karatheas safe, tucked away in their village. He taught Kaden to hunt and work hard.

Lydia

Lydia and her husband, Daneyel, raised Kaden. She taught Kaden the importance of protecting those he cares about. Lydia is an excellent baker and an even better shot than her husband, a quality she's too humble to admit. Bundled inside her petite frame, she has great wisdom and intuition. She enjoys fishing and spending time with her small family.

Asitra

Asitra is a keeper of the sacred scrolls. Though her parents wanted her to work at the farm and carry on the family legacy, she knew she was destined for more. However, she did not think of her calling until Orealus appeared in a dream and told her to depart home. Taking nothing except what she was wearing, Asitra met the wizard in Lumhagen.

Queen Luna

Everyone knows of the adoration Luna had for her children. She was a compassionate and benevolent leader who encouraged her husband to bestow mercy alongside justice. She was a charitable role model to all women who exceedingly mourned her loss. Though she is rumored to descend from elves, she was born to two human parents, a duke and a duchess. When Karatheas saw her at a ball in the castle, he courted only her, and the two fell in love.

King Karatheas

King Karatheas was a fierce, compassionate leader. The people loved his leadership and mourned his loss nationwide. He sacrificed himself for his country, dying in battle alongside his soldiers. The people knew him as a just and fair ruler. Though he perished in the Great War, his legacy lives on in his son's destiny. The royal contingency plan allows for Kaden's safety with Karatheas's beloved best friend. His other children and wife did not survive the war, which makes Kaden the only surviving heir.

Mechanimals

These odd, robotic creatures tinker throughout the city of Lumhagen. Animals like owls, horses, cats, dogs, and even tiny mice make up those engineered to assist in the daily tasks of the city's people.

Dawn Light

Though the wooden ship appears rickety, damaged, and old, she is a sturdy, clean, well-loved boat. With one top deck, one lower deck, two sets of sails, and one crow's nest, this ship spans 60 feet and can carry about 100 tons of cargo. Her sails are the color of the sunbaked canvas, and she sports the flag of Adena's family.

Mana

Utilizing yah'zhaval expends Mana. Mana is a renewable, internal energy source qualified by the amount of faith a person has in Orealus. Restoring Mana takes time and rest. Just as faith can grow, so can one's maximum amount of bankable Mana.

Bonberries

Bonberries are indigo berries that form in clusters of at least a dozen and grow on shrubs. They grow around sharp, green, shiny leaves resembling holly bushes.

Environments

Ashland

Ashland is a town of around 400 people where Kaden and his family reside.

Binicorn's Farthing

Binicorn's Farthing is an open area full of green grass dotted with trees. Several streams run through the plain, feeding the lake where the binicorns drink. The backdrop of this locale is the mountains carving into the blue sky.

Brightshire Forest

Many types of unique creatures and exotic plants inhabit Brightshire. Brightshire Forest is named after the lampi plants that spread beautifully illuminated seeds in the air, which light the forest at night with fluorescent colors.

Cragmaw

Cragmaw is the underground home of the ogres. The ogres stay underground during the day because of their sunlight sensitivity and go out to hunt at night.

Fayspire

Fayspire is home to the fairies and is located west of Brightshire Forest. The city is nestled so discreetly in the forest that the average passerby misses the camouflaged buildings.

Kel Tyrion

Home to the elves, Kel Tyrion, is a city located east near Brightshire Forest but independent from it.

Kugdor

The dwarven kingdom of Kugdor is in Bardok Peaks, the second-largest mountain in Empyrea. Kudgor is known for precious metals and a large fresh supply of grog.

Lumhagen

The home to the wizards and Grand wizard Bhalla. Lumhagen is a beautiful city shrouded by a mysterious aura crafted so no one can stumble upon the locale.

Nethopolis

Nethopolis is an underwater city hidden off the coast of Shrewswell Cove and near Empyrea.

Shroudscar

Shroudscar is the home to the goblins. Within a large fort resides a village full of mercenaries.

Westramore

Westramore is a dungy, dark city filled with scoundrels, thieves, assassins, mercenaries, and other unsavory people.

Whaldalf's Landing

Whaldalf's Landing is primarily a fishing village near a small harbor. The village's shopkeepers include a rope-maker, a smith, a tailor, a carpenter, a cooper, and a blacksmith. All the shops' products are modest yet functional.

Wildepointe
Wildepointe is a hilly plain full of caravan tents that the centaurs call home.

The Clumsy Goat
The Clumsy Goat is the name of the dwarves' grog tavern. Excellently crafted, sturdy wooden tables and chairs fill the pub crowded with people. The pub smells of roast pig and salty potatoes. People often knock into one another by mistake, sloshing grog onto each other.

Landing's End
Landing's End is a tavern located in Whaldalf's Landing. The salty, fishy smell of low tide permeates the inside of this building, full of sweaty fishermen. Though the pub has sturdy wooden tables and chairs, it seems to lack enough seating for the number of patrons.

The Salted Cod
The Salted Cod is a tavern located in Westramore. This place bustles with angry people who smell like cheap grog and soiled food.

In the following pages, enjoy an exerpt
from chapter one in the next book of the
Chronicles of Empyrea series and a bonus
never-before-seen illustration.

It was a beautiful morning, the bright sunshine overhead in a way it had refused to be for the past week of travel, the moody fog melting off quickly thanks to the heat. Dew glistened on the pine needles all around the camp, and Kaden could hear a robber jay singing—more like squawking—in the distance. He was surrounded by his friends, all alive and mostly well, and he didn't have to help cook breakfast.

He wished he could appreciate it all a little more. Still, after yesterday's battle in the goblin fortress of Shroudscar, Kaden mostly felt tired, sore, and strangely empty after the terror, exhaustion, and elation. It wasn't how he wanted to handle it, but it seemed too hard to reach for anything more.

Even sitting up out of his bedroll and putting on his boots felt hard right now, so much more complicated than such a simple task warranted. Maybe he was unwell. He should talk to Bhalla about that...once he finished waking up and found the old wizard.

His hunting hound Duke, who'd been stretched out beside him on the ground, leaned over and helpfully licked his ear.

"Ugh, Duke." Kaden pushed the big dog's head away, giving him a scratch behind the ears as he did so. The prospect of avoiding a tongue bath from his enthusiastic but smelly dog made getting up a little bit easier.

After his foster father's death, Kaden Sheppard thought he knew what hard was.

Hard was losing someone he loved and realizing that his life was based on a lie. Hard was discovering he was the son of Empyreans's greatest king, Karatheas, who had died in battle against the dark forces of Lucient, an enemy of the great God Orealus. Hard was learning that Kaden was meant to take on that role, to continue that battle and win it this time, when his father had been unable to do the same.

Hard was learning to sleep on the ground, missing his mother's bonberry buns, shivering in the cold, and eating the same thing for weeks. Hard was being surrounded by friends and still feeling alone sometimes, loving those friends and being afraid for them. The hardest of all was losing them.

Getting one of them back? That was a blessing from Orealus. Kaden gave thanks from the depths of his heart as he watched Petey. Unlike his enormous hunting hound Duke, the goblin was his first and best friend. He appreciated Petey's determination to help him reclaim the land from darkness, despite how Petey bickered with Chum as he brewed tea.

Turned out, you could be thankful and still be annoyed when your friends weren't even *trying* to get along.

"That's too much!" Petey said, jerking the bag of loose tea leaves away from Chum as the sharp-horned satyr added another pinch to the kettle. Bug, Petey's adoring hopping toadstool companion, let loose a puff of yellow pollen in matching consternation. Some of it got into Duke's nose, and he sneezed, spraying pollen and mucus all over Kaden's boot. *Gross.* "You'll use it all up before the week's out, at that rate!" His bright yellow eyes—goblin eyes—were narrow with irritation, and the corners of his long green ears twitched like nervous mice.

"Better no tea than the pale, tasteless stuff you brew," Chum retorted. He was the first satyr Kaden had ever met and, apparently, the only one he ever would since Lucient's forces had wiped out the rest of his people. Being the only one of his kind didn't make Chum any more eager to get along with others. He thought of himself first, Weylyn second, and everyone else was a distant third. "You'll have to keep it on the fire for half the day just to make it palatable!"

"I'll keep it on for as long as it needs to be on." Petey rolled his eyes. "Honesty, I was only dead for a minute, and you went and declared yourself keeper of the tea?"

"Don't joke about that," Ada said from where she was sitting closer to the fire, checking the pot to see how the porridge was coming along.

Porridge. Again. Yuuuuum.

"Nobody wants to think about you dying," she continued as she brushed one of her long black braids back from her face. Ada Davenrich, or Adena as her mother called her, was a little older than Kaden, with bright green eyes and warm brown skin. She wasn't the first person to answer the call of his quest, but she had already proven her worth despite her youth and inexperience.

In truth, Kaden felt a little better about his inexperience with her alone—having someone else to learn and discover things with, rather than already being an expert at them, made confronting his limitations a bit easier.

"*I* don't mind it," Chum said snappishly.

"Yes, but we all know what a reprobate you are," Weylyn called out from the other side of the fire, where he was painstakingly tapping out a dent in one of his massive steel pauldrons. Kaden could still barely believe he'd convinced Weylyn, Son of the Wolf, the greatest mercenary in the land, to join his crew. How did someone as green as Kaden command someone as experienced as Weylyn?

With care and deliberation, he was learning. He hoped those would be enough to help him justify his next decision because he still needed to figure out where they were going next.

A drop of dew dripped down onto the top of his head from the tree above, and Kaden flipped the hood of his cloak up with a silent huff. Honestly, he would have liked nothing more than a break from travel for a while, a chance for his mind and body to catch up with the events they'd been through, but that wasn't going to happen. Not now that Bhalla the Bright was here.

Here, but not *here*. Where had the wizard gone now? He'd arrived last night with little fanfare and listened to Kaden talk all through his watch, telling him of their adventure so far. Bhalla had laid out the next step in the quest—to find the godly imbued armor of Orealus, which Kaden would need if he were going to survive a confrontation with Lucient.

Kaden pressed to his feet, groaning at how his muscles balked and complained at getting up. He shook his head as Ada caught his eye, her unspoken offer to join him turned down. Kaden needed to find Bhalla and get some things straight before he could make his next big decision. The less Kaden shared his uncertainty with the others, the better. Duke stretched out on the ground with a doggy smile, and Kaden gave him a pat before leaving him to rest while he went to find Bhalla.

A hundred yards or so away from camp, Eldrin was shooting arrows into trees. Kaden watched his elven friend's face tighten with focus, staring out at a target only he knew before he loosed. A second later, Kaden heard, "Got it!" Redfern flew out of the dense pine forest, waving the arrow in a tiny hand. She passed it back to Eldrin with a grin, her bright red hair bounding in a braid between coppery wings. "You can fire it harder than that. I'll still be able to catch it."

"Will you? Or will I end up perforating one of Queen Pepper's bodyguards like a piece of ripe fruit and getting punished for it?" Eldrin replied haughtily, but Kaden could see it was just a front. Amazing that he noticed those things now about the prickly elf prince. There had been a time when Kaden was convinced they'd never understand each other. Time and togetherness had worn their sharper edges down, though.

"Sounds like you're making excuses to me," Redfern sing-songed before looking at Kaden. "If it's my lady you seek, she and Millicent are with Bhalla. There's an overlook about a quarter mile's distance that way." She pointed deeper into the forest. "They should be there."

"Thank you," Kaden said, then added, "Try not to embarrass Eldrin too badly."

"Hey!"

"Can't promise it, sire!"

At least someone's having fun, Kaden reflected as he headed deeper into the trees. He moved slowly, listening to the sounds around him, checking the ground for signs of those who'd passed this way before him. Kaden was still pretty green as a tracker. Still, he'd been working on it with his foster father Danyel before…everything. He was working even more difficult now that he had people relying on him.

Eldrin is better at it. Redfern is better. Weylyn is better.

Kaden knew he could count on his friends to do their part, that he didn't *have* to be great at tracking, but he felt compelled to be as good as possible. What if something went wrong, and he couldn't fix it because he couldn't find the right path? How would he move forward?

Your thoughts are spiraling. Get ahold of yourself. It was easier said than done. The miracle that was Shroudscar—the gift of beating the goblins, of killing their vile leader Garth and saving Petey, the blessing of him coming back to life—should have freed Kaden from so many of his worries. He'd done it, led his people through battle, and come out the other side with everyone hale and hearty! Shouldn't he be *less* worried now?

Why did he feel even more uncertain instead?